Praise for
Shadows in the Moonlight

'Remarkable and compelling'
JULIAN FELLOWES

'Fantastic, moving and beautifully written'
TRACY REES

'Enjoyable and engaging, I loved it'
BARBARA ERSKINE

'Totally absorbing, just brilliant!'
JUDY MURRAY

'Breathtakingly beautiful, captivating and so very romantic'
ALEX BROWN

'A love story to break your heart!'
LIZ FENWICK

'Beautifully written, haunting and enchanting'
FIONA VALPY

Santa Montefiore is the number one bestselling author of over thirty novels and has sold over six million copies worldwide. Her books have been translated into twenty-five languages and she won an RNA Award for *The Temptation of Gracie* in 2019, which is currently in development for film. Born in England in 1970, she grew up in Hampshire and now lives in London with her husband, writer Simon Sebag-Montefiore, their daughter Lilochka, son Sasha, and dog Simba.

Shadows in the Moonlight is the first novel of a planned trilogy following the character Pixie Tate. Santa loves to hear from readers and you can find her at www.santamontefiore.co.uk.

SHADOWS
IN THE
MOONLIGHT

Santa
Montefiore

ORION

First published in Great Britain in 2024 by Orion Fiction,
an imprint of The Orion Publishing Group Ltd.
Carmelite House, 50 Victoria Embankment
London EC4Y 0DZ

An Hachette UK Company

1 3 5 7 9 10 8 6 4 2

A CIP catalogue record for this book is
available from the British Library.

ISBN (Hardback) 978 1 3987 2000 8
ISBN (Trade Paperback) 978 1 3987 2001 5
ISBN (eBook) 978 1 3987 2003 9

Typeset by Input Data Services Ltd, Bridgwater, Somerset

Printed in Great Britain by Clays Ltd, Elcograf S.p.A.

FSC
www.fsc.org

MIX
Paper | Supporting
responsible forestry
FSC® C104740

To my dear friend Pippa Clark with love

In memoriam
To my sister Tara,
who will always be in my heart.
Until we meet again

I don't solve crimes
That's too easy
I settle souls

Pixie Tate

Prologue
England 1987

Pixie shuffled beneath the covers to the foot of her bed and curled into a tight ball. The shouting in the kitchen below was getting louder, penetrating the floorboards like bullets and filling her small heart with terror. In the darkness, she pressed her toy dog to her chest, but it was a useless shield against the barrage of anger that reached her through the duvet and sheets. Her parents' fighting was all too common, but Pixie suffered each stab of vitriol as if it were the very first time. She squeezed her eyes shut, dampening the cotton sheet with tears, and waited for the inevitable release.

It always came. Just when she was on the point of losing her mind to despair, she'd feel it. The gentle thrumming in her ears, the familiar heaviness in her limbs, the blissful sensation of rising out of her body, of leaving the physical part of her there on her bed and floating away as easily as if she were a wisp of smoke, her spirit expanding with joyful anticipation and an overwhelming sense of relief.

She found herself in the meadow. She couldn't remember when she had initially discovered it, only that, for as long as she had lived, she had known it. She was not crying now. She knew no one would find her here. They never had and, somehow, she understood that they never would. That it wasn't possible. This was *her* place, and she was quite alone.

She took a deep breath and savoured the smell of the countryside. The gentle breeze stroked her hair and a friendly grasshopper chirruped in the wild grasses. The evening sky was a watery blue and upon it clouds floated like cotton-wool boats with pink hulls.

The gulls that wheeled beneath it were pink too and Pixie knew she had time – she *always* had time – to play in this enchanted place, for it *was* enchanted to a child who had only ever known the city. Who had only ever known the grass and flowers from the park and the small patch of neglected garden at the back of their house.

For Pixie, the meadow was simply a welcome escape from an unpleasant situation. She was too young to know what it *really* was. She imagined she must be visiting Heaven. But she knew not to ask. Instinctively, she understood that it must remain a secret, that if she told her parents, they simply wouldn't believe her. They might even accuse her of lying. However, one day she would learn what it was and how to control it. She would realise what a special gift it was, to slip out of her body and slide through the veil. And one day she would give it a name. A good name. A name that said exactly what it was. *Timesliding.*

Knowing not what the future held, Pixie played in her own private heaven, chasing butterflies and observing the bees foraging about the daisies and knapweed. She could not know that she hadn't travelled any distance at all, that she was, in fact, in the very same place, only in a different time. A time long before she had been born. Long before her house had been built. Long before even her grandparents had come into the world.

She was ignorant of where she was and what was to come. And it was blissful and uncomplicated, and completely without jeopardy.

For now.

Chapter One
Cornwall 2013

Sea mist had settled upon the land like a sponge, choking the light and saturating the fields and hills with drizzle. In the damp, the air felt colder. Sheep huddled among the rocks to keep warm despite their woolly winter coats and the odd rabbit thought better of it and dived back into its burrow. Trees shivered without their summer foliage, spindly branches black against the grey, and only gulls dared fly into the wind, their cries like the eerie laments of sailors drowned long ago. The tide was out, leaving the estuary bed crawling with unfortunate creatures left behind to survive in the shallow pools and sodden sand that remained, and everything, everywhere looked bleak and inhospitable.

It was not a day to be on the road, but Bruce and Olivia Talwyn were determined to settle into their new Cornish home in time for Christmas. Bruce sat at the wheel of their shiny black Range Rover, paying close attention to the dulcet tones of the satnav and driving slowly due to the mist. His tousled red hair, hazel eyes and wide, handsome face revealed the remains of a once dashing appeal, but a certain weariness had dulled his radiance and robbed him of his polish, like a peach left too long in the fruit bowl; he just looked tired. Olivia, on the other hand, blonde and pretty with vivacious blue eyes and a large, toothy mouth, looked spirited. There was no way she was going to let on how anxious she was, for she had invested all her hopes in this new adventure. 'Isn't this exciting?' she gushed for the hundredth time, turning around to beam at their two children as the satnav told them they were only ten minutes from their destination.

Their two children ignored her. Zach, who was fifteen, watched a film on his iPad. He had sugar-brown hair and intelligent hazel eyes, and a sprinkling of freckles over his nose, which was still small and boyish. His younger sister, Tabitha, who resembled her mother with long, curly blonde hair and dreamy blue eyes, gazed out of the window, her thirteen-year-old imagination stirred by the desolate beauty of the countryside. Indeed, it lit something inside her; a small spark of creativity, fanned by a sense of wonder she hadn't yet grown out of. Bruce cursed the weather, Olivia tried to be positive, Zach was absorbed in George R. R. Martin's fantasy world, but Tabitha saw necklaces of pearls in the hedgerows and twinkling diamonds in the grass, and her excitement escalated as the winding lanes grew narrower and the mist darkened, for this place was galaxies away from the bright, metallic streets of Notting Hill, and held within it the promise of enchantment.

Their new home, St Sidwell Manor, was positioned at the end of a long avenue of ancient plane trees. It was a grey-stone Elizabethan mansion built in the shape of an E with three Dutch-style gables and tall, square chimney stacks. There was a pleasant harmony in the proportions and a playful prettiness in the flamboyantly carved gables, but something about the windows belied its apparent air of frivolity. They seemed to gaze upon the world with resentment, like the eyes of one who did not wish to be disturbed. Or more exactly, the eyes of one who most strongly objected to being disturbed.

Admittedly, the mist did not help. It gave the impression that the house was looming out of the past like a ghost – a ghostly galleon that haunted the seas and embroidered the talk of local fishermen who liked to scare tourists with tales of the supernatural over tankards of beer in the pub. Olivia wished the sun would come out so the children could see the size and splendour of the gardens. They had been charming, albeit unloved, when she had first seen them back in the spring. There was a walled vegetable garden, overgrown with weeds but full of potential; two stately Victorian greenhouses, which, with a good scrub, would shine like new; an orchard of apple and pear trees, and endless lawns that Bruce would enjoy mowing on a tractor. It all required a lot of work, for Bruce's distant relative, who had bequeathed him the place, had clearly run out of both money and enthusiasm, and left it to the mercy of nature. On this dreary day it didn't look charming at all, it just looked hostile, and Olivia wondered whether they had done the right thing in selling their house in London and moving down here so hastily. St Sidwell Manor was in a terrible state of disrepair, and it was the middle of winter. What were they thinking?

She glanced across at her husband, whose jaw was rigid as if he, too, was rather wishing they hadn't been so rash, and reminded herself why they had, in fact, given up on their city life so quickly to move to an estate in the middle of nowhere. Bruce's health depended on it; it was as simple as that. They had grabbed the opportunity when it had so unexpectedly presented itself, like desperate rock climbers to a rope, even though they weren't quite sure what they'd find on the other end of that rope. Bruce needed tranquillity following a nervous breakdown brought on by the accumulative stress of his trader's job – a job that Olivia had finally persuaded him to leave – and he needed an entirely new profession. The sweet promise of a farmer's life deep in the Cornish countryside had seemed to come just when he'd needed it most. Bruce knew nothing about farming, but how hard could it be?

Bruce drew the Range Rover to a halt in front of the pillared porch. As he did so, the large wooden door opened and a stout, grey-haired woman appeared in a long black dress and brightly coloured tasselled shawl, followed by a burly young man with scruffy brown hair and an unshaven face, wearing a chunky, navy-blue fisherman's jersey and heavy, lace-up boots. Olivia and Bruce had already met Elsa Tregoning and her son, Tom, when they had first visited the place in the spring and found them to be decent, quietly spoken people. Elsa had worked for the previous owner, Mrs Delaware, for over fifty years, and was keen to retire. Olivia had tried to find a replacement for her, but no one had answered her advertisement, even though it had been pinned to the noticeboard in the local newsagent's for over seven months. She had never imagined it would be so hard to find staff in the countryside. Tom managed the farm, which his late father had done before him, as well as doing useful things around the house like chopping logs and unblocking drains. He had seemed relieved when Bruce had told him that he wasn't intending to replace him, and somewhat bemused when Bruce had added that he was, in fact, intending to farm himself, if Tom had the patience to teach him. Olivia had read the man's mind – in jeans and trainers and an expensive blazer, Bruce did not look like the sort of material that could be easily moulded into a man of the land.

Fortunately, Elsa had agreed to stay on until the family settled in. 'I think it best. This old house needs time to get used to you,' she had said in her gentle Cornish lilt, a knowing smile upon her lips. 'It can be a little cranky with newcomers.' Olivia had thought that a strange thing to say, to imply that the house had feelings like a person. She had laughed Elsa off as eccentric and resolved to advertise further afield. However, as she and her son came down the steps and over the gravel to help with the luggage, Olivia was grateful to them for she would not have liked to arrive to an empty house.

Olivia was pleased to find a large fire in the hall. The flames danced vigorously about the giant-sized logs, which crackled and burned and threw woodsmoke into the air. She had hired a local building company to do the bare minimum, for the bones of the building were already beautiful and the rooms were full of grand marble fireplaces, antique wooden furniture and gilt-framed paintings. Faded tapestries hung on the walls and threadbare rugs covered the wooden floorboards, but Bruce and Olivia did not have the money to do much beyond the small number of rooms they were actually going to use. At some point they would have to rewire and replumb the entire building, for nothing had been touched since Victorian times, but that would cost a small fortune. For now, the important thing was to live in it before deciding what needed to be done. In spite of being stuck in a time warp, it was a dream house and, as the children ran off to find their bedrooms, Olivia let her anxiety go and sighed with relief; it had been a long drive, but they were here. Bruce took her hand. 'It's okay, isn't it?' he asked, hazel eyes seeking validation, for even though the decision to move had been mutual, he knew his health was the overriding motivation behind it.

'It's perfect,' she replied, giving him a reassuring smile. 'I might need another sweater, though,' she added with a shiver. Despite the roaring fire the house felt cold.

Olivia swept her gaze around the hall and wondered about the previous mistress of St Sidwell Manor, Bruce's mystery relation who had left her entire estate to him in her will. Bruce had never heard of her, and she hadn't left much of an explanation, stating simply that he was the closest living relative she had. It hadn't taken much to find out that Delaware was her married name and that her maiden name had been Pengower. Elsa had told them back in the spring that the Pengowers had built the house in the time of Elizabeth I and lived here, uninterrupted, for nearly four hundred years. Bruce had done a bit of research and discovered that there was no Delaware or Pengower in his ancestry, but what did it matter? Mrs Delaware had left St Sidwell Manor to him, and how very nice of her.

The house was much too big for the four of them, Olivia thought as she wandered into the grand drawing room with its high, moulded ceilings and tall, mullioned windows. She wondered how Mrs Delaware had lived here for so long on her own. It certainly wasn't a house for one person, but for a big family with a large retinue of staff. Olivia would not have chosen to live in such a mansion, but, when she had visited for the first time, on a clear spring day nine months before, she had fallen in love with the house, which was undeniably magnificent, and with the idea of the peaceful, wholesome life it promised. It was just the place where poor broken Bruce could put himself back together again and where Olivia could have a proper studio to paint in. She had chosen a pretty sitting room overlooking the box garden to be her den. She would no longer have to illustrate books at the kitchen table, disturbed by the children and the doorbell endlessly ringing with everyone's Amazon deliveries. It was going to be marvellous.

She was inspired, too, by the thought of living close to the sea, which was only a few miles from the house. Imagine being able to wander down to the beach? To stroll up the sand in bare feet whenever she felt like it? To lie on her back in the sunshine and listen to the gentle whooshing of waves? She looked through the small rectangular windowpanes to the garden, still obscured by mist and the impinging darkness, and tried to imagine it. Everything would be lovely when the sun came out, she told herself firmly.

She moved away from the window and felt suddenly daunted by the size of the room. She wasn't used to so much space. She didn't know what to do with it. She was overwhelmed, and, for a terrible moment, doubted she could do it. Of course, it was quite a leap of faith leaving their home and friends and everything that was familiar, but they had both agreed that Bruce's health was a priority. Without it, he had nothing. Without it, they had nothing. Besides, the children would thrive in the clean air and with all this freedom. It would do each of them the world of good. It was going to be the best decision they had ever made – the *best*, she was sure of it.

Just then her heart lurched as a sharp thought punctured her positivity like a thorn. She saw herself in her cosy London kitchen with a cup of tea and the music softly playing. How warm and snug it was in that tiny but familiar room. She pushed the image out of her mind. No, this was going to be wonderful, she reassured herself for the millionth time – a new start, a new adventure – and once she'd settled in, St Sidwell Manor would feel just as cosy as her London home had.

She folded her arms and shivered. As she'd said to Bruce, she'd simply have to wear an extra sweater, or two.

Making a home out of a mansion was always going to be a challenge, but there were certain changes they had made in order for the house to feel less cavernous. They had decided not to use the attic at all, for why did they need six small servants' bedrooms when the floor below already had ten big ones? Olivia had therefore already shut off the narrow staircase with a door. It would remain untouched with its old wooden floorboards, plain white walls and simple iron beds. 'I'm not sure the house will be happy with this change,' Elsa had said when she'd seen what was being done. Olivia had reassured her that the house would get used to it. Elsa had looked doubtful. She had put her hands on her hips and narrowed her sea-green eyes and shaken her head portentously, but that was as far as her objections had gone.

No one liked change, Olivia understood that. However, nothing ever stayed the same. That was the nature of the world. St Sidwell Manor would just have to deal with it – as would Elsa Tregoning.

The first night was strange for all of them. Bruce and Olivia had chosen the largest bedroom for themselves. It was south-facing with a view of the lawn and lake. In it was an antique four-poster bed, a sturdy wardrobe and dresser, and an elegant dressing table, all fashioned out of walnut. Big Tudor windows with small rectangular panes dominated one wall and into the panelled recesses had been built charming seats. Olivia had decorated the bedroom to suit her taste – Bennison floral wallpaper and curtains, seagrass carpet and White Company bedlinen – but it still felt oddly spooky, as if she was being watched, as if the very house had eyes and was observing her reproachfully. The mist lay low on the ground and, as darkness settled over the gardens, nothing could be seen but an impenetrable blackness through which a subdued moon occasionally shone. Out of that blackness the lake gleamed like onyx. The wind whistled about the walls and through the branches of the plane trees, and the old house creaked and groaned like a cantankerous old man who objects to the arrival of strange city folk. Olivia lay awake, ears alert to every unfamiliar sound. She missed the soft rumble of traffic and the reassuring orange light that used to trickle through the gaps in the curtains of her bedroom in Notting Hill. Here the darkness was total, as if she had been swallowed into the belly of a whale. She pressed herself against Bruce's warm back and felt better when he took her hand and drew it into his chest. In a few moments he was asleep and for the first time ever she was grateful for his snoring because it made her feel less afraid. She hoped the children were asleep too and not lying awake like she was, feeling like she shouldn't be here.

*

Zach did not want to admit that he was frightened. He was fifteen years old and had been at boarding school since the age of eight. However, the moaning of the wind sounded like someone crying and the squeaking floorboards were like footsteps, making their way along the corridor towards his bedroom. He half expected the door to open at any moment and for a Wildling or a White Walker to barge in with an axe. He found the four-poster bed creepy. In fact, the whole house was like something out of a horror film. His parents were mad to have decided to move down here, to this remote part of the countryside where they knew no one. He would have preferred to remain in London. At least there they'd had nice neighbours and streetlights. He blinked into the darkness and tried to rein in his imagination. Finally, to subdue his fear, he put on his earphones and listened to his favourite playlist until he drifted into a restless sleep.

Tabitha, on the other hand, was not at all scared. To the contrary, she sat cross-legged on the seat in the window recess and watched the cloud slowly thin until silver wisps of moonlight began to brighten the sky like angels flying slowly across it. Through the small panes, she gazed transfixed at an enchanting new world as little by little it revealed itself to her. The trees, silhouetted now, waved their delicate branches and she imagined they were coming to life, like giants convening in the midnight garden. Perhaps they were waving at her, welcoming her to her new home, recognising that she was special, because she could see them for what they really were.

Tabitha loved it here already. She loved her four-poster bed with its thick velvet curtains, the wood panelling and window seats, and the sense of history in the old corridors, uneven walls and creaky floorboards. She hoped she would see a ghost, for surely a house as old as this must harbour souls who had died long ago. When she'd been small, she had often awoken at night and seen shadowy beings moving about her bedroom. At first, they had scared her, those translucent figures, and she had switched on the light in panic, and they had disappeared. But since she had read *The Ghosts* by Antonia Barber, a tattered book she had found in the school library and read with a torch long after her lights had been turned out, she had been fascinated by the paranormal, not fearful of it. Zach didn't believe in ghosts, and she hadn't told her parents in case they had a logical explanation that negated their existence. She didn't want to hear it. Tabitha knew that what she saw was real. Therefore, she had made a decision long ago to keep her experiences to herself. But to see one here – wouldn't that be delightful? She stared up at the cloud, now parting to reveal the bright round face of night's dependable watchman, and hoped more than anything that she would see something otherworldly.

The following morning, dawn broke onto limpid skies. Frost covered the lawn and twinkled like fairy dust in the weak winter sunshine. The wind had died, and, in its place, a gentle breeze slipped up the estuary and onto St Sidwell Manor, carrying with it the sulphurous scent of brine. Olivia opened the curtains and smiled with relief at the sight of her new home, for it looked so innocent and reassuring dressed in white. The overgrown weeds and tangled shrubs, hidden beneath their winter clothes, were magical. A red kite soared in the crisp blue, its mournful whistle punctuating the silence, and a pair of mallards waddled across the surface of the lake, which had frozen over during the night. Olivia took it all in, for soon the sun would melt the frost, and the rot would reveal itself along with the immense amount of work that would be required to restore the gardens to their former glory. But restore them, she would. She had taken on no new work assignments just so that she could dedicate her time to making this magnificent house a home.

Elsa had cooked breakfast and left it on the hot plate in the dining room. The house had not been modernised and the kitchen, pantry, scullery and storerooms were still cut off from the main part of the house by a green baize door. Behind it was the servants' domain and a place where, traditionally, the family was not welcome. Olivia had wanted to open that part of the house to make a large kitchen–living area, but they didn't have the money. At least not right now.

It felt strange to Olivia, the four of them sitting at one end of the long mahogany table, leaving the greater part of it empty. But Bruce tucked into bacon and eggs with relish and suggested they go exploring straight after breakfast. He hadn't heard the creaking bones of the house and had slept soundly. In a blue plaid shirt with his sleeves rolled up and a pair of jeans, he didn't seem to feel the cold either. 'Isn't this great?' he said, looking at each child in turn. 'How does it feel to live in a mansion? I suggest you eat up and then we can take a look around. This place doesn't seem to have changed since Victorian times. It's a real time warp.'

Zach was relieved it was morning. Sunlight poured in through the windows, banishing the shadows of the night and with them his fear. His father's enthusiasm made him feel stupid for having been afraid. White Walkers, indeed! What an idiot he'd been.

Tabitha was impatient to explore the house, but Olivia wanted them all out from under her feet; there were still boxes to be unpacked and things to be put away and she did not want to be distracted by the demands of her family. They'd have plenty of time to explore the house later.

'Right,' said Bruce, draining his coffee cup and pushing out his chair. 'Ready to venture into the wild?' He grinned at Zach and Tabitha, eyes shining with enthusiasm. 'We'll need scythes and swords to cut a path through the weeds.' Then to Olivia, 'It's going to be a challenge!'

Zach buttered another piece of toast to take with him. Tabitha hurried off to put on her coat and boots. Olivia laid her napkin on the table. 'This entire place is going to be a challenge,' she replied, smiling bravely. 'But together we can turn it into a fabulous home.'

After breakfast, Olivia found Elsa in the kitchen. It was one of the rooms she most longed to change for it was woefully outdated. It had a huge pine table, a cast-iron range placed in the alcove where once there must have been a great fire, and a dresser laden with shiny brass pots and pans, which would never be used. Olivia had put in a dishwasher, but, by the sight of the plates piled up in the sink, it did not look like Elsa knew how to work it. 'Everything to your liking, Mrs Olivia?' Elsa asked. Despite being told to call her Olivia, Elsa insisted on a certain formality. She did not seem pleased to see Olivia in her territory, either.

'All good, thank you, Elsa,' Olivia replied cheerfully, determined to make a friend of her.

Elsa looked as comfortable in that room as the table. With her dove-grey hair clipped loosely to the back of her head, a white apron worn over a black dress that reached down to her ankles, and black lace-up boots, she appeared out of another era, just like the house. Her whole demeanour was, in fact, old-fashioned, except for the large prehnite gemstone at her throat that matched the unusual greeny-blue colour of her eyes. Olivia felt as if she was intruding, even though the house was hers. 'I would love some help,' she said, her tone apologetic. 'There are boxes to be unpacked. Would you mind very much?'

Elsa nodded and went to wash her hands in the butler's sink. 'How was your first night? Did you sleep well?' she asked, picking up the soap and turning on the old brass tap. The water choked and spluttered before coming out in a rusty torrent.

'A bit scary, to be honest,' Olivia replied. 'I'm not used to such a big house.'

'Oh, it's a big house, and a little surly,' Elsa agreed, bangles jangling on her wrists as she soaped her hands. 'You just need to get to know each other.'

'It's not haunted, is it?' Olivia laughed nervously. She didn't really believe in ghosts, but, nonetheless, she wanted reassurance.

Elsa turned and her face softened. 'No, Mrs Olivia. It's only the sound of the wind and the natural creaking of an old building. In a few days' time, you won't even notice it.'

Olivia was relieved. 'That's good. One always assumes places like these are full of ghosts.'

'People love to tell tales, don't they? There are plenty of people around here who will tell you this place is haunted. Don't listen to them. I've lived here for over fifty years, and I've never had a moment's worry.'

'Thank you, Elsa. I'm glad to hear that,' said Olivia. 'Silly of me to mention it.'

Elsa smiled warmly and dried her hands on a tea towel. 'Now, where would you like to start?'

In her coat and boots, Tabitha followed her father and brother through the back door and onto a wide terrace that looked out over the garden. It was framed by an elegant but mildewy stone balustrade and had mossy steps that descended onto a paved pathway. The path sliced through the middle of what would once have been an immaculate lawn but was now overrun with weeds that peeped through the frost like tufts of fur. At the end of the path was a sorry-looking fountain. It seemed lost there in that desolate part of the garden.

Tabitha watched in delight as her breath misted on the air. It was bitterly cold, and everything was white, for Jack Frost had been busy in the night. The sky sparkled with millions of ice crystals and the gulls that wheeled beneath it suggested the sea was close. Tabitha was excited to be near the sea.

Propelled by a wave of enthusiasm, she set off along the path. Giant balls of yew topiary sat in rows on either side, resembling enormous Christmas puddings resting beneath a sprinkling of icing sugar. Tabitha abandoned the path and ran across the grass, her Wellington boots leaving a trail of footprints behind her. A pair of rabbits must have had the same idea for their tiny pawprints, set down in two trails of entangled tracks, revealed their nocturnal dance.

At length she reached the end of the path and stopped by the fountain. Crafted out of grey stone, it was circular in shape and quite large. In the centre was an intriguing statue of a woman. She seemed lonely, as if no one had noticed her in a very long time. Even the blackbirds and crows seemed to stay away, pecking the ground at the other end of the lawn. The stone that shaped her was mottled with lichen, yet time had not robbed her of her beauty. Indeed, her face was compelling, being both striking and sad. Her long swirling skirts gave her slender figure the illusion of movement while her outstretched hands reached up to heaven in supplication. Tabitha stood before her, assaulted suddenly by a strange feeling of sorrow. The way she tilted her face was pitiful, as if she were searching for something precious up there in the clouds. The fountain was dry, which seemed to compound the sense of solitude and neglect. Only dead leaves collected in the basin beneath it where water had once been.

'Tabitha!'

Tabitha was pulled out of her contemplation by her father waving at her from a pretty wooden gate built into a high stone wall. Reluctantly, she left the beautiful woman to her loneliness and ran to join him.

Through the gate was a walled vegetable garden that contained two enormous greenhouses, a rusted wheelbarrow discarded on its back, disused cold frames and a barn full of giant logs. While Bruce groaned at the sight of the mildewed glass on the greenhouses and the unappealing prospect of having to clean them, Tabitha and Zach raced on ahead over the abandoned vegetable plots and through a rickety gate at the far end into woodland. Their father called after them, but they ignored him and ran on. The feeling of space was intoxicating, the sense of adventure thrilling; neither wanted to slow down to a walk. There was too much to see. Too much to discover. Having been confined to the streets of London, this sprawling land was a paradise. Even Zach was beginning to appreciate the advantages of living on a large country estate.

Eventually, the trees opened onto a lush meadow and, in the far distance, the blue ribbon of the estuary glittering in the morning sunshine. In the middle of the meadow stood a small grey chapel surrounded by gravestones. The children stopped and stared, their exuberance stolen suddenly by the sobering sight of the graveyard. The place was eerily quiet, obviously neglected, perhaps for decades. Only crows hopped about the long grasses where the frost had already melted. Among the traditional gravestones were various obelisks on plinths. One or two leant unsteadily, maybe from the fierce gales that blew off the water, or possibly, Tabitha thought as she gazed upon them in fascination, unsettled by the souls of the dead that lingered restlessly beneath.

Zach, whose imagination was not made of the same fertile stuff as his sister's, saw simply tombstones, blackened by time and corroded by wind. What interested him, however, were the inscriptions carved into the stone, for that was history, and Zach was very interested in the past. He ran on ahead to examine them.

Bruce caught up with his children. 'Wow, look at this!' he exclaimed, putting his hands on his hips and catching his breath. He regretted spending so much time sitting at his desk and not taking exercise. But he was going to be a farmer now. He was going to get fit. 'An abandoned chapel. Amazing!' He hadn't explored this far when he'd first looked around the house back in the spring. Taking Tabitha by the hand, he strode towards it. 'Let's see what's inside, shall we?'

When they reached it, Zach was already wiping the lichen off one of the memorials and trying to read the inscription there.

'Who do all these gravestones belong to?' Tabitha asked.

'Dead people,' said Zach with a laugh.

'I know they're dead, silly,' she responded, rolling her eyes. 'Do you think they're people who used to live in the house?'

'I imagine it's the Pengower family chapel,' said Bruce. 'Let me see.' He bent down to read the inscription on one of the stones. *Bernard Pengower 1821–1881.* There, you see, I'm right.'

'This one's a Pengower too,' Zach called out, picking at the moss that concealed the first name. '1886–1965. Looks like it could be Robert, Robin, Richard. R-something.'

Tabitha let go of her father's hand and skipped over to look at one of the leaning obelisks. She stood before it. On the plinth was a white marble relief of a woman's hand. Gently resting in it was the small hand of a child. Above was a brief inscription: *Cordelia Pengower 1862–1896. May she find peace in holy rest.* 'Daddy, look at this one,' she said. 'Who do you think she was?'

Bruce came over to have a look. He, too, read the inscription and took in the elegant sculpture. The hands resembled a white dove. 'Well,' he began, remembering the small amount of research he'd done after he'd been told about his surprising inheritance. 'Thomas Pengower built the manor in fifteen eighty-six, having made his fortune providing wood for the royal fleet. I'd say Cordelia Pengower was important because she's been given a big memorial. The Victorians loved elaborate gravestones. I'd guess that she was mistress of the house and a mother, too, because she's holding a child's hand. And she died young. Only thirty-four years old. Perhaps she died in childbirth. Who knows?'

Tabitha wondered whether she was the same woman as the statue in the garden. The moment her thoughts turned to the statue she felt the hairs on the back of her neck stand up. She put a hand there and rubbed the skin.

'Are they all Pengowers?' Zach asked, now going from stone to stone like a bee in clover and counting how many Pengowers he could find.

'Looks like it, doesn't it? No Talwyns?' Bruce asked.

'Not yet,' Zach replied.

Shall we go inside?' Bruce suggested, making for the door. 'Then we can go home and see what we can find in the library. The library at the manor,' he added proudly, 'is pretty spectacular.'

'Home,' said Zach with a shrug. 'Sounds funny.'

'Funny ha-ha, or funny odd?' his father asked.

'Odd,' Zach returned. 'It doesn't feel like home yet.'

'It does to me,' Tabitha interjected. 'I don't ever want to go back to London.'

To Bruce's surprise, the chapel door was unlocked. The children followed him inside and fell silent. It was a simple place of worship, built for the Pengower family judging by the commemorative plaques bearing their name that dated as far back as the seventeenth century. Wooden pews were lined in rows facing the altar and the large stained-glass window behind it. The white altar cloth was clean, but nothing lay upon it. There was little doubt that the place was no longer in use – it had an air of abandonment – but somebody clearly came in to keep it clean; there were no dead insects on the windowsills or dry leaves in the corners. It did not smell stale as one might expect of such an old, disused building and it had a pleasant feeling, like an oasis of peace and tranquillity in a landscape that was battered by sea gales and rain.

'I'd like to know more about the Pengowers,' Bruce murmured, running his fingers over the marble relief of a certain Arthur Pengower who had died three hundred years before. Bruce was speaking to himself, but Tabitha overheard.

'There can't be any left,' she said. 'Because if there were, you wouldn't have been given the house.'

'Very true, darling,' he replied.

'Was Mrs Delaware a Pengower?' she added.

'She was. She was Emily Pengower, but she married Henry Delaware, so she must be buried here,' said Bruce. 'I didn't see a fresh grave out there, did you?'

'Are you sure you're not a Pengower, Dad?' Zach asked, plonking himself down in the front pew and folding his arms. It was icy cold and he shivered. 'How are you related to Mrs Delaware anyway?'

'I don't know,' Bruce replied. 'Distantly, for sure.' He and Olivia had both asked themselves the same question, and Elsa had been unable to enlighten them either. They hadn't had the time to do much research beyond looking down Bruce's family tree, which had yielded nothing. Frankly, he had more important things on his mind than genealogy.

'How can you not know?' said Zach.

'Well, the relations I called hadn't a clue. No one has heard of either Pengower or Delaware. I'm none the wiser.' Indeed, Bruce's parents were both dead and his younger brother lived in Australia. The fact that Olivia came from such a large family had been one of the things that had first attracted him to her. He had been tired of feeling alone in the world.

'How far back *can* you trace your family?' asked Zach.

'*Our* family,' Tabitha corrected.

'Quite far, actually, but there are no Delawares or Pengowers in it. That's for certain.'

Zach chuckled. 'So, you believe you're related to Mrs Delaware because she said so?'

'Yes, Zach. I'm sure she didn't make it up. Perhaps I'm descended from a distant cousin of hers. Doesn't have to be Delaware, does it? Could be anything. There'll be a connection somewhere. She's not going to have given it to a random person who has nothing to do with her. She specifically stated that I'm the closest living relative. So, there we are. And I'm not complaining.' He chuckled, appreciating once again his extraordinary good fortune at being handed such a magnificent estate on a plate.

Tabitha grinned. 'I'd like to be a Pengower,' she declared.

'Why?' said Zach, getting up. 'What's so good about being a Pengower? As far as I can see they're all dead.'

'I like the name. It sounds like Pendragon,' she replied. She couldn't put into words how much she already admired this family who had built the beautiful house and chapel and the statue in the garden.

'There's probably a family tree in the house somewhere,' said Bruce, leading the children out into the sunshine and closing the chapel door behind them. 'We can have a look in the library. There are loads of books in there. In fact, I'll assign you both a challenge. The first to find a family tree gets a fiver.'

Zach liked the sound of that. 'I'll find it,' he said, thrusting his hands into his pockets and setting off towards the trees at speed.

Tabitha took her father's hand. 'I know you're a Pengower,' she said, looking up at him with serious eyes.

'How do you know that, darling?'

'I just do,' she replied.

Her gaze lingered on the gravestones a moment as she and her father followed Zach through the long grasses. She was sure she'd seen something pass in front of one of them. It had been fleeting and out of the corner of her eye. It might have been a bird, or a squirrel. A chilly breeze lightly caressed her cheek and the skin on her arms rippled. She searched for the eyes that watched them, because she sensed they were not alone, but she saw nothing, only the gravestones – still, silent and cold.

Chapter Two

The following morning, Olivia drove into town with Tabitha, leaving Zach still searching for the family tree in the library and Bruce being given a tour around the farm by Tom. Olivia had slept no better than the first night. She'd left the light on in the bathroom and snuggled up against Bruce not simply to keep warm, but for reassurance. However, the groaning and creaking of the house was accompanied by a faint but distinctive sound of crying. To Olivia, it resembled the plaintive sobbing of a woman. Knowing that it couldn't possibly be that, she dismissed it as the wind whistling around the corners of the building – those sea gales were robust. But it was, nonetheless, unsettling. She hoped she'd get used to it – the wind was not going to go away.

Bruce, she discovered on waking, had heard nothing and had slept like a hibernating bear, which made her feel all the more foolish for having been afraid. It was clearly nothing. She was just being paranoid.

Tabitha, too, was sure she had heard whimpering, but when she'd told Zach about it at breakfast, he had laughed at her and declared that it was just the wind, moaning round the chimney stacks. 'Really, Tab, anyone would know that,' he'd said, not wanting to admit that he had heard it too – not wanting to disclose his own fear. But Tabitha was sure it had been a ghost, and resolved to do some investigating if she heard it again the following night.

St Sidwell was a picturesque seaside town built in a sheltered cove on the southwest coast of Cornwall. The hillside was clustered with white houses that cleaved to it like mussels to rock, their grey slate roofs and shiny windows giving the place a pleasing sense of uniformity. A small harbour saw the coming and going of blue-bottomed fishing boats and the seafront boasted quaint cafés, restaurants and gift shops that entertained tourists during the summer months, but which fell quiet off-season, and a little forlorn, when winter gales swept through the deserted streets, giving the place the desolate feeling of the morning after a party. Olivia parked the car against the kerb and set off for the local convenience shop where she'd advertised for a couple to replace Elsa Tregoning.

Fat clouds trundled across the sky like sheep and a brisk wind whipped off the water. Seagulls mewed as they wheeled against the blue, and one or two greedy ones squabbled over the odd chip discarded on the pavement outside Captain Killigrew's fish restaurant. The white houses dazzled in the bright light, but there was little warmth in the sun. Olivia, in a faux-fur hat and red scarf tucked into the lapels of her dove-grey cashmere coat, long blonde hair falling in loose curls down her back, cut an elegant albeit urban figure as she clattered down the high street in her expensive black ankle boots. Tabitha trotted enthusiastically along beside her. Small and slight for her age, she still wore clothes chosen by her mother and looked much too polished for this country setting in a crimson, waisted coat and matching bobble hat and scarf. Olivia noticed the inquisitive glances of locals as they passed, but she put their interest down to small-town curiosity; newcomers like them must have stuck out like parakeets among pigeons.

A bell tinkled as Olivia pushed open the door and strode in. It was pleasantly warm inside and smelt of damp. While Tabitha wandered the aisles, Olivia went straight to the counter where two young women were bent over their smartphones looking at social media and gossiping about the evening before. When they saw Olivia, they stopped talking and reluctantly put down their phones. Recognising her immediately, a shifty exchange passed surreptitiously between them.

'Hi,' said Olivia, tapping her fingers on the counter. 'I don't suppose anyone has shown any interest in my advertisement, have they?'

The girl with auburn hair, freckles and a nose ring shook her head. 'Afraid not,' she replied, cool blue eyes taking in this impossibly stylish woman who was as alien to her as the Queen. 'You'd have more luck trying further afield.'

Olivia sighed, struggling to distinguish the words beneath the girl's thick Cornish drawl. 'I know. But I really want a local person, ideally a couple. People who know the area. If I hire people from far away it will just be a case of the blind leading the blind.' She laughed mirthlessly.

The other girl, who had black spiky hair, unfeasibly long pink nails and was chewing gum, gave Olivia a sympathetic smile. 'Have you tried online?' She said it slowly, as if unsure whether someone as posh as Olivia knew what online was.

'I've been reluctant to do that,' Olivia replied. 'I don't want a live-in couple.'

The girls looked surprised. 'In a house that size you could have ten live-in couples and not even notice them,' said the redhead with a chuckle. She caught her friend's eye, and the gum-chewer chuckled too.

'I know it sounds silly,' said Olivia, laughing with them because she could see how very silly it sounded. 'We come from a small London house and value our privacy.'

Neither girl had ever been to London, but they did not imagine that Olivia's definition of small was the same as theirs. They looked at her blankly. Olivia sighed. 'What to do?' she murmured, tapping her fingers on the counter again. She was at a loss.

'If I were you, I'd persuade Elsa Tregoning to stay,' suggested the gum-chewer. 'She knows the house.'

'She said she'd stay on until I find someone to replace her,' said Olivia.

The redhead pulled a face. 'Then she'll be staying for some time,' she said. 'I'd not look a gift horse too hard in the mouth if I were you. Perhaps you'd better keep things as they are.'

Olivia thanked them, although they had been most unhelpful,

and went to the newspaper stand near the door to buy *The Times* for Bruce. Tabitha was now browsing the sweets close to the counter. Neither salesgirl noticed her there. 'Someone should tell the poor love the house is haunted,' said the redhead in a low voice.

'She'll find out soon enough,' returned the other. 'I give them a week.'

Tabitha's hand froze over the Maltesers. She stared at the two girls in astonishment. The power of her stare alerted them to her presence, and they looked down at her in surprise. 'Oh, hello there, sweetheart,' said the redhead, smiling guiltily. 'Do you want those?'

Tabitha shook her head, mumbled that she'd changed her mind, and went off to find her mother. On the way home in the car she was pensive. She gazed out of the window at the passing countryside and wondered whether the house was, indeed, haunted. And if it was, by whom? Perhaps she hadn't imagined the sound of whimpering, after all.

'What are you thinking about, darling?' Olivia asked, noticing that her daughter was unusually quiet.

'Do you think the house is haunted?' Tabitha asked.

Olivia laughed nervously and answered a little too quickly. 'Of course not, why?'

'Maybe that's why no one wants to work there.'

'Well, Elsa and Tom haven't got a problem with it, have they? Elsa's worked there for over fifty years and Tom's grown up there. In fact, Elsa specifically told me there are no ghosts.'

'You asked her?'

'I did.'

'Maybe she's lying to stop you being frightened.'

Olivia glanced at her daughter and frowned. 'What's brought this on?'

Tabitha silently debated whether to tell her mother what she'd overheard. She didn't want to worry her, but, on the other hand, it might explain why no one had responded to her advertisement. 'I heard the girls in the shop saying that someone should tell you it's haunted,' she admitted, finally.

'Typical!' Olivia exclaimed in annoyance. 'Elsa said people like to gossip. As soon as you get an old house you get stories of ghosts! It's such a cliché. I don't believe in ghosts and neither should you,' she added tersely. 'Ridiculous.'

Tabitha bit her lip and turned her eyes back to the passing countryside. Her excitement quietly mounted. A haunted house. She couldn't think of anything more wonderful!

They drove on in silence. As they turned into the drive and made their way beneath the plane trees, Olivia hoped it wouldn't be as hard to find people to tend to the gardens as it was to find people to tend to the house.

Inspired now by the very real possibility of her new home being full of ghosts, Tabitha decided to ask Elsa about it herself. She found her in the kitchen preparing lunch. She perched on a stool and watched the old woman taste with a spoon the lamb stew that simmered on the gas stove. It smelled delicious and Tabitha's stomach growled. 'What was Mrs Delaware like?' she asked.

Elsa put down the wooden spoon and looked at Tabitha thoughtfully. The child's eyes were the colour of topaz and full of enthusiasm and inquisitiveness, but there was something wise about them, as if there was an adult behind them, looking out. 'She was a cold woman, secretive and antisocial,' Elsa began, wanting to satisfy the child's curiosity and, at the same time, get to know her. Tom hadn't married so Elsa had no grandchildren to dote on. She suspected, by the alert and curious look on her face, that Tabitha was a rather exceptional person. 'But once you won her trust, she softened,' Elsa continued. 'She was an only child and looked after her father until he died. She was a widow by then and had no children, though not for want of trying. She miscarried three, you see. That was a tragedy and she never got over it, God bless her. She never married again, either, but lived here all by herself, rattling around like a marble in a tin.'

'But she had you,' Tabitha reminded her.

'She did, indeed.' Elsa sighed and moved away from the stove. 'She had me and Tom. I was very fond of her. She was like a mother to me, in a way. When I came to work here, I was but a girl.'

'Did you have a husband, Elsa?'

'I did, but not for long. He was taken.'

'Who by?'

Elsa chuckled. 'The Lord. My Gerren died after a short illness and the Lord saw fit to take him.' She pulled a regretful face. 'We don't have much luck in this house. But that's all going to change now that you're here. It's going to become a happy house.'

'That's a funny name, Gerren,' said Tabitha.

'It's Cornish.'

'It's nice,' Tabitha added, not wanting to appear rude. 'Is Mrs Delaware buried at the chapel?'

'No, she's scattered,' said Elsa. 'I think I'd like to be scattered too, somewhere peaceful by the sea.'

'Why didn't Mrs Delaware look after the gardens?'

'She didn't have the money to do that. This big old house gobbles up money, as your parents are going to find out, God help them.' She started stirring the pot again. 'Mrs Delaware didn't do anything to it when she inherited it from her father because she liked it just the way it was. I like it just the way it is too. We oldies don't like change.'

'If Daddy is related to Mrs Delaware,' Tabitha continued, 'he must be a Pengower, right?'

'Oh, he will be,' Elsa replied with a certainty that took Tabitha by surprise. 'It was important for Mrs Delaware that the house stayed in the family, her not having children of her own. The Pengowers built it, you see, in the time of Queen Elizabeth the First. Fancy it being that old, eh? Bet you've never set foot in such an old house before.'

Tabitha was not thinking about the house, but about the Pengowers. 'Daddy says he doesn't have a family tree,' she said ponderously. 'He says there's nothing interesting about his family.'

'There's likely to be a Pengower family history here somewhere. Mrs Delaware was very interested in genealogy.'

'What's that?'

'Family trees.'

'Why?'

'Because the Pengowers used to be a big and powerful family once. She was proud of that. In fact, this house was the only thing she was proud of. It was everything to her. Poor duck, it was all she had. But she got old and let it go to ruin. She went to ruin herself, in a way, becoming more and more isolated.' Elsa's eyes looked far-away suddenly. 'It was beautiful once, but sad. It's always been sad. When I was a girl . . .'

'Are there ghosts?' Tabitha interrupted.

Elsa blinked and tossed the spoon into the sink. 'Never you mind about ghosts,' she said dismissively.

'But I heard the ladies in the shop saying the house is haunted.'

'Tales, that's all they are. Tales. People love to think the worst.'

'I think it *is* haunted. I heard someone crying last night,' Tabitha stated suddenly.

'Just the wind,' said Elsa, bending down with a groan to open the stove door and check on the baking potatoes.

'That's what Zach said.'

'Sensible boy. You London folk aren't used to sea gales.'

'Do you believe in ghosts, Elsa?'

Elsa stood up stiffly, putting a hand in the small of her back and grimacing. 'No,' she replied quickly. 'When you go, you go, and you don't come back.'

'Are you afraid of dying?'

Elsa frowned. This child was certainly unusual. 'That's a strange question,' she said.

'*I'm* not.'

'Nor should you be. You're young. You have a long life ahead of you. I'll be seventy next year.'

'That's old,' said Tabitha.

'You're right about that, my lovely. Sometimes I feel every one of those years in my bones.' Elsa chuckled and went back to the stew. 'Lunch will be in ten minutes,' she said. 'Why don't you go and tell your brother.'

That night, Tabitha lay in bed waiting for the sound of crying. It was windy once again and her windows clattered, but the moaning the wind made as it whistled about the chimney stacks was very different to the crying she was sure she had heard the night before. She stared at the ceiling of her four-poster bed. The shimmering moonlight that seeped in through the gaps in the curtains made it possible for her to see it clearly. There was a rose painted onto the wood and a pair of birds. The paint had faded, but she could still make out the picture. She wondered who had slept here before her and looked up at the same sight. Maybe Queen Elizabeth I herself. The mattress was soft, and she sank into it with pleasure. Her London bed hadn't been anything like as comfortable or as big. She was alert to every creak and scrape, and to the scratching noise of mice beneath the floorboards, but there came no murmur of crying. Eventually, she must have drifted off, lulled by the wind and overtaken by tiredness, for she was awoken sometime later by the sound she'd been waiting for.

She lay very still and listened. It was definitely someone sobbing, a woman or a child, judging by the pitch of it. Soft and mournful. Tabitha wanted to give comfort. She couldn't bear to remain in her bed while this poor creature cried with such despair. Finally, after arguing with herself, wavering between nervousness and curiosity, she slid out from beneath the covers and climbed down. Her room was cold. She reached for her dressing gown that hung on a hook on the back of the door, and slipped her feet, already snug in cashmere socks, into sheepskin slippers. She turned the brass knob and opened the door a crack.

The crying did not stop but grew a little louder.

Tabitha stepped out into the corridor. It was colder there than in her bedroom, and she shuddered. Suddenly, she was surprised by a figure looming out of the darkness. She gasped, but it was only Zach. 'What the hell . . .' she whispered crossly. Zach put a finger over his lips to silence her. His eyes glinted in the moonlight that entered through a small window and Tabitha saw the fear in them. Tabitha, however, was not afraid – in fact, she felt vindicated, for Zach would not have come out to investigate had he still thought the crying sound was only the wind.

Encouraged by his sister's presence, Zach tiptoed ahead, in the direction of the crying. He hoped he'd discover that it was Elsa and then he could go back to bed and not worry about hauntings any more. Tabitha was in no doubt that it was a ghost. It hadn't occurred to her that it might be Elsa. She'd be intensely disappointed if she found out that it came from someone living.

The two children carried on as the crying grew louder. At the end of the corridor was an L-shaped bend. A tall window cast a grid of silver squares onto the floor over which they silently stepped. No sooner had they turned the corner than they were faced with a big, wood-panelled door. The crying sound was coming from behind it. Zach shied away, for the tone of the crying told him immediately that it was *not* Elsa, and, besides, the Tregonings' quarters were not in this part of the house, but in the kitchen wing.

Tabitha pushed past him and put her hand on the doorknob. Taking a breath and gathering her courage, she turned it.

Both children could barely hear above the pounding of their hearts. Yet, when Tabitha switched on the light, they saw only an empty bedroom. The crying had stopped. They stood and listened, running their eyes over the high metal-framed bed, the mahogany chest of drawers and wardrobe, the window seat and the small panes of glass through which the moon shone keenly. An icy chill pervaded the place. It had the stagnant smell of a room whose window was never opened – the stagnant smell of abandonment.

'There's no one in here,' said Zach, stating the obvious with relief.

'Someone *was*,' said Tabitha, sensing an unhappy energy that lingered in spite of the glow of the naked lightbulb. Whoever had haunted this room might have disappeared, but they had left a trace of their emotion behind. Tabitha felt it strongly.

'Well, unless they jumped out of the window or walked through the wall, there never was anyone in here. The crying must have come from another room.' Zach chuckled. The sound of his voice dispelled his fear and he felt foolish, once again, for having been afraid. 'Perhaps it's a cat,' he added. 'There might be cat in the house, or outside the window. We're just being stupid.'

Tabitha lifted her chin defiantly. 'It was a ghost, Zach,' she declared firmly. Zach was about to disagree but chose not to. 'I overheard the ladies in the shop saying this place is haunted and that's why no one wants to work here,' Tabitha continued in a loud whisper. 'I told Mum and she said it's rubbish. But I think this house is haunted. I can feel it.'

'You just *want* it to be haunted,' he said.

Tabitha shrugged. 'I don't mind if it is.' She narrowed her eyes. 'She was in here, I know it. I *feel* it. She's left her unhappiness behind.'

Zach shivered. 'Let's get out of here,' he said, making for the door.

'You needn't be afraid,' she said, following him into the corridor. 'I don't think it's a nasty ghost, just a sad one.'

'I'm not afraid,' he replied tersely. 'I came to investigate, didn't I?'

Tabitha chuckled. 'You're as white as a sheet.'

'So are you.'

'No, I'm not.'

'Yes, you are.'

He walked back up the corridor, not caring now if his footsteps caused the floorboards to creak. If there was a ghost, perhaps the noise would scare it away. He wanted to ask Tabitha to sleep in his bedroom, but he didn't want her to think him pathetic. 'Are you okay, sleeping on your own?' he asked, hoping she'd grab the chance to share with him.

'I'm not frightened,' she told him coolly. 'But you can come and sleep in my bed if you want. It's big enough for ten people!'

He looked appalled. 'As if,' he scoffed. 'We'll find out the Tregonings have a cat and then we'll feel really stupid.'

'Suit yourself,' she said, opening the door to her bedroom and stepping inside. 'Check the bed before you climb in – there are big fat rats under the floorboards, and they love warm feet!' She laughed and closed the door behind her.

As she snuggled beneath the duvet she heard once again the distant sound of crying. She listened hard. It was not the wind, or a cat, or, indeed, a rat. It was a woman. The sorrowful, grief-stricken crying of a woman.

*

Further down the corridor, Olivia curled up against Bruce, who snored loudly; he'd drunk too much red wine at dinner. She could hear the same noise again. Wind or not, it sounded like crying. She wasn't sure she would ever get used to it. It tugged at the primordial part of her, the maternal part of her, and gave her pain. She wanted it to stop. She squeezed her eyes shut and tried to focus on Bruce's snoring. But the sobbing was pitiful, and constant.

The next day, while Bruce drove Zach into St Sidwell to buy a Christmas tree, Olivia searched through the bookshelves in the library for a history of the house. So far, neither Zach nor Bruce had managed to find one. Ever since Bruce had inherited St Sidwell Manor, her family had been on at her about her husband's connection to Mrs Delaware. They couldn't understand why someone Bruce had never heard of had bequeathed him a mansion. Olivia needed to find out as much as she could about the house and its history, or they would think her negligent. Who inherits an old house and doesn't bother to learn something about its history?

The trouble was, neither Bruce nor Olivia had had the time nor the inclination to do any research until now. Olivia had been busy illustrating a children's novel, the author of which was a pedant, sending the drawings back countless times in her pursuit of perfection. On top of that, Olivia had managed the building work of the manor and looked after the children, which had given her little time for anything else. Bruce had given it his vague attention, but, besides finding out who had built it and when, he had learnt nothing.

Now Olivia stood in the library, surrounded by shelves and shelves of beautifully bound old books that would no doubt be worth a fortune were she to approach one of those antiquarian booksellers in London. The room itself was magnificent. The walls were completely taken up by wooden bookshelves, the ceiling ribbed with sturdy beams. Rugs covered oak floorboards aged to a rich brown. In the centre was a round table laden with heavy tomes. There was a tall, mullioned window at one end with a charming window seat and, in the middle of one wall, a marble fireplace beneath a portrait of a man in a white wig, fetching white stockings and a scarlet and ermine cloak. There had been a very valuable antique French clock on the mantelpiece when she'd first viewed the property, but that had been one of the many treasures they had had to sell at auction in order to pay the inheritance tax. Olivia decided to start at one end of the room and work her way round.

While her mother searched for a family history, sneezing every now and again at the dust, Tabitha set off to explore the house. There was a large part of it she had yet to see, most notably the attic. She knew her mother had cut it off from the rest of the house by a door, because she'd overheard her on the telephone discussing it with the builder, and also justifying her decision to Bruce who had initially wanted to use that floor for Tabitha and Zach and the many friends they were going to invite to stay during the school holidays. It was not out of bounds, only ignored, and this made Tabitha all the more curious to explore it; there was nothing as exciting as a secret floor separated from the rest of the house by a locked door.

The door, as it turned out, was not locked, but that did not make her expedition any less thrilling. As soon as she set off up the narrow wooden staircase, worn in the middle of each step by centuries of treading feet, she began to feel a strange chill. It was a different sort of cold from the rest of the house, it had a heaviness to it as if it was thick with damp. It smelt different too, but that might have been caused by a dead mouse decomposing beneath the floorboards. Tabitha wasn't sure. Once again, she got the feeling that she was being watched. It seemed that eyes followed her everywhere – as if the very walls had eyes.

At the top of the staircase was a narrow corridor with doors to bedrooms and little natural light. When she looked about for a switch, there seemed not to be one. In fact, on closer inspection she discovered that there were no electric lights at all. Old cobwebs had been spun and later abandoned in the corners where the walls met the ceiling, and brown patches of damp darkened the white paint.

Tabitha knew servants had slept here once, for the rooms were modest with uncomfortable-looking iron beds. Of course, there were no sheets or blankets, just striped mattresses too thin and knobbly to give anyone a good night's sleep. The ceilings were low for this floor was built under the eaves; a grown person would have to stoop to walk safely down the corridor. Tabitha, being small, could walk with her head held high, but Zach would not be able to do so and neither would her parents.

She wandered from room to room, imagining what it must have been like for the servants who once occupied them. The air was stale and distasteful, and it was dreadfully quiet. Suddenly she heard a shuffling noise. She stopped in her tracks and cocked an ear. She heard it again. It was coming from the room at the end of the corridor. A banging noise and a strange, muffled sound. Her heart began to thump in her chest, but she didn't turn around and flee. She was more than ready to see a ghost – after all, they were vaporous things and unable to hurt her. She thought of Elsa then and realised that the housekeeper had not told her the truth. The house was haunted. But why was Elsa lying?

Slowly, Tabitha made her way towards the door. Behind it, the noise got louder. Tabitha took a deep breath and paused a moment with her hand on the brass knob. She hoped that this time, when she opened the door, the ghost would still be there.

Quietly, she turned the knob. There came another banging sound from within. Tabitha pushed open the door and winced, catching her breath and taking a step back, as if expecting whatever was inside to suddenly pounce on her.

To her disappointment it wasn't a ghost at all, but a huge crow flapping about the room, trying to get out. One look at the broken windowpane told her how it had managed to fly in. Tabitha hurried to open the window and then left just as quickly, closing the door behind her.

Chapter Three

Olivia had hoped for a quiet Christmas – she didn't want Bruce to have any stress with her large family descending on them – and had managed to use the dilapidated state of the house as an excuse as to why she couldn't invite them all to stay. However, her spinster aunt, Antoinette, was a case apart and could not be deterred. Nothing could put *her* off visiting her favourite niece in her new home and, despite Olivia's gentle attempts to defer her stay, nothing did.

The day of her arrival it snowed. Fat feathery flakes floated down from a flat white sky, shrouding the house and gardens in a downy silence. Bruce and Zach had erected the fir tree in the hall – they'd chosen the biggest they could find – and Olivia and Tabitha had decorated it with tinsel, shiny baubles and fairy lights. The effect was charming. Tom had filled the baskets with logs, bringing them round to the front in a tractor and trailer, and carrying them through the house without complaint. He had lit fires in the hall and drawing room, as well as in the dining room where they would be having dinner. Nothing seemed too much for him – he managed the farm and the estate with the philosophical temperament of a man who accepted the moment as it was, because he had little control over the land and none at all over the elements, so it was therefore pointless to fret. Every request was met with a nod and a lopsided smile, and he went about his tasks in an easy, unhurried way, but managed to complete everything. Olivia found him a pleasant person to be around and was certain he would be a good influence on her husband. She had aired one of the nicest spare bedrooms that looked over the drive for Antoinette and, with

Elsa's help, had made the bed with brand new sheets from The White Company. Bruce put electric heaters in the main rooms, but, in spite of continuously blowing out hot air, the house still felt cold. It was as if the very bones of it were made of ice.

Olivia was restless. She wanted the house to feel like a home, but nothing in it belonged to her, at least nothing felt like it did. It resembled one of those stately homes that are open to the public, beautiful to look at but vacant. The sofas and chairs might once have been upholstered in the finest damask silks, but they were now faded and threadbare and sagging in the places where the springs had gone. Rugs were moth-eaten, bookcases dusty, and everything smelt of age, like a museum. Ornaments that might have been hundreds of years old were lovely to look at, but they were impersonal and held no value for Olivia. In fact, she was a little afraid to touch them, as if she were in someone else's home, rifling through their possessions. Any minute she expected the mistress to walk in and question what she was up to. She wandered around, plumping up cushions, tentatively moving objects, even rearranging the furniture, but somehow the place still felt inhospitable. It was partly due to the inherent cold, of course, but it was something else, besides; an uneasiness, as if the house itself was unhappy. No amount of repositioning tables and chairs could impact the fundamental feeling of disquiet that lay within the foundations. Olivia knew her aunt would be impressed – it was impossible not to be – but she wanted her to feel comfortable. If Olivia didn't feel comfortable, how could she expect anyone else to?

She was in the hall, sitting on the stairs in a thick grey jersey, wondering whether she should have bought poinsettias for the refectory table, when she was alerted to the arrival of her aunt by the rumbling sound of a car making its way slowly over the gravel. Olivia got up and called through the green baize door for Tom to come and help with the bags. A moment later he sauntered out from the kitchen wing, munching on a biscuit.

Antoinette Dixon burst into the hall with typical aplomb, bringing with her a gust of icy air and a holler of good cheer. 'How lovely to be here, at last. What a magnificent house! Goodness, the tree.

Gorgeous! And the fire. Heaven. Darling girl,' she exclaimed on seeing her niece. 'How lovely to see *you*, Liv.'

Tom went outside to bring in her bag. When he opened the boot of her rickety Volvo estate, he was surprised to find a large animal lying in the back. 'Bloody hell!' he exclaimed, putting a hand on his heart. 'How much does this thing eat?'

Everything about Antoinette was oversized, from her fulsome body to her titanic personality. She wrapped Olivia in a hearty embrace, swallowing her into the folds of her favourite old sheepskin coat and almost overwhelming her with the smell of wet dog and cigarette smoke. Her once lustrous brown hair had been left to the fancy of nature and was now streaked with grey, and, as she never cut it, it was much too long to be let loose. She swivelled the lengthy strands into a knot and secured it onto her head with a pencil. She wore no make-up and washed her face with soap – when she remembered. Her nails were bitten rather than filed and she could not have cared less about her clothes; she wore what was comfortable and inexpensive, and if the colours blended rather than clashed, it was a pleasant coincidence rather than a considered choice. Antoinette was loud, cheerful and immensely charismatic.

She swept her bright green eyes over the hall. 'This really is magical, Liv,' she gushed. 'It's as if time has stood still. Really, it doesn't look like anything has been done to it for a hundred years. Splendid.' She smiled broadly at her niece, revealing crooked teeth. 'Many would baulk beneath the challenge of such a massive project, but not you, Liv. You rise like David before Goliath. I can't wait to see what you do to it.'

Olivia laughed. 'I'm finding it overwhelming, actually,' she said. Then, aware that she might sound ungrateful, she added quickly, 'But it's a fantastic house and slowly we'll make it into a home.'

'I have no doubt that you will,' Antoinette replied, striding into the drawing room. 'Goodness, what a magnificent room. Magnificent. And yet another beautiful fireplace. Aren't they lovely. Glorious. I feel as if I'm stepping back in time.'

'So do I,' said Olivia. 'There's so much work to be done.'

Antoinette looked around eagerly. 'I bet it's haunted.'

Olivia winced. 'Oh, no. I'm sure not.'

'Oh, yes! A house this old? It would be odd for it *not* to be haunted. Think of all the people who have died here.'

'I'd rather not.'

'Such fun. I shall lie awake tonight and listen out for strange noises.'

'Oh, you'll hear plenty of those.' Olivia put a hand on her aunt's sleeve. 'But let's not talk about ghosts in front of the children. I don't want to put them off. It wasn't easy persuading Zach to leave London, and Tabitha is still young and sensitive. I don't want to frighten her.'

At that moment, Bruce strode in dressed in a pair of brown corduroy trousers and a brown fleece gilet over a checked shirt. He was already looking like a farmer, Olivia thought. 'Antoinette,' he exclaimed, opening his arms to embrace her. 'You look well.'

'You need feeding up,' Antoinette replied, looking him over and allowing him to kiss her plump cheek. 'Are there any cows on this farm?'

'Yes, we have a dairy herd. Are you suggesting I eat one?' Bruce replied with a grin.

'Might not be a bad idea. You're much too thin.'

'I'd rather buy a steak in the supermarket,' he said.

Antoinette laughed. 'I think you're going to enjoy being a farmer. Beats working in an air-conditioned office in the middle of the city, doesn't it?'

'It sure does,' Bruce agreed happily. 'I'm looking forward to giving it a go. Tom, the manager, is going to learn the meaning of the word patience! What would you like to drink?'

Antoinette was distracted by Zach and Tabitha, who were coming into the room looking none too pleased at having been pulled away from the television by their father. 'Ah, monkeys! What have you been up to? You look as guilty as sin!' Antoinette narrowed her eyes and gave Tabitha the once-over. 'Pretty as a picture but as pale as porridge. My dear, you need fresh air. Get rid of that city pallor at once! Hello, Zachary. How handsome you are! And haven't you shot up. Yes, you're a weed!' She patted his head as if he were a pet. 'Bruce, I'd love a drink. Make it strong. Whisky, double, straight up. It's been a long drive.' She looked at the children in turn. 'Will one of you let the dog out? She's in the back of the car.'

'You've brought Daphne?' Tabitha exclaimed, giving a jump of joy.

'Of course. I couldn't very well leave her at home at Christmas, could I? She might eat Santa Claus, mistaking him for a big red cake.'

Tabitha dashed out of the room. Zach flopped onto one of the sofas, sending up a cloud of dust. Bruce handed Antoinette the tumbler of whisky. Olivia perched on the club fender, relishing the feeling of warmth on her back.

Antoinette sat on the sofa opposite Zach. 'Isn't it nice to be together, and in this marvellous place,' she said. She took a generous swig of whisky and smacked her lips. 'Marvellous place. Can't wait for a tour.'

They heard the front door slam and then Tabitha flew in with Daphne, an enormous marmalade-and-white St Bernard. 'Drool alert!' Antoinette exclaimed. 'Back to the car, Tabitha, at once, and fetch a towel. They're on the back seat. Olivia won't want Daphne dribbling over her sofas. And you might as well bring in her water bowl too.'

Tabitha went out to get the towel and dog bowl. Her shoes made scrunching noises on the snow as she skipped back to the Volvo. Antoinette's car looked like it could do with a good wash, and much else besides. It was a boxy old thing with patches of rust and splatterings of mud. As she was shutting the boot, something made her look up. There, in an upstairs window, she thought she saw a white face, staring down at her. She caught her breath. However, no sooner had she seen it than it vanished. She turned to the sky. The moon was shining brightly behind diaphanous layers of feathery cloud. Could it have been a trick of light? A reflection of a cloud passing over the glass? She remained a moment, gazing hopefully up at the window, but the face did not reappear. Finally, unable to withstand the cold a moment longer, she hurried back into the house.

Olivia had warmed the dining room with two electric heaters as well as a substantial fire, but even though the temperature was toasty, a subliminal chill persisted. Elsa had cooked a cottage pie, and everyone sat down at the long table to eat it. Bruce had taken trouble with the wine, knowing how much Antoinette appreciated it, and had decanted a bottle of Argentine merlot into a crystal decanter he'd found in the pantry.

'This strange relative left all this to you?' said Antoinette, lifting her fork and examining the crest engraved into the silver. 'What is it? I can't see without my glasses.'

'A lion and a unicorn,' Bruce replied. 'Yes, she left the place as it was. I inherited everything, even this crystal decanter.'

'How extraordinary,' Antoinette exclaimed. 'To leave your home to a perfect stranger.'

Bruce grinned. 'Lucky me.'

'Lucky, indeed.' Antoinette turned to the children. 'I bet you two are delighted to have such a big house with all those gardens to play in.'

Zach looked unconvinced. He stabbed the peas with his fork. 'It doesn't feel like home yet,' he said.

'Give it time, Zachary. Homes are created by memories. You have to make them.'

'We have to make it our own,' Olivia cut in quickly. 'Right now, everything feels strange and unfamiliar. But we'll get used to it. Antoinette's right. We need to give it time. Rome wasn't built in a day.'

Tabitha smiled. 'I love it here. There's so much to explore.'

'That's the spirit!' Antoinette gushed, swigging her wine. 'Don't let it defeat you. Grab it with both hands.'

Tabitha laughed. She loved Antoinette's enthusiasm. It was infectious. 'Did you bring your cards, Antoinette?' she asked.

'I always bring my cards,' Antoinette answered.

'*I'd* like to learn how to read tarot,' said Tabitha.

Zach rolled his eyes then looked to his father for backing. 'They're just cards,' he said. Bruce caught his gaze and smiled in agreement.

'Nothing wrong with a bit of fun,' Olivia interjected. She knew how important tarot was to Antoinette.

'Oh, they're not fun, Liv,' Antoinette corrected her seriously. 'One must never read the tarot for fun. In fact, rule number one with regards to any psychic work – you never enter into it for fun. The law of attraction is very powerful. Like attracts like. If you enter into it for mischief, you will attract mischief and then you'll be sorry.'

Zach chuckled. 'Tabitha thinks this house is haunted.'

Olivia put down her fork with a clank. 'Let's not talk about ghosts, Zach,' she said, feeling ever more keenly the underlying chill.

'There are no such things as ghosts,' said Bruce. 'Nor are there leprechauns, goblins or fairies.'

Tabitha was watching Antoinette closely. 'What do you think, Antoinette?' she asked.

'Well, it's important to distinguish between ghosts and spirits,' she began, ignoring Olivia's stiffening jaw and Bruce's loud sigh, and fixing her keen gaze on Tabitha. 'Ghosts are empty, two-dimensional energies that are trapped in places where trauma has occurred. They are not dead people, but the memory of dead people, replayed over and over like a roll of black-and-white film. Anne Boleyn stalking the corridors in the Tower of London is a good example of a ghost. That's *not* her spirit, but a trapped memory. It will eventually fade, in time. Spirits, on the other hand, are the souls of people who have died. They come back to be close to the places and people they love, but, sometimes, they get stuck between worlds and are unable to move on without our help.'

'Why do they get stuck?' Tabitha asked.

'Do we really need to hear about this, Antoinette?' Olivia asked. She looked at Bruce, who shrugged good-naturedly.

'Tabitha isn't scared, are you, Tabitha?' said Antoinette.

'I'm not scared at all,' the child replied eagerly.

'Neither am I,' said Zach. 'Because there are no such things as ghosts.'

'So, why do they get stuck?' Tabitha persisted, ignoring her brother.

Antoinette took a sip of wine and then continued. 'Sometimes they don't know they're dead. If they come out of their bodies too quickly, or if their death is particularly traumatic, they can be left in a state of confusion. They're bewildered, you see, Tabitha. They need to be shown the way home to Spirit, to what you would call Heaven.'

Bruce laughed and poured himself more wine. 'Is that what you do, Antoinette? Show them the way home? I'd like to see you do that. "Come on, spirits, chop chop!"' He imitated her voice and laughed.

'I wish I could, Bruce. Sadly, I'm not gifted in that way.' She glanced at Olivia and put down her wine glass in a belated act of compliance. 'I'm sure this house isn't haunted. Just because it's old, doesn't mean it will harbour spirits.'

'I hope it *is* haunted,' said Tabitha, thinking of the face at the window and the strange sound of crying.

'I'd like to see you come across a real ghost,' said Zach. 'Then you might not be so eager.'

'I'll give you a tarot lesson tomorrow, if you like, Tabitha,' Antoinette offered.

'I'd love that,' Tabitha replied, eyes lighting up.

'Not before I've given you a tour of the house,' said Olivia.

'And I've given you a tour of the farm,' Bruce added. Husband and wife smiled at each other in collusion.

Tabitha sighed and forked some pie into her mouth. It was cold.

Antoinette considered herself an amateur enthusiast when it came to the paranormal. In her childhood she had seen shadowy beings in her bedroom, but she saw them rarely these days, which was most frustrating for someone who was keen to develop her psychic ability. Meditation would have honed it, but she didn't have the patience to sit and do nothing. She was good at reading, though, and had devoured a wide variety of books on the subject, which she ordered from Watkins Books in London. She was a most enthusiastic member of the College of Psychic Studies in London, probably *the* most enthusiastic, where she attended lectures and the odd workshop, and had taken courses in palmistry and scrying as well as in tarot. She had been a professional painter in her day, which had taken her to houses all over the country where she'd had various ghostly encounters. But nothing had prepared her for St Sidwell Manor. She had known as soon as she had laid eyes on the house that it was going to be riddled with spirits, and she was ready to test her sensitivity. But that first night was something else.

She was awoken in the small hours by the sound of someone crying. At first, she thought it was one of the children, most likely Tabitha having a nightmare. She waited for Olivia to go and comfort her, but the crying didn't stop. Perhaps Olivia was a heavy sleeper, she thought. Or maybe Tabitha's bedroom was too far away for her mother to hear her. Never one to hold back, Antoinette took it upon herself to find Tabitha's room and reassure the child herself. It wouldn't be hard to find. She'd just follow the sound of sobbing.

Antoinette padded softly down the corridor in her pyjamas and bare feet. No need for a dressing gown; Antoinette did not mind the cold. The way was lit by the moon that shone in through the odd window. It cast its silvery light onto the walls, bringing into relief the portraits hanging there so that the eyes of Mrs Delaware's ancestors seemed to watch her warily. The crying got louder. Antoinette followed the sound until she reached a door just beyond an L-shaped bend. She realised then that it was not the crying of a child, after all, but that of a woman, and one in great distress. She shivered, but not from the cold. That sorrowful sound cut her to the quick.

Spurred on by the urgent need to comfort this person who was so unhappy, Antoinette gently pushed open the door. The crying stopped at once. The icy cold in the room had a particular quality to it, alerting her to the fact that the presence wasn't a person at all, but a spirit. Antoinette had encountered them before.

She knew not to switch on the light. She would see nothing if she were to do that. Spirits, like stars, could only be seen by

41

amateur enthusiasts like her in the dark, when she was in a certain, somnolent frame of mind. The switching on of lights would shift her out of that mindset, like moving the dial on a radio and losing reception. But even in the darkness, Antoinette saw nothing. What lingered, however, was the sense of someone having occupied the room – an energy, deeply sad and disturbing. Antoinette knew that the spirit hadn't gone very far, but she knew, too, that she was not equipped to deal with it. However, she was acquainted with someone who was. Someone who understood exactly how to deal with cases like this. She'd tell Olivia first thing in the morning. Whatever happened, this poor, unhappy creature had to be settled.

Olivia did not wake up due to the sound of crying, but to a light knocking on her bedroom door. She opened her eyes with a start and stared at the door in fear. Panicking, suddenly, that it might be a ghost, she shook Bruce's shoulder. 'Bruce, there's someone at the door!'

Bruce awoke with a jolt. He sat up in alarm. 'What? What door?' His first thought was that they had an intruder.

'*This* door. There's someone knocking,' Olivia hissed.

'For God's sake, Olivia. It's probably one of the children. Come in!' he shouted.

Olivia felt foolish when Zach's pale face appeared round the door.

'Are you all right, Zach?' Bruce asked.

'I'm fine. There's just a strange noise. Sounds like a dying cat.'

'Really?' said Bruce. 'I can't hear anything.'

'It's probably just the wind,' Olivia lied. She wasn't going to let on that she had heard it too. 'Why don't you sleep with the light on?'

'Like that's going to help!' Zach sighed despondently. 'I just find it hard to sleep here.'

'You'll get used to it,' said Bruce, laying his head back on the pillow and closing his eyes. 'Count sheep.'

'That's never worked for anyone,' Zach returned. 'Wish I was in London. I never had trouble sleeping there.'

Olivia felt a pang of guilt. 'It'll be fine, darling. Give it time. Old houses make strange noises. It's just the wind and mice beneath the floorboards. You and Tabitha can share a room if you prefer.'

'Yeah, right. Well, I'll play some music or something.'

'Great,' said Bruce without opening his eyes. 'See you in the morning.'

Olivia watched her son leave the room and then lay on her back, wide awake and anxious. This wasn't going the way she had expected. There was something intrinsically wrong with the house. The crying was persistent, and it wasn't the wind. Someone was haunting the place and it needed to leave. But how could she even begin to deal with a ghost, when she didn't really believe in them?

The following morning when Antoinette came into the dining room after having taken her dog around the garden and smoked a cigarette, she found Olivia sitting alone at the table, reading the newspaper. 'Morning, Antoinette,' she said, putting the paper down. 'Now, what would you like for breakfast? Elsa can make you anything you want.'

Antoinette sat down beside her niece with a serious expression on her face. 'We need to talk, my dear,' she said gravely.

'About what?' Olivia felt nervous suddenly. What could be so worrying to induce such an ominous tone of voice.

'I didn't sleep much last night.'

Olivia was relieved. 'Oh? Was the bed uncomfortable? The sheets are brand new but the mattress is old. I didn't have time to try it out before you arrived. Was it too soft?'

'I'm not talking about the bed, Liv. I'm talking about the noise.'

'Mice.' Olivia shook her head. 'They make a right old racket beneath the floorboards. And the wind . . .'

'It's not the wind. It's not the mice. It's a woman crying.'

Olivia felt a little sick. She rubbed the back of her neck where her skin felt prickly and hot. 'A woman crying? Really? Are you sure? Might be a cat . . .?'

Antoinette inhaled through her nostrils and looked squarely at her niece. 'You have an earthbound spirit, Liv, and you need to settle it.'

Olivia glanced at the door, aware that Bruce could walk in at any moment. 'How do you know it's a ghost?' she asked, lowering her voice. 'I mean, I don't really believe in ghosts . . . but . . .'

'It's not a ghost,' Antoinette corrected. 'It's a spirit,' she said with emphasis. 'She's stuck. The poor thing needs to be shown the way to the light.'

Olivia's head told her that this was ridiculous, but somewhere in the pit of her belly she felt it to be right. She sighed, wishing she wasn't being put in this position. 'Did you see it?' she asked uncomfortably.

'No, I didn't see it. I heard the sound of crying and followed it to a room on the other side of the house.'

Olivia dropped her shoulders. 'You don't think it's a cat?' she asked hopefully.

'It's not a cat,' Antoinette replied.

'A mouse?'

'Mice don't cry.'

'No, I suppose they don't.'

'It's a woman, Liv. She might have been here for hundreds of years. Poor thing. She's very unhappy.'

Olivia inhaled sharply. She really didn't need anything else on her plate right now. 'Then we have to get a vicar to exorcise the place,' she suggested.

Elsa, who had slipped in and was putting a dish of fried eggs on the sideboard, turned around. 'Excuse me for interrupting,' she began, wringing her hands. 'But it won't do any good. We've tried everything already.'

Olivia stared at her. 'But you said . . .'

'I know. I didn't want to alarm you.'

'So, the house *is* haunted?' Olivia felt a sharp wrench in her stomach.

'It is. Mrs Delaware never invited people here because of the ghost,' said Elsa. 'Word got out and put the fear of God into people. No one wanted to come and stay.'

'It's not a ghost,' Antoinette repeated. 'It's an earthbound spirit. They're not the same thing at all.'

'It's true, then, that I can't find a couple to replace you because no one wants to work here?' said Olivia, her heart sinking. The situation was hopeless.

'I'm afraid so,' Elsa confessed, guiltily dropping her eyes to the floor.

'So, what do I do? I can't tell Bruce. He'll think I'm mad. He doesn't believe in gh . . . earthbound spirits.'

Antoinette filled her cup from the teapot. 'There's only one thing to do,' she said in a tone that suggested she had the answer. 'You need a professional.'

'We've tried,' repeated Elsa. 'We've even had the house blessed by a priest, *and* a vicar.' The housekeeper dropped her shoulders in defeat. 'If God can't do it, I don't know who else to call.'

Olivia chuckled mirthlessly. She was inclined to agree with her.

Antoinette was not to be deterred. 'When I say professional, I mean the very best. There is only one person who can move your earthbound spirit on to the place where she needs to go.'

'And who is that?' Olivia asked.

Antoinette put down the teapot. There was an excited glint in her green eyes. 'Pixie Tate,' she said, articulating each syllable with relish.

'Pixie Tate?' Oliva repeated. Was she meant to have heard of her?

'I'll make the call as soon as we're done with Christmas. After all, she knows me from the college.' Antoinette smiled jubilantly and dropped two sugarlumps into her tea. 'A lovely girl and quite extraordinary.' She gave her niece a reassuring smile and patted her arm. 'Fear not, my dear. Everything happens for a reason. The universe brought me to *you*, and I will bring *you* Pixie Tate.'

Olivia would have dismissed her aunt's suggestion as ludicrous had she not been so desperate. Everything rested on this move working. For Bruce, for the children, for her. St Sidwell Manor *had* to be a success. They had nowhere else to go. 'Very well,' she agreed. 'But leave me to square it with Bruce.'

Chapter Four

Pixie Tate was nervous. Not scared nervous, more like excited nervous. Pablo was coming home today after spending Christmas with his family in Spain and she was going to sneak into his apartment and surprise him.

She cut a slim figure as she strode purposefully down Gloucester Road. With an orange beanie pulled low over her brow, long pink hair cascading down her back, a grey knitted coat that was elegantly waisted and showed off her small frame, and a pair of black biker boots, she certainly didn't look like anyone else. Pixie Tate, impish face and vivid sapphire eyes that had seen more than a person should, was her own woman.

The pavement was wet after a night of heavy rain, but this morning the sun was dazzling, hanging low in a sky washed clean to a shimmering blue, and the air refreshingly cold. Pixie never complained about the weather. She accepted whatever nature threw at her, for there was beauty even in the bleakest winter's day. Only human beings managed to make things so ugly.

There was little traffic. The week between Christmas and New Year was always quiet. Pixie had spent Christmas Day in the countryside just outside Leicester with her grandmother, who had brought her up, but one night was as much as Pixie could tolerate. Family was complicated, even if she had only one member – well, two to be accurate, but the second one didn't count for she hadn't seen her mother since she was a child.

Just then she heard the buzz of her phone. She delved into her handbag and pulled it out. She read the text with a smile.

Good luck, Pix. I hope he takes you to the moon and back. Ulysses – with emphasis on the y – who was from Brazil, was the family she had chosen. Currently, he was in Paris with a man he had picked up just before Christmas at an art exhibition in Mayfair.

Right back at you, darling, she replied, then returned the phone to her bag.

Pixie and Ulysses had met at Manchester University, at a society for students interested in the paranormal who gathered once a week in the dingy basement of an unfashionable pub, in an unfashionable part of town. Pixie hadn't made friends in her history classes, nor in the hall of residence where she'd spent her first year; she just wasn't like anyone else. Yet, she'd found kindred spirits at the society – likeminded people who were interested in phenomena beyond the scope of scientific understanding. She and Ulysses had bonded at the first meeting – Pixie had displayed an undeniable psychic gift, but Ulysses was searching for his, and they had laughed over his comical and unsuccessful attempts to find it.

They had lived together in their second and third year, and then rented a flat in London when they'd graduated. For the past six years, they had been sharing a small apartment in Little Venice. Ulysses was hardworking and made good money in journalism. Pixie had tried and failed at various conventional jobs – she couldn't bear to work in an office and anything on a computer turned her blood cold. She knew her life's purpose was in a different area. Eventually, she had found herself drawn to the College of Psychic Studies in South Kensington and gradually earned a reputation for being a trustworthy and effective psychic. She hadn't, as yet, told Pablo what she did for a living. But she would tonight. Tonight, she would tell him everything.

Pixie purchased some flowers at a stall outside Gloucester Road Tube station and then nipped into a shop to buy milk and other essentials so that Pablo wouldn't arrive to an empty fridge. She'd cook him a simple pasta and open a bottle of wine. She pictured his face as she put the items through the till. His raffish smile and sensitive brown eyes, his sensual lips, unshaven chin and cheeks. His thick black hair. Her spirits fizzed at the thought of his return.

She had missed him. They'd only been going out since the summer, but he'd already told her that he loved her. No one besides Ulysses had ever told her that. But Pablo's *I love you*, was in a totally different category to Ulysses', whose love was platonic. Pixie had absorbed those three words greedily, like a dry sponge soaking up water.

Pixie stepped lightly over the shadows and turned into the mews. Pablo's apartment was a converted stable, which had been built into two residences. His was the top half and the most luxurious. Below him lived an elderly lady who smoked marijuana and had a feral cat. Pablo was an aspiring scriptwriter, but had yet to produce a script or find an agent. Notwithstanding, his parents believed in him to the point of compensating for his lack of income by giving him more money than he needed. Hence his apartment was in one of the most expensive boroughs in London.

Pixie glanced up to see that the curtains were closed. She wondered why the cleaner hadn't come while he was away. She sighed with irritation, anticipating spending the next hour doing the cleaning for him. However, she rallied at the vision of him returning to an immaculate home, with the dinner made, flowers on the table, and she, Pixie, lying in wait on the freshly made bed in pink satin underwear. Her irritation evaporated. She placed the flowers and shopping on the ground and then lifted the cobblestone to retrieve his spare key. She'd noticed he kept it there one night after he'd drunk one too many martinis and left his keys in the cab.

She unlocked the front door and pushed her way in. She would have picked up the post piled on the hall table, but she didn't have a free hand. She made her way upstairs and managed to unlock the door at the top without having to put everything down again. The lights of his apartment were off, the blinds closed, the place shrouded in semi-darkness. She went to the kitchen and put the bags and flowers on the table, then switched on the lights. The place was a mess, as she had expected. She cursed the cleaner but channelled her annoyance into action, focusing instead on the delighted look on Pablo's face when he'd arrive later that afternoon to find his home so clean and tidy. She took off her coat and hat, selected a playlist of Lana del Rey songs on her telephone and put on her headphones.

Pixie set to work. She pulled up the blinds and threw open the windows, allowing the crisp winter air to blow in. She could smell Pablo's aftershave and it brought him back to her in a delicious wave of memory. She almost felt his arms around her and his body pressed against hers; solid, warm, energetic. With Lana del Rey's sultry voice in her ears and the growing anticipation of the night to come, she opened the bedroom door.

Something stirred beneath the duvet. A lump moved like an awakening creature in the gloom. Pixie stared, aghast. At first, she thought it was an intruder; someone using Pablo's apartment while he was away. Then she thought he'd come home early without telling her. She was about to back away so as not to disturb him when she caught sight of a tendril of blonde hair spilling out over the pillow. There wasn't just *one* person in the bed, but *two*.

Cold fingers squeezed her heart. She felt for the switch and turned on the light. Two faces shot out of the duvet: Pablo – and a woman Pixie didn't recognise. They stared at her, horrified. Then Pablo put out a hand. 'This is not what it looks like, *mi amor . . .*' he began, blinking at her in panic.

Pixie noticed a pair of stilettos on the carpet. She picked one up in disgust and threw it at him. She aimed well. The woman dived beneath the duvet with a squeal. 'Ouch! Pixie, please!' Pablo shouted, trying to defend himself from the second shoe that winged past his left ear. But Pixie wasn't listening. Her temper unleashed, she was now rampaging about the room, throwing everything in reach at the man who had betrayed her. Pablo disappeared beneath the duvet, taking shelter from the barrage. When there was nothing left to throw, Pixie stormed into the kitchen and flung every item of food she had bought onto the floor, spilling the milk and sending peas rolling across the carpet.

As she gently picked up the flowers, for they were living things and she was not going to desecrate *them*, Pablo came running out in his boxer shorts. 'Pixie, please, she's a friend. Just a friend. Staying

49

over. It's not what it looks like.' But Pixie was no fool. At least, not now. She grabbed her coat and hat.

As she made for the door, she noticed a wooden knife block on the sideboard. The sharp blades were concealed within slits, but it wouldn't take much to unsheathe them. Pixie knew what a carving knife was capable of. She went cold. For a moment she was paralysed with fear. The red mist that had taken her over evaporated and she was a child again, lost and alone and petrified. Her father's surprised face swam before her, then her mother's horrified one, then the clattering sound of a knife falling onto the tiled floor. Pixie began to cry. Sobs rose up from the darkest place inside her. A place too dark even for Pixie, who was afraid of almost nothing. She stopped crying and stifled her sobs with her fist. The fear passed. She pressed the flowers against her chest and took a conscious breath.

Pablo came towards her, slowly, hand outstretched, hoping for calm.

Like a snake, she turned, blue eyes blazing with hurt. 'Stay away from me, Pablo!' she hissed, and then slammed the door behind her.

As soon as she was a safe distance away from the mews, she slipped into her coat, pulled her hat over her head and texted Ulysses. FOUND PABLO IN BED WITH ANOTHER WOMAN. GOING HOME.

She switched off her phone in case Ulysses tried to call her. She couldn't speak about it right now.

Overwhelmed by the feeling of rejection, she marched into a newsagent and bought a large bottle of vodka. The flow of pain needed to be cauterised at once. She made her way home by Tube. With Lana del Rey still playing, she felt even more disconnected from the world than usual. She was alone in the music, alone in her despair, alone because she was never going to be like other people. Alone because she couldn't keep a man. Always alone.

She was weary of being lonely.

She saw a couple necking by the doors. The woman was laughing softly, the man whispering something into her ear. They weren't especially attractive, but that didn't matter. They had found something beautiful in each other. Pixie's heart ached with longing. Was she unlovable? Was that why her relationships never worked out? There was always a Pablo to break her heart.

She arrived home and shut the door behind her. Then she climbed into bed and opened the bottle.

Pixie knew very well what would happen if she drank excessively. She'd been here before.

But right now, she just wanted to go to sleep and not wake up for a very long time.

Visions came in fits and starts. Images of her parents. Her father's face, ruddy and cross. Her mother's, pleading, pathetic. She could hear them fighting. Her mother's high-pitched yelling, like a fishwife. Her father's sporadic roar. She curled into a ball, but she did not float off as she had done as a child; the vodka kept her firmly grounded. She saw her mother being taken away. Her father too, but he was already gone. He would never come back, not even when she asked him to. She began to cry, crushed suddenly by the unbearable weight of loss.

Pixie felt a pair of hands on her shoulders, shaking her vigorously. 'Pixie . . . Pixie . . . wake up!' Pixie blinked. Her vision was blurred. She saw the outline of a person. The person shifted in and out of focus for a moment before remaining stable. Tanned face, floppy dark brown hair, intense olive-green eyes. So handsome it was almost a joke: Ulysses. 'Pixie . . . come on . . . wake up.'

Pixie threw her arms around him and sobbed uncontrollably.

The following morning, Pixie awoke with a shocking headache. She blinked up at the ceiling and tried to remember what had happened. Then the memory of finding Pablo in bed with another woman emerged out of the fog in her mind and she cried all over again. Eventually, she got up and went to the bathroom. She brushed her teeth and took a couple of painkillers. She looked at her reflection in the mirror. Her eyes were red, the skin under them looked like bruises. Her face was grey. She took a shower and washed herself clean.

When she went into the kitchen–living room, she was surprised to see Ulysses sitting at the table in front of his laptop. From the sound coming out of it, he was watching another Ingrid Bergman movie. Ulysses was obsessed with 1950s cinema, but most of all by Ingrid Bergman. 'What are *you* doing *here*?' she asked.

He grinned and pressed pause. 'You don't remember?' His Brazilian accent was musical, and soft as if the words were covered in fur.

'Remember? What should I remember?'

'I found you in a state last night.'

Her eyes landed on the near-empty vodka bottle on the sideboard, and she sighed. 'Oh, I see.'

'You're a crazy witch, Pix,' he said fondly. 'And all because of that asshole you thought was The One.'

She sighed again and went to make herself a cup of black coffee. 'I should have listened to you.'

'You know, for someone as psychic as you, you really have a blind spot when it comes to men.'

'I'm never falling in love again,' she said resolutely, taking a cup down from the cupboard.

'If I had a pound for every time you've said that, I'd be a rich man.'

'You're already a rich man.'

'Everything is relative.'

'Well, relative to me.'

'Everyone's rich relative to you, Pix. But I have a job for you.'

'I don't want to know. I'm not ready.'

'The best way to get over a heartbreak is to throw yourself into work.'

'I don't have the energy.'

'You will when you hear this one.'

She put the cup under the Nespresso machine and pressed the button. 'Let me have my coffee, then you can tell me about it. Did you leave Paris just for me?'

He got up and took his laptop to the sofa, plonking himself onto the cushion and placing it on his knee. 'You know I did. I'll do anything for you.'

'What did you do with . . .?' She couldn't remember his name.

'Jean-Michel.'

She laughed. 'Seriously?'

'Jean-Michel. What can I tell you? He's a walking cliché.' Ulysses grinned, his smile handsome and playful, his canine teeth pronounced like a wolf's. 'He's divine. Absence makes the heart grow fonder. I'll see him when he comes to London, which he will because he finds me irresistible.' His grin broadened. *Everyone* found Ulysses irresistible.

'Are you in love?' she asked anxiously.

Ulysses looked appalled. 'In love? Now you're being ridiculous.'

She relaxed and brought her coffee cup over to the sofa. She sat beside him. 'If you leave me, I'll . . .' She wasn't joking.

Ulysses gazed at her affectionately, then reached out and curled a lank strand of pink hair behind her ear. 'I'm not going to leave you, ever. And if I do fall in love, we'll be a happy trio. If you don't like him, he's out.'

'Promise?'

'Promise.'

She backed into the corner of the sofa, folding her legs beneath her, and took a sip of coffee. Sunlight tumbled in through the glass doors that led out onto a small balcony. She began to feel better. 'So, what's the job?'

'The college emailed this morning.' He scrolled to retrieve the email from the College of Psychic Studies. 'It's a haunting in Cornwall. A linguini.' *Linguini* was the word they used for a lingering earthbound spirit. 'The usual stuff. They've tried everything, exorcism, mediums, you name it. The spirit won't budge. They say the woman who called knows you. Antoinette Dixon. You've heard of her?'

Pixie smiled. 'Yes, I met her at the college. She's wild. A real character.'

'It's an Elizabethan house and they've invited us to stay the first week in January.'

Pixie pulled a face. 'I'm not sure I'm ready for this, Ulysses.' She put a hand on her heart and looked at him mournfully. 'I'm hurting.'

Ulysses stood up. 'Too late. I've already written back.'

'You haven't!'

'I have. You need the money, Pixie,' he said seriously. 'And they need you.' And by *they*, Pixie knew he did not mean the living.

Ulysses sat at the wheel of 'Morris', his vintage blue Morris Minor while Pixie processed the Great Betrayal. 'You're the worst picker of men I've ever come across,' he told her.

'I know, but what can I do about it?' she replied, popping a handful of chocolate raisins into her mouth.

'Take your time. You rush into relationships much too quickly.'

She laughed. 'Coming from you.'

'Mine aren't relationships. I don't think each man I sleep with is The One.'

'Neither do I.'

He gave her a sidelong glance. 'You do. You're looking for your father in every man you date.'

'If he was the man my mother said he was, then I wouldn't want him.' But Pixie didn't believe her mother.

Pixie turned her face away and looked out of the window. They were now off the motorway and heading into deep countryside. She tried to picture her father but only managed to conjure up his face from the few memories she had of him. She had only ever found one photograph, in her grandmother's house, stuffed beneath random papers in a desk drawer. It had been of both her parents together, but Pixie had cut out her mother. Pixie looked like him, she could see that. They had the same blue eyes and brown hair – he had not dyed his pink – the same mouths, something similar in the proportions of the face in general. But she knew nothing about him besides what her mother and grandmother had told her: he'd been an alcoholic; he'd been abusive; he'd been a bully; he'd deserved it. Pixie didn't believe any of it. They were biased; Granny was her maternal grandmother, after all. He'd never come to Pixie in spirit, either. She was still waiting.

'Let's not talk about my father,' she said, taking another handful of chocolate raisins. 'Tell me about Paris. What did you do? What did you see? Did you go up the Eiffel Tower?'

Ulysses laughed and shook his head. 'I saw every angle of Jean-Michel and the inside of his bedroom.'

Pixie grinned. 'Typical.'

'Naturally.'

'So, who are *you* looking for in every man you date?'

'The devil,' said Ulysses, pulling a face. They both laughed.

'Beware of the power of manifestation,' she replied. 'If you keep joking about him like this, he'll find you!'

They arrived at St Sidwell Manor early that evening. It was dark. Scudding clouds obscured the moon and stars, and a high wind blew through the avenue of plane trees and about the walls of the house. Ulysses parked Morris beside an old Volvo. 'Wow, what a house!' he exclaimed excitedly. 'You're going to have your work cut out here, Pix.'

Pixie glanced up at the façade, at the pretty gables and windows. It really was a beautiful place, but so sad. She could feel the energy already. It hung over the place like fog. A dense and gloomy fog.

The front door opened. Antoinette burst out, her exuberant smile in stark contrast to the glower of the unhappy house. 'Darling girl, you are a dear to come so quickly. You have never been needed more. Come in, come in.' Antoinette enveloped Pixie in a hungry embrace. Pixie, being slight, almost disappeared completely. 'And this must be your friend,' Antoinette said, resting her warm gaze upon Ulysses and putting out her hand.

'Ulysses Lozano,' said Pixie. 'We work together,' she added, in case Antoinette thought they were a couple.

'Welcome, Ulysses,' Antoinette gushed.

Ulysses shook her hand. It was firm and rough, like stale bread. They took off their coats, although Ulysses would have rather left his on; the place was freezing. Pixie walked softly into the hall. There was a hearty fire in the grate. The Christmas tree was still up and twinkling with fairy lights. A wide wooden staircase ascended to a landing and a tall, mullioned window, and then disappeared off to the right. There were grand, gold-framed portraits on the walls and worn Persian rugs on the floor. The ceiling was held up by exposed wooden beams that looked like the ribs of a prehistoric animal one might find in a museum. It was cold. The particular cold that spirits carry with them. 'Do you feel anything?' Antoinette asked eagerly.

Pixie felt a great deal. Ulysses and Antoinette stood watching as she walked slowly around the hall, taking everything in. If she had been a dog, the hackles would have risen on her neck, and her ears would have pricked up. She felt a terrible sadness, but something more sinister too. She was surprised anyone had managed to live here at all. 'There's a lot going on in this place,' she said thoughtfully.

'How many are here?' Antoinette asked.

'I don't know,' Pixie replied. 'Too early to tell. But I'm glad you called me. I'm sure I can help you.'

At that moment, Olivia appeared with Tabitha. Neither had expected to see a woman with pink hair. 'Hello, I'm Olivia.' Olivia shook their hands. 'This is my daughter, Tabitha. My son, Zach, is about somewhere, and Bruce, my husband.'

'I'm Ulysses,' said Ulysses. 'Pixie and I work as a team.'

'I couldn't do without him,' said Pixie.

'Like Ulysses from James Joyce's novel?' said Olivia with a smile. She'd never met anyone by that name before.

'Pronounced Oo-lee-ses,' said Pixie. Everyone mispronounced it.

Tabitha stared at Pixie in wonder. She thought she was the coolest person she had ever seen. 'Is your hair really pink?' she asked.

'Tabitha!' Olivia baulked, embarrassed.

Pixie grinned, revealing small, crooked teeth. 'I dye it pink,' she replied.

'It's pretty,' said Tabitha, immediately warming to Pixie.

'Thank you, Tabitha. If I had beautiful hair like you, I wouldn't have to dye it.'

'Come and have a drink. What would you like?' Olivia asked, inviting them into the drawing room.

'I'd love a cup of tea,' said Pixie, following after her.

'Me too,' said Ulysses, although he would have preferred something stronger.

Olivia turned to Tabitha. 'Darling, can you go and ask Elsa to make some tea and to bring some biscuits and cake and, while you're at it, find Zach and Daddy? Tell them our guests are here.' Tabitha huffed crossly and ran off towards the kitchen. She didn't want to miss a minute of being with Pixie.

'It's a very pretty house,' said Pixie admiringly, entering the drawing room. She'd seen some magnificent houses in her line of work, but this one was special.

'I fell in love with it the moment I saw it,' said Olivia, offering them the sofa and sitting down on the club fender so that the fire could warm her back. She seemed never to be warm in this house, in spite of the layers of cashmere she put on. 'We haven't told the children that you're here to rid the place of ghosts. Bruce knows, but he thinks we're mad.' She smiled sheepishly at Antoinette. 'I've put my faith in my aunt. She's assured me that you can deal with the problem, and quickly. I hope she's right.'

'I should be able to,' said Pixie, sinking into the sofa. She could feel the heat from the fire, but the house would remain cold until the place was cleared of spirits. 'Tell me what's going on?'

Olivia put her hands in her lap and looked at Pixie hopefully. 'There's the sound of a woman crying at night. It's coming from one of the bedrooms. Antoinette has heard her, so has Zach. I'd like to say it's the wind, but I don't think it is. I don't really believe in gh—'

'I can tell you the very room, because I followed the sound, but when I opened the door there was no one inside,' Antoinette said.

'Anything else?' Pixie asked.

Olivia continued. 'Elsa Tregoning, who has worked here for over fifty years, tells me that they've tried everything to get rid of her.

57

Exorcisms, you name it. But the gh . . . spirit, won't leave.'

'And you've just moved in?' Ulysses asked.

'A couple of weeks before Christmas,' Olivia returned. 'My husband inherited it. We've done nothing to it. No renovations, nothing. Just a little decoration in the bedrooms.'

'Do you know who lived here before?' Pixie enquired.

'A widow named Mrs Delaware. She died childless, in her late nineties, and left it to Bruce. He didn't even know he had such a relation. It came as a big surprise. We were going to sell it, but, when we saw it, well, we fell in love with it. We sold our house in London and moved down here for good. Bruce doesn't know how he's related to Mrs Delaware. I don't suppose it matters, really. We've been left this house. It's rather wonderful. Mrs Delaware's maiden name was Pengower. They built the house in the sixteenth century. It's Elizabethan. There's a family chapel near the estuary, at the edge of the estate. All the graves seem to belong to them. And their family crest is everywhere – a lion and unicorn. The chapel hasn't been used in decades and most of the house hasn't been used either. I've shut off the attic, which was where the servants slept, because I can't bear not to use all of the house. Rooms under dust sheets are creepy. There's nothing up there, anyway, just old beds and furniture. When we do redecorate, I'll convert it into a children's floor, but until then I don't want to know about it.'

'Quite right, Liv. What you don't see won't hurt you,' rejoined Antoinette. 'Ah, tea.'

Elsa came in bearing a tray, followed by Bruce with the cake. Tabitha returned with Zach and Daphne. Pixie and Ulysses stared at the giant dog in amazement. 'Sorry, darling, I was in the library,' said Bruce, putting the cake down on the centre table. He shook hands with Pixie and Ulysses. If he thought them charlatans, he had the manners not to show it. He politely asked after their journey and offered them cake. Ulysses tucked hungrily into his slice and then asked for another one.

'And this is Daphne, who belongs to Antoinette,' Olivia said as the dog bounded up to sniff them.

'Slobber alert!' cried Tabitha, chasing the dog with a towel.

'She's beautiful,' said Pixie. She stroked Daphne's big face as Tabitha wiped the dog's chops.

'And so big!' added Ulysses. 'Are you sure she's a dog and not a pony?'

Antoinette laughed. 'Lie down,' she commanded, but Daphne ignored her. 'If you don't give her attention, she'll settle,' she added, deciding not to waste her energy on trying to discipline a dog that couldn't be disciplined. Pixie stopped petting her and the dog gambolled off to lie down at the other end of the room where it was coolest. Tabitha sat on the club fender beside her mother and as close to Pixie as possible. She couldn't take her eyes off her long pink hair.

'Look what I've found in the library!' Bruce held up a thin book in triumph. 'A book about Ivan Pengower.' He showed them the title: *Ivan Pengower 1855-1930* by Robert Pengower.

'No way!' Olivia exclaimed happily.

'I found it hidden among Samuel Pepys' diaries. It's so slim, I almost missed it,' said Bruce, sitting on the sofa opposite Pixie and Ulysses.

'Have you had a chance to look at it?' Antoinette asked.

'I've glanced over it, but I have no idea where I come into it.'

'You mean, there are no Talwyns?' said Antoinette.

'No. I must be very distant.' He opened the book. 'Mrs Delaware, Emily, was the only child of Robert Pengower, who died in nineteen sixty-five. His father was Ivan. Ivan had two brothers, Cavill who died on his way to South America in eighteen ninety-five, leaving no children, and Albert who died of typhus in nineteen twenty-six and who had two daughters. Now I could be related to one of those daughters.'

'Of course, you're descended from the female line, otherwise you'd be called Pengower,' said Olivia sensibly.

'Genius,' Bruce agreed. 'Now I know why I married you.'

'Intriguing,' Antoinette murmured. 'I'm so glad I stayed.'

'So am I,' said Olivia. 'Not least because of Daphne. I feel very reassured having a dog in the house.'

'Has she been upstairs?' asked Ulysses.

'No,' Antoinette replied. 'She's not allowed to go up there.'

Ulysses caught Pixie's eye. 'I think she's happier down here,' he said.

I think everyone's happier down here, thought Pixie.

Chapter Five

After tea, Olivia and Antoinette accompanied Pixie and Ulysses to their bedrooms. Tabitha had wanted to go with them, but Olivia had suggested she watch TV with Zach. Zach was grateful for the company. He didn't want to be alone, especially after dark. 'You know why they're here, don't you?' he said, flopping onto the sofa and grabbing the remote control. 'They're ghost hunters.'

Tabitha frowned. 'What's a ghost hunter?'

'Someone who hunts ghosts.'

'Well, I know that, duh! What do they do once they've found them?'

'They get rid of them – that is, if you believe there are ghosts in the first place.'

'How do they get rid of them?'

'I don't know.' He shrugged. 'Perhaps they put a stake through their hearts.'

'That's vampires, silly.'

'Can ghosts be killed? Aren't they dead already?'

'I'm going to ask Pixie.'

'She's cool,' said Zach. 'I think you should dye your hair pink.'

'Mum would kill me.'

'Then you'd be a ghost too.' He laughed and, pointing the remote at the TV, flicked through the channels.

'I'd be a ghost with pink hair – a *spirit* with pink hair,' she corrected, wanting to get the terminology right. Tabitha curled into the corner of the sofa beside him. 'I want to help Pixie find the spirit.'

'They won't let you. They think it'll frighten you.'

Tabitha was about to confide in him that she'd always seen spirits, like for ever. But she held back. 'Why would I be afraid of dead people? They're like smoke. They have no body, so they can't hurt me.'

Zach settled on a superhero film, even though it was already halfway through. 'I've had enough of ghost talk,' he said dismissively. 'Let's watch the film.'

Tabitha crossed her arms and sighed irritably. She decided she'd never confide in her brother, ever.

Pixie felt the sense of unhappiness intensify as they climbed the stairs to the first floor. Something dark had taken place here. They made their way down the corridor and her whole body began to bristle. 'I can't believe you've been living here since mid-December,' she said to Olivia. 'It's now January. How have you coped? This place has a very heavy energy. Can you feel it, Ulysses?'

'Not really,' he replied with a shrug. 'It just feels cold.'

Pixie chuckled; Ulysses never felt anything. 'Can you feel it, Antoinette?'

'Absolutely,' Antoinette exclaimed heartily. 'It makes one's hair stand up, doesn't it.'

Olivia wished she felt it too, but she didn't. A part of her thought this whole ghost thing was crazy, but the other part longed to be convinced that it was true. She decided she'd go along with it and keep an open mind. Pixie didn't seem like a fraud, and she trusted Antoinette.

After putting their bags in their rooms, Olivia suggested Pixie look around the rest of the house. 'Just so you know what you're up against,' she said. 'I do hope you can sort it out. I don't know what I'm going to do if you can't.'

'Of course, she will,' said Antoinette confidently. 'Have you ever not been able to move on a spirit, Pixie?' she asked.

'Sometimes they just don't want to leave,' said Pixie truthfully. 'But I'll do my best.'

Olivia felt anxious. If Pixie didn't release the ghost, they might be forced to sell up. They couldn't live in a house that was haunted – no one would want to come and stay.

Pixie followed her intuition right to the bedroom where Antoinette had heard the crying. 'It's in here,' she murmured to herself, opening the door. Although she didn't hear the sound of crying, she felt the woman's grief as soon as she entered. It was like a grey shadow that enveloped her. She focused a moment and tuned into the finer vibrations of the spirit dimension. There, by the window, was the slim figure of a woman looking out. She was wearing a long black dress with a veil over her head that covered her face. When she turned, her eyes shone through the silk, wet with tears. On seeing Pixie, she stiffened. Pixie knew she was about to disappear. *Don't be afraid*, she said in her mind. *I'm here to help you.* The woman did not move. She stared at Pixie, astonished perhaps to be visible to this strange creature with pink hair. Pixie wondered if any of the mediums had tried talking to her before. The woman certainly appeared surprised to be spoken to. *I'm here to help you*, Pixie repeated.

You cannot help me, the woman replied at last, her voice as thin as ribbon. *No one can.* She turned back to the window with a sob.

I can, said Pixie, her heart flooding with pity. *And I will.*

Then find my son.

Before Pixie could say anything further, the woman vanished.

Olivia, Antoinette and Ulysses stood quietly in the doorway, knowing not to disturb Pixie by asking questions. She was standing very still and staring at the window, a look of concentration hardening the contours of her face. After a few moments she turned to them. 'It's a lady. And she wants me to find her son.'

'But her son is surely dead,' said Ulysses. 'Or very, very, very, very old.'

'She doesn't know that. I doubt she even knows *she's* dead,' Pixie explained.

'Are you going to tell her?' Olivia asked.

'It's not as easy as that. If I told you *you* were dead, would you believe me?'

63

'No,' said Olivia, confused suddenly. How could a spirit not know they were a spirit?

Pixie looked at Ulysses. 'I'd say she's Victorian or early Edwardian. She's wearing a long black dress with a veil. Late twenties, early thirties. No older than that.'

'We can look in the book Bruce found and see if we can work out who she is,' Olivia suggested. 'Who she *was* . . .' she corrected quickly.

'That's a brilliant idea,' said Antoinette enthusiastically. 'Perhaps there's a record somewhere of the fate of her son. Then you can tell her.'

'That's a good start,' said Pixie. But she sensed by the stubborn energy of the spirit that this was going to be a difficult case. She had worked with the paranormal long enough to know when a job was going to be challenging. 'It would be helpful to know something about her before I meet her again,' she added.

They gathered in the drawing room once more. Bruce poured wine. Pixie declined. Ulysses gratefully took the glass. Tom came in and put another log on the fire. On the sofa, Olivia looked down the family tree in the book Bruce had found, which only included names of the direct family members. But it was enough to identify the spirit. Olivia's finger swiftly rested on a likely candidate. 'Cordelia Pengower was Mrs Delaware's grandmother,' she said. 'She was married to Ivan and died at the age of thirty-four, in eighteen ninety-six. And, yes, she had two sons, Robert, who was Emily Delaware's father, and Felix.' Olivia looked up, eyes shining with excitement. 'Felix only has a dash by his name, and the words *disappeared night of 29th June 1895.*'

'Must be the spirit, don't you think, Pixie?' Antoinette asked with rising excitement.

'Yes, that's her. She was young, in late Victorian clothes. She's not leaving St Sidwell Manor until we find out what happened to her son.'

'So what do you do?' Antoinette asked. 'You just tell her?'

'Once I've found out what happened to him,' said Pixie.

'Okay,' Olivia said. 'How are you going to find out what happened to him? I mean, if no one managed to find out at the time, how are you going to find out now?'

Pixie inhaled deeply, unsure about whether or not to tell them. 'It's . . .' She hesitated and looked uneasily at Ulysses. Even he only knew a small part of what she did.

'Complicated?' Ulysses arched his eyebrows.

Pixie did not feel ready for this.

'What does *that* mean?' asked Antoinette keenly. She had not missed the silent communication that had passed between their two guests.

'It means that I have to go back in time and find out what happened,' said Pixie. Normally, she would not have told the clients this information, as most sane people would think her mad, but Antoinette was an ally and a friend.

Bruce, who had been sitting quietly, listening, frowned. He'd agreed to invite Pixie to the house only to please his wife. He hadn't heard any crying in the night and most certainly did not believe in ghosts. As for time travel, he'd really heard it all now!

'How do you do that?' Olivia asked, suddenly feeling a little sick, because this woman was beginning to sound like she was two sandwiches short of a picnic.

'I didn't notice a Tardis in the back of your car,' said Bruce with a chuckle. Olivia shot him a warning look.

'I timeslide,' Pixie replied simply.

'What the hell is timesliding?' Bruce asked, looking at his wife, who shrank. 'Am I the only person here who's never heard of it?'

'Darling, why don't you go and find something to do in your study?' Olivia suggested tersely. She didn't want Bruce's scepticism to put Pixie off – and if she was, indeed, a little loopy, she did not want him to know.

Bruce didn't protest. The whole situation was ridiculous. He decided to go and look through his emails and leave the witches to their witchy business. He hoped the two charlatans would be gone first thing in the morning.

Once he'd left the room, Pixie knitted her fingers and took a breath. Timesliding was hard to explain to people who had no understanding of metaphysics. Even *she* didn't fully grasp it. But having slid to different times since childhood, it was second nature to her. 'If you accept that there is no time, then you will agree that there is only infinity,' she began. 'If there is infinity, then there is no beginning and no end, in which case there can be no past or future, just a continuous present.'

'That sounds like a riddle,' said Ulysses, who had heard Pixie explain it various times and still didn't understand it.

'You don't need to get your head around it,' said Pixie. 'Just know that that is the way it is. No time. Just now. Which means that everything is happening all at once.'

Antoinette chuckled. 'I don't suppose our human minds can grasp that,' she said, wanting very much to have one of the rare human minds that could.

'Mine certainly can't,' said Olivia. She glanced at her watch. Would it look indecent to have another drink?

'You don't have to understand it, or even believe it,' Pixie went on. 'It is what it is, regardless. What it means is that some, like me, can slide through time, like walking through a veil and arriving in another era.' Pixie, however, had never met anyone else who could do that.

'That's crazy,' said Olivia. 'You can actually time travel? Is that a thing?' The sick feeling in her stomach intensified. Did Antoinette appreciate what sort of people she had allowed into their house? *Please*, she thought feverishly, *don't let them be mad*.

Pixie nodded. 'It's not as extraordinary as it sounds. It's really quite simple. And it's not that exciting. I link into a spirit via an object of theirs and follow them to where *they* are. Tomorrow, I'll link into Cordelia. There must be something of hers in this house.'

'I'm sure there will be,' said Olivia, not sure how she was going to know unless it had the name Cordelia on it.

'How will you get back?' asked Antoinette. She didn't want Pixie getting lost in the past.

'Sliding back is easy because this is where my body is. I can return to my body at any time.'

66

'And how long do you stay, um, out of it?' Olivia asked.

'I stay for as long as I need to. Sometimes, I stay a day, other times a couple of weeks. It just depends.'

'You're going to disappear for two weeks?' Olivia gasped, panicking suddenly that these crazy people were going to stay in her house for an entire fortnight.

'I won't disappear, and it won't be two weeks to you. Remember there is no time. To you it will seem like I've been sitting with my eyes shut for merely minutes, maybe a few hours.'

'You just sit with your eyes closed?' said Antoinette.

'Yes, but I must not be disturbed. That's why I work with Ulysses. I need him to stand by me, to keep me safe.'

'What happens if he doesn't do his job properly?' asked Olivia, who had a tendency to think of the worst-case scenario.

'Let's just say it's dangerous,' said Ulysses, knowing Pixie wouldn't want to talk about the time she had ended up in hospital after being shaken out of her trance by her worried grandmother. 'I do my job properly, every time,' he added firmly.

'Can you change the past?' asked Antoinette. 'I mean, if you find Cordelia's son, you'll change her destiny, won't you?'

'I can only witness what happened. I cannot, and must not, change it. That is a responsibility I must bear,' said Pixie seriously. 'I have to be careful not to change the future, by altering things that happened in the past.'

'Are you *you*?' Antoinette was so enthralled by this fascinating information that she had forgotten to take a sip of her whisky.

Pixie did not want to tell them too much. She hadn't even told Ulysses what really happened. It was too weird. 'I'm me,' Pixie replied simply, which was partly true.

'Sounds like a movie,' said Olivia, praying hard that she wasn't being fed a load of garbage.

'Timesliding has been around for thousands of years,' said Ulysses helpfully. 'The thing is that most people don't believe it's possible. They write it off as science fiction.'

'Which is a good thing,' Pixie added. 'If novices tried to do it without proper guidance it could be really dangerous. Like astral projection and any other psychic experience, it's unwise to attempt it if you don't know what you're doing.'

'I must admit, it's not an easy one to comprehend,' said Olivia, wanting very much to believe it. 'I mean, most people accept there's some sort of life after death, many believe in spirits, some even believe we come back time and again to live other lives, but timesliding feels like one step too far. It sounds unbelievable.'

'It does,' Pixie agreed. 'But the good thing is *you* don't have to believe it. You don't have to do anything at all. Just leave me to sort it out for you. If I help this soul move on to where she's meant to be, then you can pay me. If not, I'll leave, and you will have lost nothing.'

To Olivia, that was only mildly reassuring.

After dinner, when Pixie was in her bedroom getting ready for bed, there came a soft knocking at the door. She knew it wasn't Ulysses, because he never knocked, and she knew it wasn't a spirit, because they didn't knock either. She did not expect it to be Tabitha.

The child's pale face looked up at her inquisitively.

'Are you all right, Tabitha?' Pixie asked, standing aside to let the child into the room.

'I'm scared,' Tabitha replied. The truth was that she wasn't scared at all. She just wanted to talk to Pixie on her own.

'You don't need to be scared,' Pixie replied, although she understood why she was. Children were often sensitive to the spirit level of vibration, having so recently come from there. Pixie went over to the bed and sat down. 'Come here and tell me why you're scared.' She patted the space beside her. Tabitha climbed up and sat cross-legged on the quilt.

'Zach says you're a ghost hunter,' she said, eyes wide with curiosity and not a trace of fear. 'Is that why you're here? To hunt down the spirits?'

Pixie laughed softly. 'I'm not a ghost hunter, Tabitha. I help spirits find their way home.'

'Why are they here?'

'Because they're stuck.'

'Why can't they get unstuck?'

'Because they don't know they're dead.'

Tabitha frowned. 'How can you not know you're dead?'

'Well, when you dream, do you know you're dreaming?'

'Sometimes.'

'But most of the time you don't, right?'

'I suppose.'

'It's a bit like that. It's like they're in a dream. Things look strange, just like they do in a dream, but they're lost in the strangeness, just like when you're lost in your dream. It's only when you wake up that you realise it wasn't real.'

'Why do they get lost?'

Pixie put her hands in her lap and smiled at Tabitha. Her childish curiosity was endearing. She had none of the adult's cynicism, only a sense of wonder – that precious quality so quickly lost in puberty. 'When we die, we leave our bodies behind. We still look like us, only more transparent, because the spirit world is made of a quicker frequency than the earth world, which is made of matter. Imagine a fan.' Pixie waved her hand. 'When it's spinning slowly, like this, you can see it, right?' Tabitha nodded keenly. 'But when it's spinning really really fast, like *this*,' Pixie made her hand move at speed, 'you can't see it. It becomes invisible to your eyes. Spirit is just like that. So, when you leave your body, most people can't see your new form. I can, because I'm psychic and I can see that level of vibration, but most people can't. If they could, they would realise that there is no death, only transformation. The spirit, on leaving its human form, goes home. But some, either because of fear, or hate, or because of some terrible trauma where they slip out of their bodies but don't realise they're dead, fail to see the light that's leading them home. They don't realise where they're meant to go. Those poor souls get stuck. That's where I come into it. I can help them find their way home. I simply lead them to the light.'

'Are all spirits just souls who are stuck?' Tabitha asked.

'Not all of them. Some are people who love us and want to visit us. They've returned home to where they belong but choose to keep an eye on us, so they come back. In fact, we're surrounded all the time by those we love who are in spirit, but most people can't see them. Even animals come back to be near us.' Tabitha's face lit up. She liked the sound of animals coming back. 'For spirits, we're only a thought away. There is no distance or time. But you never need to be afraid, Tabitha. You have an angel looking after you constantly.'

'An angel? Really?'

'Of course. You don't know about angels?'

'They're in the Bible,' said Tabitha, remembering the angel Gabriel from the nativity play at school.

'The angels mentioned in the Bible are archangels, which are very powerful beings. Those angels work with everyone. I'm talking about your guardian angel who works especially for you to keep you safe. That angel has been with you from the moment you were created as a soul. You are never alone, ever.'

'Do horrible people have angels, too?' Tabitha asked, scrunching up her nose, hoping that they didn't. Horrible people didn't deserve to have an angel looking after them.

'Everyone does, regardless of whether they're good or bad. But some people don't listen to their advice. They don't hear that small voice within. If they listened to it, they wouldn't be bad.'

'Where do evil people go when they die?' Tabitha was warming to the subject. It was wonderful to be able to talk about these things with someone who knew the answers.

'Let me explain to you the law of attraction.'

'Aunt Antoinette told me about the law of attraction, but I didn't really understand it.'

'Then let me try to explain it to you better. It's the most powerful law in the universe. Basically, it means "like attracts like". Have you ever heard the expression "birds of a feather flock together"?'

'Yes,' Tabitha replied keenly.

'That's not just a fun saying. It's true. You tend to get on with people who are like you. It's the law of attraction and it applies to everything. If you think positive things, you'll attract positive things into your life. If you think negative things, you'll attract negative things into your life. You're like a magnet. Whatever you put out, you'll get back. If you complain about things all the time, you'll just attract what you complain about and get more of it. If you notice the beauty and good in things, you'll attract that. So, with that in mind, after we die, our souls, by the law of attraction, go to a place of equal vibration to our . . .' Pixie was going to say 'consciousness', but she didn't imagine Tabitha would know what that was. 'To our state of being. Imagine a balloon filled with hot air – it will rise very high, won't it? A balloon with cold air will drop. Love is like hot air that fills a person's soul, like a balloon. Life is all about love, Tabitha. Each of us is here to learn about that. If you're loving, you'll find yourself in a beautiful place after your body dies. You'll rise like a big balloon. Cruel people find themselves somewhere very different. Everyone has a choice to be loving or not. We all get what we deserve, and no one judges. It's up to us to decide how we want to be.'

'Is the crying woman a spirit?' Tabitha asked.

'She is.'

'Will she go to Heaven?'

'I'll try to encourage her to move on.'

'Why doesn't she go on her own?'

'That's what I'm here to find out.'

'Do you ever get scared?'

'Not really, although sometimes unhappy spirits can be mean. This one isn't mean. She's just lost.'

Pixie was keen to get back to Cordelia. She hoped that in the quiet of night she might be able to persuade her to find her way home without having to timeslide. Most likely her child was in spirit, waiting for her to join him. Pixie put a hand on Tabitha's shoulder. 'You should go to bed. It's late. You're not scared any more, are you?'

'Not now,' Tabitha replied, reluctantly slipping off the bed; she wanted to stay and talk.

'We can chat more tomorrow,' said Pixie.

'I'll show you the chapel and the fountain.' Tabitha smiled broadly. 'There's so much to show you. This is a really cool house.'

*

Once Tabitha had left, Pixie tiptoed down the corridor to the room where she had encountered Cordelia Pengower. She sat on the edge of the bed in the darkness and closed her eyes. She then called out to her with her mind. *Cordelia.* A moment later, Pixie sensed the presence of a spirit. It carried in its energy the heavy, cold weight of unhappiness. *I want to help you.*

She felt Cordelia's presence and opened her eyes. In the darkness she could make out the dim figure standing by the window. *Cordelia, I want to help you*, Pixie repeated. She knew Cordelia could hear her; she was deciding whether or not to respond. Pixie continued to sit patiently and wait. She'd wait all night if she had to.

The woman's energy was thick, the light she carried within her frail and dim, like twilight. There was no way she was going to be able to return home to Spirit on her own. She needed Pixie's help, but she seemed not to want it. Why?

Pixie decided to take another tack. *Cordelia, are you happy here? Is that why you wish to stay?*

At last, the spirit answered. *How can I be happy when I have lost my child? When I have lost everything? Everything that was dear to me has been taken away.*

I can help you reunite with your son.

You lie. No one can help me.

I can show you the way home.

I am home.

You are between worlds, Cordelia.

Who are you? Why do you tell me this?

Because I want to help you. You have died a physical death. You must leave this place and go home, to the light. Your child waits for you there.

You know nothing. My child is lost. If you want to help me, find him. Find my son and bring him home to me. The woman's voice broke into a sob. The little light she emanated faded so that Pixie could barely see her.

He's not out there. He's already in that light. You can go to him any time you want. Why not go now?

What are you talking about? You know nothing about it. Nothing. He is lost, somewhere out there. Alone in the dark. Alone and afraid. Your talk of light is the Devil's work. Perhaps you are the Devil. I will not be lured away. I wait here for my child to come home, as any good mother would do. I wait for him, and I pray. That is all I can do. No one can help me. Least of all you.

Cordelia's energy faded further. Then she was gone. Pixie was baffled. There was something evasive in the way she refused even to consider that her child might already be in spirit. It didn't make sense.

Cordelia didn't *want* to leave – that was the problem. Given that she had lost her child, that was understandable. But Pixie sensed there was more to it. There was something else. The only way she could find out what that was, was to slide back to her time. Pixie didn't imagine it would take very long. She knew the date on which the child had disappeared. All she'd have to do was observe the events that had taken place on that night and then return and tell Cordelia what happened.

It was still dark when Olivia climbed out of bed. She hadn't slept well. She'd been worrying about the stuck spirit – if there truly was one – and whether Pixie and Ulysses were the real deal. She hoped she hadn't invited a pair of frauds into her home. The very idea of timesliding sounded ridiculous. Olivia considered herself pretty open-minded, but, really, this was way out there. Beyond what an educated, intelligent person could accept as truth. She was too embarrassed to discuss it with Bruce, and he had had the tact not to mention it or tease her about it. She was ashamed to have even listened to such nonsense. However, as she had invited them down to do a job, she felt compelled to go along with it. And a part of her *wanted* to believe in Pixie, so that the house would warm up and they could make it a home. So much depended on it: Bruce's health, the children's happiness, her own happiness. This *had* to work.

She dressed in the bathroom so as not to wake Bruce, and then went downstairs to see if she could find something that had belonged to Cordelia Pengower. The room she had chosen to be her studio had previously been a study. By the pretty wallpaper and curtains, she deduced that it had been a woman's room. However, the chance of finding something of Cordelia's in there was pretty slim, for Cordelia was Emily Delaware's grandmother. The objects could have belonged to Emily's mother, or to Emily herself. Elsa had explained that Emily had changed very little, preferring to live among memories rather than creating memories of her own, so there might be something lying around that had once been treasured by her grandmother. And if it hadn't belonged to Cordelia, did it matter? If Pixie was a fraud, it wouldn't matter whom the object had belonged to.

She switched on the light. The window was laced with frost. Elaborate patterns in the shape of ferns caught the weak glow from the rising sun and shone like gold. Olivia didn't want to linger in there for long; it was too cold. She hurried, opening drawers and cupboards. At last, she came upon a miniature portrait of a woman in an oval locket. She was arrestingly beautiful, with fair hair curled and pinned to her head in the Victorian fashion, and deep blue eyes that stared solemnly out. Her naked shoulders sloped prettily to the indigo top of her bodice. Around her neck was a pearl choker with a diamond centrepiece at her throat. Olivia turned it over. On the back, the initials *CJP* were engraved into the silver. Triumphant, she put it in her pocket and went to the dining room for breakfast.

When Pixie and Ulysses came down for breakfast, Bruce was reading *The Times* at the head of the long table, Olivia and Antoinette were discussing the weather, and Zach and Tabitha were eating their cooked breakfasts, arguing once again about the existence of ghosts. As soon as Pixie and Ulysses appeared, they stopped their debate. Bruce lowered his newspaper and grinned. 'Did anything go bump in the night?' he asked.

Ulysses smiled mischievously. 'Only the poor devil dragging his ball and chain.'

'Oh really, Ulysses,' said Olivia, feeling uncomfortable again.

'I heard that woman crying,' said Tabitha. 'But I wasn't frightened.'

Bruce ignored his daughter and turned to Pixie. 'How long is this going to take?'

'I'm not sure,' Pixie replied.

'It'll take as long as it takes, Bruce,' interjected Antoinette, pretending she hadn't noticed the cynical look on his face.

'I found this,' said Olivia, turning to Pixie and holding out the locket.

Pixie took it and looked it over carefully. The spirit in the bedroom had hidden her face behind a veil. From this portrait, Pixie could see that Cordelia Pengower had been a very beautiful woman. 'This will do nicely,' she replied.

'Can *I* help?' Tabitha asked.

'I'm afraid not.' Pixie smiled at the girl. 'This is something I have to do on my own. But I'd love you to show me around the garden when I'm done.'

Tabitha nodded enthusiastically. 'And I'll show you the chapel and the statue too,' she said.

Bruce closed the newspaper and got up. 'I'm going to the farm to find Tom,' he told Olivia. Then he turned to Pixie and Ulysses. 'If you're gone by the time I get back, it's been nice meeting you. I hope you find your ghost and send it on its way.'

Olivia winced at his flippant tone, but Pixie did not seem at all offended. 'It's been nice meeting you, too,' she replied. It made no difference to her whether or not people believed in the existence of spirits. She was here to settle Cordelia's soul, not to win over Bruce Talwyn.

After breakfast, Pixie and Ulysses set off to do their work. They requested only that they be left alone in the bedroom on the first floor where Pixie had encountered Cordelia Pengower. Olivia and Antoinette decided to leave them to it and drive into town to see if there was any information about Cordelia Pengower in the local library. Zach and Tabitha didn't want to join them. They remained in the hall, listless and cold, wondering what to do with themselves.

*

Pixie sat on an upright wooden chair. The spirit of Cordelia Pen-gower had chosen not to appear, but Pixie did not require her to be present. She could link into her energy through the locket, and, by holding her in her thoughts, she would ensure that she slid to the right time. That was of vital importance. Pixie needed to slide back to the summer of 1895 in order to find out what had happened to Felix, not to a time long before, or after. Therefore, she envisaged Cordelia and the child, and put out the desire to be transported into the past to ascertain why Cordelia was unable to move on into Spirit in the present. Then she waited to travel on the vibration of that desire. The thought was the deed. Together with the locket, it was a powerful combination.

However, what she hadn't mentioned to Ulysses, or indeed to Olivia and Antoinette, was that linking into an earthbound spirit in this way in order to investigate a possible crime that had happened in the past was a new technique for Pixie, which she had only recently discovered and was gradually refining. Right now, it wasn't an exact science. In fact, it wasn't exact at all. What she had to factor in was the existence of a higher intelligence – which people called the universe, a higher power or God – that also played a part in her slides. Pixie put out the desire and together with the law of attraction, the higher intelligence set about fulfilling it. But she had no control over divine power. She just had to put her trust in it.

Pixie had come a long way in her development, from astral pro-jection in childhood, which took her back in time as herself, to actually possessing another person's body, which enabled her to remain in the past for longer and experience a physical life. But she wasn't even close to perfecting it. This case gave her the ideal opportunity to hone her ability. She hoped it would work.

Ulysses lay on the bed, crossed his ankles, and chose his favour-ite Ingrid Bergman movie to watch on his iPad: *Casablanca*. 'Okay, Ulysses. Are you ready?' Pixie asked.

'Are you?' he said, putting on his earphones.

'As ready as I'll ever be,' she replied.

Pixie wrapped her hands around the locket and closed her eyes. She took three deep breaths. In her mind's eye, she imagined a silver cord extending from her solar plexus and wrapping around the locket, linking her to its owner. As she sank into trance, she heard the familiar thrumming in her ears, she felt the heaviness in her limbs and then she gave herself over to the gentle lift and floated out of her body.

'Safe travels, Pix,' said Ulysses, before turning his attention to his movie.

Past

Chapter Six

I open my eyes. I'm standing in front of the weathered old walls of St Sidwell Manor. For a moment I'm not sure that I've slid. The house looks the same with its mullioned windows, curvy Dutch gables and square chimney stacks, but then I become aware of the heat. I've left winter and arrived in summer – and it's glorious. The skies are a rich sapphire colour, and the breeze is sugar-scented. The smell of the gardens is so delicious, I want to fill my lungs with it. I inhale, but my breath barely travels further than my chest. It's as if I'm being held in a vice. I become aware of my dress, which is tight and uncomfortable. It's suffocating. I wiggle about and try to expand my ribcage to give me some room. But I'm well and truly trapped, like a caterpillar in the claws of a bird. I look down to see that I'm wearing a long black dress embellished with little round buttons, and lace-up boots. Beside me, on the gravel, is a tatty brown suitcase and a round hat box. If I'm the lady of the house, why am I in a black dress with luggage? Have I been to a funeral? I reach up and discover that I'm wearing a hat. It's small and discreet, not the hat of a great lady.

I look at my hands. They're elegant with long fingers and pretty nails. In my normal life I don't have elegant hands – I chew my nails when I'm nervous. Cordelia Pengower is clearly not a nail-biter.

Just then the front door opens. An austere-looking man in a tailcoat steps out. He glares at me, then lifts a watch from his waistcoat pocket and makes a great show of examining it. 'You are late, Miss Swift,' he says.

Miss Swift? Who the hell is Miss Swift? I'm *meant* to be Cordelia

81

Pengower. I panic suddenly. I've slid into the wrong body. How has this happened? The locket was supposed to link me to Cordelia. But I'm Miss Swift. This is not at *all* what I expected. But now is not the time to reflect on the provenance of the locket, or on the law of attraction and the higher intelligence that have also been at work to bring me to this time and place, and body. I will work it out later. For now, I have to go with what I'm given and trust powers greater than myself. Anyway, I'm on for an adventure and maybe Miss Swift will enable me to complete my mission. I put out the desire to be transported back to 1895 and I trust that *that* part of the slide has succeeded.

I pick up my suitcase and hat box and walk quickly towards him over the gravel, my boots scrunching on the stones. 'Mrs Pengower is expecting you,' he tells me in an imperious tone. I'm relieved to hear that Mrs Pengower is in residence. That's a promising start. I've slid to the right era at least. 'She will be surprised that the governess is late on her first day.' Ah, so I'm a governess. Well, that makes sense. The position will give me the opportunity to observe. This is looking more positive. The butler slips the pocket watch back into its pouch and sniffs. 'I might tell you that you are fifteen minutes late. It is now a quarter past three.' He looks at me down his long nose, a haughty expression on his face. I notice the nasal hair in his large nostrils, like spiders hiding in caves, and the broken blood vessels on his cheeks. He has hooded, watery eyes, so pale it's as if the colour has been washed away, leaving but a trace of blue.

'I apologise for that,' I reply, hastily thinking of an excuse. 'I was delayed at the station. There were no cabs. I had to wait.' I hope that I sound plausible.

I'm relieved to see that I do. He's satisfied. He leads me inside and closes the big door behind us. I see a mirror hanging on the wall and seize the opportunity to look at the woman I have borrowed for this slide. I'm astonished to see how lovely she is. Well, this is going to make my slide more pleasurable, for sure. I'm not a beauty in my real life, but Miss Swift is truly gorgeous.

Gripped by my new face, I stare at the reflection in amazement, my pink lips parted prettily. My brown hair is tied up beneath my hat, but tousled strands have come away from the pins and are loose about my rosy cheeks and slender neck. My nose is small and straight and delicately freckled. My hazel eyes shiny and bright, more green than brown, and I gaze into them, searching for myself behind them, for I'm in there somewhere, looking out. If it wasn't for the butler, glaring at me from the hall, I'd trace my fingers over every contour of my face and bask in my beauty.

'Come along, Miss Swift,' he calls, an edge of impatience in his voice. 'Mrs Pengower has already waited fifteen, now eighteen, minutes.'

I follow him through the hall. It's the same magnificent hall that I know, only there's no fire in the grate, and there's a generous display of white flowers on the refectory table – cow parsley, roses and lilies. They're spectacular, bathed in the beams of sunlight that stream enthusiastically into the room. I linger a moment to admire them. I'm struck by the energy in the house. It's soft and full of joy. So different from the energy in the present, which is heavy and sad. I'm curious to find out what happens to Cordelia's boy and wonder how long I've got. I need to find out what day it is, but I can't ask the snobby butler, who turns to me again and says impatiently, 'Do come along, Miss Swift.'

Just then a man comes skipping down the stairs in riding boots and breeches, tapping a black top hat against the palm of his hand as if in rythmn to a tune he's humming. He's tall with scruffy brown hair, and strong eyebrows positioned low on a wide, handsome face. His sky-blue morning coat is dashing, his gait self-assured, and I assume he's the children's father, Mr Pengower, and I smile. He returns my smile, a jaunty curve on his lips. He has a witty expression, as if he's about to crack a joke, and I warm to him at once. He fits very nicely in this sunny, cheerful hall.

'And you are?' he asks, looking me over with intelligent eyes as blue as cornflowers.

'Miss Swift, sir, the new governess,' the butler informs him.

'Ah, good, good.' Mr Pengower carries on through the hall and out of the front door, slamming it behind him. I expected him to introduce himself. But he seems in a hurry and, as the master of the house, I suppose he takes it as a given that I know who he is. He has left me a little dazed, however, and the hall too, for it seems to reverberate in his wake as if a strong wind has just swept through it.

Cordelia Pengower is in a small sitting room situated down a wide corridor. It's a pleasant room with a high ceiling supported by a spine and ribs of dark wooden beams, a large, open fireplace and those typical Tudor windows overlooking the garden. The walls are papered in blue-and-yellow flowers and the flouncy curtains, which hang on sturdy poles, are a shiny blue damask and break luxuriously onto the floor. It's a happy room, bathed in sunlight, and Cordelia looks very happy in it. She turns and smiles at me with such charm and grace that I'm caught off guard; I hadn't expected the miserable soul haunting the Talwyns' home to be so radiant with joy.

'Miss Swift, how delightful,' she says.

Her beauty is startling. She is indeed the woman in the portrait. The likeness is undeniable. I wonder again how I slid into Miss Swift's body when I was holding a locket that clearly belonged to Cordelia Pengower. It doesn't make sense.

I curtsy, which is what I imagine I'm expected to do. 'Madam.' I return her smile, but not too much. As a governess, I assume that I'm born into a good family, but I won't be her social equal. It's important that I remember that. As friendly as she may be, she won't like her superiority challenged. I must know my place. I've learnt, through my previous timesliding, that human nature doesn't really change, whatever era I'm in. Cordelia Pengower is my boss, and I must treat her with respect. And I must behave like a Victorian woman, and not like a modern girl in fancy dress.

'I trust your journey was not too arduous,' she says, and her voice has a warm tone to it, like a flute played low. She's stunning; the bones of her face are well defined, her blue eyes wide-set and very bright, like tanzanite. Her skin is almost translucent and flawless. And her hair, swept off her face and falling in waves over her white lace blouse, is the colour of sundried hay. She is mesmerising and her graceful manners make her lovelier still.

'Not arduous at all, thank you, madam,' I reply, careful not to say too much in case I give myself away. Although, the last thing anyone would expect is a visitor from the future. I think I'm quite safe. At worst she would think me eccentric.

'Come, let me introduce you to the children. They are upstairs in the nursery with Gwen.'

Cordelia talks to me as we climb the stairs and I listen and learn so that I can copy her and pass myself off as a Victorian woman. She asks after my mother, who apparently is a widow. Not knowing anything about Hermoine Swift, I have to make up the answers. Aware that I'll get Hermione into trouble if my lies are too elaborate I answer her questions briefly and allow her to do the talking. I need to find out as much as I can about Cordelia and her family. I still don't know how long I'm going to be here. It's imperative that I find out today's date, and fast.

Cordelia tells me how very lucky she is to be so blessed as to live in this enchanting house with such lavish gardens. She stops on the landing and we look out of the big window at the ornamental garden below. There's a paved path that cuts through it with perfectly trimmed balls of hedge on either side like giant green hedgehogs slumbering contentedly in the sunshine. Tall, leafy trees shimmer in the distance and I look forward to walking there. It's all so beautiful. 'When my husband and I moved in here, upon the sad death of his father, I took it upon myself to transform the gardens into a paradise. I had such a vision for them. That was eight years ago. How much one can achieve in so little time. Everything grows very fast here, even my children, as you will see.'

We continue up to the first floor and down the corridor, past the bedrooms where Ulysses and I slept, and on to what I assume is the children's part of the house. Our skirts rustle as we walk, and I try not to look ungainly. Cordelia's gait has a charming bounce to it, which makes her long blue skirts rustle ever more vigorously. Through the windows I get to see further glimpses of the gardens: borders of purple delphiniums, a wistful iron gate, big terracotta pots of hydrangeas, a statue of a boy playing a flute, all bathed in the languid light of late afternoon.

I can hear children's laughter as we approach the nursery. 'I hope they are behaving,' Cordelia says. She arches an eyebrow and gives me a sidelong glance, and a smile. I can see that she's joking. I sense she's indulgent of her two boys.

'They sound like they're having fun, which is what children ought to be doing,' I reply and she nods in agreement.

She opens the door and I see two small boys. The older one is playing with a train set on the rug. The little one has made a den out of blankets and chairs and is peeping out, like a hamster from its burrow box. When they see me, they fall quiet. The older boy jumps to his feet and the little one emerges through blankets. The nursemaid gets off her chair and curtsys. 'Ma'am,' she says to Cordelia.

'This is Master Robert,' says Cordelia proudly, patting the taller boy on the head. He's a fair child with his mother's colouring and good manners. He looks at me gravely and doesn't smile. He appears very serious.

'Hello, Master Robert,' I say. 'I am Miss Swift, and I'm going to be your governess. How old are you?'

'I'm eight,' he replies. 'I shall be nine in October,' he adds, and I can see that he's impatient to be nine. I want to tell him not to rush through life. That every moment is precious. His little brother, who stands beside him with a mischievous look on his face, has few moments left. As I lay my gaze upon him, something catches in my chest, for his eyes shine with sweetness and innocence, and I'm immediately saddened by the future that lurks in the wings like an ogre, poised to steal him away. The weight of knowing is too heavy for me to carry but carry it I must if I'm to do my job well.

'And this darling little thing is Master Felix.' Cordelia reaches out and draws the boy to her skirts. By the affectionate expression on her face and the tender way she strokes his hair, I think Felix must be her favourite. 'He's six and growing so fast. He wants to catch up with his brother.'

'I am sure he does,' I say, but my voice is tight. I clear my throat and take a breath. I must compose myself. I'm not here to save him and change the past, I'm here to save his mother in the present.

Felix appraises me with curiosity and grins, proudly displaying a missing front tooth, the first of his milk teeth to go, I assume. I can tell already that he's a character.

'And this is Gwen,' Cordelia continues, and Gwen smiles at me shyly. She's a voluptuous girl with a pretty round face, and big round eyes to match, the colour of peat. Her curly brown hair is pinned up in a bun on the top of her head, but strands have come loose about her hairline in a sweaty frizz. She wears a long cotton dress with puffy sleeves beneath a white apron stained with earth. I imagine she's been playing with the children in the garden.

'Pleased to meet you, miss,' she says, and gives me a shallow bob.

'Gwen is very fond of Master Felix, aren't you, Gwen?' says Cordelia with a laugh, as Felix wriggles away from his mother and puts his arms out for his nursemaid, who gathers him into her apron. 'He used to sneak off and sleep in her bed, didn't you, darling?' she adds. 'But he's a big boy now. Big boys sleep in their own beds.' She turns to me. 'I do not allow the boys to come to my room at all. If they need something in the night they find Gwen, or you. Is that understood? I do not want this rule broken under any circumstance. It is not appropriate for boys of their age to be knocking on their mother's bedroom door.'

I nod. 'That is very clear, Mrs Pengower,' I reply.

'Now, let me show you your quarters. Then I'll leave you to familiarise yourself with the place. I don't need to tell you your duties; you have come highly recommended. Indeed, I was very impressed with your letters of recommendation. I have no doubt that you'll turn my little rascals into proper gentlemen.'

'That's my intention, madam,' I reply. But their education is the last thing on my mind.

My 'quarters' are on the first floor, close to the nursery, and are very cosy. They comprise of two rooms: a bedroom with a robust-looking four-poster bed, and a pretty sitting room next door where Cordelia says I might find some peace. Both rooms have fireplaces, but it's too warm to light them. In fact, it's so hot, it's stifling. I'm grateful that the windows have been thrown wide open, but there is no breeze. The air is still and heavy. I don't know how these women tolerate the heat with all the clothes they have to wear. I can feel the sweat trickling down my back and my drawers are sticking to my legs. I don't think I've ever been so uncomfortable. The bathroom is a short distance down the corridor. I'd like to fill the tub with cold water and lie in it like a hippo.

'I would very much like you to join us for dinner when we do not entertain guests,' says Cordelia, hovering in the doorway. 'We are few, my husband, his brother Mr Cavill, who is unmarried and lives here with us, and I. We often invite my mother-in-law, Mrs James Pengower, for she is a widow and on her own, and Mr Bray, the foreman at Mr Pengower's mine and a dear friend, to dine with us. You will give the table balance and, I hope, refresh the conversation.'

'Thank you. I would very much like that,' I reply.

Cordelia is in no hurry to leave. She looks at me intensely and I sense an eagerness in her. 'I do hope you will be happy here, Miss Swift.'

'I'm sure I shall,' I reply. I'm surprised by this sudden glimpse of neediness. 'This room is beautiful,' I add, because I feel I must reassure her.

She smiles, pleased. 'It is, is it not? I did not want you in the attic with the servants. I am glad you like it. If anything is not to your liking, you must tell me at once, is that understood?'

'Of course.'

I realise from the way Cordelia is treating me that she's keen for me to be a part of the family. I imagine the servants won't take kindly to that arrangement. I remember the novels I read as a teenager, *Jane Eyre* and *Agnes Grey*, written by the Brontë sisters, and how common it was for a governess to fall between two stools. On the one hand they are of a higher social standing than a servant, but on the other hand they are not on the same level as their employers. They earn money just as the servants do, but the servants resent them anyway.

'Very good. I believe it is important to speak plainly. This is going to be your home, Miss Swift. It matters to me that you're happy in it.' She lingers a moment longer, as if reluctant to go. I wonder whether, being in such a remote part of the countryside, she's lonely and starved of female company.

I see that my suitcase and hat box have been brought up and placed on the bed. She notices me glancing at them.

'I will let you unpack,' she says. 'Gwen will introduce you to the rest of the household and show you where everything is.'

'Thank you, madam,' I say and watch her leave, her skirts swishing merrily as she makes her way down the corridor. I was not expecting her to be so friendly. There's a surprising vulnerability beneath the veneer of poise, which has made her instantly likeable. Her beauty led me to believe that she is a woman both confident of her power and happy in her skin. But her neediness has revealed that she's not quite as confident or as happy as she first appeared. I shudder suddenly at the knowledge of what is to come. How long have I got? How long until Felix goes missing? I open the suitcase and hope to find a clue buried among the clothes and toiletries.

I'm relieved to see a letter placed on top. It's addressed to Miss Hermione Swift, Seaview Cottage, Topsham, Exeter, and is unsealed. I pull it out of the envelope and open it. It's dated 30th May, 1895, and is from Cordelia to Miss Swift, confirming details of her position. I notice the date of arrival is specified on the last line: Wednesday 19th June. I take a breath – I have eleven days, counting this one, to find out what happens to the boy. That is way too much time. I wish it was the evening of his disappearance so I could lie in wait in his bedroom and watch, then slide back and tell Cordelia what became of him. But timesliding is not an exact art. I put out my desire and trusted that the law of attraction would draw me to the moment of his vanishing. It has brought me to this moment now. What on earth am I going to do here for eleven whole days, and in this tight corset? There's nothing I can do but go with it. I shall put my trust in the universe and hope that it knows what it's doing. There's no such thing as coincidence, so there must be a reason for my early arrival, and for sliding into Hermione Swift. No doubt I will find out soon enough what that reason is.

Another thought crosses my mind. I assume that whoever takes Felix will creep into his bedroom in the middle of the night and bundle him away, and that I will see it happen from my clever hiding place, most likely behind a curtain. But what if I don't recognise the perpetrator? What if I'm unable to follow them because it's too dangerous and I risk being seen? I can't put Hermione Swift in danger. I have a responsibility to her. I warm to my argument, but it makes me go cold. What if the events of the night are not what I expect, and they turn out to be more challenging? I realise then that I cannot pin my hopes on that one night. I have to find out who takes Felix *before* it happens. Maybe that is why I have slid back eleven days in advance of his disappearance. Because I need this time to investigate. I must explore every eventuality, for Cordelia's sake. I feel a little sorry for poor Hermione, who is unknowingly lending me her body for almost two weeks. I decide not to think about that and focus instead on my work.

It is at times like these that my history degree comes in handy. If it is 1895, I know that Queen Victoria is on the throne – she still has six years before she dies. The Liberal Earl of Rosebery is on the point of resigning as prime minister and will be succeeded by the Marquess of Salisbury, who is Conservative. Oscar Wilde, at the height of his fame, has been convicted of gross indecency and imprisoned. I imagine his plays are still being performed in London.

I open the hat box and find what appears to be a black top hat, nestled in purple silk. I guess it's for riding. I haven't ridden in years, but I used to ride as a child when my grandmother signed me up for an equestrian club in the village. I think it was an attempt to help take my mind off the trauma of losing both parents, and in such a violent manner. I'm not sure if it did any good, but it might come in handy now. I hope I can remember how to do it. Eleven days is a hell of a long time to pretend to be what I'm not.

I put the clothes away in the wardrobe and chest of drawers. I could do with some hangers, but they haven't been invented yet. There are hooks in the wardrobe and I have to make do with those. It doesn't take long; I don't have many possessions. I clearly wore my most elegant dress today in order to make a good first impression.

It'll do for church. I imagine a good Christian family like the Pengowers will go to church on Sundays and I'll be expected to dress smartly. The only alternatives I have are a few blouses and skirts. I suppose those are what I'll wear when I'm with the children. The black shirt and jacket must be for when I'm on a horse. There are petticoats and nightwear – it's all so unfamiliar, I wish I had a manual that told me what everything was for. I suppose I'm just going to have to work it out from the hours I've spent watching period dramas – or wing it.

Once again, I stare at myself in the mirror, keen to familiarise myself with my new shape. This time it's a full-length mirror, standing by the window on little wooden feet. It's a strange thing to inhabit someone else's body, yet it feels normal. I'm still me inside it. Me, Pixie, looking out.

I examine myself from every angle. I'm slim. In fact, my figure is the quintessential hourglass shape, and I'm taller than in my normal body. I unpin my hat and smooth the stray strands of hair off my forehead. I think I'm going to enjoy being Hermione Swift for a while.

I look out of the window. Below are the gardens, lush and green in the early evening light. Hazy in the heat. The lawn is mown into tidy stripes and the topiary clipped into balls. The yew hedges are manicured, the borders ablaze with flowers. How different it is from the white, winter garden I've slid from.

I finish unpacking and return to the nursery. Gwen is by the window, engrossed in something going on outside. The children are playing together on the rug and she's not watching them. She jumps when I say her name. She puts a plump hand to her chest and gasps. 'Oh, dear God, you startled me, miss.'

'I'm sorry, Gwen.'

She laughs it off. 'You settled in, then?'

'I am, thank you.' I need to find out what my duties are and realise that Gwen can help me. I sweep my skirts out of the way and sit down on a wooden spindle-backed chair. 'Tell me, Gwen,' I begin breezily. 'Have the children had a governess before?'

I hold my breath, expecting her to frown at my strange question, but she simply plonks herself down on one of the other chairs. She lowers her voice. 'Master Robert didn't like Miss Archer,' she tells me gleefully. 'She only stayed six months and then left. He's a sensitive boy, you see, and she was very strict. Mrs Pengower wouldn't have it.'

'Is Mrs Pengower a loving mother?' I ask.

'She's soft. Mr Pengower disapproves. He wants his boys to grow up to be men. Master Robert is a gentle boy.'

'And Master Felix?'

'Master Felix likes to be with me,' she says, lifting her chin. I can tell that she's proud of their bond, and possessive of it, perhaps. 'He's too little to have a governess. He still needs his nurse.' Her expression softens as she looks at him playing in his den. 'Master Robert is ready to be moulded into a young gentleman, but Master Felix is still a child. Your job is to teach Master Robert and leave Master Felix to me.'

'Of course, I know that,' I reply, and she smiles, pleased to have staked her territory.

'And what was Master Robert's routine? I would like his life to be as consistent as possible.'

'Miss Archer got him up at six. He practises the piano before breakfast at seven and has lessons until lunch. He rides out most afternoons. He loves horse riding.'

'And how long have you worked here, Gwen?' I ask.

'Four years,' she replies. 'Master Felix was two when I arrived. In those days he used to sleep in his mother's bed, but she put a stop to that about a year ago. He's good most of the time, but occasionally he creeps upstairs to my bed. I can't turn him away. Not my sweet Master Felix.' Felix hears her talking about him and leaves his game to sit on her knee. She draws him against her generous bosom. 'Why don't you let Master Robert here show you his bedroom?' she suggests, looking at Robert, who doesn't appear happy to have to stop his play. 'Go on, Master Robert. Be a good boy and show Miss Swift the rest of the house.'

'Thank you, Master Robert,' I say and watch him put his wooden soldier down and get to his feet.

'I will show you Felix's and my bedroom first,' he says solemnly and leaves the room. I smile at Gwen, and she smiles back. She seems pleasant enough, if a little dreamy.

Robert leads me down the corridor. We get to the L-shape corner, and he opens the door to the room where I found Cordelia crying. 'This is Felix's bedroom,' he says.

'How charming,' I reply as I look around. I feel a moment's sadness at the memory of the woman crying by the window. It's no wonder that her poor soul gets trapped in here. It has changed little. There's the same single bed with its carved wooden frame, the same fireplace, even the same chest of drawers and sturdy wardrobe. But the walls are papered with little yellow flowers and there's a rocking horse by the window. The room is full of childish things – books, toys and trinkets, the usual paraphernalia of a little boy's bedroom. Gwen needs to teach him how to keep his room tidy, I muse. 'Show me yours, Master Robert,' I ask.

He opens a door on the opposite side of the corridor. The room is much the same as his brother's, but with blue walls and two large windows looking out onto the stable and carriage block, a harmoniously proportioned, red-bricked building with a tall clock tower capped by a lead dome and weather cock. I can see one of the stable boys standing by the wall, smoking idly. In a tweed cap and brown jacket, his black hair curling about his neck, he cuts a surly figure. He's lost in thought until someone calls him, then he drops his cigarette to the ground and saunters back through the giant archway, beneath the clock tower, and disappears.

Robert shows me his possessions. He's proud of his books and the way they're neatly lined up on the shelf in alphabetical order. He tells me that he likes to ride, play tennis and swim in the sea. He also enjoys history and writing poetry. I sense he's a quiet child who enjoys his own company. 'Shall I show you the rest of the house?' he asks.

'I would very much like that, Master Robert,' I tell him. Although I have already been in this house in the present, I need to familiarise myself with it in this time as quickly as possible if I'm to find out what's going on.

Robert shows me around with enthusiasm. No longer the solemn little boy, but a child full of self-importance. He knows many of the characters in the portraits and reads out their names and dates with gravitas; they are Pengowers, and he's clearly pleased to be descended from them. He tells me who built the house and when, and how Queen Elizabeth herself came to stay and that the stairs had to be widened especially to accommodate her dress. 'That is why it is as it is,' he says, taking me down it. 'On account of the Queen's dress. I am sure Queen Victoria will visit too,' he says loftily, 'but we won't have to widen the staircase. I would think it is wide enough for her dress.' I decide not to deflate his hope by telling him that the Queen is an old lady now and unlikely to go anywhere. Robert is full of information, and I imagine that he must be a pleasure to teach, for he's alert and interested in everything.

When we get to the dining room he goes and stands beside the antique carved fireplace surround. The walls are covered in wood panelling upon which hang gilt-framed portraits and landscapes. He grins at me. 'Shall I show you something special?' he asks.

'Are you going to disappear up the chimney like Santa Claus?' I ask.

He laughs. It's the first time I've seen him laugh. 'I'm going to show you a secret hiding place where priests used to hide. Did you know that Queen Elizabeth killed Catholics?'

My curiosity is piqued. 'Are you telling me there's a priest hole in here?'

'This house is full of treasures, Miss Swift. Come and I'll show you.'

I go and stand beside him. He waits a beat, enjoying the suspense, and then puts his hand on the relief carving of a rose and presses it. To my delight, a hidden door in the panelling to the left of the fireplace springs open. Robert pulls it wide to reveal what looks like a stone pit.

'Where does it lead to?' I ask, intrigued.

'A room. There's nothing in it. No bones of dead priests.'

'What a horrid thought!' I exclaim.

He laughs again. 'I would not want get stuck down there. No one would find me and I would starve to death. It's a hole, you see. Papa said there would have been a ladder there once, but there's no ladder now. There is no way out.'

It crosses my mind that Felix could fall down there by accident and never be found, but I discount the theory because surely this would be one of the first places they would search after he goes missing.

'Papa says there are likely to be other tunnels and secret hiding places in the house. This one was discovered by one of the house-maids when she was polishing the wood. She pressed so hard the door popped open. She nearly fainted with fright.'

'I can imagine.'

'Shall I show you the rest of the house? We can look for other priest holes if you like. Papa will be very pleased with me if I find a new one. He says the house is riddled with them.'

In showing me the house, Robert omits the servants' side and their sleeping quarters on the second floor. I imagine, to him, those areas don't exist. The servants move about the place as ghosts, unseen, unheard, quietly going about their business. For me, the servants are of great significance. Felix does not disappear on his own accord. He's taken, and I need to find out why, where and by whom. I know that I won't be able to prevent the abduction, for I mustn't alter the future. That is the most important rule for a timeslider – to be mindful of the Butterfly Effect, the theory that comes from the Chinese proverb 'the flapping of the wings of a butterfly can be felt on the other side of the world' that every tiny action can have a far-reaching effect. When the time comes, I should leave this place having disturbed nothing.

Robert leads me outside. It's a beautiful evening. The sky is a great expanse of blue, the clouds that float in it like candyfloss, moving slowly on the breeze. Robert shows me the gardens. They're magnificent. Cordelia has a gift for beauty. Her inner playfulness and charm have manifested this glorious place. There are flow-ers everywhere, and shrubs and trees and fountains and statues and secret walled gardens and arboretums and grottos. Mayflower adorns the hedges with its frothy white blossom and cow parsley grows in abundance beneath an avenue of lime trees, like heaps of exquisite lace. Dappled light shimmers on the grass where daisies and buttercups grow, and butterflies flutter through the sunbeams with tiny insects and bees. It's a paradise and I wonder whether Bruce and Olivia Talwyn will be able to restore it when spring comes. I'm particularly struck by the quiet. There's no drone of airplanes overhead, or the whizzing of cars in the lane. Only birdsong and the lazy humming of bees.

Robert does not introduce me to the groundsmen, nor, when he shows me the stables, does he present me to the grooms. He does, however, stop to talk to the coachman, who doffs his cap and greets me cheerfully in the stable yard. He has grey whiskers and sage-green eyes, crooked teeth and an engaging smile. 'Mr Grantly at your service, madam. I have just the mare for you, Miss Swift,' he tells me, his enthusiasm infectious. 'She's gentle but bold. This young lad here likes to ride fast, don't you, Master Robert?'

Robert laughs. 'If Miss Swift is anything like her name, *she* will want to ride fast too.'

Mr Grantly looks at me and his eyes twinkle. 'You see, he's a clever boy is Master Robert.'

'I'm going to take great pleasure in teaching him. I enjoy a child with a quick mind,' I reply, rather enjoying the part I'm playing. I'm settling in well, I think, and I can tell that Robert is warming to me.

'Oh, he's quick, all right.' Mr Grantly ruffles Robert's hair and Robert grins proudly.

Just as we set off, that surly stable boy I saw smoking by the wall comes through the archway, leading a horse by the reins. We catch eyes and he holds my gaze. He has an arrogant look and I find that it is *I* who averts my gaze first. 'Come, Master Robert,' I say, putting my hand on his shoulder. 'What else have you got to show me?' I smile at Mr Grantly. 'Good day.' The coachman doffs his hat once again. I glance at the stable boy to see that he's still staring at me. His eyes are very dark, almost black, and they're not friendly like Mr Grantly's. I lift my chin and walk away, but I can still feel his gaze on my back. I don't like him. I don't like his energy. I sense he's resentful and devious.

I ask Robert his name. 'Mr John Snathe,' Robert replies. I'd better watch out for John Snathe.

I sit with Gwen at the table in the nursery while the children have their tea. Felix is sweet, playful and endearing. He loves Gwen, who must sit next to him otherwise he cries. He's very attached to her and she to him. She looks at him with adoration and laughs at everything he says, however banal. Robert finds his brother annoying and snaps at him impatiently. They are typical brothers with their petty jealousies and annoyances. Gwen defends Felix with an indulgent smile. 'He's only little,' she says, which I imagine excuses him for every misdemeanour.

Later, after the children have gone to bed and I've read to them both, I leave them with their mother, who has come to kiss them goodnight. 'Gwen tells me that Master Robert gave you a tour of the house,' she says before I leave the room.

'He showed me the priest hole in the dining room,' I tell her.

'This house is full of secrets,' she says, eyes brightening. 'One never knows when one is going to find another surprise. Those Elizabethans were an ingenious lot.'

'I suppose they had to be. Those were dangerous times, for both Catholics and Protestants, depending on who was in power.'

'How glad I am to live now,' she says and, knowing what the twentieth century holds, I'm inclined to agree with her.

I watch her sit on Felix's bed. He snuggles up against her and she rests her cheek against his hair and inhales the sweet smell of him. It's clear that she loves him very much.

I leave them to share this moment in private and return to my bedroom to change for dinner. As I survey the few clothes that Hermione owns, an image floats into my mind of travellers in the modern day lugging enormous suitcases full of fashion around crowded airports. At least I won't waste hours rummaging through my wardrobe trying to decide what to wear.

I'm pleased to find the house has running hot and cold water. I run a cold bath and wallow in it luxuriantly. It's a relief to be naked and free after the tight-fitting corset. I'm not free for long, however. I dress, having learnt from *un*dressing in which order the items of clothing go on. I slip into the long white shirt, which I believe is called a chemise, and a pair of white drawers that reach my knees. It feels strange not to wear knickers, but they haven't been invented yet. I can hardly bear to put on stockings. It's too hot. I wonder for a moment whether I can get away with bare legs beneath my skirts, but I don't want to get anything wrong on my first evening. I step into the crinoline and spend far too long figuring out how to fasten the corset, which goes over the chemise. There's a white lace blouse to wear over the corset. It buttons up to the neck. There are so many little buttons that by the time I've finished fastening them, I'm sticky with sweat again and could do with another bath. Finally, I pull on the long blue skirt and cinch it in at the waist with a belt. Trussed up like a Christmas turkey, I can barely breathe. I'm not sure how I'm going to survive eleven days like this.

I appraise myself in the mirror. I might be boiling hot in all these clothes, but I certainly cut a dash. The corset makes me stand erect, with my shoulders back, and I know that I look feminine and demure in it. Satisfied that I'm sufficiently elegant, I make my way down to the drawing room at eight. I hear voices wafting up from the hall and feel nervous for I'm about to be formally introduced to Mr Pengower and his brother, Cavill, and I'm aware that as the governess I'm highly fortunate to be permitted to join them. I hope I don't put my foot in it.

When I enter, two men get to their feet. I recognise Mr Pengower from earlier. The other must be Cavill. Cordelia, in a pale yellow gown that reveals the milky skin of her décolletage, and a dazzling array of jewellery, is seated in an armchair. 'Ah, Miss Swift,' she says, her voice soft and warm. 'You have yet to meet my husband.'

I smile at Mr Pengower and am once again pleasantly surprised by the lively expression on his handsome face. 'I had the honour of meeting him earlier,' I tell her and put out my hand. He looks at it and frowns. Aware that I have just made my first faux pas, I hastily withdraw it and nod my head.

'Ah, you are mistaken, Miss Swift,' he replies, watching me with curiosity, as if I'm a rare bird. 'I am Cavill, Mr Pengower's brother.'

'I am Mr Pengower,' declares the more solemn-looking man. He does not smile but appraises me with condescension. I should have known – *he* has the bearing of the master of the house with his cold, dark eyes, serious face and sweeping black moustache. His hair, the colour and texture of a wild boar, is thinning. His brow is furrowed and his ruddy skin coarse, as if he's constantly worried. Cavill, with his clear, untroubled eyes, tousled hair and smooth brow, has the bearing of a man who takes life lightly and with humour.

'I do apologise, I assumed . . .'

'Of course, you did,' Mr Pengower interrupts gruffly, glancing resentfully at his brother, as if he's only too aware of his superior good looks, and annoyed at being reminded of them.

Cavill chuckles and I'm struck by the charm in the lines around his mouth and fanning out at his temples as he smiles. He's clearly amused by the misunderstanding. 'It was an easy mistake,' he says. 'I do have the air of a man weighed down by responsibility and obligation.' He's joking, of course. Mr Pengower grunts. He is not so amused.

'The only responsibility you have seems to be towards your horse,' Mr Pengower replies with a sniff.

'Do you ride, Miss Swift?' Cavill asks, ignoring the resentment in his brother's voice.

'I do,' I answer, and hope to God that I remember.

'Good, then you can help me instil in the boys an understanding of how to take command of a horse and to have it do his bidding.'

'Certainly.' I'm much less confident than I sound. Cavill is staring at me intensely and I'm disarmed. His blue gaze has a way of penetrating straight through a person, like a laser. Does he see something in me that looks out of place, or is he just entertained by my ineptitude? I've been here a matter of minutes and I've already put my foot in it, twice.

'Please sit down,' says Cordelia. I do as she asks and sit beside her on a chair upholstered in pale blue silk.

The lofty butler appears with a tray of drinks. I take a crystal glass and thank him, although he doesn't look me in the eye. 'Thank you, Symons,' says Cordelia. I take a small sip of wine and remind myself to be careful not to drink too much and let down my guard. I must remember who I am.

Cordelia smiles at me warmly. 'I want you to feel at home here, Miss Swift,' she says quietly. 'It is important to me that you do. You see, we have more in common than you can imagine.' Her smile broadens and there's a whisper of collusion about it. 'I do so want us to be friends,' she adds softly. I wonder what it is that we have in common besides being women.

Mr Pengower goes and stands in front of the empty fireplace and hooks his thumbs in the pockets of his waistcoat, giving a glimpse of a fine gold watch on a chain and a paunch. He's of a sturdy build with a barrel chest, a thick neck and short legs. He lifts his chin and appraises the room with an imperious gaze, as if he's about to launch into a speech. Cavill flicks up the tails of his coat and perches on the sofa. His eyes shift to me and he gives me a jocular smile, as if he's aware that his brother is pompous and is tacitly apologising for him. Mr Pengower asks after my impressions of the house, visibly pleased by my enthusiastic response. He then proceeds to enlighten me on its illustrious history, without knowing that his son has already done so. I listen – Mr Pengower is a man who is used to being listened to.

I watch Cordelia. She's not looking at her husband but gazing into the middle distance, lost in thought. There's a subtle smile upon her lips, as if she's thinking of something pleasant. I imagine she's heard this speech before, maybe many times. Ivan Pengower does appear to be a man who loves the sound of his own voice. 'The exterior of St Sidwell Manor was altered in eighteen hundred by John Nash . . .' On he drones and I try to look interested, for this soliloquy is for my benefit. The history would be interesting were it not for his self-important and monotonous intonation. There's something very unappealing about him and I wonder what

SANTA MONTEFIORE

inspired Cordelia to marry him. Perhaps she didn't have a choice.

I'm acutely aware of Cavill. He has a charisma that his brother does not. It's powerful and I can't help but be drawn to it. I catch his eye more than once and am embarrassed to be caught looking at him. But he is looking at me, too. I can feel the intensity of his gaze, burning through my clothes. There is between us an undeniable frisson, and I'm excited by it. I'm very far away from Pablo. Very far away from my world and the disastrous love affairs I've had. And I'm beautiful. That in itself is a novelty. I'm not at all surprised that he's looking at me. None the less, I mustn't allow myself to be drawn into a flirtation. I'm not here to enjoy a romance, but to save Cordelia Pengower's soul. I focus my attention on the boorish Mr Pengower and try to ignore the magnetic allure of his brother.

Chapter Seven

The following morning I awake at five to the cheerful sound of birdsong. For a moment, in the darkened room I don't remember where I am. I blink up at the canopy of the four-poster bed and believe that I'm in the present – that Ulysses is about to come into my room and tell me I'm being a lazy troll. But as I take in the dress hanging over the standing mirror and the brown suitcase placed against the wall, the day before comes flooding back. I know where I am. It's 1895, 20th June, the second day of my slide. I have ten days to find out what happens to Felix.

I lie on the crisp sheets and think how strange it is not to see any light switches on the wall or a lamp on the bedside table. Of course, electricity hasn't yet been rolled out in homes. It's at least another ten years before that starts to happen. You only realise how much you rely on these things when you don't have them. These people can't imagine how much their lives are going to change with the wealth of inventions that are to come.

I open the curtains and gaze onto the garden, serene in the pale dawn light, and I don't believe I have ever seen a garden more beautiful. The greenery is still fresh with newness, the grass and flowers still abounding with the enthusiasm of early summer. They're not yet tired; they've only just begun to take pleasure in their aliveness. And everything looks so positive in the sunshine. It's impossible to imagine the darkness that is to come.

I awaken Robert at six and he dutifully practises the piano for an hour before breakfast. I leave Felix to Gwen, mindful that my duty is to turn Robert into a gentleman and give him an education. I'm also aware of the responsibility I have towards Hermione Swift. I believe that when I leave, her memory of these days will be non-existent. Apparently, the hosts put their amnesia down to trauma or fever – at least that's what I've read in the small amount of literature that exists on the subject, which, by the way, is called astral projection possession. Timesliding is my own term. Hermione will continue from where I leave her, so it's imperative that I do the best I can for her while I'm in possession of her body. I don't take that responsibility lightly.

The four of us meet at the breakfast table in the nursery at half past seven, and I notice that Gwen is sleepy. Her round face is pale and the shadows beneath her eyes are accentuated, making them look almost purple. The eyes themselves have a sparkle, though, and a dreaminess, as if she hasn't fully awoken. Felix demands her attention, and she gives it, but without the zest of the day before.

I watch her, curious about her demeanour, and make polite conversation but get little in return. I focus my attention on Robert instead, and we make a plan to ride after lunch. He wants to show me the chapel and the beach and the gypsy encampment. 'They're a rotten sort,' he says crossly, and I hear his father's voice and know that the boy has picked up this blinkered attitude from him. 'They make a frightful mess and have no respect for anybody.'

'Perhaps we should steer clear of them then,' I say, but he wants to show me all the same.

He lifts his chin. 'I'm not afraid of them.'

I realise his fervour needs to be tempered. 'They are probably here temporarily to find work picking fruit and later to help with the harvest. It's unkind to judge them when you do not know them. They are likely going about their business and doing the best they can just like everyone else.'

'Nonsense, they are up to no good, I tell you.' He believes this passionately and I have to remind myself that we are in 1895, not 2013, and people's attitudes are different. However, I can't help but see them through the lens of my own time. I want to encourage Robert to view them as people and to understand our shared humanity. Just because they're different doesn't mean they're bad. I don't want him to grow up with a sense of superiority simply because he's born into more favourable circumstances than others. I'm mindful of the Butterfly Effect, but, surely, influencing someone for the greater good of the world is a positive thing?

After breakfast and before we begin our lessons at nine, I take the opportunity to meet the servants. I make my way through the hall and down a passageway that leads to a green baize door. The same door that exists now, separating Elsa's domain from Olivia's. On the other side of this door is a different house. No more the fine furnishings and grand log fires. Here the floors are tiled, the walls white, the furniture simple and functional. I introduce myself to the cook, Mrs Moyle. She's a large-boned woman with an air of authority and the weary patience of the sorely tried. She greets me briskly, pausing her rolling pin for a only moment before resuming her work, indicating that she doesn't have time for niceties. I'm not at all surprised that she's stretched considering there are no kitchen appliances to lessen her load, or ready-made meals from the supermarket. I meet Miss Prideaux, who is Cordelia's lady's maid. She's plump and comely with shiny brown hair, fine features and a wily expression in her eyes, which are almost the colour of amber. She's friendly and not at all harassed like Mrs Moyle. When she speaks, she has an air of education, as if she's a cut above the usual women of her station. I sense she's a rare jewel, and that Cordelia is fortunate to have found her. There's Mrs Petworth, the housekeeper, and Mr Lanyon, the steward, a cheerful kitchen maid called Esther, Mr Pengower's valet, Mr Roskelley, who is handsome and self-satisfied, a couple of housemaids named Ida and Rose, and various under-butlers. They are all welcoming enough. I feel none of the usual resentment, only from Mr Symons, who is the most important member of the household being the butler. He has no reason to feel threatened by me for I, as the governess, answer directly to Cordelia and not to him. Perhaps he's supercilious with all the servants.

I spend the morning teaching Robert in a room upstairs, which has been converted for this very purpose. It has a view of the stable block and every now and then I look out and see John Snathe, smoking against the wall, or bringing round the pony and trap, or saddling up a horse, or loitering. He loiters a lot, I've noticed. He looks like a character from Central Casting. But this is no film set. This is real, and soon a little boy will go missing.

I teach Robert French. My French is basic, but I manage to convince him that I know what I'm talking about. He frowns when I mention the word geography and, after some explanation, I realise that he calls it 'Use of the Globes'. The same happens when I declare that we're going to do some maths – he knows that as arithmetic. He looks at me with a bewildered expression, as if I've come from a different land. If only he knew! But once we get going, he's quick to learn and keen, soaking up information like a greedy sponge. I slip very comfortably into my role. The dress makes it easier to act the Victorian governess. Because of its restrictive structure, I find it simple to take on the deportment and manners of a woman of this time, as if I'm in a period drama and therefore mindful of the character I'm playing. However, I'm not sure how I'm going to keep it up for nine more days. At least actors get to go home in the evenings and slip into a pair of jeans and a T-shirt.

After lunch we both need fresh air. The day is too lovely to spend inside. We change our clothes and head out to the stables. I pray that I can remember how to ride. It's been a long time.

As we walk through the archway beneath the clock tower my heart gives a little skip, for there, on the cobbles mounting his horse, is Cavill. When he sees me, he takes his foot out of the stirrup and smiles, his eyes lighting up with pleasure. He exudes an energy that's so spirited I'm infected by it and feel spirited too.

'Miss Swift,' he says, lifting his hat. His hair is tousled beneath it and the blue of his eyes very bright against his tanned skin. 'Robert, where are you off to?'

'I'm going to show Miss Swift the chapel and the beach,' the child declares importantly.

Cavill grins. 'Then allow me to come too, for I would very much like to see the chapel and the beach for myself.' He's joking, of course, because he's more than familiar with both, but there's a playful twinkle in his eye. 'Grantly, mounts for Miss Swift and Master Robert,' he shouts, and Mr Grantly appears in the doorway and waves an acknowledgement, before disappearing again to do as requested.

We chat in the sunshine while Robert runs in to help Mr Grantly. I feel myself flowering once again in the appreciative light of Cavill's gaze. He admires me and isn't shy to show it. This is a novelty for me. As Pixie Tate, I do not receive so much male attention. I tell him how much I love the gardens and how grateful I am that his family has made me feel so welcome.

'Mrs Pengower is an admirable woman,' he says. 'She has no airs, only grace.'

'And her children are delightful, just as she is,' I reply.

'My brother is not an easy man to live with,' he confides, running a hand down the blaze on his horse's face. 'But Mrs Pengower is a soothing influence. He is quick to temper and to find fault, but she always understands the bigger perspective and enables him to see beyond his often narrow viewpoint. He has married a sensible and patient woman. He is fortunate. St Sidwell needs a mistress like that.' He smiles at me, and I notice the slightly pronounced canine teeth that give his mouth a jaunty charm. 'She is keen to make a friend of *you*,' he adds, arching an eyebrow, aware perhaps that friendship between mistress and governess is unusual.

'It is uncommon for her to seek my friendship,' I reply. 'A governess is usually a lonely figure, neither fish nor fowl, but something in between.'

'Not in this household. We are remote here, and my sister-in-law is in need of female company. You are obviously intelligent and level-headed, a natural friend for her. However, I would understand if you have incited the jealousy of your previous mistresses.'

He's flirting with me. I imagine that, being undeniably attractive, he flirts with all women. I must tread carefully. How would the real Hermione Swift respond to that, I wonder? 'Mrs Pengower is above jealousy,' I reply tactfully. 'And has every right to be, being so lovely.'

'You are lovely too, Miss Swift, if I may be so bold.'

I'm at a loss of how to answer. He's moving in fast and I'm not ready for him. I laugh, for what else can I do? 'I fear you are toying with me, Mr Cavill,' I reply at last, attempting to deflect his comment gracefully and with the modesty of a woman of my situation. I turn my eyes to the stable, hoping that Robert will come out, or Mr Grantly, or even John Snathe. I don't trust that Cavill is altogether sincere.

'I am not toying with you, Miss Swift,' he says seriously. 'Merely admiring. You cannot pretend that you have not been admired before?'

I'm sure Hermione Swift has been *much* admired before, but it's not my place to answer for her, or to put her job and reputation in jeopardy. I remind myself once again that I'm not here to enjoy a flirtation, but to investigate a possible crime. That is my *only* job.

'I thank you for your admiration, then, Mr Cavill.' I smile with feigned confidence, but my heart is thumping in my chest. I cannot deny that I'm enjoying his attention.

'It is sincerely given,' he says.

Just then Robert skips out, shadowed by John Snathe who is leading a small brown pony by the reins. Mr Grantly follows with a grey mare in tow. 'Ah, your steed, Miss Swift,' Cavill declares.

Mr Grantly leads the mare to the mounting block. I realise from the shape of the saddle that I'm expected to sit side-saddle. I've never ridden like that before. I conceal my panic behind a frozen smile and walk towards the horse. I stroke its long nose, playing for time. From the shape of the saddle it's quite obvious where to put my legs. At least I think it is. I really don't want to get this wrong. I climb the steps of the mounting block and, as Mr Grantly holds the horse steady, shift my bottom into the seat, placing my right knee behind the lump of leather designed to hold it in place and, I presume, to stop me falling off. I hold my breath. It feels strange, but not uncomfortable. Mr Grantly slips my boots into the stirrups, and I arrange my skirts, relieved that I've got this far without betraying my ignorance.

Robert swings himself into his saddle with ease. I thank Mr Grantly, who pats my horse's neck and tells me what a good-natured creature she is. 'You'll have no trouble from her,' he says, and I hope he's right.

'Lead the way, Robert,' says Cavill, who is dashing in the saddle, being so at home there. He then looks at me. 'After you, Miss Swift.'

We walk our horses up a track that leads away from the house and into the open countryside. After an initial apprehension, I begin to feel more confident. Robert rides ahead while Cavill and I ride side by side. I ask him about his growing up here at St Sidwell Manor, and about his other brother, Albert, who I learn is in India. Cavill is the youngest by twelve years. We slip into an easy conversation, and I'm relieved that we're no longer talking about me. I keep my wits about me. It's all too easy to lose oneself in the past, and I don't want to get lost.

He tells me that Ivan not only inherited the house and the estate, a vast amount of farmland and various cottages which are rented to tenants, but a tin mine that their father purchased in 1857. It's a given that Robert will inherit it one day, being the firstborn son. 'I hope that he will treat his workers more kindly than his father does,' Cavill says, and I'm surprised that he's confiding in me an aspect of my employer's nature that is less than flattering. 'My brother is a hard taskmaster,' he continues. 'If you can instil in Master Robert a sense of fairness that will ensure he treats those who work for him with courtesy, that would be a fine thing.'

'I hope I will,' I reply, determined to do so. He nods, satisfied. I'm impressed that he cares.

A breeze brushes my face; it smells of the sea and pine, and I feel the fullness of summer. It's hot. Too hot to be wearing these clothes and this corset. What I would give for a pair of shorts and a T-shirt. But the countryside is breathtakingly beautiful. Periwinkles and dandelions shimmer in the sunlight and the long grasses gently sway, and there's not a telegraph pole or a pylon to ruin the view. The hills and vales extend for miles, uninterrupted by the ugliness of the modern world. My heart aches at what is to come – for the wider world, and for this small world here at St Sidwell Manor. They cannot imagine how their lives are going to change and what the twentieth century will bring.

The track takes us through a small copse, and I spot through the trees the chapel that Tabitha wants to show me. It's serene and quiet there, resting sleepily among the gravestones, with the big sky above it and the estuary glittering in the distance in a line of blue.

'Is this where your family is buried?' I ask as we approach.

'Yes, and where I will also be buried someday.'

The thought appals me. I'm suddenly aware that, where I come from, he's already in the ground. 'When was it built?' I ask, deflecting his comment, not wanting to talk about death. Not wanting to be reminded of why I'm here. Wanting very badly, suddenly, to be lost in this innocent moment of sunshine and splendour and not to have to think of my purpose, which is so dark.

'It dates back to the seventeenth century,' he replies.

'How wonderful to be able to trace your family that far into the past.'

'We can trace our ancestors much further back than that, Miss Swift.'

'Does it give you a heavy sense of responsibility?' I ask. 'Knowing that this beautiful place has been in your family for so long. That it must remain so?'

'It is certainly a concern of my brother's. It matters a great deal to him that the house and estate remain in the family. But he has two sons. The continuation of the line is assured. Master Robert will inherit it and *his* son thereafter. My brother sees himself as a caretaker. He would like to hand the estate to the next generation in a better condition than that in which he found it.' He puffs out his chest and imitates Mr Pengower's pompous voice. 'Each generation must improve it, nurture it, love it.' He laughs. 'That is the way he feels and he never tires of telling us about it.'

'And you?'

He turns to me and grins. 'I cannot think of anything worse than being stuck here for the rest of my life. In fact, I think I would rather gnaw off my left arm.'

I laugh with him. 'That would be a pity. So, instead of gnawing off a perfectly good arm, what are you going to do?'

'I leave shortly to seek out my own fortune.'

'Where do you intend to go?' I ask.

'South America,' he answers. 'Argentina to be precise. I am hungry for adventure, Miss Swift.'

'That's brave,' I reply. 'To go all that way on a boat.' Then a cold hand squeezes my heart. I suddenly remember the book Bruce Talwyn found about Ivan Pengower, written by Robert. Cavill dies in 1895, on his way to South America. I realise with a shudder that he doesn't make it to Argentina at all. I want to tell him not to go – but I mustn't interfere. It's a burden that only a timeslider will ever know.

'How else am I going to get there?' he asks, looking at me in amusement. 'Am I to fly?'

I suppress the sick feeling in my stomach and laugh bitterly at the irony. 'I'm sure that one day people will fly all over the world.'

I expect him to laugh at the absurdity of my comment, but he doesn't. His eyes gleam. 'You have heard of Otto Lilienthal, then?' he says.

I frown, aware that I'm showing my ignorance, but unable to lie. 'Who is he?'

'The Flying Man, Miss Swift. Have you not read about his glider in the papers?'

I shake my head and he looks bemused. I suppose everyone has heard about him but me. I rally. 'Then I am right. One day people will be travelling by air rather than by sea. Perhaps they will even fly to America.'

'That would be fine thing,' he replies. 'I would be the first to buy a passage on an air machine to America.'

'Then they will fly to the moon,' I add merrily.

I've gone too far. He frowns and chortles with scepticism. 'You have a strange way of looking at the world, Miss Swift. An adventurer's spirit. But I think the moon is . . .'

'A pie in the sky?'

I laugh and he laughs with me. 'Well, I suppose, yes, as unlikely as a pie in the sky.'

I realise then that that's a phrase he's never heard before. 'Why do you want to go to Argentina?' I ask, changing the subject and reminding myself to watch my language or else he'll think me eccentric beyond redemption.

'I want to make something of my life,' he replies.

'Of course, you do.' My question was a silly one. Why else would a Victorian gentleman want to go to Argentina? Certainly not to see the Casa Rosada – Eva Peron, who will make that balcony famous, hasn't even been born yet!

'Ivan's life is mapped out for him,' Cavill continues. 'His life is here, at St Sidwell. It has ever been thus.'

'It seems unfair,' I say, even though I know it's been tradition for centuries. 'Your brother inherits everything. What is left for you and Mr Albert?'

Again, he looks at me, surprised, I suppose, by the ignorance of my question. 'It's the way it works, Miss Swift. If one were to cut up estates, after a few generations there would be nothing left.'

'That is true,' I concede. 'It just seems unfair,' I repeat.

'I wouldn't want St Sidwell,' he says with a shrug. 'I would hate to have my life planned out, with no way of escape. I am delighted to have the freedom to choose. I can go anywhere, be anything, do exactly what I want. Not many men can boast of that. I will make my fortune in Argentina and live a great adventure.'

But I know that he won't, and my heart hurts for the light of ambition in his eyes that will soon be snuffed out.

We reach the chapel. Cavill dismounts and then takes my hand to help me down. I look into his eyes and thank him. He holds my gaze for a long moment, and I stare back at him, transfixed by the intimacy I find there. It's as if we're seeing each other for the first time. I avert my gaze, bewildered. I could swear that he's seeing through Hermione's eyes to Pixie looking out, but I know that he isn't. That it's not possible. I'm invisible, even to myself.

Robert is already wandering around the gravestones, and I gather my skirts and walk hastily after him. I must not allow myself to be attracted to Cavill, or to encourage him to be attracted to me. There's no point. I will depart in nine days and Hermione will have to deal with whatever I leave behind.

We read some of the inscriptions. Robert is proud to show off his grandfather's large memorial, and I'm reminded of the transience of life, the brevity of it. I stare at the inscriptions, at the dates carved into the stone, the numbers separated by a dash. I think for the first time how inadequate that dash is in marking the span of a whole life lived. It tells nothing of the love, nothing of the joy, nothing of the tragedy, the ups and downs, the heartaches, the ecstasy, the sheer fullness of a life.

Soon Cavill's gravestone will be here too, carved with another set of meaningless numbers. Numbers that will never capture the cornflower blue of his eyes, or his zest for adventure.

I feel him at my side. He, too, looks upon the gravestone. He has no idea what I'm thinking. How could he?

'We must seize the day,' he says. I nod thoughtfully. He looks at me with concern. 'Are you all right, Miss Swift?'

'I find graveyards sad places,' I confess. 'Life is too short. There is so much to do and not enough time in which to do it.'

'That is why when one is taken by an idea, however wild, one must grab it by the collar.'

'And not waste a moment.' I feel him close, as if he's a flame and I'm a moth, fluttering into it.

He wanders to his father's memorial. The names James Ivan Clarence Pengower are carved into the stone at the base of the giant obelisk. He stands solemnly before it and takes off his hat. 'My father,' he tells me.

'I'm sorry,' I say.

'I am not,' he replies. His profile hardens and his mouth twists with bitterness, even the dimple on his chin seems to toughen. 'He was not a sympathetic man, Miss Swift. In truth, he was cold, selfish and unforgiving. I would even go as far as to say he was cruel. Albert and I did not receive his love, if you can call what he gave to our brother Ivan love. Such as it was, he gave it to the son who would succeed him. His other sons counted for nothing. We were as understudies in a play. But I should thank him. He taught me the most valuable lesson I have learnt in my life.'

'And what is that?' I ask.

'That I do not want to embody a single one of his qualities,' he replies. 'Unfortunately, Ivan has not yet seen the lesson in his example. Perhaps he never will.' He puts his hat back on and lifts his chin. 'One cannot control events and people in one's life, but one can . . .'

'Control how one reacts to them,' I cut in without thinking.

We look at each other in surprise. I had not intended to interrupt. He frowns. 'You spoke my mind, Miss Swift.'

'Because I have learnt that lesson too, the hard way.' My mind springs back to my childhood and for a brief and painful moment I am Pixie Tate, curled into a ball at the bottom of my bed.

His eyes soften and for the first time I see behind the humorous twinkle to the seriousness lying like a shadow beneath the light. 'If you have suffered, then I am sorry for it, for I know what it feels like and I would not wish it on anyone.'

'Don't be sorry. Life is not meant to be easy. It's meant to be laden with potholes and ruts so that we grow wise and compassionate. If it were easy we would all be selfish and unfeeling.'

'Then like me you are the product of a life laden with potholes and ruts and are the wiser for it.'

'Let us just say it is a work in progress.'

'As it is for me, Miss Swift. The two of us are alike.'

I smile at him and he smiles back with understanding. He's no longer flirting with me. He's taken off the mask of entertainer to reveal an empathetic man beneath whose life has not been as carefree as I first imagined.

'It is comforting when one finds another on a similar path,' I tell him.

'A pleasant surprise,' he replies with emphasis. 'I had not expected *that* when I met you in the hall yesterday.'

I want to talk more but Robert calls from the door of the chapel. He wants us to go inside. I take a breath and reluctantly walk towards him. It feels cold away from the flame.

Inside, the chapel is cool and smells of candlewax. I walk around, looking at the memorials on the walls, reading their inscriptions, but I'm not taking anything in. I'm aware only of where Cavill is. I need to get a grip. I'm not here to lose myself, or my heart. I'm not here to lament *his* death, but Felix's disappearance. That's *all* I'm here for.

Cavill goes up to the altar and bows. There's a simple white cloth upon it and a vase of yellow flowers and cow parsley. 'We used to keep the silver candlesticks and plates out, but since the gypsies have been camping nearby we have had to lock it all away,' he says.

'Would they steal it, Uncle Cavill?' Robert asks, standing beside him.

'One can never be too sure. There are always a few rotten apples in a barrel of fruit, and those rotten apples are giving your father a dreadful headache poaching birds and rabbits on his land.' Cavill looks at me steadily. 'If it were me, I would turn a blind eye. But my brother is less forgiving.'

'They are a rotten lot,' Robert interjects. 'They need to be moved on at once.'

'I'm afraid they are here for the summer,' his uncle tells him. 'They won't be gone until the harvest is over and there is no more work for them to do.'

'How near are they?' I ask, joining them at the altar.

'The other side of the estuary,' Cavill replies.

'We'll show you, won't we, Uncle?'

'I don't think that is prudent, Robert. Best keep our heads down and not give them any ideas,' Cavill suggests.

Robert looks disappointed. 'I'm not afraid of them,' he says, lifting his chin.

Cavill chuckles. 'You should be.'

'Why?'

'Because sometimes fear is a good thing. It keeps us safe.'

'But we're safe at St Sidwell, aren't we, Uncle Cavill?'

Cavill ruffles the child's hair. 'Of course, dear boy. St Sidwell is the safest place in the world.'

*

We gallop through the long grasses to the estuary, and I give over to the rhythmic movement of the horse beneath me. I'm not at all afraid – in fact, I'm filled with exhilaration. With the wind against my face and the sweet, marshy smell of the sea in my nostrils, I laugh with the sheer joy of being alive. We leave the gravestones and death behind and ride out with the enthusiasm of the living. The horses relish their freedom and so do we. Even Robert, who's on a small pony, manages to kick up quite a pace.

We reach the estuary. The tide is out. The sea glitters in the distance, but where we stand there's only a narrow stream and a wide expanse of sand and grassy dunes. We draw our horses to a halt and gaze out over the stunning view. There are no houses anywhere, just nature, uncorrupted by the human hand. I look up and see gulls circling, their wings shining white in the sunlight. Their cries are mournful, and I'm reminded once again of my short stay here in this place and time. Soon this world will fade, and I will slip away. Soon it will all be gone.

I glance at Cavill. He's watching me with a curious expression on his face. I smile and he returns it, but the frown does not ease. He knows there's something on my mind, but he can't, for all the world, know what it is. I usually fear being swallowed into the dream, but suddenly I want to forget where I come from. I want to forget who I really am. I like it here. I like him.

Cavill turns his attention to the estuary and points out a pair of goosander fishing in the low water channel. 'And there is an oystercatcher, do you see? Are you familiar with birds, Miss Swift?'

'I regret that I am not an expert,' I reply. 'But I love them all the same.'

'It is a hobby of mine.' He pats his saddlebag fondly. 'I like to draw them, thus keeping a record of the rare birds that fly into the estuary.'

'I think that is an admirable hobby, Mr Cavill. You must be very knowledgeable on the subject.'

'There is always more to learn. I'm an amateur. A keen amateur.'

'Might I look at your drawings? I would love to see them.'

He smiles bashfully, reaches into his bag and pulls out a

sketchbook. 'I'm no artist, Miss Swift,' he says, passing it to me. 'But they might amuse you.'

I open it and am surprised to find that he's very talented. I look closely at the first drawing. It's of a dunlin, sketched in January 1887. The detail of the bird's brown-and-grey plumage is meticulous. 'But this is exceedingly good,' I protest. 'You are very accomplished, indeed.' I turn to Robert, who's been forgotten at my side. 'Have you seen your uncle's drawings?' I ask.

'Of course,' he replies. 'He paints too. He especially likes painting ducks, don't you, Uncle Cavill?'

Cavill chuckles. 'Indeed, I do, Robert. They are plucky little fellows.'

It's not long before I find a sketch of a duck. '*Teal*,' I read out. '*December 1889*, and what a plucky teal he is.'

'I have a special fondness for teals,' says Cavill. 'There's something about the curve of their chests that I find pleasing to draw.'

'The males are pretty,' I comment. 'The females are drab by comparison. I find it unjust that the males have all the fun with their plumage.'

'But the females hold the power,' Cavill argues. 'The males have to work hard with their fine feathers and beautiful song to attract their mates' attention.'

'Is it correct that they mate for life?' I ask, handing him back the book.

'They mate for the season,' he replies. 'Their reputation is a romantic one, it is true, but I'm afraid they must disappoint you. They are not as romantic as people think. They do, however, pair up in a way that other birds do not. During the season it is charming to watch them together, and painful when one of them loses a mate.'

'I would like to know the birds by name,' I say, watching the oystercatcher prising open a shell with its beak. 'Like trees and flowers, I think it's important to know the natural world.' I look down at Robert who's watching the birds too. He's curious about everything. 'I think it is important for Master Robert to know about these things too.'

'Then I will make it my duty to teach you *and* Master Robert,' says Cavill, then, in a low voice that is meant for me alone, he adds, 'It will be a pleasure to spend time with you.'

I can sense where our acquaintance is headed and wish suddenly that I had not only days to be with him, but months and years and decades. I envisage us together on the bank, he drawing in his sketchbook and me observing the birds through a pair of binoculars. It's a beautiful image, but one that's as illusory as a mirage.

Robert, bored of watching the birds, suggests we gallop again, and I'm happy to, for galloping will throw me into the present moment and distract me from dreaming impossible dreams. We set off and I toss my regret into the wind.

When I return to the nursery, Gwen informs me that Cordelia has taken Felix into the vegetable garden to pick sweet peas. Keen to get to know the object of my mission, I hastily change out of my riding habit and set out over the lawn to find her.

The vegetable garden is contained within a tall wall covered in heaps of pink and white roses and giant purple clematis. Cordelia, in a wide straw hat and elegant white dress, is talking to one of the gardeners at the mouth of a tunnel made out of bamboo and wire, up which sweet peas have begun to climb. They look like multicoloured butterflies gently flapping their wings in the breeze. When Cordelia sees me she waves. She says something to the gardener, who nods and then strides off in the other direction. I look about for Felix, but he's nowhere to be seen.

'Aren't these splendid?' she says as I approach.

'I can smell them from here,' I reply.

She sighs with pleasure. 'They are my favourite flower. I especially love the deep violet ones.' She presses the bouquet to her nose and closes her eyes. 'Wonderful,' she breathes.

'Where's Felix?' I ask.

'Pretending to be a rabbit, or a fox, I cannot remember which.' She laughs. 'He's always something with four legs.'

I laugh with her. 'How does he do that?' I ask.

'He has made a burrow in a hollow tree. Come, I will show you.' She puts the secateurs and flowers in a wicker basket she's brought with her and leads me through the tunnel. We head up one of the gravel paths that slice through the raised vegetable plots, richly planted with all sorts of cabbages and carrots, until we reach an old, gnarled chestnut tree. There is a clear opening in the trunk, revealing a dark cavity and Felix's mischievous face peering out.

'Look, Mrs Pengower, there's a rabbit in there!' I exclaim playfully.

Felix grins. 'I am not a rabbit, I'm a fox,' he retorts.

'Of course you are,' says his mother. 'How could we mistake you for anything else.'

'May I come in?' I ask, but I'm much too big. The hole is barely large enough for a small boy to squeeze through.

'You are not a fox, Miss Swift,' he says.

I pretend to look disappointed. 'You are so right. Besides, there is only room in there for one fox.'

Cordelia smiles indulgently at her son. 'Is the fox hungry, do we think?'

Felix crawls out. 'Yes,' he says. 'Foxes are always hungry.'

'What do they eat?' I ask.

Felix thinks about this for a second. His mouth opens into a giant smile. 'Boiled eggs and buttered soldiers,' he says with relish.

'Then we'd better feed him,' says Cordelia, putting out her hand. Felix takes it and with a laugh, the three of us return to the house.

That evening, Mrs James Pengower comes for dinner, escorted by Pascoe Bray, the foreman at Mr Pengower's mine and a family friend. He's a man of about fifty, with a slim, athletic build, a long, noble face partly concealed behind an auburn beard, and intelligent hazel eyes. I'm struck at once by his eyes, because they're sensitive and wise, the eyes of an old soul. Cordelia has requested that I join them, claiming that, without me, the two women will be overpowered. Cavill is on edge because his brother is in a foul mood – he's angry that the gypsies have been trapping hares on his estate. He stands in front of the empty grate, thumbs hooked into his waistcoat pockets, holding forth as his face reddens with indignation. Cordelia tells him to ignore them. 'What do you care if there are a few less hares running about your woods?' she says with a smile, but I can tell from the shadow of disdain in her eyes that she despises his lack of charity.

Mr Pengower turns on her and growls. 'It is best if you do not voice an opinion, my dear, when you know nothing about it.' His tone is surprisingly sharp, and Cordelia blinks a few times to mask her hurt. Her smile remains fixed. However, two pink stains bloom on her cheeks. Mr Bray looks uncomfortable. He stiffens on his chair and sweeps his auburn hair off his forehead with a strong hand. He glances at Cordelia and his expression is one of concern. He's clearly troubled by Mr Pengower's harsh words but is in no position to do anything about it. I don't suppose anyone contradicts Mr Pengower, and certainly not when it involves his wife.

Mrs James Pengower is not as I expected her to be. She's a small-boned woman, like a chihuahua, vivacious, with high cheekbones and the same bright blue eyes as Cavill's. Her smile has a sweetness in it that belies her age, and she exudes a light, joyful energy that lifts us all, even Mr Pengower who, for a moment, forgets his fury as she turns the subject to a more cheerful one. 'Did you hear the wonderful news that Mrs Tally was delivered of twins?' she says happily. 'After losing so many, it is simply lovely to be blessed with two, and a pigeon pair.'

'That is indeed wonderful news,' Cordelia agrees. She has shaken off her husband's rebuke and is serene once again. 'It is always magical when a new soul comes into the world.'

Mr Bray smiles. 'They bring with them hope,' he says.

'And love,' Cordelia adds. 'A mother wonders how she can love another child and yet they seem to bring their own love with them.'

'That is a lovely way to put it,' says Mrs James approvingly.

I want to add that sometimes their love isn't enough, but instead, I say, 'One cannot help but look into the eyes of a baby and wonder at the adventures in store for it. They are at the beginning of their journey. Where will it take them?'

'To the moon,' says Cavill pointedly, giving me a meaningful look, and I laugh, embarrassed, because no one else understands the reference but me.

Mr Pengower grunts; he's not interested in babies or the moon.

The conversation inevitably turns to the travellers once more as we sit with glasses of wine in the drawing room before dinner. Mr Pengower can't leave the subject alone. Like a tongue craving the aching tooth he goes back to it time and again. He has nothing nice to say about them. 'They are filthy and immoral, and have no respect for our laws and our ways and live by thievery,' he declares hotly, tossing out every cliché as if they're facts.

'Shame on you, Ivan,' Cavill snaps. 'Those are absurdly wild generalisations.'

'If I were making wild generalisations, Cavill, I would not have seen fit to have a pair of them locked up in a cell for the night. They should have languished there for a week I tell you, to teach the rest of them a lesson. Poaching is a crime and it needs to be managed with the full force of the law. They steal a rabbit one day, what might they steal the next? No, they need to be halted and reprimanded. A soft heart will only encourage more thievery and I am not a charity.'

Cavill chuckles with derision. 'You make it sound like they're an army poised to swarm St Sidwell and rob it of every living thing.'

Mr Pengower curls his lip and flares his nostrils. 'Foreigners like them who wander from place to place cannot be trusted. They have no sense of community besides their own. They are criminals, no less. It might sound like exaggeration to you, Cavill, but while you are gallivanting about the countryside on your horse, some of us are trying to keep this family safe.'

Cordelia attempts to voice another opinion, which is brave of her considering the reception she got the last time. 'My dear, they are human beings like anyone else,' she says patiently. 'They are simply poor and have no fixed abode. In God's eyes they are no different from you and I.'

Mr Bray adds, 'It is a shame that a few bad ones tarnish the reputation of the rest. I have met them, and they are, on the whole, decent folk doing their best, raising their children and feeding their families. Most earn an honest wage when they manage to find work.'

'Well said, Mr Bray,' Cavill exclaims. 'If one treats people well, they most often respond in kind.'

Mr Pengower scowls. 'We cannot have people trespassing on our land and laying traps for animals that do not belong to them,' he says irritably. 'You give these people an inch and they will take a mile, goddamnit.'

'Ivan, dear, do mind your language,' says his mother softly. However, she doesn't seem at all offended by her son's raised voice. She's probably used to it.

'We certainly don't want them coming to the house,' Mr Pengower continues.

'They already have,' says Cordelia in a steady voice.

'Cordelia?' Mr Pengower is horrified. 'When?'

'Only a few days ago. Two of them, a couple, with a young child. They wanted food. I took pity.'

Mr Pengower's face goes the colour of a beetroot. 'You took pity?' He spits out the words in disgust as if pity is a dirty thing.

'I did.'

'One cannot turn away a woman and child,' says Mr Bray in Cordelia's defence, and she looks at him with gratitude.

Mrs James agrees. 'When one is fortunate to have so much, it is only right that one shares.' She smiles sweetly at her daughter-in-law. 'So good of you, Cordelia, to take pity.'

Mr Pengower is struggling to hold his temper. 'That was unwise of you, my dear,' he says, clipping his consonants with forced patience. I get the feeling that, if we weren't present, he'd have called her a fool or worse. 'They will be back.'

'For food,' returns his wife. Her eyes shine suddenly. 'Is that such a crime?'

'It is Christian to help,' adds his mother.

'It is human,' rejoins Mr Bray.

'They are a rotten lot,' explodes Mr Pengower.

'Enough, Ivan,' Cavill exclaims. He's no longer chuckling and being good-natured. For the first time I see his face harden with fury. 'Let us talk about something else. This is no discussion to have in front of the ladies.'

Mr Pengower ignores him. 'Nothing good will come of this,' he says with a snarl. 'Mark my words. Give them an inch and they will take a mile,' he repeats and shakes his head portentously. 'Symons, another whisky and make it a double.'

The drawing room falls silent. Mr Pengower is angry, and his energy has dampened the mood. Even his mother's light is unable to disperse the shadow that has suddenly darkened the room. Symons goes to the drinks cabinet and pours his master another glass. The only sound is the clinking of the crystal decanter as Symons removes the lid and pours. I catch Cavill's eye and he sighs and shakes his head. Mr Bray turns his face to the black grate. The muscle on his jaw is strained with suppressed emotion. Cordelia sips her wine and appears as placid as a swan on a peaceful lake – however, I suspect her feet are paddling fast beneath the waterline.

Mrs James turns to me. 'Do you play the piano, Miss Swift?'

I can only play two tunes and they haven't yet been composed. 'I do,' I reply, lifting my chin and feigning confidence. 'I'm afraid, I am not accomplished,' I add, hoping that I won't be asked to perform.

Cavill is looking at me expectantly. I imagine he suspects I'm being modest. I wish I was. I've never had a piano lesson in my life and only taught myself two tunes because my grandmother had an upright piano in the house, and I was bored. I pray that I won't have to expose my lack of talent. My prayer, however, is ignored.

To my horror, Mrs James claps her small hands cheerfully. 'What a lovely evening,' she says with a sigh. 'Just lovely. How very blessed we all are to be here, together, and that Miss Swift is going to give us a rendition on the piano after dinner.'

I cannot wriggle out of it. I contemplate falling into a faint or feigning a headache, but neither of those is a credible excuse; I look perfectly well. I'm sure Hermione Swift can play the piano – isn't that a qualification every governess is expected to have? The prospect of shaming myself – and Hermione – ruins my dinner and I can barely eat or speak.

Finally, the moment arrives. My audience take their seats in the drawing room, and I take mine at the piano. I lift the lid and rest my fingers over the keys. I take a deep breath. Then I begin. I have no alternative but to play one of the only tunes I know. It's not Beethoven, or Bach. It's the Beatles – 'Let It Be'.

There is a horrified silence as I sing. I'm surprised to find that I have a rather good voice, which is encouraging. I sing it with emotion, because I figure that if I'm going to do it I might as well do it with aplomb. When I finish, no one moves. They're all staring at me in astonishment, as if I've just turned into an alien. I put down the piano lid and stand up. There's nothing for me to do, but smile.

'Good Lord. Is that what they teach young people these days?' says Mr Pengower at length, clearly appalled.

'What is it?' asks Mrs James slowly, and I see the joy drain from her face, leaving it ashen with confusion.

But Cordelia is amused. 'Most original,' she says.

'I concur,' agrees Mr Bray, and the two of them look at one another and laugh together.

Cavill roars with laughter. He gets to his feet and claps loudly. 'I do declare,' he says, eyes shining with enjoyment. 'I have never been quite so entertained!'

At that moment, I smile to myself. It is true then. The music of the Beatles really is timeless!

I'm grateful they don't ask me to play the only other tune I know: 'Patricia the Stripper' by Chris de Burgh.

Chapter Eight

Mrs James Pengower departs in her carriage, attended by Mr Bray. 'How kind he is to always escort my mother-in-law home,' says Cordelia, standing on the doorstep and watching the carriage make its way slowly down the drive. 'Mr Bray lives close by, you see, and Mrs Pengower only a short distance from him on the edge of the estate. He is such a gentleman, always insisting on looking after her. Truly, she relies on him in her widowhood, and he is as solicitous to her as a son.'

'What was her husband like?' I ask, interested to know more about Cavill's father.

Cordelia slides her eyes about to make sure we are not being over-heard. 'Mr James Pengower was not an easy man,' she tells me in a low voice. 'He commanded respect and won it. His workers and tenants held him in high regard, but he was unforgiving when any of them stepped out of line. He was particularly hard on his sons, and his wife. Poor Mrs Pengower was cowed. I do believe her widow-hood has been a relief. She was as quiet and meek as a rabbit when he was alive. Since his death, she has transformed into a lively parrot.'

'She is certainly vivacious,' I agree. Then I take a chance. 'I think you were very brave standing up for the gypsies.'

I hold my breath, aware that I might have overstepped the mark. But Cordelia looks at me and gives me a grateful smile.

'My husband and I disagree on many things, as you will dis-cover.' She sighs and turns her eyes away. 'But I have my allies. Mr Cavill and Mr Bray are of the same mind as me, and, being men, their voices carry more weight than mine.'

I would like to disagree with her, but she is a woman of her time, and it's very much a man's world. 'Nevertheless, you were brave and fierce. I admire you for speaking your mind.'

When she turns to look at me again, I notice her eyes are shining once more and her cheeks are pink. She takes a deep breath. 'It is my duty to stand at my husband's side and support him in all his endeavours, but there are some things I cannot condone because they go against my nature, and my beliefs.'

'I think you will discover they go against mine too,' I say, but I can't explain that I come from a culture that is, on the whole, more inclusive and tolerant of other people's differences than hers.

She smiles and rallies. 'Thank you, Miss Swift. It is nice to know that I have an ally in you, too.'

We leave the men smoking in the library and retire for the night. I follow Cordelia into the hall. It's still light. The sun has sunk behind the trees, but a beguiling pink dusk has settled over the gardens, and I'm gripped suddenly by a yearning to walk in it. Cordelia smiles wistfully when I tell her. 'I love the night,' she declares with longing. 'The silence, the stillness, the peace. Sometimes I find it stifling in the house. One is never alone, you see. Never.' I sense frustration in the pause that follows, as she sighs heavily and drops her shoulders. The eyes that gaze at me seem to yearn for understanding. 'From time to time I need so very much to be alone. Away from Mr Pengower and the servants. Away, even, from my children. My soul cries out for seclusion. Therefore, I take myself off and sit on the bench in the vegetable garden. It is tranquil there with only the owls for company and the moon and stars above. In those solitary moments I feel close to God. To that wonderful source of love and might. God gives me strength and I feel restored.'

I imagine she needs strength being married to Mr Pengower. 'I need time to myself as well,' I reply. 'There are many corners here where one can be sure to find solitude.'

'But take care not to come in too late,' she warns. 'Mr Pengower is a stickler for locking the doors and closing all the windows before he retires. He is concerned for our safety and the security of the house. In fact, I would go as far to say that he is quite paranoid about it. If you get locked out in the garden, you will have to sleep there and wait for Symons to let you in in the morning. My husband and Symons are the only two people who have keys.' I wonder why she doesn't have a set of keys of her own, but I don't know her well enough to ask. She makes her way up the stairs, her silk gown trailing down the steps behind her. I leave by the back door, mindful not to stay out too long.

As I set off across the lawn, I wonder about Mr Pengower locking all the windows and doors before going to bed. Whoever takes Felix in just over week's time has to get him out of the house. If Mr Pengower and Mr Symons are the only two people with keys, it begs the question, do either of those men have something to do with the child's disappearance? But then, the police investigating the case would have asked themselves the same question and come to the conclusion that they did not. Therefore, there must be more that I haven't discovered yet.

A stillness as soft as down bewitches the estate. The birds have settled in the branches and gone quiet. The lawns and borders are sinking into slumber. Their lines are blurred in the roseate light, their colours muted. It's too beautiful and my heart aches with longing. I've been here but two days, yet I feel as if it's been weeks.

I walk through the arboretum and find myself thinking about Cavill. Men are not like him where I come from. Indeed, we are novelties to each other. I know I shouldn't yearn for him – that he is not my mission and I must not allow myself to be distracted by thoughts of a romance. But I find him irresistible. I find the way he makes me feel – irresistible. I like who I am when I'm with him. I realise now that my past love affairs were pale imitations of what love should be. The feelings Cavill is arousing in me are surprisingly strong, and I'm bewildered by them. Are they more intense because I know a romance is impossible? Because I know I can't have him? Or am I really connecting with him on a deeper level? Am I forgetting myself? I fear I'm being swallowed into this reality, living the dream – and gradually getting lost in it.

As I stroll over the grass I remember the wise words of the woman who taught me how to control my gift, Avril Merivale. She was a brilliant psychic medium I met at the College of Psychic Studies after I left university. She recognised my potential and, over time, nurtured it, giving me private guidance sessions in her flat in Earl's Court. Astral projection possession, she explained, was an ancient practice, like astral travelling and other paranormal experiences, but the technique was lost, along with many esoteric mysteries known by the ancients. Human beings simply forgot how to do it. She was excited to discover that I came into the world doing it naturally, and I was grateful to have found someone who understood. She lent me an ancient book, translated from Sanskrit and given to her many years before by a guru she trained with in India. It was the only book I ever read that spoke about what I called timesliding. I was excited to discover that I was not the first to experience this. I wasn't so very different, after all. Just fortunate, perhaps.

She told me, 'Anything is possible, Pixie. It's not about what you're allowed and not allowed to do, but about what you deem acceptable and appropriate. Your gift comes with great responsibility. You can choose to create havoc, or you can choose the highest good. It's up to you. It is always up to you.' I remember Avril's advice now and realise that I must not allow myself to get lost in the dream. It's not my dream, after all; this is Hermione Swift's life and I'm just passing through – it's not my place to fall in love.

I wander on, through an archway in the yew hedge and on up a winding path that leads through an ornamental stumpery. The stumps are adorned with spikey ferns and soft mosses and wildflowers that have seeded themselves and flourished. The air grows damp, the shadows deepen. I spy a stone folly nestled in a leafy corner, hidden away as if it doesn't want to be found. It's a classical building with a triangular pediment and pillars. A whimsy, a delight, built long before the current Mrs Pengower added her creative touches to the gardens. Curious, I walk towards it.

I hear a peal of laughter coming from inside. Quickly, I retreat into the ferns, and hide. Another peal of laughter disturbs the quiet. The low voice of a man follows, and then feverish whisper-ing. *She* is wanting to leave; *he* is persuading her to stay. They are playing a game. I lie in wait.

It's getting dark and dew is settling upon the grass. An owl hoots in the woods, a pigeon is disturbed and flies out of a tree, its clumsy wings flapping loudly. A figure emerges from the folly. It's John Snathe. He looks from left to right, checking that there's no one about. Then he gestures to the woman. Gwen emerges tim-idly, smoothing down her dress, making sure that the buttons are fastened on her blouse. They kiss. He grabs her around the waist, holding her against him. She pulls away. He pulls her back and buries his face in her neck. She giggles and wriggles free. There's an urgency in her movements. She must be keen to get back to the house before the doors are locked. He's more reckless; after all, who's going to catch them out here at this time of night?

Eventually, they go their separate ways. He back to the stable block, she towards the house. I wait until they've gone and then I, too, make my way back and sneak up to my bedroom. As I climb the stairs, I can hear the low murmur of Mr Pengower and Cavill's voices. They're still talking. They've moved to the library. The smell of cigar smoke wafts out and fills the hall.

I lie in bed and focus on the job I'm here to do. I try not to think about Cavill. Yet, every time I turn my mind to Felix and Cordelia and my mission, Cavill invades the picture until he takes it over, pushing them out so it's only him I see as I close my eyes and drift off to sleep.

The following day, I resume my lessons with Robert. I join Gwen and Felix at lunchtime. Gwen is cross because Felix has sneaked 'yet again'. He's told his mother that she fell asleep while he was playing and that he had to wake her up. As a consequence, Cordelia scolded her for her lack of vigilance. 'He tells his mama everything,' she complains, rolling her eyes. Felix, who's on his chair, tucking into his food with a fox's enthusiasm, looks bashful.

'That is only natural,' I tell her. 'It is not healthy for such a small child to have secrets from his mother.'

'It wasn't a secret,' says Gwen. 'Sometimes I find it hard to keep my eyes open, that's all.'

'You're not getting enough sleep,' I suggest, thinking about what I saw the evening before.

'I'm not a good sleeper at the best of times.'

'Have you tried warm milk and honey before bed?' I'd recommend Xanax if I could.

'No, miss,' she replies.

'It might help.'

'My head is so full of things,' she complains, but her eyes gleam.

'What sort of things?'

'Dreams, Miss Swift.' She turns her gaze to the window and sighs longingly. 'I have dreams, you know. But good things don't happen to girls like me.'

'What do you mean? What sort of girl are you?'

'Not the lucky sort, miss.' She shakes her head and sighs again. 'I don't want much. Just a husband and a child and a roof over my head. That's not too much to ask for, is it?'

'It's not too much at all. Why do you think it will not be given to you?'

'Because I fall for the wrong sort of man.' She grins sheepishly and shifts in her chair. 'I fall for the ones who don't want what I want.'

'Have you fallen for the wrong sort of man now?' I ask, hoping to extract information and win her confidence.

She reddens. 'Oh no, miss.' Felix puts out his hand and she takes it. 'Why would I want a man when I have a handsome little boy here who loves me?' She smiles at him fondly. 'You love me, don't you, Felix?'

'Yes,' he replies.

'See! I'm busy with Master Felix. I don't have time for anyone else.'

That afternoon I ride out with Robert once again. I'm thrilled to see Cavill waiting for us in the stable yard. 'Shall we show Miss Swift the town?' he asks his nephew, and Robert nods enthusiastically.

Grantly and John Snathe bring out the horses, saddled and ready, and we ride out together. As we're setting off down the track, I glimpse Cordelia and Felix through the trees feeding the birds. It's a tender sight, mother and son, hand in hand, bathed in the soft, dappled light of a summer's afternoon. She's wearing a straw hat and a pale blue dress, and her waist is tiny. She might be in a Monet painting. She looks down at her son and laughs. He gazes adoringly up at her. I smile with pleasure, wanting to forget the tragedy that lies only eight days away. The tragedy that will steal their happiness. Cordelia, distracted by the movement in her peripheral vision, lifts her eyes and sees us. She waves. We wave back and Cavill takes off his hat and flourishes it theatrically. Cordelia tells Felix to wave and the little boy puts up his hand and waves heartily. It's a jolly scene, a jolly summer scene, and I'm charmed by it.

Our conversation flows easily. I feel as if Cavill and I have been friends for a long time. 'Master Felix is adorable,' I say. 'Yesterday he was playing in a hollow tree, pretending to be a fox.'

Cavill chuckles. 'He has got quite an imagination, that boy, and is fearless. He will climb to the top of a tree like a squirrel and swim in the lake like a duck without a moment's hesitation. His mother is often baffled by him, for his brother is by nature more cautious.'

'Perhaps he takes after his uncle with his thirst for adventure.' I glance at Cavill and grin.

He nods, appreciating the compliment. 'He might be a famous explorer one day, like Dr Livingstone.'

I wish I could agree with him. 'Maybe *you* will be like Dr Livingstone,' I say, diverting the conversation away from Felix's future. But I know that Cavill doesn't have a future, either.

Cavill is pleased with that idea. 'I shall explore South America. There is much to discover there. Although, I doubt very much I will make such a name for myself as Dr Livingstone. Sufficient it will be to make a fortune. There is money to be made in railways and tramlines, agriculture and livestock, and I shall learn to play polo at the Hurlingham Club. Indeed, I shall very much enjoy riding out there. They say that the Argentines are the best horsemen in the world and their horses are of the highest quality.'

'If your enthusiasm is anything to go by, I suspect you will make a great success of it.'

'I hope you are right, Miss Swift.' He turns his gaze to the countryside. To the shadows that pass over the land as the clouds move slowly in front of the sun. 'I will miss St Sidwell.'

'I can imagine. But the spice of life is in the diversity, is it not?'

'The Argentine Pampa is very flat. I shall miss the hills and cliffs and the sea. I shall miss the birds too.' He looks wistful suddenly. 'There will be different birds there, of course.' He turns to me. 'Would you like to paint with me tomorrow?'

'I would love that,' I reply. 'With Master Robert, of course,' I add hastily, aware that I must do my duty as the governess. I'm not here for *me*.

'Naturally,' Cavill returns. 'We shall set up on the estuary and find some ducks to sketch.' He looks at me and grins, and once again I feel that he's looking straight through Hermione to me, Pixie, beneath. 'You are not like other women,' he says softly, narrowing his eyes and scrutinising me. 'I cannot say what it is about you that is so different – your manner of speech, your intonation, the unusual way you look upon the world. But there *is* something undeniably different about you, and I like it. I like it very much.'

I drop my gaze into my hands and try to control the excitement rising inside me. The affection swelling in my heart. 'And you are different to me, Mr Cavill,' I reply. But unlike him, who struggles to define the difference and the reason for it, I am able to explain exactly why. Where I come from, women are emancipated, independent, outspoken, ambitious to succeed and able to do so, on their own terms. As much as I try to blend in to this time, I know I bring an air of the future with me. I can't help it. It must infuse everything I do and say. In the same vein, perhaps many of the things I'm loving about Cavill are foreign to me too. He's chivalrous and gallant, with beautiful manners seldom found in my post-feminist culture. I feel that he sees me, which is a contradiction, because I don't look like myself. How can he see me when I look like Hermione? I don't know, but I believe that he does.

We reach the town. I'm shocked by how poor it looks. How poor the people look. It's far from the picturesque, quaint, charming English coastal town I expected. The small cottages are ramshackle, the squalid streets narrow and cobbled, the locals weatherworn and unwashed. Women sit in groups mending nets, their white aprons stained, their faces haggard, their hands rough from their labour. Men are scarce. I imagine they're in their boats, fishing, or up at the tin mine. Filth-covered children play, their clothes ragged, their feet bare, their gaiety belying the true nature of their lives, which is hardship and deprivation. The difference between this place and St Sidwell Manor is stark. There's no sheen of elegance, no glamour, no opulence, and little beauty. The sun shines upon the white walls of the cottages and floods the streets with jubilance, and that, certainly, endows the place with a certain bucolic charm, but, I imagine, on a drizzly day in winter, it must look miserable.

We dismount and Cavill tethers the horses to a post. Robert tells me excitedly of the time he came with his father to watch the fishing boats returning from their day out on the sea. 'They had barrels full of fish,' he says, skipping on ahead. 'Papa bought some and we ate them for supper.' We wander through the town. The people are wary, hostile even. They look us over. They recognise Cavill and greet him by name, but they don't smile. I feel their stares sticking to me like barnacles as they try to work out who I am and what I am to Cavill. The children stop what they're doing and stare at Robert. I imagine they must envy his fine clothes and shoes. I wonder what happens in winter when it snows. Do they wander barefooted then? 'Why are they so unfriendly?' I ask Cavill under my breath.

He leans in so that he won't be overheard. 'This is a mining town,' he answers. 'If my brother treated the men better and raised the standards of their living and working conditions, they would greet us with smiles. As it is, they resent us and everything we stand for. They have little when we have so much.'

'Would they harm you, or your family?' I ask, wondering whether this animosity might be to blame for Felix's disappearance.

'No,' he says firmly. 'They are all bark and no bite.'

I hope that he is right.

There is a commotion on the beach. Men and women are gathered there in a huddle. People are shouting. Cavill tells us to stay where we are, and he hurries off to find out what it's all about. I try to see through the crowd but am unable to. I suspect something has been washed up on the sand. Robert is impatient and asks why he can't go too. 'Because it might be dangerous,' I tell him. 'If there's a brawl, you don't want to be caught up in it.'

'But it's an adventure, Miss Swift.'

I laugh. 'An adventure that might end in tears.'

'I'm going to be nine in four months,' he reminds me.

'Still too young, Master Robert.' I glimpse through the mass of people then and spy a large mammal lying on the beach, half in the water, half on the sand. 'It looks like a whale,' I tell him, and I grimace at the sight of the poor creature beached and helpless.

'A whale!' he exclaims, jumping up and down. 'What's it doing?'

'Nothing. It doesn't look like it's moving,' I tell him. I feel a wave of pity and hope that it's dead. If it isn't, I'm sure the locals will kill it and maybe even eat it.

Suddenly, the child runs off. I shout at him, horrified. My instincts are to give chase. He is my responsibility and if anything happens to him, I'll be blamed. I lift my skirts and set off down the sand as fast as I can go. Robert is much too quick for me. I'm barely able to breathe in my corset. It wraps about my body, holding it in a vice. It's hard to run across sand, even in trainers. In these boots I'm slow and ungainly. Robert disappears into the throng, which is getting restless. There's a nasty strain of tension in the air. I sense there's going to be a fight. I search frantically for Cavill. I see his hat for it rises above the heads of the other men. He's tall, and his hat gives him an extra five inches, at least. I call his name. But he doesn't hear me above the excited voices of the locals. I understand that they're arguing over who gets to keep the whale. A woman cries, 'If it be alive, for God's sake, put it back in the water.'

I reach the throng and start to push my way through it. I feel an elbow in my stomach, another against my chest. My boots sink into the wet sand the closer I get to the sea. 'Robert!' I shout. 'Robert!'

Just as I see Robert with his hand safely in Cavill's, I'm knocked to the ground. A man falls on top of me. My instincts take over and I forget myself. 'Get the fuck off me, you idiot!' I cry out angrily, thumping the body with all my strength. I see the horrified expression on the face of the man as he takes in my foul language and, in haste, pushes himself up and hurries away as if I've bitten him. A fight breaks out. A woman screams. The gathering becomes a mob, heaving and swelling around me. I feel a kick to my stomach and am suddenly unable to breathe. I try to cry out again, but no sound comes, only a strangled hiss.

Then Robert is by my side. 'Miss Swift! Miss Swift!' He's shouting. Cavill is shoving people out of the way, swearing at them, raising his voice and forgetting his manners. Then he's lifting me up and carrying me away from the brawl. Robert has begun to cry. I can hear his sobs and feel sorry that he's blaming himself. I want to reassure him that it doesn't matter. That I'm not badly hurt, only bruised. But I'm winded and can barely breathe.

Cavill lays me on the sand. The noise of the crowd is distant now. He hastily unfastens the buttons on my bodice, but that gives little relief, for it's the corset beneath that needs loosening. Bloody corset! I put a hand on his. He stares down at me in alarm. I blink up at him, catching my breath. 'I'm all right,' I tell him.

'Are you hurt?' he asks. I can see the panic in his eyes.

I take his arm and with his help, haul myself onto my feet. Robert is snivelling at my side. 'It's not your fault, Master Robert,' I tell him. He gazes up at me with glassy eyes, apologetic, contrite. 'You didn't know there was going to be a fight.'

'I'm afraid the locals are not welcoming to outsiders. They see them as a threat,' says Cavill. He puts a hand around my waist. 'Come, let us get you away from here. It is not safe.'

We walk slowly up the sand. One or two people who are making their way down in the direction of the drama glance at us, but they don't stop. I put a hand on my stomach for I've received quite a punch.

A voice calls out behind us. 'Mr Pengower!' We stop and Cavill turns. An elderly man with fluffy grey whiskers and a face the colour of bull's blood hurries up to us, holding out my hat. 'The lady dropped this,' he says. He gives a bow. If he'd heard my language he wouldn't be calling me a lady! That thought amuses me as I nurse my aching shoulder.

Cavill takes the hat and thanks him. I touch my hair, which has come loose from its pins. I hadn't even noticed the hat was missing. 'What a sight I must be,' I murmur and laugh, for if I don't laugh, I shall cry.

'You are a beautiful sight,' Cavill reassures me quietly.

I'm suddenly keenly aware of my body pressed against his, of his hand holding me around my waist and of his face tantalisingly close to mine. I can hear his breath as we walk together towards the harbour. I can almost feel it brushing my cheek. I forget the pain in my stomach and the ache in my shoulder. I feel safe and protected and bask in the novelty of being cared for by this chivalrous, valiant man. I feel like a heroine in a historical romance and play up to it a little by pretending to be feeble. Then Robert's voice pipes up.

'You won't tell Mama, will you?' he says.

I look down at his anxious face. His big grey eyes are red from crying. 'What is there to tell, Master Robert? There was a beached whale on the sand, and we went to look. That is all. There is no drama.' I put my hand on his shoulder. 'You were very gallant coming to my rescue,' I tell him. 'If it wasn't for you, I might have been trampled.'

'But I shouldn't have run off,' he says quietly.

'No, you shouldn't. I'm sure you will not do that again.'

'Papa would have lost his temper,' he adds.

'There is no point in losing one's temper,' says Cavill. 'Sometimes, one's own remorse is the best teacher.'

I smile across at him. 'Wise words, indeed,' I say. 'And thank *you*, Mr Cavill.'

He doesn't remove his hand from my waist even though I'm more than capable of walking by myself now. In order that it doesn't appear improper should anyone witness it, I feign a limp.

*

We walk to the harbour wall and Cavill suggests I sit there in the sunshine for a moment to compose myself. I do as he suggests and set about fastening the buttons on my bodice and tidying up my hair. He holds my hat while I repair the damage, and brushes it with his hand to get rid of the sand. Robert, feeling better now, stands on the wall and watches the commotion, which is far enough away to be of no threat to us. 'Is it dead, Uncle?'

'I believe it is, Robert,' says Cavill regretfully.

'Was it alive when it got washed up?'

'I believe so.'

'Did they kill it?'

'I am not sure.'

'Maybe it died of fright,' says the child.

'I don't think they last very long out of the water,' says Cavill.

'Poor thing.' I sigh.

'Will they eat it?' Robert asks.

'If they're hungry enough, I dare say they will eat anything.'

'Those gypsies are a rotten lot,' Robert says, echoing his father once again.

'Don't be hard on them, Master Robert,' I interject. 'Perhaps they didn't start the fight, and besides, maybe they're desperate with hunger and saw the whale as an opportunity to feed themselves and their families. It is unwise to judge when you know nothing about the situation.'

'Very true, Miss Swift,' says Cavill. 'It is also unwise to write off all gypsies as rotten. I'm sure the majority of them are decent people. They simply choose to live outside society. People should be permitted the freedom to be themselves.'

I press my ribs to check that nothing is broken, but it's hard to feel them beneath the bones of my corset. Bones that, ironically, must once have belonged to a whale.

Cavill's eyes settle on me with concern. 'You are sure you are not hurt, Miss Swift? You need not be brave in front of me and Robert.'

I chuckle. 'I suffered blows to my stomach and chest, but nothing serious. I simply feel a little bruised.'

'Poor Miss Swift,' says Robert with feeling.

Cavill smiles sympathetically. 'Come, let us get you back home where you can rest. A cup of sweet tea, or something stronger, will put you right.' I could really do with some ibuprofen or paracetamol, but I won't find anything like that in their medicine cupboard.

We walk back to where the horses are waiting for us, and Cavill lifts me onto the saddle. There's an intimacy between us now that wasn't there before, and an affection. I know that neither of us will mention what took place to Mr Pengower and Cordelia. The three of us are bound by a secret. It's delicious to share it with Cavill, to have something that is ours.

That evening, my presence is not required at dinner. Mr Pengower and Cordelia have guests and I'm left to eat alone in my sitting room. It's just as well, for the bruises are tender and I don't feel like dressing up. I long for some painkillers or a vodka shot, or two, to dull the aches. But there's nothing besides a glass of hot milk and honey that Rose brought up. That won't do any good at all. I stand by the window and watch the sunset turn the light golden. I know it's foolish to indulge in what can only be a dream. I'll wake up and when I do, I won't be able to bring Cavill with me.

Yet I still have eight nights before the 29th of June. How will I resist him?

I gaze upon the trees, their tips are alight with the final rays of the dying day. It's a beautiful sight, and my heart floods with longing. But I drag myself out of my reverie. I must stay focused and not get distracted by fantasies that are purely selfish. I remind myself why I am here and push Cavill to the back of my mind.

My thoughts turn to the folly, and John and Gwen within it. What if Gwen is with John the night of Felix's disappearance, and because of that the thief is able to enter the house and steal him away? But that doesn't feel right. Mr Pengower and Symons ensure that all doors and windows are locked every night before they go to bed, so how would the villain get in and then make off with the boy without breaking a window or knocking down a door?

It's a compelling mystery and I'm consumed by it. How does the villain get into the house? Unless they are already inside . . .

Chapter Nine

The following day, being a Saturday, I'm given the afternoon off. Cordelia has requested that the children spend the time with her and she disappears in her carriage, taking Gwen with them. I wave them on their way and then retreat into the house. With the children out of my care, I can't help but wonder where Cavill is. He's on my mind all the time and taking up more space in my heart with every moment that passes, despite my attempts to shut him out. I know I mustn't feel tender towards him, but I can't help it. I can't help but throw myself unreservedly into this reality, even though I'm aware that it won't last.

With the focus of my investigation departed, I decide to go for a walk and take a book with me to read in the shade somewhere. It's another fine day, hot and still. The gardens are bathed in sunshine, and fauna and flora appear to be basking in it, for the birdsong is a clamour and the flowers are more radiant than ever. Through the lens with which I see the world, everything appears to be heightened – the colours, the sounds, the sensation of warmth on my skin and the smell of roses in my nostrils. It's because it's transient, because I know I'll have to leave it. I want to live it to the full and savour every moment while I can.

I set off across the lawn. Daisies grow in the grass among white clover and dandelions, and fat bumblebees toddle about in search of nectar. I'm reminded of the meadow where I slid to as a child when I needed to escape the unhappiness in my home. I feel the same sense of peace and safety here. I can smell the lavender and hear the distant cooing of pigeons from the rooftops. The cooing dies away as I leave the lawn and enter the shady woods. I'm enjoying my stroll and the beauty of my surroundings. St Sidwell is an enchanting estate, bursting with extravagance. Everything is abounding with life, with fertility, with joy. There are giant red rhododendron bushes and wild jasmine that climbs the ancient oaks. There are damp corners where laurel grows, and ferns yet to fully unfurl. There are purple forget-me-nots and pink campion, yellow primroses and chamomile. I wander through the wildflowers, taking pleasure from the butterflies that bask in the sunlight and the dragonflies that whizz through the sunbeams, and I know that this is paradise. That paradise is right here where I am, for nature has never looked more glorious.

I hear someone call my name and stop. It's Cavill. I turn and see him striding up the path towards me in a linen suit and straw hat, with what looks like his sketchbook under his arm. 'Miss Swift,' he says as he approaches. He lifts his hat. 'Forgive me. I saw you leave the house alone and remembered I promised to sketch with you. Besides, it is not safe to be out on your own.'

I smile because I know that's not true. I haven't even left the property yet, nor do I intend to. 'That is very kind of you,' I reply.

'Please, allow me to escort you.' His eyes drop to the book in my hand. 'Oh, you were planning on reading?'

'Only because I had no one to talk to. I would much prefer to talk to you.'

He returns my smile enthusiastically. 'Then I'm not disturbing you.'

'Of course not. Please.' I walk on.

'We will find a nice place to sit down and then we will sketch.'

'Very well,' I agree. I think my sketching will be as embarrassing as my piano playing.

'It's such a fine day,' he says, walking in step with me. 'I don't think I have ever seen a more beautiful summer.'

'I cannot believe that is true. I imagine every summer at St Sidwell to be as beautiful as this.'

'We get plenty of rain down here, you know. Why else would it be so green?'

'Then I am fortunate to have arrived in fine weather.'

'Perhaps you have brought the sunshine.'

I laugh. 'I wish that were true, that wherever I went I endowed the place with sunshine.'

He looks at me seriously. 'You have endowed *me* with sunshine, Miss Swift.'

I train my eyes on the path ahead. 'It will rain tomorrow and then you will tell me that I have endowed you with that.'

'I will not,' he protests. 'Ever since you arrived, I have been up-lifted. Every time I look at you, I feel happy. I care not if it rains or if it's fine. If I am in your company, the sun shines within me.' He takes my hand. 'May I?' He brings it to his lips and kisses it.

I try to remind myself that I'm not here to embark on a love story, and yet . . .

Just then Pablo's face pops into my mind. The thought of him is so incongruous here, in this time. He feels very far away and so does the heartache. I can't believe I was ever taken in by him. Ulysses' image follows, mocking me for being so gullible, so quick to fall wholeheartedly for someone – so desperate to be loved that I'll believe any old romantic cliché that's fed to me. I pull my hand away. Is Cavill playing with me, or can I believe he's sincere? As sensitive as I am, I seem, to my cost, incapable of telling the difference.

I walk on beneath the trees, struggling to sound cheerful because the little voice in my head is filling me with doubt and self-reproach. 'Teach me about the birds,' I ask him, changing the subject and deliberately putting a little distance between us as we stroll side by side. 'What is that one called?'

Cavill seems not at all put off by my sudden demurring. 'That, my dear Miss Swift, is a green woodpecker,' he says, and smiles in a way that suggests he's rather enjoying the challenge. Does he think that I'm playing a game with *him*?

'What a fine red stripe it has on its head,' I reply. 'Have you sketched it?'

'I have, many times.'

'And that, what is that one?' I point to a dull brown bird scurrying among the ferns.

'A quail.'

'Dinner?'

'Not tonight. One tends to eat quail in winter. This quail is lucky.'

'Lucky quail, indeed. I am familiar with the pheasant and the dove, the blackbird and the blue tit. I especially like blue tits. Can you distinguish a bird's song without seeing it?' I ask.

'Indeed. Do you know which is my favourite birdsong?'

'I could never guess. But let me try. Goldfinch?'

He laughs. 'Not the goldfinch, although his song is pretty. No, the bird with the best voice, in my opinion, is the simple blackbird.'

'I would never have known.'

'The blackbird is not blessed with pretty feathers, but he has the most beautiful voice of all the birds. It is with that exquisite voice that he wins the heart of his mate.'

'I will never listen to a blackbird now without being mindful of that.'

'Shall we sit down, Miss Swift? It is hot in the sun, and you might enjoy a rest in the shade.'

Cavill spreads his coat over the grass, and I settle myself onto it while he leans back against the trunk of a beech tree. 'Will you tell me your name?' he asks, then before I can respond he adds, 'No, let me guess.'

'Very well.' I know he will never guess right.

'Rose?'

'Wrong.'

'Violet?' he says with confidence.

'No. Why do you think I am named after a flower?'

'You are as beautiful as a flower, Miss Swift. But you are right. You are not fragile like a rose or a violet.' He narrows his eyes, taking me in, trying to find the right word. 'You are more like a queen,' he announces with satisfaction. 'Wise, open-minded, intelligent, bold.'

I laugh, enjoying the game. 'I am not named after a queen, Mr—'

'Cavill,' he interrupts, looking at me steadily with those intensely blue eyes. 'Just Cavill.'

'I am not named after a queen, Cavill,' I repeat, and the word tastes sweet – as well as a little forbidden – on my tongue.

'It sounds better when you say it,' he tells me. 'Say it again.'

'Cavill.'

He grins, pleased. 'You must have a magnificent name then,' he continues. 'Like Joan of Arc, Florence Nightingale or Catherine de' Medici?'

'No, no and no.'

'Boudicca?' We both laugh.

'Wrong again, Cavill.'

He sighs dramatically. 'I will have one more guess. If I am wrong, you will have to tell me.'

'Very well.'

He looks doubtful, but gives it a go all the same. 'Mary?'

I shake my head and smile triumphantly. 'Hermione.'

He smiles back and his eyes light up as if they have rested on something magical. 'Hermione. What a beautiful name. Just like you. Are you named after the famous Hermione?'

I have absolutely no idea what he's talking about – the only Hermione I know is Hermione Granger. 'Which one?' I respond vaguely.

'Hermione of Troy, King Menelaus and Helen of Troy's daughter. But I think Hermione Swift has its own charm.'

'Hermione *Penelope* Swift, if you please.' I gasp at the audaciousness of saying that word out loud, for Penelope is *my* name. But I cannot pretend that it was an unconscious mistake. I yearn for Cavill to know something of me, the real me. Now he does, even though he's unaware of it.

'Cavill Henry James Pengower, if *you* please.' We both laugh and I avert my gaze, because I'm overwhelmed with a desire to kiss him and know I mustn't.

He's brought two sketch books with him and a wooden case of chalks. We sit in the shade and begin to draw. I lean against a tree stump and, with the book open on my lap, I sketch a foxglove, because it doesn't move like a bird does. Cavill declares that he's going to draw a squirrel, but he has to be quick, because the creature remains still for a moment only before scaling a nearby tree and disappearing into the leaves. 'So, what do you do now, Cavill Henry James Pengower? Draw the squirrel from memory?'

He looks at me quizzically and I wonder what I've said to amuse him. 'You have an original turn of phrase,' he comments, shaking his head. 'I will draw the squirrel from memory, but I dare say it will return. Squirrels are curious creatures, and they will want to know what we are doing.'

'I'm curious to see whether you are as good at drawing squirrels as you are at drawing birds.'

'Oh, I think you will find my squirrel is every bit as good as my spoonbills and gannets. Perhaps even more so.' There's a hint of mischief in the curl of his lips.

'I'll be the judge of that, my friend,' I return smartly, and he smiles secretively to himself as if perfectly confident of his talent.

We sketch in silence, until it's too hot to sketch any more and I close the book and fan myself with it instead.

'Show me your squirrel,' I ask at length, when he puts down his piece of chalk and looks with satisfaction upon his sketch.

He holds up his book. He hasn't drawn a squirrel at all. He's drawn me.

He beams at my reaction, elated to have surprised me. 'What do you make of it, my dear Hermione?'

I don't know what to say. It's beautiful. *I'm* beautiful – or rather Hermione is. 'I think it is a very fine squirrel,' I joke. It's come as such a shock, I can't think of anything clever to say.

He grins. 'I believe it is the finest squirrel in the wood. Indeed, in *any* wood.'

'The resemblance is astonishing,' I tell him, staring at it in wonder. I can't help but ask myself whether he would think me so appealing if he saw me as Pixie with my long pink hair. Something inside me deflates because I know that he wouldn't. He likes Hermione. Despite my wishing it, he doesn't see *me*.

'I'm glad you think so,' he says. 'Your opinion matters to me.'

'Does it?'

He looks deeply into my eyes, and that deflated feeling inflates into optimism. 'It does. Very much.'

'You have my high regard,' I tell him quietly.

'Might I have your affection too?' he asks, holding my gaze steady with his.

'I am a governess, Cavill,' I remind him.

'What difference does that make? You're a woman, Hermione. One that I greatly admire.' And, as I sink into his stare, I'm hopeful that his admiration is inspired by something more profound than the superficial Hermione that he sees with his eyes.

That evening, there is a grand dinner party at the manor. I watch from an upstairs window as the carriages draw up in front of the house. The guests alight in their finery – the ladies in their elegant dresses and sparkling tiaras, the gentlemen in white tie. I imagine Cavill and how dashing he must look, and I wish that I were there to see him. But my presence is not required tonight. It's a blessing for I would not have anything suitable to wear.

I'm too agitated to remain in my sitting room. I need to move. I can't sit still in this airless house. It's much too hot, and I'm restless with anxiety. I know I shouldn't be falling in love. I should remain detached and focused on my mission. I'm not here for my own pleasure. But four days feels like four weeks. I'm sinking into this dimension and growing accustomed to it. My own life seems very far away, as if *that* is the dream and *this* is the reality.

Timesliding really messes with my head! I have to remain focused and not forget who I am.

I decide to go for a walk. I set off in the golden evening light, avoiding the front lawn where the guests are enjoying a drink before dinner. I have no plan. I follow my instincts and allow myself to be led into the woods and out the other side, eventually winding up at the chapel. It rests quietly here in the dusk, as if it's asleep. A pair of fat pigeons coo from the roof, but, besides them, all is still. I sit on the iron bench, which is set against the chapel wall facing the graveyard, and allow my thoughts to wander. It's startling how quickly one gets used to a way of living. How quickly one sinks into a new reality and how normal it feels. I don't think about Ulysses any more, and I'm so invested in this dimension that I've all but forgotten Pablo. It's as if he's part of another life lived long ago. I can't believe I ever cared for him. That I suffered because of him. Now my heart is full of Cavill, spilling over with him, to the point where I can't ever imagine it otherwise. I want to believe that he's honest and sincere about the way he feels about me. I want to believe that it's possible to fall in love in a few days, that it's not only the stuff of novels and films, but reality too, and that it can happen to *me*.

I gaze up at the pale evening sky and feel that familiar tug somewhere in the depths of my being. In the place where my loneliness dwells and silently yearns for connection. Am I a dreamer to hope that Cavill might see beyond the physical and into my very soul? That he connects with the deep, eternal part of me that lies beneath the personality, beneath the woman, beneath Hermione and even beneath Pixie – the *real* me. Is it possible to sense in another that dimension that exists beyond time and space? Do I sense it in him? Am I a hopeless fool to search for it, to want it? If we were to meet in another time, would a light in our eyes lead us to recognise each other when our appearance is that of a stranger?

I don't belong here. I'm an imposter. Shortly, I'll have to pull myself away. I can't stay beyond Felix's disappearance. Or longer than it takes to discover the truth about what happens that night. That wouldn't be fair. I mustn't forget my responsibility to Hermione. Eleven days of her life is a very long time.

I remain on the bench. The setting sun caresses my face; it's lost its power now and is not so hot. The wind blows in off the water and cools the air, which is a relief. I listen to the roosting birds and take pleasure in the moment. I'm disturbed then by the sound of voices. I don't recognise them and sense that they're strangers, locals perhaps, or travellers trespassing on Mr Pengower's land. I get up at once and hide around the corner of the chapel. Gingerly, I peep out. I see two scrawny, filthy-looking men in ragged clothes. One is carrying a dead rabbit by the feet. It looks like the first square meal they've managed to find in days. The other, with his sharp, rapacious eyes and pointy face, is carrying a knife. They're a pitiful, yet menacing, sight. I know that they mustn't see me.

They try the door. It's unlocked. I suppose if the family left it locked, the trespassers would only break a window to get inside. They disappear into the interior, and I edge closer to listen to what they're saying. Their accents are so strong, curling their 'r's and leaning on their consonants, that I can make out only a little of their conversation. By the tone of their voices, however, I deduce that they're put out that there's nothing in there worth stealing. Could these men be linked to Felix's disappearance? They're certainly desperate, and on the prowl. Whether they're evil, I cannot say. What can people hope to gain from stealing a child? A ransom? Or do they hope to inflict pain on people who have so much when *they* have so little? Is that what it's about – resentment?

The men come to the door again and I dash back to my hiding place. They've found nothing. Besides the rabbit, their hands are empty. They shuffle off in the direction of the estuary and I'm alone once more. No wonder Cavill didn't want me walking about the place on my own. He's right – it's not safe.

I decide to make my way back to the house. The sun has now dipped behind the horizon. The moon is beginning its nightly climb and the first star twinkles in the cobalt sky. It'll be dark soon and I need to return while I can still see the way. I hope I don't meet anyone else skulking about the woods.

I reach the garden from the rear of the house. The track leads me past the stable block where the golden light of a gas lamp glows in one of the upstairs windows. I make my way towards the servants' entrance. It's then that I notice a shadowy figure climbing the drainpipe. It clings to the building like a giant rat. I stop and stare in horror. My heart thumps. I wonder if I should scream to alert the household. It's my instinct to tell someone. But then I remember that I'm not here to change things, merely to witness them. I crouch down and watch. Closer now, I can make out who it is.

It's John Snathe. He's climbing nimbly into one of the attic windows, where I can just make out the silhouette of a woman. It must be Gwen. Something about the sight of him climbing the drain-pipe gives me an uneasy feeling in my gut.

After he's disappeared inside, I walk on into the house by way of the servants' door. I take the stairs to the first floor and creep down the corridor to my bedroom. I hear the distant sound of voices rising up from the hall. The gentlemen must be smoking in the dining room while the ladies have moved into the drawing room. I think of Cavill there and wish that I could be with him. I wish I could warn him of what is soon to happen, but, if I did, I would change the future and who knows what the consequences of that would be? I cannot and must not tamper with time.

As the grandfather clock sounds the hour from somewhere deep within the house, edging closer to the dreadful night of Felix's disappearance, I sense evil has already slipped one of its dark tentacles beneath the door of St Sidwell Manor and I'm powerless to do anything about it.

I'm awoken by a twisting feeling in my belly. I reach for the light, but of course there isn't one. The room is dark but for a sliver of silver that trickles through the curtains from the crescent moon. I find the box of matches and light the gas lamp. I attempt to look at my watch, but I'm not wearing one. The clock on the shelf tells me it's two in the morning. I think of John Snathe climbing the drainpipe and then my mind turns to the men I saw at the church, and the twisting feeling in my belly grows tighter. Is that how the intruder breaks in to steal Felix away? Up the drainpipe? Driven by a sense of disquiet, I put on my dressing gown and step out into the corridor. I tread softly down it, towards the part of the house where Cordelia sleeps, and beyond her bedroom to her husband's suite of rooms. I know that in families such as this one, husbands and wives do not sleep together but have their own quarters.

I don't know what I'm looking for, but, spurred on by a strange nervousness, I follow my instincts. They prove to be on point for I notice the vanishing glow of a gas lamp at the bottom of the stairs. I turn my own lamp low and quietly descend. My feet tread silently on the wooden steps and I'm grateful that they don't cause the floorboards to squeak and betray me. I decide that, if I'm caught spying, I'll claim to have suspected an intruder.

Whoever it is has gone into the library.

I reach the hall and hurry across it to hide behind the door to the library, which has been left ajar. I peer through the crack. My heart is pounding wildly against my ribcage. I breathe as quietly as I can. I'm terrified of being caught snooping. Terrified for Hermione as well as for myself, for if I'm discovered the consequences for her will be dreadful.

It's Cordelia. She's standing in front of the bookshelf to the left of the fireplace. I'm astonished to see a cleverly disguised door open among the books. She's walking through it. I can see from the light of her lamp that there's a narrow staircase behind it. I imagine it must be another priest hole, perhaps leading into a tunnel that runs beneath the house and into the garden. She goes down a couple of steps and then twists round and closes the door behind her.

I wait a few minutes to make sure that she's not coming back, then turn up my lamp and go straight to the bookcase to see if I can find out how she opened the secret door. I look hard among the books, pressing them as well as the wooden spines that separate the sections in the hope that I'll trigger some clever mechanism, like the rose in the dining room. Nothing happens. The door is completely concealed. If I hadn't seen her walk through it with my own eyes, I would not believe it to be there. I go to the window to see if I can spy her in the garden, but all is still, bathed in the weak silver glow of the waxing moon.

I'm triumphant. Now I know how Felix must be taken out of the house when all the doors and windows are locked. I wonder who else knows about this secret exit, or has Cordelia stumbled across it, as the maid stumbled across the one in the dining room that Robert showed me, and kept the knowledge to herself?

I realise, too, that this is how Cordelia escapes from the stifling atmosphere of the house. I imagine her sitting in blissful solitude on the bench in the vegetable garden, wrapped in the soft cloak of darkness, and I smile to myself. Is this perhaps a small and harmless act of rebellion on her part, defying her husband who is so certain that he has locked everyone inside his fortress?

The following day is Sunday. I accompany the children and the rest of the family to the chapel in carriages. The silver has been laid out on the altar and the candles are lit. The building no longer appears to sleep but resonates with music and song and prayer. The children, in their Sunday best, are well behaved, in spite of Felix whispering loudly that he would like to make a den beneath the altar cloth and pretend to be a badger. Mrs James Pengower attends with Mr Bray. He seems to escort her everywhere. I'm intrigued to know what their relationship is. He's clearly a close family friend as well as an employee, which seems a little unusual in a household where there is a vast distinction between the family and those who work for them. But then I think of myself and Cordelia. The fact that she wants to make a friend of me, and invites me to join them at dinner, is unusual too. As I observe them, I see that Mr Pengower, Cordelia and Cavill all treat Pascoe with familiarity, as if he's one of them. I wonder whether it's Mr Pengower or Cordelia who is driving these intimacies. Judging by what I've seen, I would say that it's Cordelia herself. She told me that she and Mr Bray share the same concerns about the miners and their welfare. Perhaps she knows that Mr Bray can help her in her endeavours to improve their conditions and that is why she keeps him close. Cordelia's opinions might not be tolerated by her authoritarian husband, but I think it is she who sets the tone of the household.

Unlike Pascoe Bray, who sits with me and the family at the front, the servants take their places at the back, along with the gardeners, Mr Grantly and the grooms. It appears that only Mr Symons remains in the house, with Mrs Moyle, who I imagine is cooking lunch. Cordelia has told me that the children will join the adults at the dining-room table, and so shall I. She says it's an opportunity for Robert to show off his manners and for his little brother to watch him and learn.

Cordelia is glowing and in high spirits. She has clearly been recharged by her nocturnal visit to the vegetable garden. Gwen, on the other hand, is drowsy and glum, and I'm not at all surprised. I don't know what time John Snathe left her bedroom, but by the weary look on her face and the endless sighing, I imagine it was late. She sits at the back with the other servants and tries not to nod off during the sermon.

There appears to be an awful lot going on in this house under the cover of darkness. I resolve to lie in wait tonight in the library for Cordelia – that way I will find out how she opens the secret door and then I can discover where it leads.

I sit with the children and their mother in the front pew. Mr Pengower sits with his mother, Pascoe Bray and Cavill in the pew on the other side of the aisle. Most of the seats are empty. I wonder if there was a time when the family was large enough to fill the whole place. We are so few, it seems almost indulgent to require a priest just for us. Wouldn't it be more convenient to attend the church in town?

I catch Cavill's eye and he gives me a secretive smile. I avert my gaze and settle it upon the paintings of saints and angels that surround the arched window behind the altar. It is then that I notice a phrase from the Bible written in gold lettering: *Suffer the little children to come unto me*. It makes me think of Felix. I look across at him, so innocent and sweet, and my heart aches. This time next week this child will be gone. He'll simply vanish. I pray to God that I'll find out what happens to him. What I do then, with the information gleaned, can only be guessed at. Will it be enough to move Cordelia on?

During the ride back to the house, I find myself seated beside Miss Prideaux in a carriage driven by John Snathe. Mr and Mrs Pengower are in the bigger one with the children and Mr Bray, and the other servants are walking, for it's only a short distance away and the weather is fine. I haven't spoken to her much since I arrived. She's busy with Cordelia. The job of lady's maid is a relatively elevated one, and it's all-consuming. I've occasionally crossed paths with her on the stairs as she takes her mistress's breakfast up on a tray and when she's coming down with a dress to mend, or a stain to be removed. She always smiles and greets me politely. Now we have time to talk. She's lively and indiscreet. 'Didn't he go on so?' she says of the vicar. 'Have you noticed how they all sound the same? They have a common pompousness in their tone of voice, an air of superiority, as if they have exclusive access to God. Perhaps that is part of their training, learning how to be pompous.'

I laugh. She's absolutely right. 'I suppose they consider us ignorant sheep who need to be herded so we don't stray off the path,' I reply.

'And that path only leads in *one* direction. Theirs.' She lifts her chin and offers her pretty face to the sun.

'I'm afraid being in the right is a prerequisite to being a member of any religion,' I add. 'It is by putting everyone else in the wrong that they reinforce their sense of identity.'

'You speak wise words, Miss Swift. And have you noticed how, after holy communion, those who have received it return to their seats with a look of moral superiority on their faces, as if they have been elevated? It lasts until luncheon and then they forget that they have been blessed and return to their usual ways.'

'You are very observant,' I tell her and we laugh together.

'I enjoy watching people. It makes life more enjoyable. The priest puts himself on display every Sunday, so it's easy to observe him. However, I do not always observe to mock, Miss Swift. Some characters I am very fond of. Take Mr Bray, for example. He is an upstanding, and sensitive man – handsome too. You may not know but his wife died some years ago. Poor woman. She was very sick. She simply faded away. It's a wonder that he has not remarried. I imagine an attractive man like him would not have trouble in finding a new wife. I'm sure they are queuing up at his door.'

'Perhaps he doesn't want one. Perhaps he wants to remain loyal to his wife.'

'There is no point in remaining loyal to someone who is dead, Miss Swift.' She sighs and I wonder whether she rather sees *herself* by his side. 'He needs someone to look after him. Men are not very good at looking after themselves.'

'Maybe he's too busy with his job to think about love,' I suggest.

'You might be right.' She leans towards me and lowers her voice. 'He's constantly fighting with Mr Pengower over the miners' living conditions, which are shoddy. You would be horrified. He's their knight in shining armour. You will not know this, but last year there was an accident up there and Mr Bray went into the collapsed tunnel with no thought for his own safety and saved one of the men. Another young lad was killed. Terrible thing. The poor boy died instantly. But Mr Bray is a hero among them. Apparently, Mr Pengower only arrived on the scene when it was over. They say he was having luncheon and did not want to be disturbed, but I don't know whether that is true.'

'I'm sure that's not true,' I cut in, but I have no reason to say that other than in disbelief that anyone could continue eating under such circumstances.

'I have overheard Mrs Pengower fighting with her husband in Mr Bray's defence,' Miss Prideaux continues. 'She, like Mr Bray, is a compassionate person. Occasionally, when Mr Pengower is away on business, Mr Bray takes Mrs Pengower up to the mine so that she can talk to the men and give them encouragement. She listens to their complaints and tries to reassure them that things will improve. Mr Pengower would be furious if he found out. He would accuse her of undermining him. I can tell you, he has lost his temper with her for less. But the miners respect Mrs Pengower. No one throws eggs at her when she goes into town – they throw eggs at her husband though.'

I'm horrified. 'They throw eggs at Mr Pengower?' I repeat.

'Indeed, they do. I have seen it with my own eyes.' She lowers her voice further. 'I should not speak out of turn, but you will soon learn for yourself, so I might as well enlighten you now. Mr Pengower is *not* a kind man. Oh, he can appear perfectly charming when he wants to. I have watched him with guests he needs to impress, then he is all sweetness and light and butter won't melt in his mouth. But sometimes the manner in which he treats Mrs Pengower is cruel. I would not want to be married to a man like him, however much money he had. Mr Bray is gentle and sympathetic. If he remains a bachelor out of respect for his wife, then it is simply testament to his loving heart, and only makes him more noble in my eyes.'

'Why doesn't Mr Pengower improve the mines? Could he not pay the men more? He's a wealthy man.'

Miss Prideaux widens her eyes theatrically and grins. 'Because he is greedy, Miss Swift. He wants to keep it all for himself. I do not imagine he pays Mr Bray very much.'

'It is a curious relationship,' I begin carefully. 'Mr Bray is a gentleman and a friend, but he also works for Mr Pengower. How is that so?'

'Mr Bray is, indeed, a gentleman. I do believe that he and Mr Pengower were educated together. Mr Bray's family lost their money and Mr Pengower, on inheriting the mine from his father, took Mr Bray on to help him run it. That is what I have gleaned from keeping my ear to the ground.' She sniffs and pulls a face to show that she's proud of her craftiness. 'Mr Bray is loyal to Mr Pengower, and Mr Pengower respects him, even though they do not agree on many things, otherwise they would have parted ways long ago. I think Mr Pengower knows the high regard in which the miners hold Mr Bray, and that prevents him from laying him off. Without Mr Bray, there would be serious trouble up at the mine.'

'Have the miners ever threatened the family besides throwing eggs?' I ask, thinking of Felix and what is to come.

'If I were Mr Pengower, I would be very careful,' she replies portentously. 'With a bit of drink in them, there are some that might easily do something they might later regret.'

That afternoon, Cordelia summons me to her sitting room. She's looking anxious and alert. She closes the door behind me and invites me to sit with her in the window seat. I can tell from her cautious, conspiratorial air that she's about to confide in me something that she doesn't want anyone else to know. We sit and she takes a breath. 'I consider you my ally, Miss Swift, as well as my friend. I need you to come with me today. I am going to drive to the gypsy encampment and give charity to the women. I want the children to come with me. Mr Grantly and John will take us in the carriage. Mr Pengower, as you know, does not agree with me in this case, therefore I have not told him.' She smiles suddenly and her eyes shine. In them is both fear and excitement.

'What if he finds out?' I ask. I imagine Ivan Pengower has a formidable temper.

'He is away all afternoon, returning for supper. I can count on Grantly and John to keep it secret. There is little chance of him finding out, and, if he does, well . . .' She lifts her chin defiantly. 'I will hold my ground.' Her courage lasts only a moment, however. She sighs and drops her shoulders, the sheen of excitement dimming in her eyes. 'It grieves me to hear Robert speak of the gypsies with intolerance and judgement when he has never even met one. He copies his father, who he admires, echoing his intolerant opinions like a parrot. Much of the time what my husband says is in stark contrast to what I believe. I don't want Robert growing up to be prejudiced and dogmatic like him. He is afraid, you see, my husband. Afraid of foreigners. But that is human nature, isn't it, to be afraid of the unknown, and suspicious of it?'

'It is,' I agree. 'And when people are afraid they turn aggression to protect themselves from the perceived danger. Most of the time there is no danger at all. It is all in their heads, anticipating it.'

She smiles wanly. 'Those poor gypsies are outsiders therefore people are mistrustful of them. They accuse them of all sorts of terrible things. They should not be treated with disdain simply because they want to live differently to the rest of us. I am a Christian woman, Miss Swift, and Jesus taught us to love our neighbour as ourselves. Well, the gypsies are my neighbours and I want to do the right thing and help them. We are all the same in the eyes of God. But we are all different in the eyes of man.'

'You are a good woman, Mrs Pengower.'

'I do my best. I try to be a good wife, but, truly, my higher purpose in this world is to be a good mother. That is my priority. Therefore, I will take children to meet the gypsies to broaden their horizons. To give them perspective and clarity. To make them understand that there are people who are less fortunate than them, and to know that there is much that can be done to help them.'

'You do not consider Master Felix a little young for the experience?' I ask. I cannot help but wonder whether those men who were thrown into a cell on account of Mr Pengower's complaints might be looking for revenge.

'I did consider that, Miss Swift. But I do not believe he is too young. Perhaps it will make a greater impression on him because of his tender age. Maybe the experience will ignite something inside him that will inspire him to be charitable one day. I am afraid he is not going to learn to be charitable from his father. Besides, he is always being left out. His father has eyes only for his first-born, moulding Robert into a miniature version of himself. Felix is overlooked and he minds. He craves his father's attention and admiration. Therefore, he will come with us.' She grins at me and the excitement is restored in her impassioned gaze. 'It will be an adventure for all of us!'

We set off in the early afternoon with the roof of the carriage folded down. I sit beside Felix, facing Cordelia and Robert. It's another sunny day, but there's a haze in the air that seems to make the heat more intense. I fan myself and feel my skin grow damp inside my dress. As we near the sea, a gentle breeze begins to blow, and I turn my face into it in search of relief. It gives little, but it's pleasant none the less.

Cordelia is elegant in a pale pink dress and matching hat, complete with flowers and ribbons, and a white lace fan, which she waves in front of her beautiful face. Once again, she's like a painting and I can't take my eyes off her. My dress and hat are modest compared to hers. I feel like a moorhen beside a flamingo, but I don't mind. I mind only of what Cavill thinks.

Robert and Felix are excited to be out with their mother and chat away without restraint, asking questions and making comments. Cordelia indulges them with patience, pointing out things that might interest them, answering their questions thoughtfully. Then she turns her gaze to the landscape and becomes quiet suddenly, as if disturbed by the infiltration of something dark and unwelcome in her mind. Her expression changes from serene to troubled. I wonder whether she's worrying about her husband finding out and getting angry. I recall Miss Prideaux's words about Mr Pengower being cruel. I wonder what she meant. How cruel *is* he? He was coldly dismissive of Cordelia the other evening when she spoke about the travellers, but I haven't yet seen him lose his temper. It doesn't take much of a stretch of the imagination, though, to envisage it. Might Cordelia be struggling to cope with him? Is that why she's looking to find a friend in *me*?

She notices me watching her and shifts out of her reverie with a couple of blinks and a wistful smile. I return her smile. However, I can't help but frown at her inquisitively. She responds with a sigh. 'It's too lovely,' she says, looking once again at the faraway hills. 'It breaks the heart.'

The carriage rattles up a track that cuts through a meadow of buttercups and long grasses. On the right is the sea, glittering and sparkling in the sunshine. Felix points at a gull wheeling above us and then waves at it gleefully. When he stands up, his mother tells him to sit down. 'We don't want you falling out, my love,' she says, and gazes at him with tenderness, her troubled face relaxing into tranquillity once again.

Ahead is the encampment. From a distance it looks picturesque, for there are green and red caravans, white tents, muscular cart horses, and linen hanging from the branches of trees and blowing in the wind. But as we get nearer, the scene takes on a very different hue. Robert comments on the squalor and his mother reprimands him, telling him to keep his voice down. 'Remember, my dear, that these people do not have the luxuries we do. They deserve our respect and compassion, not our condemnation.' Then she turns to me and smiles wistfully. 'There is something terribly appealing about their way of life.' She laughs at herself. 'It reminds me of the poem *The Raggle Taggle Gypsy*. About the lady who runs off to live in freedom with the gypsies. "What do I care for a goose-feather bed?"' She sighs deeply. 'Indeed, sometimes I wonder.'

Shortly, the people come into view. They stop what they're doing when they see us and form a group, like deer coming together for safety. The women's long skirts are colourful and bohemian, their peasant blouses billowing and embellished with embroidery. They wear headscarves and tasselled shawls, beads in their hair and bangles on their wrists, and their skin is a rich, golden brown. They certainly look different to the pale, weathered faces of the locals, which explains the hostility they arouse in people who, as Cordelia acknowledged, are afraid of strangers. Even in my own time, where people are generally more accepting of those who are different, there is, unfortunately, still mistrust. Mr Pengower's view of them is the common view. Cordelia is unusual, and I admire her for having her own mind, and heart.

As the carriage draws up, the children break away from their parents and come running towards us excitedly. Their clothes are a patchwork of bright colours and they're shoeless. 'I wish I did not have to wear shoes,' says Felix, gazing at them with longing.

'You would be sorry not to have shoes in winter,' Robert retorts.

Cheerful and friendly, the gypsies are quite the opposite of Mr Pengower's descriptions. In fact, they're exuberant and their laughter and cries of delight fill the air like the squawking of gulls. I look out for signs of malice but see none. I see only curiosity as Mr Grantly halts the horses in their midst. The poverty of their living conditions is impossible to ignore, and I feel a wave of pity, for I haven't seen poverty like this before. Cordelia's expression is full of concern. 'We are here to help these people just as we help those in St Sidwell,' she tells her children. 'You must be polite and kind and friendly. They might be dressed differently, but in God's eyes they are the same as us.' Cordelia is determined that her children do not grow up with the same prejudices as their father. She is set upon broadening their experience and deepening their understanding of people, in all their many variations, and I admire her. She is a woman ahead of her time.

Mr Grantly helps us down from the carriage, then he and John set about unloading the baskets of food, children's clothes and blankets, and other items that Cordelia no longer needs. I take Felix's hand and we accompany his mother, who takes it upon herself to talk to the women and to distribute the offerings. They're grateful. Their hands reach out and their eyes shine with gratitude. They're far from the menacing thieves and rogues that Mr Pengower and Robert have made them out to be.

There are a few men among the group and I search for the two I saw at the chapel the evening before, but they're nowhere to be seen. I imagine they're out working or looking for work. Perhaps they're not even travellers at all, but miners, or vagrants who wandered onto Mr Pengower's land and have since moved on. Children gather around Robert, gazing at his fine clothes and putting out their fingers to touch them. Robert, ever his father's son, pushes their hands away and crinkles his nose with repulsion. Felix, however, is the focus of the mothers' and grandmothers' attention. They pinch his pink cheeks and coo at him like colourful pigeons, and he relishes their curiosity and giggles joyfully. He has picked up none of his father's prejudice and is as inquisitive as a puppy. After a while he runs off to play with the other children, while Robert goes to help Mr Grantly and John – anything to get away from the strange people he so abhors.

Just then an old woman with long white hair flowing out of a brightly patterned scarf grabs me by the hand. I turn and notice at once that the eyes gazing up at me are opaque, like peeled lychees. She's blind. She presses my palm into the hollow of her weathered brown cheek and gives her head a little shake, as if she's trying to sense something that's just beyond the powers of her perception. She narrows her eyes that do not see and cranes her neck, listening hard. I recognise her kind at once. She's a seer. I suspect, from the realisation dawning on her face, that she has recognised me too. Her bony fingers find my face and cup it, pulling me towards her own, which is strangely beautiful despite her great age. Wisdom is embedded in the deep lines that scratch it with a thousand crosses. 'Who *are* you?' she whispers and her lips part to reveal an incomplete set of stained teeth.

'No one,' I reply quickly. My head is like an egg in the clutches of an eagle. I pull myself out of her grasp.

'I *see* you,' she says and nods with satisfaction. 'You are special, like me.'

I glance at Cordelia, but she's busy distributing charity to grateful women. Felix is surrounded by a group of children, laughing merrily. The gypsy women are rummaging through the baskets with enthusiasm, pulling everything out and shrieking in delight. Robert is sulking and staying close to Mr Grantly.

The seer and I are alone.

For a moment I feel as if we are a million miles away from the encampment, on another plane entirely.

'Take care,' she says softly, and, even though her eyes don't see, she looks at me keenly. 'It is a dangerous game to play with time.'

'I don't know what you're talking about,' I protest weakly. But one cannot hide from a seer. Is it possible that she's a timeslider like me?

She ignores my denial. 'You are young. You have much to learn.' She takes my hand again, sandwiching it between her brown ones and squeezing it meaningfully. 'One thing you must know: love will bring you back,' she says. 'Love will *always* bring you back. It is very important that you do not forget this for you will need it. Yes, with your gift you will surely need it. There is no force more powerful in the universe than love.'

I wonder with a pang of anxiety what she has seen in my future to inspire this warning.

That night, I lie in wait for Cordelia in the library. I hide behind the curtain as if I'm in an Agatha Christie movie. At least I can sit on the window seat and look out onto the garden and big black sky. The stars are very bright tonight and the moon, growing fatter with every lap, will soon be at its fullest. I wish I had a smartphone. I'm not used to waiting and doing nothing. I hear the grandfather clock in the hall mark the hour of midnight with twelve loud chimes. They echo through the silent hall. I wait. And I wait some more.

I hear the clock chime one, then two and finally, I realise that she's not going to come.

At least, not tonight. I will try again tomorrow.

Present

Chapter Ten

There was a strange atmosphere in the house, as if it was holding its breath. Tabitha and Zach lingered in the hall, not knowing what to do with themselves. 'I wish I could watch Pixie getting rid of the spirit,' said Tabitha, gazing longingly up the stairs. 'I wonder how she's going to do it.'

'There are no such things as spirits,' Zach scoffed, putting his hands in his pockets. 'Dad thinks they're fakes.'

'Did he say that?' Tabitha asked, offended; she knew that Pixie wasn't a fake.

'He called them charlatans.'

'What does that mean?'

'That they're full of shit.'

'He's wrong.'

'And *you* know.' Zach grinned at her in that superior way of his that made her blood boil.

'Actually, I do.' She went to the cupboard for her coat and hat.

'Where are you going?'

'Into the garden.' She didn't want her brother to come with her. 'I'm going to explore on my own.'

'Suit yourself,' Zach replied, sauntering off to the library, which was his favourite room in the house.

Tabitha slipped into her red coat and pulled her bobble hat over her head. She ran out into the frosted garden with a rising sense of exhilaration. It felt good to be outside in the sunshine and away from her cynical brother and the tense mood in the house. It was bitterly cold, but the light was dazzling, shining onto the hoary grass and causing it to sparkle like glitter on an advent calendar. Her breath turned the air to fog and she pretended she was a dragon, exhaling fire as she skipped over the lawn, leaving a trail of footprints behind her. Her joy overflowed and she laughed out loud with the sheer delight of being in the midst of such loveliness.

She adored the gardens and, unlike her mother, did not find fault in the weeds that had taken over the borders or in the bushes that had grown into each other. In Tabitha's eyes nature was beautiful just as it was, in its wonderfully chaotic and uninhibited way. Just then a robin alighted on the ground in front of her and pecked at the frozen earth. Finding it barren, it flapped its wings and flew off to try its luck elsewhere. Tabitha followed it through the trees, wandering deeper into the wood. Shortly, the bird landed again and thrust its beak into the grass. Tabitha stood very still and observed it. The robin seemed to notice her and lifted its little head to observe her back. Tabitha inched closer but the bird fluttered off, only to land once more a few hundred yards away, as if it wanted to entice her into a game. Tabitha was only too happy to oblige and ran in pursuit, stopping each time the robin came down to land.

Eventually, the robin flew out of the trees into a clearing and dropped onto the remains of a post-and-rail fence that surrounded a quaint little cottage. Tabitha was astonished and delighted to have stumbled across this unexpected treasure. St Sidwell Manor was full of surprises. The building was obviously abandoned for the windows were opaque with dust, glass panes were missing or broken, and there was a hole in the pitched roof where the tiles had fallen in. It looked like a dinosaur had taken a bite out of it, then thought better of the tasteless meal and stomped off. The entire edifice was being slowly swallowed by ivy, which had crept upon it with its greedy green tentacles. It wouldn't be long before the cottage became a part of the wood. Maybe one day no one would know that it had ever been here.

Tabitha was thrilled. She loved to explore, and this was more exciting than anything she had explored before, even the house. It was like something out of a fairy tale – the cottage in *Hansel and*

Gretel where the witch is pushed into the oven. Tabitha wondered who had lived here and why it had been deserted.

She was about to venture inside when she noticed a little boy standing in the doorway. She jumped, for she hadn't seen him standing there and was taken by surprise. He was watching her warily, unmoving, as if he were a statue. 'Hello,' she said.

The boy blinked then and stepped out of the shadows. He was wearing what looked like a white sailor suit. Tabitha noticed that he had nothing on his feet. Her first thought was that he must be freezing. Her second thought was that his mother must surely be nearby, for he couldn't have been more than six years old. Of course, he didn't live here, in this cottage, did he?

'Who are you?' he asked at last.

'I'm Tabitha,' Tabitha replied. 'Aren't you cold?'

'Cold?'

'You're not wearing any shoes.'

The boy looked at his feet. 'No.' He shrugged. 'I don't feel the cold.'

'Lucky you,' she said. 'I do. It's freezing. Look.' She blew a cloud of smoke into the air. 'I'm like a dragon.'

He laughed as if she'd performed a magic trick. 'Do that again,' he said.

She blew out another smoky puff and laughed with him. 'What are you doing here?' she asked.

'Playing,' he replied casually.

'Who are you playing with?'

'No one, there aren't many children who live around here.' Tabitha's heart sank. She was used to having lots of friends nearby in London.

'Do you live near here?' she asked.

'Yes.'

'We've just moved into the big house. I wonder who used to live in this cottage.'

'They've gone,' he replied. 'There is no one here now.'

'Have you been inside?'

'Yes.'

'What's it like?'

'Messy. Do you want to play hide-and-seek?' he asked suddenly.

'If you like.'

'I'll hide,' he declared, and before Tabitha could discuss the rules of the game, he scampered off, the sound of his bare feet soft on the frosted ground.

Tabitha started to count to one hundred.

Olivia and Antoinette drove into town to do some research in the local library. There were sure to be records. If a child had gone missing, it would have got into the newspapers. The whole county would have known about it.

'It really is very beautiful here,' said Antoinette, looking out of the frosted window at the undulating white fields and old drystone walls that separated them. Wheeling gulls surfed the wind, their wide wings a dazzling white in the glare. 'You wait until spring when the flowers come out and the leaves are on the trees. It'll be glorious.'

'And the house will warm up,' said Olivia hopefully.

'The house will warm up when Pixie gets rid of the spirit,' Antoinette reminded her.

'Do you really think she can?'

'I know she can. I saw her in action once. I was working at a house in Burnley. It wasn't a big house like yours, but it was quite old. I was painting the sitting room, which required an expert dragger. Pixie was called in to get rid of a nasty earthbound spirit who refused to budge because he didn't want anyone in his house. There was no trauma around his death, he just refused to leave. Pixie sorted him out.'

'She didn't slide back in time, did she?'

'I'm not sure.'

'Do you think she really does that? I mean, time travelling sounds like science fiction to me.'

'It does, and this is the first I've heard about it, to be honest. I don't think it's something she advertises. Most people would think her batty. But I trust Pixie. She wouldn't lie about anything. She's not capable of it. Bad karma.' Antoinette looked across at her niece and grinned. 'What you sow, so shall ye reap. That's a good one to remember. Whatever you put out will come back, good *and* bad, like a boomerang.'

'Look, I have no problem with ghosts,' Olivia said. 'I believe we live on after the body dies and some of us hang around, for whatever reason, but the past is in the past – gone – how on earth can a person slide back there? And if Pixie *can* slide back, then surely she can slide forward too, which means that the future has already happened. If the future has already happened, what about free will? Is any of it our choice? Do you see what I'm trying to say? It doesn't make sense.'

'That's because you're trying to understand it with your limited mind, Liv. The mind cannot grasp infinity because there's nothing infinite in our experience. Try telling a frog who lives in a pond about a fish tank in your local pet shop. It's beyond his experience. We're like frogs. So just go with it and don't try to get your head around it, because you'll simply make yourself dizzy.'

They arrived in town and parked the car against the kerb. The library was easy to find for it was clearly marked, just off the high street. 'I love the smell of books,' Antoinette gushed when they entered. 'Don't you just love the smell of books, Liv?' she repeated, smacking her lips with pleasure.

'I love being in the warmth,' Olivia replied. 'The smell of books is a bonus.'

They walked up to the desk where a young woman with glasses, lank brown hair and no make-up sat staring at a computer and typing at speed. Antoinette did not wait for her to look up. 'Good morning,' she said.

The girl stopped typing and reluctantly lifted her eyes off the screen. Her lack of interest did not bode well for their mission. Antoinette explained what they were after. 'There must be newspaper articles from that time or perhaps a book on the history of the house.'

The girl looked bored. 'I think you'd better talk to the manager. He'll know,' she said. She got up from her chair with a sigh and moved slowly into a back room. A moment later she came out and plonked herself down on the chair again. 'He'll be with you in a minute,' she said and then returned her attention to the screen. Her expression enlivened and her fingers began tap-tapping once more over the keyboard.

Antoinette caught Olivia's eye and pulled a face.

They didn't have to wait long. The door flew open and a small man with an eager expression, round glasses, and wiry grey hair curling beneath a bald lid, sprung out with a vivacious bounce. He looked incongruous in a three-piece tweed suit and tie. Smiling enthusiastically, he introduced himself. 'Victor Pollard at your service. What can I do you for?' His eyes were large and brown behind the magnifying glass of his spectacles.

Antoinette and Olivia introduced themselves and then Antoinette explained once again while Olivia cut in when she had the chance, which wasn't often.

Victor turned his bright eyes onto Olivia. 'So you and your husband have moved into the manor, have you?' he asked.

'That's right,' she replied.

'And how are you getting on?'

'Good so far.'

He looked sceptical for a second. 'Well, that *is* good. Very good.' He chuckled. 'Most people are too frightened to even set foot in the front door. But it's good so far.'

'I can't imagine what they're frightened of,' said Antoinette briskly.

'We just want to learn something of the house's history,' said Olivia.

Victor rubbed his hands together. 'Well, you have come to the right place, Olivia Talwyn,' he said. 'You have, indeed. Just the right place. You see,' he beamed proudly, looking from Olivia to Antoinette and back again, 'I'm an amateur but avid local historian. There's not much that I don't know about the history of St Sidwell and the surrounding area.'

'That's very encouraging,' said Olivia.

'Let's go and sit down over there, shall we?' he suggested,

pointing to a circle of soft chairs arranged around a table by the window. 'Would you like some tea or coffee?' They declined. 'Very well, let's cut to the chase.'

They sat down.

Victor Pollard put his hands on the table and knitted his short fingers. 'Before I direct you to newspaper articles that will give you more detail,' he began, 'I can tell you what I know about Ivan and Cordelia Pengower. It's been a thrilling mystery in these parts for over a century, but I have my own theories. I'll share them with you. It'll be my pleasure. It's not often that I get to talk to people who are really interested in local history. It'll be a veritable pleasure, to be sure.'

Victor Pollard took a breath, clearly savouring this moment to show off his knowledge. 'You are indeed right, little Felix Pengower disappeared on the night of the twenty-eighth of June eighteen ninety-five. His body was never found. His mother, Cordelia Pengower, was married to a man called Ivan and they had another child, older than Felix, called Robert. Now Ivan was a hard and pompous man, and not well liked in the town. Not well liked at all. But Cordelia, being a charitable and graceful woman, was loved and admired by everyone she met.' Olivia caught Antoinette's eye. Victor Pollard was now running with the ball.

'The newspapers were full of the story. Indeed, the whole of St Sidwell was buzzing with it. No one could believe that a child had been abducted. St Sidwell was a relatively peaceful little town. The police reports show that they searched the house and the grounds of the manor and found nothing. The windows and doors, which had all been locked for the night by Ivan Pengower himself, had not been broken or disturbed in any way. The only people to have the keys were Ivan Pengower and the butler, Mr Symons. Mr Symons was questioned and released. The nursemaid, a certain Gwen Blight, was also taken in for questioning, as was Ivan, the child's father. But there was no motive, you see, and no body. Nothing. There was no reason whatsoever why any of those characters would have wanted to be rid of the boy. Suspicion then fell on the travellers. They had settled onto land the other side of the estuary. Some of the men had been caught stealing and there had been the odd brawl outside the public house here in town, so they weren't popular. Travellers had a bad time of it in those days and it was natural that the finger of suspicion was pointed at them. Their campsite was searched, people were taken in for questioning, some were kept for a few days. But again, there was no evidence and no motive. Why would the travellers want to take a boy? They had no dispute with Mr Pengower or the family. None at all. No motive, you see. That's important.' Victor rubbed his hands, relishing his captivated audience. 'There has to be a motive to fit a crime.'

'But *you* have a theory, don't you, Victor?' said Antoinette, indulging him.

Victor smiled the smile of an amateur sleuth who believed he had solved the crime. 'It was a miner,' he declared confidently.

'A miner?' Olivia repeated. 'Was there a mine?'

'There was, indeed,' he said. 'Indeed, there was.' He took a long breath through his nose. 'Ivan Pengower's father, James, had bought a tin mine back in the middle of the century, which Ivan inherited upon his death. Ivan was not a benevolent man. He was ambitious. He didn't treat the men well. In fact' – and now Victor wagged his finger at the women – 'there had been a nasty accident up at the mine the year before. In the winter of ninety-four. Seven men were killed, among them a young lad of fifteen, Billy Tonkin. As a result of this accident, there was a riot and Ivan and his brother Cavill were called up to assist. It wasn't pretty. The manager, Pascoe Bray, had warned Ivan not a few months before that the tunnels of the mine were unsafe. That they were digging too fast, without the necessary precautions. But Ivan Pengower didn't listen. He wanted more and more tin, and quickly. Now it's my belief, and I have looked into this very carefully, that Billy Tonkin's father, Frank Tonkin, did away with Felix Pengower in an act of revenge and buried his body in the mine. In the part of the mine that had collapsed, you see, where his son was killed. No one was going to look in there. In fact . . .' Again Victor wagged his finger, his eyes taking on a feverish sheen. 'No one bothered to look in the mine at all. They simply didn't connect the two events. Is that not strange? Can you not hear alarm bells? To me it's simple, but then everything is simple with hindsight, isn't it?'

'Frank Tonkin was never questioned?' Antoinette asked.

'He was not, but Pascoe Bray left some months after and was never heard of again. That is suspicious, is it not? I suspect he'd had enough of working with Ivan Pengower and left St Sidwell altogether. I wonder whether Pascoe suspected Ivan knew what had become of his son, but somehow diverted the police's attention away from the mine because he didn't want to be blamed for the boy's death – and he didn't want the men to stop mining.'

'But the child might not have been killed. They never found a body, did they?' said Olivia.

'They never found a body,' Victor repeated. 'Cordelia Pengower, the child's mother, died the following year of a broken heart.'

'That's terrible, considering she had another son to live for,' said Antoinette.

'She did, indeed. Indeed, she did. And, I must say, Robert Pengower turned out to be an interesting fellow.'

'How so?' asked Olivia.

'He wanted sons. It was very important to him, as it had been to his own father, Ivan, to leave the estate to a son. But he only had a daughter, Emily.'

'Mrs Delaware!' said Antoinette.

'Yes, and, sadly, when it came to continuing the Pengower line, Emily Delaware bore no children. A great misfortune for her, and then her husband passed away from cancer. She lived alone in that big place for years. A strange woman she was. A recluse.'

'So, she finds the closest male relative, my husband, Bruce, and leaves the estate to him?'

'Yes, indeed,' said Victor.

'But how is Bruce related to Mrs Delaware?' Antoinette asked.

'Now, that I haven't been able to uncover, I'm afraid. You'll need to find a family tree,' said Victor. 'If Emily Delaware found him, the information must be available somewhere.'

'We've been looking for one in the house, but so far my

husband has only found a book Robert wrote about his father,' said Olivia.

'There's no mention of any Talwyns in there,' Antoinette added.

'As far as we know,' Olivia interjected. 'To be honest, we've only just moved in, so we haven't had much time to look into it. We'd love to read any newspaper clippings from that time. The mystery of Felix Pengower is a compelling story. I'm much more interested in that than in finding out how my husband is related to Emily Delaware.'

Victor set up the microfilm so that Antoinette and Olivia could read the newspaper articles that came out in response to the child's disappearance. The two women sat in front of the screen and scrolled through them. According to contemporary reports, there was no sign of a forced entry into the house. The doors and windows had been locked as usual the previous evening by Mr Pengower himself and were still secure when the butler came down to unlock them in the morning. They were intrigued to see a black-and-white photograph of Ivan and Cordelia Pengower. Ivan was dark-haired with a sweeping moustache and hard eyes staring out impassively beneath thick, forbidding eyebrows. Cordelia was beautiful at his side, her face long and soulful, but serious. There was a sketch of the child. His heart-shaped face cherubic, his eyes wide and innocent. There was an article about the travellers accompanied by a sketch of a man in a cap running away with a bundle, supposedly Felix, wrapped in a blanket in his arms. Olivia found the picture chilling, as well as unfair – if the travellers were innocent, the sketch made them look decidedly guilty.

'To think this happened in our house,' she murmured. 'If I'd known, I might have persuaded Bruce to sell it. I don't think I'd have wanted to move into a house with that sort of history.'

'A terrible tragedy,' Antoinette agreed. 'But it happened a long time ago.'

'It did, but if Pixie is to be believed, Cordelia Pengower is still in the house.'

*

'Ninety-eight ... ninety-nine ... one hundred!' Tabitha took her hands off her eyes and peered about looking for the boy. The sunshine was gradually melting the frost, but scatterings of white lingered in the shadows beneath the trees and the evergreen bushes where the light did not reach. The sun did little to warm the air, which was still bitterly cold. An icy wind whistled through the spindly branches that reached up to the sky, but down where she was, near the ground, all was still. She listened out for him, straining to hear the snap of a twig or the rustle of leaves underfoot. He was so little, she didn't imagine he'd be very good at hiding. But she heard nothing besides the wind and the occasional cawing of a crow. After half an hour, she still hadn't found him and was plodding about wearily. She was tired of the game. It wasn't fun if someone was too good at hiding. She wanted to call out his name but then she remembered that she hadn't asked him what he was called. 'Hello?' she shouted tentatively. Perhaps it had been unwise to play hide-and-seek in a wood like this, that stretched out for miles. He could be anywhere.

She called out again. 'Hello!'

Nothing.

Tabitha hoped he hadn't got lost. She was bored now and wanted to go back and explore the cottage, but she couldn't just leave him.

'I'm going to go now,' she shouted. 'I don't know where you are, and you're obviously in a very clever place, but I can't find you. You have to come out, or I'll just have to leave.' She waited. Nothing. 'Okay, I'm leaving now.' Again, no answer.

Perhaps he'd already gone home. She thrust her hands into her coat pockets and turned back towards the cottage.

If the little boy was still hiding, hopefully he'd get bored soon and come to find her.

Past

CHAPTER ELEVEN

On Monday morning, our French lesson is interrupted by Mr Pengower. He strides into the schoolroom and declares that he wants to take Robert to the chapel to give him a critical lesson on the importance of family and legacy. Robert jumps down from his chair. He delights in his father's attention. I remember what Cordelia said about Felix always being left out and I feel sorry for him. 'I would like you to accompany us, Miss Swift,' Mr Pengower declares. 'I dare say it will be of interest to you, too.'

I put on a bonnet and follow them outside to where the carriage awaits us in the sunshine. The hood is down and two black horses are standing patiently, nodding their heads to fend off the flies. It reminds me of our excursion to the travellers' camp the day before and I hope that Robert doesn't let his mother down by telling his father about it. Excitement is a dangerous thing when one has secrets to keep.

Mr Pengower offers me his hand and I climb in, taking the seat with its back to the horses. I don't mind facing the wrong way, but I sense Mr Pengower would rather face the direction in which we are travelling. Robert sits beside his father. His eyes are dancing with happiness. A movement in one of the upstairs windows draws my attention. It's Felix. He's got his nose pressed against the glass and is watching us with a sad look on his face. I want to tell Mr Pengower to bring him too, but it's not my place. I'm here to observe, not to interfere. But the more I'm drawn into this family's dynamic, the more I want to influence it. I must remain detached.

The carriage drives through the grounds, up the track beneath the plane trees and over the stones and long shadows that are shortening gradually as the sun makes its slow climb up the sky. I sit quietly and take it all in. Robert is asking his father questions, much like those he asked his mother the day before, and I leave them to it and listen to the cheerful twittering of birds and the gentle rustling of leaves as the breeze slips through the branches. It's another hot day and I cool myself with my fan, but it gives little relief. I feel the sweat forming beads on my nose and down my back, beneath the corset. How women can wear these things all day, every day, is unimaginable. They are tight and uncomfortable. I suppose, if I were a Victorian woman, I would get used to it. But I'm not and I won't. I shift on my seat and try not to let the heat get to me. I'm wearing too many layers. If only I could take them all off and sit in my chemise and drawers!

Unlike his brother, Cavill, Mr Pengower does not include me in his conversation. Mr Pengower is a man who is keenly aware of status and of people's places in the world. He doesn't understand our shared humanity, as Cavill and Pascoe Bray do. To him I'm a lesser being because I'm a governess. The gypsies are beneath contempt. The miners are there simply to extract the tin and make him money. He sees not the soul, travelling through life, through many lives, growing and learning from the challenges thrown at it, expanding its inner light. One life a pauper, another a prince. Shakespeare knew: *All the world's a stage and all the men and women merely players*, he wrote so wisely. He knew very well what life was about. But Mr Pengower is limited, narrow-minded, primitive and unenlightened. I wonder what blinkered views he's going to impart to his son this morning. I won't be able to contradict him for even if I wanted to, I don't have time. I have five days left before I wake up from this dream. Robert will carry his father's words in his heart and only life's experience will have the power to wake *him* up to the truth.

When we arrive at the chapel, Mr Grantly jumps down from the box and comes and opens the carriage door. I take his hand and step lightly down. Robert remains close to his father, eager to hear what he has to say. This is a treat for him to spend the morning with his dear papa. But I fear it's going to lead him in the wrong direction, and I won't be around to put it right. I remind myself then that we are not responsible for another's state of consciousness – we only have power over our own.

I follow them towards the gravestones and wonder what Mr Pengower makes of them. Cavill was inspired to seize the day. How will they inspire Mr Pengower?

'Now listen to me, Robert,' he says, stopping in front of his father's six-foot Egyptian stone obelisk. I remember what Cavill said about his father. I wonder what Mr Pengower will say. 'Beneath your feet is the grave of your grandfather, James Pengower. Do you know the one thing that the three of us have in common? James, myself and you, Robert?'

Robert frowns. He wants to give the right answer. I can see it on his face. 'We are Pengowers?' he replies uncertainly.

His father is elated. 'Clever boy! We are all Pengowers. But more than that, we are *firstborn* Pengowers. D'you know what that means?'

'I will inherit St Sidwell,' Robert answers, more confidently now.

Mr Pengower glances at me and smiles, as if I'm somehow responsible for his son's fine mind. 'Very good. Very good,' he exclaims proudly and pats his son's back. Robert puffs out his chest and beams. 'You will inherit St Sidwell, as I did and my father, your grandfather, did before me. St Sidwell was built by a Pengower, and it will remain in the hands of trusty Pengowers for generations to come. But that depends on you, my boy. Being a Pengower comes with great privilege but also great responsibility. It is an important house, and we are an important family, but money is easy to squander, to flit away, to lose by carelessness and stupidity. You must marry a sensible woman like your mother and have sensible sons to ensure it passes into good hands. You must bring your children up wisely as we are bringing you up. St Sidwell must not pass into the hands of strangers. Do you understand that, Robert? Do you understand how very important that is?' I understand that when he speaks of St Sidwell, he does not mean the town, but the house. There is something grandiose about that too.

Robert nods at his father, but how can a child of eight comprehend such a notion? He's but a boy. However, Mr Pengower continues regardless. He's on a roll now and enjoying the sound of his voice and his captive audience. He assumes, quite wrongly, that I'm as riveted as his son. 'One day I will be in the ground like my father. One day, you too will be in the ground, Robert. What will we have left behind? How will people remember us? What will they say? What do we want them to say? I will tell you. They will remember us as being competent caretakers of St Sidwell. *That* is our legacy. *That* is our purpose here on this earth. This house and this land and the fact that we have improved it, preserved it, nurtured it and kept it intact so that it may pass down the line, to another Pengower. On into the future. That is our legacy, yours and mine, dear boy. That is our responsibility and our duty. The Pengowers who built St Sidwell were an eminent family, blessed by God, favoured by the Queen, and envied by many. They watch us from up there.' He raises his eyes to the sky and points with his index finger. His son raises his eyes too. 'They watch to make sure that we are honouring their legacy and ensuring that it continues for many generations to come.' Again, he pats his son on the back. 'There, that is your lesson in family and legacy.'

What a lot of rubbish, I think to myself, and I'm distracted momentarily by a beautiful seabird. It makes me think of Cavill and I wish that he were here. He would dare to put his brother right. He's the only one who can. But I fear Ivan Pengower will listen to no one but the voice of his own ego.

Mr Pengower looks at me and nods approvingly. He believes that I've swallowed his nonsense, but I haven't. He's got it all wrong, every bit of it. We're not here for material gain and social status. However much one cherishes matter, everything in the world dies eventually, even our structures that appear so indestructible. We're here to recognise the eternal, divine part of ourselves, and to grow in love, but Mr Pengower has no interest in something that people can't see and admire. He's only interested in himself and his ego, which is the very thing that keeps him from finding true fulfilment. I look at him, this arrogant man in his fine clothes with his air of entitlement and superiority, and I pity him. I pity him for what is to come. I wonder, after losing his wife and son, whether he'll continue to put all his energy into cherishing his name and his house, or whether he'll come to realise the value of love.

We ride back to the house in the carriage and my mind wanders. I think of Cavill. How very different he is to his older brother. Where Ivan Pengower is unyielding, narrow-minded, weighed down by the enormous responsibility he's placed upon his shoulders, and materialistic, Cavill is compassionate and deep-thinking. Beneath his cheerful, carefree exterior lies a man who has suffered and grown wise from his suffering. How did it become thus? I long to see Cavill. I hope that we'll ride out together this afternoon and that he'll teach me more about the birds he's so passionate about. I crave his lightness after the heaviness of his brother's company.

I turn my eyes to the horizon and sense ever more keenly the rapid expiring of time and with it, the diminishing window of opportunities available to us. My mind tries to find a way around it, like water in a bucket searches for the smallest crack, but our fate is immutable. It can't be changed. The only thing we can do is accept that it's so and make the best with what little time we have.

The carriage draws up in front of the great door and Mr Grantly helps me down. Symons is on the step looking more solemn than usual. 'Mr Bray is waiting to see you in the library, sir,' he says to Mr Pengower. Mr Pengower nods and strides past him into the house. Robert is still in the carriage, disappointed that his outing with his father is over. He gazes at the grand façade of his home, and I wonder whether he's seeing it now in a different light, giving it more importance than it should have.

'Come now, Master Robert,' I call. 'It is almost luncheon.'

Robert jumps down. 'Papa won't be happy to see Mr Bray,' he says.

'How so?' I ask, following him into the dark interior of the house. It takes a moment for my eyes to adjust, for the summer light outside is so bright. It's pleasantly cool in the hall and I want to linger there and recover from the heat. I glide past Symons, who gives me a warning look, as if telling me to mind my own business.

I lift my chin and sail on. What business is it of *his* what I discuss with my charge?

We're in the hall. The grand fireplace is empty, like the black mouth of a calcified beast. Even though the lilies on the table fill the air with their sweet perfume, there's a strange atmosphere. It's as if that dark tentacle has not only slipped beneath the door but has begun to make its way up the stairs. I can feel it. I can feel it sliding over the rug. It brings with it a chill, and I have felt that chill before.

Robert turns to me. 'Listen,' he says, narrowing his eyes.

I cock my ear. I can hear raised voices coming from the library. Mr Pengower and Mr Bray are having an argument. I can't make out the words and, as Symons is loitering close by, I'm unable to move closer. Mr Pengower's voice is more dominant and I sense that, whatever they're arguing about, Mr Pengower will win. I assume he *always* wins.

'Come, Master Robert,' I say, putting my hand on his shoulder. 'Let's go upstairs.'

We set off up the stairs. 'Mr Bray and Papa are always arguing,' says Robert.

I want to ask what they argue about, but I must take care. I must not appear to be seeking gossip. 'They are in business together; there are bound to be things upon which they do not agree,' I reply diplomatically.

'Mr Bray says there is going to be another riot.'

'How do you know that?' I ask.

'Mr Snathe told me.'

'John Snathe? Why does John think there is going to be another riot? When was the last one?'

He shrugs. 'Mr Snathe told me that Papa doesn't treat the miners well and that they are poor and can barely feed their families and that they are going to rise up against Papa.' He looks at me with wide eyes. 'They defiled the gate with paint.'

'Which gate?'

'The front gate.'

'I haven't seen it. What did they write?'

'An eye for an eye.'

I feel cold suddenly. 'An eye for an eye . . .?' Will they take Felix because Ivan Pengower caused the death of one of theirs?

Robert looks frightened suddenly. His eyes widen. He looks like a small boy, not the haughty young man in his father's image. 'Do you think they'll come and riot *here*?'

'At the house? No. You don't need to worry about that. I'm sure Mr Snathe is exaggerating, and, besides, he shouldn't be gossiping with you. It's inappropriate.'

Robert walks on down the corridor. 'Papa will show them. They must know their place,' he says, confident suddenly, and another chill passes over me. It's his father's voice again. The voice of foolishness.

'They are people, Master Robert,' I reply firmly. 'No one should be treated badly, and everyone deserves to be appreciated for the work they do.'

'Papa says they are lucky to *have* work to do. Many people do not.'

I put a hand on his shoulder to deter him. 'Look at me, Master Robert.'

The boy sighs impatiently but does as I say. 'What?' he asks bolshily. The very fact that he's bolshy exposes his unease. Deep down inside he *knows* that he's wrong. But how can one expect an eight-year-old child to question his father?

'My dear Master Robert,' I say, crouching down and holding him gently by his upper arms. 'Life is unfair. We are all born into different circumstances. Some are born into great wealth, some into abject poverty. Some are born to parents who love them, others to parents who care not whether they live or die. Each has their own path to tread. You cannot change those things. They are out of your control. It is pointless to dream to change the world. But you, *you*, Robert, can take care of your own *small* world, right here, right now. You can be kind to those around you. You can smile at people, whoever they are, wherever they come from. Like the sun you can shine indiscriminately upon everyone, as God does. Do you know what will happen then?'

He frowns, trying to take in what I'm telling him. 'What?'

'People will smile back at you.'

He scrunches up his nose. He doesn't care for that.

'You spread kindness around you and kindness will come back to you. Whatever you send out into your little world, will come back to you. Do you understand?' He nods, but he's still frowning. His father's words resonate louder than mine. 'If you spread unhappiness by treating people badly, that will come back to you. It's your choice, every moment of the day, to be either kind or cruel. Whatever you choose to be will come back to you, make no mistake, so choose wisely.'

He looks at me, narrows his eyes and I feel, finally, that I've got through to him. 'I'm hungry,' he says, pulling away. 'Shall we have lunch?'

I find Gwen in the nursery with Felix. She's been crying. Her eyes are pink and her cheeks blotchy. I wonder if it is to do with John Snathe. Felix is sitting at the table, drawing. He's so absorbed in his project that he doesn't even notice me leaning over his shoulder and admiring his picture. It's of a mole. 'That's very good, Felix. I think you might make a fine artist one day.' I stop myself, remembering that 'one day' will never come. The dark tentacle is already making its way up the stairs. Felix's destiny is tracking him down and he can't evade it.

I join them at the table for lunch. Robert sits on the chair beside Felix. I tell Gwen about our trip to the chapel and how lovely it was for Robert to spend time with his father. Felix pauses his sketching. 'I wanted to go,' he says.

'You did not miss anything,' I say to reassure him.

'Robert always goes. I am always left behind. It's not fair,' he complains.

Gwen puts a finger on the paper where his mole is slowly emerging. 'Why don't you give him a pair of spectacles?' she suggests. 'How is he to see without spectacles?'

Felix grins and bends over the paper again. 'Because moles can see in the dark, silly. Like me. I don't need spectacles either.'

Shortly, lunch is brought up to the nursery and we tuck into roast chicken and vegetables. Robert is inspired by his visit to the chapel and can't stop talking about it.

'I will inherit this house one day,' he announces.

'My dear, please wait until you have finished your mouthful before you speak,' I tell him. 'It is not very attractive to see your food being churned about like that.'

'When I am master of this house, no one will tell me what to do.' He looks at me and there's a defiant glint in his eye.

I laugh, not unkindly. 'But while you are a boy, you will be told what to do, because you need to learn how to use your power wisely. If you use it unwisely, you will only end up being very unhappy, and making those around you unhappy too.'

He carries on chewing, and I'm not sure if he's even heard me. I turn to Gwen. 'Are you all right?'

She nods and sniffs. 'It's only a summer cold.' But it doesn't look like a summer cold to me.

After lunch and before I go riding with Robert, Gwen and I have a moment of peace together. Felix is in his bed, having his afternoon sleep, while Robert is having some time to himself, looking through a book of the world.

'You have been crying,' I say, and I reach out and touch her hand. 'You know you have a friend in me, if you need one.'

Gwen takes her hand away and rubs them together in agitation. She pushes out her chair and goes to stand by the window. I wonder whether she's searching for John for the view is of the stable block and I've often watched him loitering there, smoking a cigarette. I join her and can't help but search for Cavill, for I'm certain he'll wait for me to come down with Robert for his riding lesson. How ironic it is that we both have secret flirtations and are looking out for them in the same place.

'Are you crying over a man, Gwen?' I ask quietly.

She turns to me, startled. 'How do you know?'

'I don't know, but I recognise an aching heart when I see one.'

She sighs heavily, as if she's carrying an unbearable weight. She puts a hand on her breast. 'I am, miss . . .'

'Is he worth it, this man?'

She turns her face back to the window. 'Oh, he is, miss. He's worth it, all right.'

At that moment, John saunters out beneath the arch. Gwen catches her breath. He goes and sits on the mounting block and takes out a packet of cigarettes from the pocket of his waistcoat. We both watch as he puts the cigarette between his lips and strikes a match to light it. A few puffs and he's smoking pensively. I wonder if he's thinking of Gwen. 'Is it John Snathe?' I ask.

She thinks about my question a moment, weighing up whether or not to trust me. She decides not to answer directly. 'He's doing well for himself,' she says. 'He'll be promoted one day. He started as a gardener and now he's a groom. Mr Grantly says he'll take over from him when he retires. Shouldn't be too long to wait . . .' Her voice trails off and she frowns. 'Mr Grantly can't go on for ever, can he?'

'No one goes on for ever,' I reply.

She nods. 'Waiting is a woman's lot.' She pulls away from the window.

I continue to watch John. He's making smoke rings with his mouth. I wonder whether he's putting off marrying Gwen by telling her that he can't commit until he's promoted. I imagine he's having his way with her and making promises he never intends to keep. He has an air of deceitfulness and cunning about him, like a rat. I wouldn't trust him to tell me his own name. But there's no point in disclosing my thoughts to Gwen. My opinion means nothing to her, nor should it. Perhaps I'm wrong. I hope that I am.

Chapter Twelve

I change into my riding habit and head out to the stables with Robert. I'm on the point of leaving the house when Cordelia detains me in the hall. 'May I have a word?' she says. She looks worried. Her beautiful face is pale, her blue eyes fearful. I tell Robert to go and ask Mr Grantly to saddle the horses and then follow Cordelia into the drawing room. She closes the door but remains standing there, facing me. 'Miss Swift, I understand Mr Pengower took Master Robert to the chapel this morning.'

'Yes, that is correct,' I reply, surprised. 'I assumed you knew.'

'I did not. Did he mention anything about taking him up to the mine?'

'No, not that I recall.'

Her shoulders relax. 'Good.' She moves away, wringing her hands, and casts her gaze out of the window, at the lake. The sun is reflected on it in a dazzling blaze of fire. 'I am having a terrible time, Miss Swift.' She takes a breath and turns to face me again. 'Mr Pengower and I have such different values, sometimes I wonder how we manage to be together at all.' She shakes her head and gives a mirthless chuckle. 'Mr Bray came by this morning, and they had a terrible row. Mr Bray is worried that the miners are going to kick up again.' Her voice goes quiet, and I have to lean in to hear her words. 'You see, just over a year ago there was an accident, a terrible accident, and seven men were killed. Among them was a young boy. He was only fifteen and he was small, like a child. It was dreadful. Dreadful. They blamed my husband, of course, and they had due cause, for he will not put a penny into it that he does not deem absolutely necessary. The more money he makes, the harder he tries to hold on to it. Those families are terribly poor. But Mr Pengower does not see them as men, but workers, and will happily squeeze every last drop out of them without a thought for their safety and comfort. Without a thought for their families.' She inhales deeply and I can tell from the way she braces her shoulders that she's about to divulge something shocking. 'What my husband doesn't know, Miss Swift, is that I went into town to see the boy's mother. The little mite wasn't yet buried, and they were keeping vigil over his body. I'll never forget the sight of him.' She turns her face once again to the window and lets out a sob, pressing her hand to her mouth to smother it. 'God forgive me.'

'What did she say, the boy's mother, when she saw you?' I ask.

'She said . . .' Cordelia's lips are now white and trembling. 'She said . . . Oh God, I can barely utter those words. She said, "I curse Ivan Pengower and his bloodline, that they and their house may be dogged by unhappiness. That tragedy will follow them like a shadow and not release them, so they know what it is to suffer loss."' A shiny tear trickles down her face. She looks at me with desperate eyes and two red stains blossom on her cheeks. 'She cursed us, Miss Swift.'

'They are only words, Mrs Pengower. They will do no harm if you do not believe them.'

She frowns, not understanding that words have no power if they're not accepted as truth. They are just dead sounds; it's her belief that gives them life. 'I feel responsible for that family now. The accident was nothing to do with me, but, nonetheless, I feel guilty and want to help them. There is nothing in the world that is more dreadful than the loss of a child; I cannot imagine the pain that poor woman has to endure.' Cordelia puts a hand on her breast, and I can't help but notice the terrible irony. 'Perhaps I am oversensitive, but there is a small hope in my heart that if I can somehow alleviate that woman's suffering, the suffering of her community, then the curse will not hold. That it will not happen. That we won't suffer loss.' She turns and looks at me steadily. 'Now you see why I am worried about Ivan taking Master Robert up to the mine. I am afraid for his safety.'

I want to tell her that it is not Robert's but Felix's safety that she needs to be concerned about.

'Master Robert will be safe with his father,' I reassure her, but she shakes her head.

'He is not safe with his father. Those men are angry. There is no telling what they will do. Only this morning Mr Bray was trying to convince my husband to give them more pay, to decrease their working hours and to ensure the safety of the mine. Dear Mr Bray, he tries so hard. But my husband will not listen. He does not want to hear it. Once, he was grateful for Mr Bray's advice and they were as close as brothers, but since the accident last year Mr Pengower and he have been at loggerheads. My husband won't admit his guilt and digs his heels in. He cannot admit that the accident was his fault. Every time he looks at Mr Bray, he sees condemnation. Every time Mr Bray reports on the morale of the men or the danger in the tunnels, Mr Pengower feels resentment, rather than a duty of care to those who work for him. It is terrible. But what can I do? I am a tiny voice in a storm. Mr Pengower will not listen to me. Now he wants to show Master Robert his inheritance. He says he needs to know that when he dies, his son will continue in his footsteps. It is absurd, the boy is but a child. He understands nothing.'

'What can I do to help?'

She comes to me and takes my hands. 'You have already helped, by listening.' She manages a wan smile and steadily holds my gaze. 'Thank you for that, and for looking after my boy. But you can tell me if he takes him to the mine. I suspect he will do it without my consent, even though he knows how much I am against it.' Then, in a small voice, she adds, 'And thank you for being a friend to me, Miss Swift. I cannot tell you how much I am in dire need of one.'

I find Robert waiting for me in the stable yard. He's already mounted. Beside him is Cavill. He's waiting for me too. When he sees me, he smiles and lifts his hat in salutation. I smile back, thrilled that he's decided to join us again. Grateful to be close to him once

more. Mr Grantly leads my horse to the mounting block, and I
settle myself into the saddle and arrange my skirts so that they fall
prettily over my legs. I'm getting the hang of this now. We set off up
the track and through the woods. Beams of sunshine fall through
the canopy of leaves and every now and then the sun itself dazzles
in between the branches. Birdsong fills the air, which is alive with
midges. Their tiny wings catch the light and glint like fireflies. The
wood is so beautiful, like a temple with trees for pillars. The waxy
petals of the pink and red rhododendrons have opened, and bees
and butterflies settle upon the purple, cone-shaped buddleia flowers. Cow parsley grows among foxgloves, ferns and red campion,
and the smell is woody and sensual. My horse walks beside Cavill's
while Robert rides ahead; he's keen to get to the beach. Cavill tells
me that tomorrow we shall picnic there for his mother's birthday.
'It is tradition,' he tells me. 'Every year since I was a boy, we have
enjoyed a picnic on the beach for her birthday. I do not recall a
single one of those days where it rained.'

'Your mother is surely blessed,' I say.

'She is, indeed. I believe tomorrow will be a special day for us
all.' He looks at me and there's an intimacy in the way he holds my
eyes. I feel myself opening like one of those rhododendron flowers.
It's an intoxicating feeling to be so admired, and a novel one I don't
think I'll ever get used to.

'I look forward to it,' I reply. But the truth is that I do not. I will
be one day closer to losing him. One day closer to losing Felix. One
day closer to returning to my world. And I don't want to go.

The sea comes into view, a glittering blue line meeting the sky
on the distant horizon. There's something stirring about that sight.
A sense of infinity, of the bigger picture, of God. It reminds me
of where I come from and where I'm going, not from an earthly
perspective, but from a spiritual one. The beauty of it touches me
in that deep and silent place at my very core and moves me. I don't
know why it makes me sad. Why beauty makes me sad. Perhaps
it's because our human lives are transient and that one day all of us
will have to say good-bye.

We make our way down a sandy path in single file towards a

sheltered cove. I can smell the sea in the breeze that caresses my face like the softest silk. It roars as the waves crash against the rocks at the far end. The giant body of water swells and subsides, is forever moving, corroding the land, slowly expanding, and I'm filled with excitement at the sense of drama it evokes. Robert, too, is excited and asks if he can roll up his trousers and put his feet in the surf.

We tether the horses to a rock and Robert takes off his boots and runs down the sand. Cavill and I set off at a gentle pace. 'Hermione,' he says softly, brushing my hand with his as we walk side by side along the beach.

I glance at him and return his smile. I can feel the light dancing in my eyes. 'Cavill,' I say, and the word feels delicious on my lips.

'I have a confession to make,' he begins.

'Oh, how bad is it?' I ask.

'It is bad,' he replies, but I can tell from the humorous lines around his eyes and mouth that he's playing with me.

I laugh. 'Then what is it?'

He stops walking and settles his eyes upon me, a serious expression on his face. 'I am falling in love with you,' he says solemnly.

I catch my breath. That is, indeed, quite a confession. 'Oh, Cavill . . .'

'I think I fell in love with you the first time I laid eyes on you at the bottom of the stairs.'

'When I thought you were the master of the house,' I remind him.

'I'm glad that I am *not* the master of the house, for then I could not marry you.' He glances at Robert, who's playing in the water, kicking it with his feet, giggling as the waves charge at him, one after the other.

'Marry me?' I repeat, astonished. We haven't even kissed yet. Really, he barely knows me.

'Say you will.'

I'm aware that in these times people marry quickly, often scarcely knowing each other at all. Indeed, most marriages are arranged. So for Cavill, this is normal. For me, however, this sudden proposal is incredibly fast, and, of course, impossible to accept, for I shall soon be gone. I want to yield. But I think of the real Hermione Swift and the mess I'm creating for her once I've slipped back. When she wakes up, she'll remember nothing of this. I can't commit her to something she might not want, even though *I* want nothing more than to throw myself into his arms.

'You scarcely know me, Cavill,' I protest.

He gazes at me raptly, as if he's probing beyond into the deep part of me. The deepest part of me. 'For what do I need time when what I feel for you is timeless?' he asks.

That word 'timeless' reaches the craving in my soul and I feel, suddenly, that longed-for connection satisfied at last. I feel the stinging of tears behind my eyes because I know that I will never feel such a connection in my own life. That it is the kind of thing that happens but once and I'm full of sadness that it is happening now, for I cannot keep it.

His brow creases with a frown. 'Do you not feel it too, Hermione? A bond, a knowing that renders history and biography trivial? Anyone can see that you are beautiful. That you are intelligent and charming. That you are well educated. If they are observant, they can also see that you are original and spirited and, dare I say it, mischievous. But they won't feel what I feel. They do not understand you like I do, with the heart.'

'Do they not?' I ask.

His eyes soften and he looks on me with tenderness. 'I think you want adventure like I do, Hermione. I think you want more than what this world has to offer you. I think that, beneath the veneer, there is something original in you that is yet to be expressed – you just need to be given the opportunity to be yourself.'

I'm astonished. 'You see all that in me?' I say. And I wonder, is it possible that he sees Pixie beneath the veneer?

'I want to be the man to allow you to express it. I want *you* to be the woman to allow me to express the original and creative in *me*. You see, I feel I am the best of men when I am with you. I feel uplifted. Inspired. With your love I can achieve anything, be anyone, do anything, whatever my imagination can conjure up. I am an eagle, and you are the wind rising beneath me and elevating me. I want to be the wind that elevates *you*.'

'That's a lovely image,' I say, touched. No one has ever spoken to me like this before. No one has ever looked at me like this before, with such sincerity and affection.

'When I come back from the Argentine, I will marry you, Hermione,' he continues, gazing at me with fierce intention, and I believe him. I believe every word, despite the fact that it can never happen. 'I will come home a rich man and we will start our life together. We'll soar high together like two magnificent birds.'

'You have known me but six days, Cavill,' I say, even though I feel I have known him six years. 'You might discover that I am not the woman you think I am.'

'I know my heart.' He frowns, apprehensive suddenly, and looks at me searchingly. 'Do *you* know *yours*?'

'I need time,' I tell him. 'You must give me that.'

He smiles again, a little sadly. 'Very well. If that is what you want. I'll give you anything. The whole world.' He glances again at Robert, who is now facing out to sea. Cavill takes my hand. He turns it over and caresses with his thumb the place where the skin is exposed between my glove and sleeve. Then he presses his lips there. They are warm and soft. For a moment I feel as if I might swoon. 'Dear Hermione of my heart,' he whispers.

'Oh, Cavill . . .' I look into his eyes and sink further into the dream. I search frantically for an argument to support my desire, and then I seize upon one. Does it matter if I allow this romance to flower? After all, Hermione will never know Cavill. He leaves for South America and never comes back. If I indulge myself, no one but me will remember it.

He lets go of my hand then and I'm aware of Robert, now staring at us with a bewildered look on his face. I hold my wrist against my breast, and we continue to walk, this time towards the child.

'When are you planning on leaving for South America?' I ask. It dawns on me then that the swiftness of his pursuit of me must be due to a lack of time on his part.

'I depart for Portsmouth this Friday,' he says, and the joy is suddenly sucked out of the air. I feel despondent, as if the world around me has lost its lustre. The sun retreats behind a cloud and the beach falls into shade. 'Don't look sad, my darling. The sooner I leave, the sooner I will come back and the sooner we will marry.'

I'm shaken out of my stupor as I realise how futile those words are. We can never marry. He thinks he's going to Argentina, but he will never reach it. He can't know that, and I can't tell him. There's much that I can't tell him. Oh, if only I could warn him of what is to come, but that's not the way it works. I cannot warn him of his own misfortune, any more than I can warn him of Felix's. I can do nothing but watch as the drama plays itself out. But I can try, as best I can, to help that poor soul who is stuck in her pain, to let it go. That's what I'm here for. I mustn't forget. I must not fail. Cordelia Pengower is relying on me, and she doesn't even know it.

I am not here to rescue Cavill.

Robert calls to us, and we watch him jump and splash and play. He wants our attention and although we wish we were alone, we do our duty and clap and laugh and give praise. The wind picks up and ruffles my skirt, in fact it nearly robs me of my hat. The clouds thicken and move ever more swiftly across the sky. The sea darkens, the air grows heavy and sticky. We decide to make our way back. Cavill looks at his pocket watch. It's nearly four. I can't believe we've been on the beach for that long. I forgot myself. How easy it is in Cavill's presence to forget myself and what I'm here to do.

We ride back to St Sidwell Manor. Cavill is full of cheer because he believes I will marry him. After all, I haven't said that I won't. I've just asked for him to give me time. He encourages Robert to lead the way so that we can talk, but I'm pensive and taciturn. He looks at me inquisitively, but I cannot explain what I feel. What's in my heart. All I can do is reach out and give him my hand.

That evening, it is just the four of us at dinner. Mr Pengower is in a surprisingly good mood. In spite of the argument he had this morning with Mr Bray, he's full of bonhomie. He drinks his whisky and tells anecdotes that both his wife and Cavill have obviously heard before. But they indulge him with laughter and encourage him to tell more, because it's a rare boon to see him so cheerful. He's certainly charismatic when he allows himself to shine. When he's cross, his mood affects the whole house and pulls the energy down so that you feel as if you're languishing in shadow. Now he's happy, we're all infected by a sense of optimism and joy. I watch Cordelia. She appears to have shed her anxiety and is looking at her husband with a serene expression on her lovely face. However, I now know her serenity to be a mask, concealing a seething resentment beneath. She has a public face and a private face, and the two are very different. Perhaps tonight she will leave the house by the secret passage. Maybe the anticipation of a moment's solitude on the bench is the reason for her tranquillity.

The anticipation of that is a reason, too, for my heightened alertness.

After dinner, Mr Pengower is seeking entertainment. We move into the drawing room and he settles his eyes on me like an eagle on a mouse and asks whether I might recite a poem. 'Yes, Miss Swift, a verse or two of Tennyson or Browning.' No one is suggesting I play the piano.

'Perhaps I can read one of your favourites,' I suggest hopefully. I really don't know any poems, at least, not off by heart. I'm also aware of the real Hermione Swift, who is very likely well educated in the reciting of verse.

'The children enjoy Edward Lear,' says Cordelia. 'That wonderfully fanciful poem about a pussy-cat sailing to sea in a pea-green boat.'

'And hand in hand, on the edge of the sand, they danced by the light of the moon, the moon, they danced by the light of the moon,' Cavill recites with a chuckle. 'Surely, you know that one, Miss Swift?'

I've never heard of Edward Lear. 'Of course,' I reply, laughing lightly as if I, too, find his poems hilarious. I lift my chin and look directly at Cavill. 'Would you like to hear *The King's Breakfast*?' I ask. There is nothing for it. I must distract them at once from finding out how ignorant I am. I had to learn A A Milne's classic at school and recite it in front of the class. I entertained my class-mates then, by putting on all the voices – I hope I can entertain the Pengowers now in the same way. If I'm going to do it, I might as well do it properly.

Cavill frowns. '*The King's Breakfast*? I have not heard of that one.'

'Who wrote it?' asks Mr Pengower.

'I did,' I lie. In my time it's a famous poem that everyone knows.

'Oh, how lovely,' Cordelia exclaims happily. 'I should so like to hear a poem that *you* have written, Miss Swift.'

'How very accomplished you are,' says Cavill. He has an amused look on his face as if he's expecting another bizarre performance and is impatient to hear it.

I take a breath.

'Stand up, Miss Swift, so we can all see you,' Mr Pengower in-terrupts. 'If this poem is composed by you, then we would like to see you perform it appropriately.' He laughs, no doubt thinking back to my rendition on the piano as his brother is doing. 'I did not take you for a poet.'

Reluctantly, I stand on the rug in front of the fireplace and ar-range my skirts. I hope I don't forget any lines. It's been a long time. I sweep my eyes over the expectant faces and silently tell myself to be brave. I take another deep breath and then deliver the poem. Rather than the bewildered expressions I received for my piano playing, I'm surprised to find my audience laughing with merriment. Encouraged by their enjoyment I ham it up even more. I put on the posh, high-pitched voice of the Queen, the low, whin-ing voice of the King and the cockney accent of the Dairymaid. By the time I finish with the King's plaintive final line, Cavill is wiping a tear from beneath his eye, Cordelia is pressing a hand to her belly and even Mr Pengower is chuckling.

'A triumph, Miss Swift. A triumph,' cries Mr Pengower in de-light. 'You are quite the poet, after all.'

'And the entertainer,' adds Cavill. 'Why listen to Tennyson or Browning when we can listen to Swift?'

'You would do well on the stage,' says Cordelia, fanning her face that's flushed from laughing.

'Thank you.' I feel mildly guilty for having stolen A A Milne's work. 'I am glad you enjoyed it. Just a little poem I wrote for children.'

'You must write poems for ours,' Cordelia suggests. 'Isn't it wonderful, to have our very own poet in the house?'

It's not yet dark when Cordelia retires to her room. It's only nine thirty, too early to take up my vigil in the library. I tell her that I'm going to stroll around the garden. It's a lovely evening and I need to keep myself occupied. The pink light of dusk is gradually subsiding, and a purple twilight is creeping up over the lawn. I know that Cavill would like to walk with me, and I wish that he would, but his brother wants to smoke a cigar and he doesn't want to do it alone. He's had one too many glasses of whisky and is a little unsteady on his feet. I can feel Cavill's eyes upon me as I leave the room. I know that he wishes he could follow me. 'Well, my dear Cavill, what do you think about . . .' Their voices grow faint as I walk through the hall.

I wrap a shawl around my shoulders and leave by the back door. I set out over the grass. I can feel the moisture in the air and the dew settling on the ground at my feet. The scents of the garden rise to fill the night with a sweet perfume and I inhale it greedily. Love renders everything more beautiful and tonight the beauty reaches every corner of my being. I walk past the stable and once again see that lone light in the upstairs window. I wonder whether John Snathe is climbing the drainpipe into Gwen's bedroom and what the consequence of that might be. But I'm intoxicated with a desire of my own and I don't waste time thinking about Gwen Blight. I think only of Cavill and hope that he might follow me into the garden after all.

One by one the stars shine above me as the sky deepens to a rich blue. An owl hoots in the woods and its mate hoots back. There are rustlings and scratchings of nocturnal animals prowling about in the undergrowth. I have always loved the night. It's secretive, soft, mysterious and alluring. The moon sets the garden into eerie relief, accentuating the shadows, bringing the trees and shrubs into a watery silver light, and it's magical. I want to dance, to spread out my arms like wings and to twirl round and round in my own secret ball. I want to lie on my back on the grass and gaze up at the heavens and see only the velvet darkness and the pinpricks that twinkle and shine from stars that have perhaps already died. I want to think about Cavill and, with the power of my mind, draw him to me. Here in this garden. Now.

I sense then the presence of someone behind me. I turn to see Cavill's familiar silhouette walking towards me across the lawn. He puts out his arms and I run into them. And I think not about the little time we have. I press my face to his shoulder and close my eyes and feel the vibration of the beating heart beneath. That's all that matters. The now.

'You are wonderful,' he says. 'There is no one in the world like you.' He looks at me through the darkness and I feel as if he's look-ing straight through me, right into my innermost being – to me, Pixie, beneath the exterior that belongs to someone else. He rests his hand against my cheek. His thumb gently traces my chin. And then he bends down and places his lips upon mine. He parts them gently and kisses me.

Hermione Swift floats across my mind followed by the shadow of guilt, which I am quick to dismiss. Cavill leaves for South America on Friday and will never return. Hermione will awake and know nothing of what she has done. No one will know but me. I can in-dulge in this beautiful fantasy confident that it is all mine.

I think no more of Hermione Swift, or Cordelia Pengower, or even Felix. In this moment it's only me and Cavill and the dream is real. At least for now.

I yield at last. My body sinks against his and I close my eyes and kiss him back.

But our time together is limited. Symons will shortly lock the door and I have a job to do that requires my fullest attention. Re-gretfully, we separate. We walk back to the house side by side but without touching. It is agony to have to be so discreet. All I want is to feel his hand in mine. To feel his touch. We enter the house and cross the hall, feigning formality in our manners and speech so as not to give ourselves away in the likely event that we are being watched. We part on the landing. We cannot even say goodnight with a kiss. I hear Symons' key in the lock and then the hall is plunged into darkness.

I wait in my room until midnight, replaying the kiss over and over in my mind. I trace my lips with the tips of my fingers, barely believing that it really happened. Barely believing that I allowed it to happen. But now it has, I want more.

At the sound of the clock chiming midnight, I steal down to the library as before and take up my position behind the curtain. The moon is high in the sky, presiding over the heavens with her dispassionate gaze. She shines her eerie light on the garden and I wonder what she sees out there in the night. Will Cordelia sneak out into the vegetable garden and take up her solitary communion on the bench beneath the stars? Will she find peace away from the growing tensions in the house? Or will they find her there in the shape of dark thoughts and fears that cannot be ignored? Will God give her the strength she craves?

My heart is fretful, my senses alert. I'm certain that she'll come. The clock chimes one o'clock and then a faint glow lights up the doorway. I hold my breath. Through the crack in the curtain I see Cordelia. She glides in swiftly and goes straight to the bookcase. She puts her hand on one of the shelves, at the height of her shoulder, and pulls something there. At once, the concealed door springs open. With a deftness that comes from practice, she eases it wider and slips through the gap. She descends a couple of steps, turns and closes the door behind her.

I give her a few minutes and then light my lamp and go to the bookcase to see if I can open it myself. Holding the lamp high I run my fingers over the wooden rib of the shelf. There's nothing there for me to pull. At least, I can't find it. Frustrated, I push and pull everything within my reach.

Then I notice letters engraved onto the surface of those ribs. I hold the light closer. To my amazement there is a quote from the bible carved into the wood. *Suffer the little children, and forbid them not, to come unto me.* They are the same words as the ones written in gold on the wall of the chapel. But this sentence has an additional phrase that the one in the chapel doesn't have. *Forbid them not.* Why would it be different?

I put my fingers there and feel a little ridge running along the surface beneath the spines of the books. It's subtle but unmistakeable. I clasp the shelf and pull. It's a secret lever. With a soft click the door pops out.

Present

Chapter Thirteen

Tabitha had been walking back to the cottage for a good fifteen minutes when she heard the sound of someone approaching through the trees. Relieved, she turned around, expecting to see the little boy. Instead, she saw Daphne, trotting in her ungainly manner over the frosted ground towards her. Weren't St Bernards trained to find people in the snow? Tabitha thought as she reached out to pat her. The dog leant against her legs, panting puffs of foggy breath into the icy air. If anyone could find the boy, Tabitha reasoned, Daphne could.

'Come on,' she said, and set off again with Daphne following keenly behind. The dog stopped every now and then to thrust her big nose into a shrub, occasionally putting up the odd partridge and watching in wonder as it flapped its wings and took to the air in clumsy flight. Tabitha called out, but not even the echo of her own voice responded. She was beginning to think that the boy must have gone home and was put out that he hadn't told her. There were certain codes to games like hide-and-seek, and he hadn't observed the most fundamental of them.

Shortly, the sun slipped behind a cloud and the wood was plunged into a gloomy half-light. The shadows vanished and a strange mist gathered around the tree trunks, floating above the grass like shrouded spectres. Tabitha wasn't afraid. There was something magical about the sight, as if a strange enchantment was falling over the wood. As if she had unwittingly stepped onto sanctified ground. She stopped calling, understanding instinctively not to disturb the hush. Daphne stayed close by her side, no longer interested in the smells of rabbit and fox, but sniffing in the air a scent she did not recognise. Then she stopped and refused to go any further. Tabitha stopped also. They stood, the two of them, in the midst of the gathering fog.

This part of the wood was quiet. No birds sang, even the pheasants and crows were silent. There was no flash of hare diving into the undergrowth or deer darting into the thicket. It was as if no living creature dared come to this place. Tabitha stood beside Daphne and put a hand on her back. They remained very still, and alert, for something was about to happen. They both felt it.

Then the boy appeared. He was no longer smiling and playful but concerned. For a child he wore an oddly grown-up expression and Tabitha was reminded of her father and the way his face darkened when he was worried. It had darkened the time she and Zach had been on a big wheel at a fairground and something had gone wrong, leaving them stranded high above the ground. The boy looked like that now, as if he knew that she was in danger.

'You mustn't come here,' he said gravely. 'It isn't safe.'

'Where were you?' Tabitha asked. 'I've been looking for you for ages.'

'Here,' he said. He gave a shrug. 'I'm always here.'

'What is this place?'

He gazed at her with big eyes, sad suddenly and old, the eyes of a very old man. 'You must go.'

'Shouldn't you go too? Isn't your mother worried about you?'

The light faded and with it the boy seemed to fade too, as if he was merging with the trees. 'Who are you?' Tabitha asked.

'Felix,' he replied.

Then he was gone.

Past

Chapter Fourteen

After I watch Cordelia leave through the priest hole, I return to my bedroom. I lie in bed, but I can't for the life of me sleep. My heart is a frantic cricket, throwing itself against my ribcage. I am certain that Felix is spirited away through the priest hole in the library. It's the only way anyone can come in or out of the house besides using the doors or windows, which are always locked at that hour, and I have no reason to suspect Mr Pengower or Symons who are the only people to hold keys. I'd like to know who else is aware of the priest hole besides Cordelia. Might one of the groundsmen know of it? Has someone gossiped in the pub in town, or been overheard talking about it? I'm pretty sure now that whoever takes the child, does so by that route. But who can it be and why?

I must have drifted to sleep eventually because I wake up and it's dawn. I begin my daily routine of washing myself with the jug of water and china basin as if on autopilot. I'm getting a little sick of living this way. It was a novelty at the beginning, but now I'm missing things I usually take for granted, like electricity, a hairdryer, shampoo and conditioner, an electric toothbrush, pants, a pair of jeans and a T-shirt. What I would give for some chocolate raisins!

I put on my chemise and corset and marvel at how quickly one gets used to things that were at first strange. Everything about this world was strange when I first found myself in it. But now it doesn't feel strange at all, and I don't feel like a stranger any longer; I feel as if I belong. But I don't belong, and I mustn't forget that. I shake my head and try to get this voice out of my mind. It is not mine.

I have been here seven days, but the present seems very far away, like another universe, and I am aware that I am beginning to think like Hermione Swift. I am sinking into this dimension and immersing myself in it to such an extent that I am forgetting who I am. If I am not careful, I will get lost. I will get lost in the dream.

I say every swear word I can think of out loud to connect me to my world, to who I really am. I stare at myself in the mirror and repeat them many times. No Victorian lady would ever be so vulgar.

I pull my skirt over my head and fasten it at the waist. I'm used to the mode of dress now, the chemise and corset, the drawers and stockings and the lace-up boots. I'm used to the smell of gas lamps and the golden quality of the candlelight, and I no longer reach for the light switch and find nothing but the wall. I'm used to the way they speak and to the formal way they interact. I'm even used to being Hermione Swift and speaking like her. But in five days I will have to give her up and be myself again. Me, Pixie. Pixie Tate.

I wonder whether Gwen and John Snathe have had a fight. Her eyes are pink from crying, and there's a shifty look about them, for she doesn't meet mine but fusses unnecessarily about Felix so that she does not have to look at me directly. I ask her how she's feeling, and she gives me her usual answer: tired. However, Felix makes her smile. He has the power to drag her out of her pessimistic thoughts, for she truly loves him and every little thing he does delights her. I suggest she take him into the garden to play hide-and-seek. I tell her that the fresh air will do them both good. She nods in agreement. Hide-and-seek, she tells me, is his favourite game.

I see them a little later from the window of the schoolroom where I'm teaching Robert his French lessons. They are at the stables. John Snathe is picking up Felix and putting him on a pony. The pony has no saddle, but Felix is secure there in the curve of its back. He grabs its mane and John leads the pony slowly around the yard. Gwen walks along beside them, telling Felix to hold on tightly, but the boy is fearless and doesn't appear at all anxious. They are laughing. Gwen is no longer tired or upset so I imagine they've made up. From where I'm standing the three of them look like a family. It's a heartwarming sight, for they're enjoying themselves immensely. I wish that John would give Gwen what she wants and ask her to marry him without delay. But I don't imagine his intentions are honourable. I sense he's exploiting her naïvety for his own gratification.

That afternoon, we set off to celebrate Mrs James's birthday on the beach. Mr Grantly brings the carriage round to the front of the house for Mr and Mrs Pengower, Cavill and Robert. John comes with the pony and trap for Gwen, Felix and me. Symons has gone on ahead with Mr Roskelley the valet, and Rose the housemaid, to set up the picnic. Mrs Moyle has baked cakes and made meat pies for the men, who are always hungry. It's another hot day, in spite of the wind. I wonder when this streak of unusually hot weather will break. The air seems to be getting thicker with every day that passes. I know it will eventually collapse into a storm. But when?

A few clouds waft across the sky but the sun is fierce, and we open our parasols so that it doesn't burn our skin. Cordelia is in a powder-blue dress with a matching hat adorned with white flowers. Beneath her hat her flaxen hair is curled and pinned, which emphasises the angles of her lovely face. Her parasol is the same colour as her dress and must have been made especially. She's as pretty as a picture, sitting in the carriage with the top down, shading herself from the sun. She smiles at Cavill and then laughs at something Mr Pengower says, and the atmosphere is jolly and carefree. Once again my thoughts are pulled into the darkness, which is closing in on this merry family scene. They do not know that shortly the sun will go out and their summer will be over, and every summer after that. I glance at Gwen, who is sitting between myself and John up on the box. Her eyes are no longer stained with tears. She is cheerful, as well she might be. Although she and John are both careful not to give away their secret, it is obvious to me, in every peal of laughter and gentle teasing.

I turn my eyes away and watch the countryside, focusing on the light and keeping my thoughts away from the shadow. It is a curse to know and to be prevented from doing anything with that knowledge. It is better to be like them, blissful in their ignorance.

Today I intend to advance my friendship with Cordelia. The better I get to know her now, the more equipped I will be in the future to encourage her to move on. I will hopefully discover what happens to Felix; that shouldn't be hard. I know the night. I will simply lie in wait and see who shows up. I will enlighten her to his fate, but I sense it will take more than simply giving her the information to get her to leave St Sidwell and cross over into the light. She's a mother whose son is stolen right out of her nest. It's natural that she will blame herself.

The ride is pleasant. Felix sits on Gwen's knee and points out the things that thrill him. He's a curious child, delighted by everything. He loves the sheep, who graze in the fields, the donkeys that nod at us over the fence, and the seagulls that circle above, hoping for scraps upon which to feast.

We arrive at the beach and Mr Grantly and John pull up the horses on the sand dunes a short distance from where the picnic is laid out, further down the beach in the shelter of rocks. Mrs James's carriage is already here, and her footman waits with it. Down on the beach I can see Mr Bray, in a straw hat and white jacket, attending her.

Robert and Felix run on ahead, while Cavill offers me his arm so that I do not trip on the dunes. I slip my hand around his sleeve and take the opportunity to lean my body against his. I'm certain that the energy between us is plain for everyone to see, but no one pays us any attention. Cordelia walks in front of us with Mr Pengower. There is a jaunty swish in her gait that reveals her happiness. She has clearly forgotten her concerns of the day before or she is burying them. I glance back to see Gwen talking to John. They are hidden from Mr Grantly's keen eye by the pony that stands conveniently between them. John sweeps a tendril of hair off her face. I look away. It's nice to see Gwen so much happier than she was this morning. Right now, in this moment, we are all happy. I focus on that and try not to be drawn into the tragedy that is imminent and unavoidable.

We reach the rocks where the picnic has been set up. Symons and his two helpers have put out four folding chairs, a large parasol, and spread blankets upon the ground. The picnic baskets are open. There's enough food for a banquet: lobster, fish, meats, bread and goodness knows what else. The children, like gulls, hover about the cakes, but Gwen hurries down to shoo them away. She takes Felix's hand and leads him to the water to paddle. Robert goes with them. I notice a scrawny dog in the distance, sniffing about the sand. There doesn't appear to be anyone with it, so I assume that it's a stray. Perhaps it will come over and we can offer it some of our leftovers.

I greet Mrs James, who smiles sweetly and thanks me for wishing her a happy birthday. 'Every year I go *down* a number, not up,' she says, blue eyes gleaming with mischief. 'That was a decision I made a long time ago, so really, I am in my prime.' Everyone laughs, for her girlish delight is winning.

I greet Mr Bray and he bows formally. We don't speak for long for he is quick to turn to Cordelia and offer his hand so that she can sit down beside her mother-in-law. Mr Pengower takes the third chair beside his mother. Mr Bray offers me the fourth, but I don't accept it. 'Thank you very much, Mr Bray, but I am perfectly content sitting on the blanket,' I reply, and watch him sit on Cordelia's right. She turns to him and smiles softly, and they engage in quiet conversation. I am pleased that there is nowhere else for me to go, but to join Cavill on the blanket. We are immediately separated into two groups. The four on the chairs and the two of us on the blanket. Symons passes around drinks while Rose and Mr Roskelley serve the food. I notice that I am served last and with a certain derision, as if they are keen for me not to forget my place. If they were not beneath the gazes of Cordelia and Cavill, I'm sure they would leave me to help myself.

Gwen returns with the children and my conversation with Cavill has to be curtailed. She plonks herself on a rock a short distance from where we are seated and forms a third group with Robert and Felix. Cordelia is deep in conversation with Mr Bray. As we eat, gulls begin to drop onto the sand nearby. The children find much amusement in them, for their beady black eyes are on the fish and they are determined to steal one. Every now and then Symons shoos them away and they flap their wings and rise a few feet, before dropping a little further down the beach. Gradually they edge their way back, only to be shooed away again. Felix thinks this is tremendous fun. When he has finished eating, he jumps up and rushes at them with his arms outstretched. They are not afraid of him and only bounce out of his reach. Felix bubbles with laughter and does not tire of the game. Neither do the birds.

We finish our meal and sit chatting in the sun. A peaceful languor falls over the group. It is mid-afternoon. The sun has turned mellow, and a softness has settled over the sea. Silver spangles jump and dance on the water. The gentle rhythm of the waves breaking onto the beach is hypnotic. Slowly the tide inches its way out, leaving small creatures in the sand for the birds, who turn their attention away from the picnic, which does not reward them so well as the sea.

Cavill lowers his voice. 'I enjoyed meeting you in the garden last night,' he says, and he furtively brushes my hand with his little finger.

I glance at Cordelia and then at Gwen. They are neither listening to us nor watching us. Cordelia is engrossed in the conversation she is having with Mr Bray and Mr Pengower is talking to his mother.

'I enjoyed meeting you, too,' I whisper back.

'Did you go out on purpose, just so that I could follow you?'

I smile coyly. 'Perhaps.'

He smiles too and holds my gaze with his. 'I was hoping that was the case.'

'It is not easy to be alone together, is it?' I say. 'Maybe the garden at night is the only place we can meet safely without being caught.'

'If I may be so bold, Hermione.' He shifts his eyes to the four chairs, then back to me. His voice is so quiet I have to lean in to hear. 'Might I find you in your room?'

I catch my breath and glance once again at the others. They are now discussing a scandal. Cordelia looks positively appalled. Her mother-in-law simply laughs as if she has heard it all before. She appears not to be the sort of woman who is easily shocked. 'You may,' I reply, and the thought of him coming to my room gives me such a strong feeling of desire that I have to turn my face to the water so that the others do not see me blushing. In a moment of awareness, I chuckle inwardly at myself. How far I have sunk into this reality that I blush at the mere suggestion of intimacy. I would never blush at such a suggestion in the present. I realise that I'm turning into a proper Victorian woman and losing myself in the process.

We continue to talk in this way. I forget where I am and who I am with and withdraw into a bubble where it is just me and Cavill, removed from the world, absorbed in each other. His voice is sweet in my ears, his scent powerful in my nostrils; even his eyes give the sensation of caresses upon my skin. I am consumed by him, until, suddenly, Cordelia speaks, and the bubble is burst.

'Where is Felix?'

I'm brought back to my senses with a jolt. I turn to Gwen. She clearly nodded off because she's blinking furiously and looking around her as if she, too, has been far away and is reminded now of where she is. We all look about for Felix. Robert is contentedly playing beside a rockpool a short way off. I scan the surf. Felix is not there. Gwen scrambles to her feet. It does not take long for panic to set in.

I am panicked. I question whether I somehow got the date of his disappearance wrong. Could it be that he disappears today, never to be seen again? Have I missed my moment? Was I so distracted by Cavill that I failed to watch Felix? But I never expected him to vanish here. Not with Gwen and his parents nearby.

I feel guilty because I should have been keeping an eye on him too. He's Gwen's responsibility, of course, but I'm also employed to look after the children. I put a hand to my chest and take a deep breath. Have I failed them? Have I failed Cordelia Pengower? The emotion rises into my throat and squeezes it hard. I kick myself for indulging in a romance when I should have been doing my job.

Cavill looks at me, his face grave. 'Come, let us scour the beach.' I lift my skirts and follow his long strides over the sand. Mr and Mrs Pengower and Mr Bray are setting off too in search of the

child. 'I will never forgive myself if he has got lost,' I say as I struggle to keep up with Cavill.

'He will be somewhere. Children don't simply vanish,' he says,
but he does not know what I know.

We head towards the sea.

'He was chasing seagulls when I last saw him,' I say, trying to be
helpful. Trying to remember some small detail that might at least
push us in the right direction.

'It is always prudent to check the water first,' Cavill replies. My
heart contracts as tightly as a fist. Is that what happens? Does Felix
drown? Has history got it wrong? Does he in fact, vanish today?
My mind whirrs with possibilities. I stand beside Cavill and sweep
my eyes over the water. There is no sign of Felix.

'Let us look about those rocks,' I say, pointing hopefully. 'You
know how he likes to make dens. Perhaps he's playing in one of
those caves.' Mr Bray and Cordelia have gone in the other direction and Mr Pengower is heading up the dunes to the carriages to
get Symons and the others to help. Gwen is standing with Robert,
gazing about her like a bewildered sheep. The beach is not very
long, but there are lots of dunes and rocks and it's perfectly possible
that Felix is playing quietly behind one of them. A moment ago we
were enjoying the pleasant languor of a sunny afternoon, but now
the beach appears dark and menacing, as if the sun has turned her
face away because she cannot bear to look. How quickly life can
change. Am I now witnessing that change in the Pengowers' fate?

Cavill calls Felix's name. I hear it echoed by his father and then
by his mother. Her voice is tight. It breaks and then she begins
to cry and can shout no more. Mr Bray puts his arm around her
shoulders.

I want to cry too. I can't have let them down. I just can't have.

When I think all is lost, I see, coming round from behind a large
peninsular of rock, a gypsy woman leading little Felix by the hand,
followed by the dog I saw earlier. Relief washes over me and I jubilantly call out. 'He's here!' I spot the small shape of Cordelia break
into a run from the other side of the beach. She lifts her skirts
and races over the sand towards us, her face radiant with joy. Mr

Pengower and Mr Bray follow at a brisk walk. The relief is tangible. It is as if the sun has turned back and is shining on us again.

Cavill and I reach the woman first. I recognise her at once as being one of the mothers who was pinching Felix's cheek and cooing over him the other day at the gypsy camp. Felix clings to her skirts, perfectly happy to be with her. Cavill lifts him into his arms and holds him tightly. 'Where did you get to, you little devil?' he asks, but he looks to the woman for the answer.

'He wandered round with the dog,' she explains. I notice that she only has a few yellowed teeth. Her strong foreign accent makes her hard to understand. 'He wanted to play with it, bless him.'

'Thank you for bringing him back,' Cavill says. The woman pulls something out of her pocket and takes Felix gently by the wrist. The boy lets her hold him as she ties a leather strap with a blue-and-white bead about him. 'To keep you safe,' she says. 'To ward off the evil eye.' I'm struck by those words. Does she know something terrible is going to happen? Can she sense it? Or is this just an extraordinary coincidence?

Before I can think any more about it, Cordelia reaches us. She takes her son out of Cavill's arms and presses her face into his neck, closing her eyes and sighing with relief. 'I thought we had lost you, my darling.' She inhales him, as if she wants to consume him.

Felix is bewildered by the attention. He puts his finger in his mouth and replies, 'I found a dog.'

'And you followed it?' Cordelia asks, spotting the dog who is now trotting down to the water.

'Please, Mama, can we have a dog?'

Cordelia is so happy, I think she'll agree to anything. 'Perhaps,' she replies.

Gwen and Robert finally reach us. She's panting, her hair has come out of its pins and is sticking to her sweating face. The moment Felix sees her he puts out his arms and whines that he wants to be with her. Cordelia reluctantly hands him over. She looks at Gwen and for the first time I see that beautiful, serene face harden. 'You and I will have words later,' she says, and Gwen's eyes fill with tears.

SHADOWS IN THE MOONLIGHT

She nods. 'Yes, ma'am.'

My heart is finally slowing from its frantic beating and I feel a strange sense of relief, but I know it will be short-lived. Today was only a taster of the disaster yet to befall this family. On Saturday night he will be lost for good and I'm suddenly afraid of what happens to him, for I cannot bear for this little boy to suffer. I ache to save him from his terrible fate but know that it would break all rules of timesliding to do so and possibly instigate a tidal wave of change that would engulf future generations. No, I cannot save him, but I must find out the truth. I look at Cordelia, her cheeks flushed, her hands still shaking. I have a few days yet to rescue her, to find a way to settle her soul, but time is running out and I feel I'm no nearer to discovering who takes her child and why.

As she fusses over Felix, Mr Pengower tips the gypsy woman to thank her for her trouble. By the curl on his lip he does not want to remain in her company a moment longer than he has to. He drops the coins into her outstretched palm, taking care not to touch her skin, and turns quickly on his heel. The fact that she brought Felix back has in no way elevated her, or her people, in his eyes. They are gypsies and cannot be trusted. As we walk up the dunes towards the carriages, he turns to his wife. 'I will have words with Felix when we get home,' he says crossly. 'It is unacceptable to run off like that. He could have drowned. He could have been taken. Anything could have happened. I will talk to Robert too. This is an opportune moment to teach them both a lesson. They need to learn to be vigilant and wise.'

'Felix is but a curious and fearless little boy,' says Cordelia. 'You should be proud of him, Ivan. I know I am.'

'Teach them when they're young,' her husband replies in that habitual tone of voice that carries authority. It is the tone of a man who, as undisputed head of the family, is not to be questioned or contradicted. 'The world is not a safe place, Cordelia, my dear. Clearly, I cannot count on you, or your servants, to be their guide in this matter, therefore I will take care of it myself.' He sighs and shakes his head. 'If it wasn't for me, they would both be as undisciplined as monkeys.'

Cordelia catches my eye and gives me a weary look. It is not an unhappy look, however, more a look of resignation and amusement. Nothing can dampen her mood now that Felix is safe.

The picnic is over. Mrs James is driven off in her carriage, escorted by Mr Bray who will see her to her house, and we head home in the same manner as that in which we came. I do not join in the conversation with Gwen and John, but turn my eyes to the countryside. I have been gravely rattled. The job of a timeslider is to remain detached and objective. It's not to get involved with the players in the game, but to watch from the sidelines. But here I am, involved with Cavill – *in love* with Cavill – and fond of Cordelia, Gwen and Felix. I'm much too close. I shut my eyes, feel the warm wind on my face and the hot sun on my skin, and try to restore balance to my shaken spirit. I must try to focus on my purpose. There are many pieces in this puzzle; I need to find out how they all fit together. I have four days in which to do it.

We arrive at the house and John jumps down to help me and Gwen descend. I catch his eye as he offers me his hand. I don't want to take it, but I have no choice. I can't step down without it. I suspect he knows I don't like him. I can see the animosity in his black eyes and with it a certain disdain.

It's not long before Gwen is summoned to Cordelia's sitting room. We are in the middle of tea in the nursery when the housemaid, Rose, appears in the doorway with the command. Felix and Robert are tucking into eggs and toast – they're both ravenous after the drama, and Gwen and I are drinking cups of tea and processing the afternoon. Gwen blanches. I'm sure she believes she's about to be dismissed. Stifling a sob behind a white handkerchief, she takes a deep breath, as one might before plunging into cold water, and then leaves the nursery.

Soon after, I'm summoned with the children to see their father in the library. Rose appears again, breathless but excited by the goings on. 'He's in one of those moods,' she tells me with a grin.

'I am beginning to get used to those,' I reply and follow her down the corridor with the boys.

'He likes his soapbox,' she says, lowering her voice. 'If he wasn't lord of the manor, I think he'd be a vicar.'

I laugh and prepare myself for another soliloquy of rubbish.

Mr Pengower is in the library at his desk when I knock. He puts down the paper he's reading and gesticulates for us to come in. Then he stands up and walks round to position himself in front of the fireplace. The boys sit dutifully on the leather sofa. I'm about to leave when Mr Pengower asks me to sit down. He tells me that he wants me to hear his speech so that I can enforce it. I wonder whether he just wants an audience.

Robert and Felix sit as still as a pair of marble putti. Robert is attentive, Felix, however, is fiddling with the buttons on his shirt. His father notices and reprimands him. 'Now you listen to me, young man,' he says. 'You ran off today and that was not clever. You could have been swept away by the sea or stolen by gypsies. What do you have to say for yourself?'

Felix smiles. It is a smile that can mollify the hardest heart, but it does not mollify his father's. Mr Pengower glares at him. 'Eh? What do you have to say for yourself?' he repeats.

'I found a dog,' Felix replies. 'Can we have a dog, please, Papa?'

His father frowns impatiently. 'Absolutely not. Whatever do we want a dog for? Now, I don't care whether it was a dog or a dragon, you will not run off like that again, do you understand?' Felix's face falls and he nods solemnly. 'You have to be wise, Felix, and you too, Robert,' Mr Pengower continues. 'You have to be on your guard. You're Pengowers. People are always going to want something from you, but you're not to trust anyone. You can trust your own family and, if you choose wisely, you can trust your friends. But you cannot trust gypsies. You cannot trust people who have nothing because they will always resent you for your wealth and your name and for your standing in the world.' I sense he is on a roll now and there will be no stopping him. He lifts his chin, rocks on his heels, puffs out his chest. He goes on and on, about the importance of being a Pengower and the responsibility that comes with it. Robert listens dutifully, but Felix's attention is drifting. Mr

Pengower points his finger at Felix and jabs the air in rhythm with the words. 'No more running off,' he says. 'Is that understood?'

Felix nods. 'Yes, Papa.'

'And you, too, Robert. You must look out for your brother.'

'Yes, Papa,' Robert replies, pleased to be given responsibility by his father.

'Good. I think I have made myself clear.' He turns to me. 'You may take them back to the nursery, Miss Swift.'

I get up and reach for Felix's hand as he slips off the sofa. It is then that Mr Pengower notices the bracelet on the child's wrist. 'What is that?' he asks, pointing to it and frowning in disgust. 'Did *they* give that to you?' He turns to me. 'What is it, Miss Swift?'

'The gypsy lady gave him the bracelet to keep him safe, sir,' I reply.

'Why, goddamn it!' Mr Pengower explodes and his face goes as red as a tomato. 'Take it off at once. I will not have my son wearing such a thing.'

Felix's bottom lip wobbles. His eyes well with tears. 'But I like it, Papa.'

Mr Pengower strides over and pulls it so hard that it comes undone. Felix squeals and nurses his hurt wrist. His father throws the bracelet onto the carpet at the child's feet. Felix scoops it up and clutches it to his chest.

I lead Felix towards the door. He's keen to get away from his father and comes quickly, his small shoulders hunched, his head bowed.

'And young men don't cry,' Mr Pengower calls after him. Felix takes a deep breath to hold his emotions in check, and my heart breaks for him. He's only a child.

'Come on, my dear,' I say. 'Let's go and have some tea.' I usher both boys through the door.

As I turn to close it, Mr Pengower gives me a wry smile. 'I don't think we'll have any more vanishings,' he says with satisfaction.

He does not know how very wrong he is.

Chapter Fifteen

I find Gwen in the nursery tidying away the toys. She has not been dismissed, only reprimanded for falling asleep when she should have been watching Felix. But Cordelia is not an unforgiving woman. 'She told me she'd been frightened for Master Felix,' Gwen tells me. She's no longer crying, but her eyes are still swollen and bloodshot. 'She said it mustn't happen again. I told her it wouldn't.' I wince because I know that it *is* going to happen again, and in only four days' time.

Thankfully Mr and Mrs Pengower have guests that evening, so I do not join them for dinner. I am emotionally drained after the day on the beach and by my knowledge of what is to come. I wish I could speak to someone about it, but I must carry the burden alone. I feign a headache and retreat to my bedroom as soon as the boys have been put to bed.

I take the pins out of my hair so that it falls in curls about my shoulders. I use the water in the jug that has been placed beside the chest of drawers to wash, and change into my linen nightdress and robe. I then recline with my feet up on the sofa in the little sitting room adjoining my bedroom and try to read a penny dreadful I found in the drawer of my bedside table. It must have belonged to Miss Archer, the governess who worked here before me. I see the words, but they do not enter my head. How can they? There's no space for them, for it's already crowded with dread. If the fire was lit, I'd watch the dancing flames, for that's restful. I'd like to listen to music, but that's also impossible. I have nothing to do but think and my thoughts keep dragging me down to where I do not want to go.

I'm beginning to doze off when I hear a soft knocking on the door. I awake with a start. For a moment I'm not sure where I am. 'Come in,' I reply. The door opens slowly and Cavill slips through it. He quietly closes it behind him. I'm caught off guard; in the turmoil of the day I completely forgot that he was coming.

I get up off the sofa and go to him. He pulls me into his arms and, without a word, kisses me. I forget about Felix and the future and through the power of my senses, root myself firmly in the moment. I'm aware only of his lips on mine, the taste of wine on his tongue, his arms around my body, the feeling of strength in his embrace.

He takes my hand and leads me to the sofa where we sit together. 'I was so frightened today,' I tell him, relieved to articulate my fear and wanting so very badly to be reassured even though there is no reassurance to be had.

He runs his fingers down my hair. He's never seen me in my nightclothes and I can tell that he's pleasantly surprised. 'He is found, my dear Hermione,' he murmurs softly, but I can see from the desire in his eyes that he's not thinking about Felix. 'You must not worry about it any more.'

But how can I not?

Cavill kisses me again and I realise that he does not want to talk. I grow warm as his kisses become more urgent and the heat intensifies between us. I remind myself that I am Hermione Swift, not Pixie Tate. It's already improper that he is here, in Hermione's room, kissing her in her nightdress.

I must not forget that I am she.

It takes all my inner strength to pull away, because I know I must not allow this to go further than it already has. I get up and go to the window. He follows. We look out into the sky that extends in its eternity above St Sidwell Manor. A frontier of dark cloud is moving in slowly over the trees, extinguishing the twinkling stars, one by one. We sit together. The window is open wide and the moon shines onto the garden below and also onto our faces, casting us in its mysterious silver light. 'How small we are down here,' Cavill says softly. 'How keenly I feel God's presence on a night like this.'

'The wind has changed,' I remark, and so it has. Everything will change with it.

'I thank God for bringing me you,' he says, and pulls me closer.

I stare into his eyes, wondering how far I dare go. Then I take his face in my hands and trace his cheeks with my thumbs. 'Cavill, look at me.'

'I am looking at you.' He laughs. 'I love everything I see.'

'Can you see beyond the physical? Can you see the real me, the one who is looking out?'

He frowns. He must think I've gone mad. 'Of course, I can see you,' he replies.

'One day this body will die, but the real me will live on. The real you will live on, too. Will we recognise each other when we no longer have our physical bodies? Will we recognise each other when we are made of light?'

He's concerned now. 'My darling. What are you saying? Are you talking about the soul?' He smiles reassuringly. 'Of course, I will recognise your soul. I'd recognise your soul if it was a ray of light among a thousand rays.'

Cupping his face, I press my lips to his. I close my eyes and a tear squeezes through the lashes. In three days' time I'll say goodbye and never see him again. Not in this life. Does he love me, or does he love Hermione? How *deep* does his love go?

It's unfair to ask him that, of course. It's unfair to expect him to distinguish between *two* when he believes there is only *one* 'me'.

I look up at the stars. They are the same stars in my time too. The same sky, the same moon, the same planets and the same eternal space. It's all the same. The universe seems not to change, it's only we who change within it. We come and we go, and our lives are brief. What is it all for? Love. Only love endures. Only love lives on. Love is the only thing we take with us when we depart. And I shall take my love for Cavill with me when I go.

It's of little consolation, however. Shortly, we'll be separated by one hundred and eighteen years. I can hardly bear it.

It's insurmountable.

Cavill wraps his arms around me, but he cannot imagine that when we say goodbye, it'll be for ever. And I cannot tell him.

It's one in the morning when I sneak down to the library. The moon is almost full so I have no need for my gas lamp, but I bring it with me for I'll need it to illuminate my way in the tunnel. Cavill left my room a little after midnight. I did not want him to go, but I was fearful that if he remained I would fail in my duty of care to Hermione and allow things to get out of control. It's bad enough that we've kissed.

Tonight, I have an important mission. I need to find out where the priest hole goes.

I wait for Cordelia in my usual place behind the curtain and hope that she won't come. The clock chimes twice and still she does not appear. The house is as silent as a museum. I gingerly emerge and hurry across the rugs to the bookcase. My senses are alert for any sound, but all I can hear is the pounding of blood at my temples and the frantic beating of my heart. I fumble for the lever and pull it. The door pops open. I slip through and close it behind me. Once inside and out of danger, I strike a match and light the lamp.

I see before me a narrow stone staircase. The place smells musty and old, like a crypt. I sense a heightened energy and wonder how many terrified Catholics escaped persecution through this tunnel. They certainly left their fear here, trapped in this airless burrow to fester and stagnate. It makes the hair on my arms bristle. With the lamp to light my way I reach the bottom. It's colder down here and damp. I'm surprised, though, by the care of the workmanship for the bricks are neatly laid along the walls and the barrel ceiling. The floor is made of stones and they are smooth, as if polished by hundreds of treading feet. I have to stoop a bit, and if I was with others we would have to walk in single file.

The tunnel must be a couple of hundred yards. At the end are steps leading to a wooden trapdoor. I push it and find myself peering into a shed. I climb out and look through a window. I see the stable block, resting quietly beneath the stars. This shed must be a storage shed or workshop. There's no way that Cordelia is the only person who knows about this tunnel. Anyone who comes in here can see the trapdoor. Sure, the place is full of old sacks and bailer twine, and shelves of paint pots and other paraphernalia, but the trapdoor resembles something you might find in the cellar of a pub and is certainly not hidden or disguised. Perhaps the stable boys assume it's a storage space or a cellar, and don't bother to investigate, but if any of them have an ounce of curiosity they will have explored it.

I'm one hundred per cent certain that Felix is carried out through this tunnel. The question now is by whom and why? The travellers, the miners, a disgruntled local, or someone closer to home whom I haven't yet thought of?

I feel an overwhelming sense of hopelessness. How on earth am I going to find out who takes him in the little time that remains?

The following morning, Mr Pengower summons the boys. Gwen and I bring them down to the hall where their father is waiting for them with Mr Bray. 'I'm taking them to the mine,' he declares. 'It's about time they knew what their papa does.'

I stare at him in astonishment. This is exactly what Cordelia fears. I wonder whether she knows. Do I have time to tell her? Before I can work out what to do, Cavill appears. He's dashing in a sky-blue coat and black boots. He smiles at me, the light still warm in his eyes from the night before. 'Good day, Miss Swift,' he says. His gaze is probing, and I recall the intimacy we shared with a frisson of pleasure. However, I'm caught off guard by Mr Pengower's plans that I can barely smile back. Cavill frowns at me inquisitively, but I'm unable to voice my fears without Mr Pengower overhearing me. Cavill turns to the children. 'Right, you two little devils. Are you ready for an adventure?'

'I am!' Felix exclaims. He's jumping up and down excitedly. It's not often that he's included in these excursions. My stomach churns with anxiety. My suspicions are aroused. I'm like a dog who senses danger. Why is Mr Pengower taking them to the mine? Why is he taking Felix? I notice Mr Bray is looking concerned, but Cavill seems in favour of it, laughing with the boys. Perhaps I'm worrying over nothing. Maybe Mr Pengower simply wants to show his sons his business. Or does he want to show the miners his sons?

I look about for Cordelia, hoping she will appear. Surely, she is aware of this. I know she will disapprove. It will put the fear of God into her. It seems that everyone knows the mines are unsafe, except for Mr Pengower, who perhaps knows but does not want to acknowledge it. There's nothing I can do. The boys are thrilled. Felix, especially. Robert is none too happy that his little brother is going with him, but he's pleased nonetheless to be taken away from his studies. I imagine there will be more lectures about the importance of being a Pengower.

I'm about to retreat upstairs when Mr Pengower informs me that I'm to go as well. 'To keep an eye on Master Felix,' he says. I want to warn Cordelia, but don't know where to find her and I have no time. I look about for Gwen, but she's disappeared and there's no sign of Symons. There's no one I can ask to deliver a message to Cordelia. We are leaving right away.

Reluctantly, I accept Mr Bray's hand and climb into the carriage. He follows after and takes the place beside me. Mr Pengower and Cavill sit opposite us, Felix sits on his uncle's knee. As a treat, Robert rides on the box with Mr Grantly. I catch Cavill's eye and recall the evening before with a virgin's blush, the irony of which is not lost on me.

The weather has been hot since I arrived the previous Wednesday and has been getting increasingly humid. Indeed, a heaviness hangs in the air, as thick as fog, but transparent like vapour. It's close and getting closer, like the tentacles of that dark evil that is slowly making its way through the house.

The carriage wheels turn on the gravel and I'm struck at once by the sensual smell of jasmine that grows up the wall of the house. It's sticky and strong. There's no breeze to blow it away, so it has gathered, intensifying in the heat of the sun. All around me the shrubs, flowers and trees glow with vitality. Everything is full of life. The birds tweet merrily, the bees buzz, the butterflies flutter and the dragonflies dart, and yet my heart is heavy with the knowledge of what is to come. The beauty of St Sidwell Manor is almost an affront, in the light of the ugliness gathering in the wings.

It's not long before we reach the mine. It's a drab hamlet of stone huts, cylindrical-shaped towers and what looks like frames of scaffolding built on the cliffs overlooking the sea. The sky darkens but it's not with cloud. A brick tower belches black smoke into the air, choking the sunshine and soiling the land, which is barren. Nothing grows here. Not even a blade of grass. It's as if the earth is diseased.

The boys fall silent. Felix gazes upon the place with wide eyes and an open mouth. I don't know whether he's fascinated or horrified. Mr Pengower is talking to Mr Bray. They're speaking a language I don't understand. Mr Bray is very grave. His face is still etched with concern, but he seems to be keeping his reservations to himself and listening dutifully to Mr Pengower. I look at Cavill for reassurance. He smiles at me. 'I do not imagine you have ever been to a mine, Miss Swift,' he says.

'You imagine right,' I reply. 'You will have to explain everything to me.'

'It will be my pleasure.'

'I hope it is safe,' I add, trying to communicate my apprehension with my eyes.

'It *is* safe,' he replies with a frown. 'I can assure you, neither you nor the boys will be put in any danger.'

But with every fibre of my being I want to get out of this place. It's dark and sad and desolate. There's no beauty anywhere, except for the sea, but even that looks as if it's covered in soot beneath a flat grey sky.

We climb out of the carriage. Cavill lifts Felix down and then offers me his hand. I take it and step down onto the baked earth. I notice the men watching us and feel horribly conspicuous in my elegant white blouse and black skirt.

Men emerge from the wooden sheds in grubby trousers and shirts, their heads protected by hats that look woefully inadequate. One or two are smoking pipes, some look as if they're still boys. Their faces are grimy, their expressions weary, and hostile. Their dark, mistrustful eyes watch us, and I fear for Robert and Felix.

This is not a safe place for them. Those eyes are full of resentment. I sense it in their body language and snarling mouths. These people do not like Mr Pengower. They do not like him at all.

An eye for an eye . . .

Mr Pengower seems oblivious to the palpable antipathy in the atmosphere. He's in a very good mood. 'Come along, boys,' he shouts cheerfully, putting out his hand for Felix, who takes it. His voice is so loud it's as if he wants the entire mine to hear. 'And you, too, Miss Swift. No dallying. This is an exciting day. An opportunity to see how tin is mined. To see how these clever people excavate the earth for treasure.' He strides on, a spring in his step. Robert, with an air of importance, straightens his shoulders, lifts his chin and walks beside his father. Cavill, Mr Bray and I follow behind, listening to Mr Pengower's booming voice telling his sons about the mines.

'Now you listen to me, Robert and Felix. This mine was built in seventeen ninety-one. It began as a small enterprise but now employs three hundred men, forty-four women and one hundred and eighty-six children. Yes, boys only a little older than you. Imagine that!'

I really don't want to. I'm appalled that children work in those tunnels so far beneath the ground.

Mr Pengower continues. 'The workings extend below the water table and about a mile out under the sea. When your grandfather bought the mine back in eighteen fifty-seven, they had to walk down precarious paths in the cliffs and enter through openings in the rock. Now we are much more efficient. We have man engines, run by steam, that carry the miners up and down. You, Robert and Felix, are going to experience what it is like to be a miner and go down into the earth on one of those man engines.'

I turn to Mr Bray in panic, and panic further when I see the alarm on his face. 'Is that wise, Mr Bray?' I ask.

He shakes his head. 'It is not wise at all,' he replies briskly.

I turn to Cavill. 'Is he really going to take the boys into the mine?'

Cavill's brow creases into a deep frown. He glances at Mr Bray.

'I will talk to him,' he says and his voice is deep and serious. The gaiety has evaporated. Only Mr Pengower thinks this is a good idea.

Cavill strides ahead and talks to his brother in a low voice. I can't hear what he's saying, but I can tell from the irritated expressions on both men's faces that Cavill is unhappy about his brother's plans, and his brother is not happy to be contradicted.

Mr Pengower strides on regardless. Felix is skipping excitedly beside him. Robert is walking tall, pretending to be a grown-up. Cavill is failing to change his brother's mind.

'They'll be all right,' says Mr Bray, settling his kindly eyes on mine. 'However, Mr Pengower said nothing about taking the children down the mine. Had I known, I would have tried to persuade him otherwise.'

I realise suddenly that my suspicions are not unfounded. Mr Pengower wants to show the miners how safe the tunnels are, and how better to prove their safety than to take his own sons down them? I'm horrified at the negligence of such an act. Mr Bray is unhappy about the condition of the tunnels, and nothing has been done to improve them since the disaster of last year where people lost their lives. It seems staggeringly irresponsible to put two small children in danger in this way, simply to hoodwink the poor miners. No one should be going down those tunnels. No one.

We group together at the entrance of a stone building and Mr Pengower looks me up and down. 'You wait here, Miss Swift. The mines are no place for a woman dressed like you.'

I'm relieved I don't have to go down. As Pixie, I wouldn't hesitate; I'm not afraid of small places. But I'm aware of my responsibility towards Hermione. It would be wrong of me to put her in danger. I'm fearful, however, for the children. I think of Cordelia. Does she know now where they've gone? Is she at home, worrying?

Mr Bray has no option but to carry out Mr Pengower's orders. He takes charge, summoning the men. They're clearly surprised to see the two children but pleased to be chosen to assist. They greet Mr Bray and Mr Pengower politely and then disappear into the building. The men who have not been selected to help stand around, watching warily. Some whisper to each other. By the curling of their lips and the hostility in their eyes, I don't imagine they're saying anything nice.

'I will take care of the boys,' Cavill reassures me before following the group into the building.

'And take care of yourself,' I add. But I know that he's not in danger. The danger he faces is to come.

Time goes slowly. The heat is intense. The air is thick with smoke, I feel polluted with every breath I take. I tell myself that I don't need to worry about the children's safety. Felix does not disappear today, and Robert lives on to marry and father a daughter, Emily. What concerns me more than the danger in the mine is the danger in the men. They are boiling with rage. I understand their bitterness. They are poor, they work long hours, their labour is hard and the conditions of those tunnels are insufferable. Many of their wives and children work here too. The children are young and spend most of the day in darkness underground. I don't imagine they get paid very much. It's pure exploitation. But Victorians thought nothing of putting their children to work, sending them up chimneys and into the sewers to search for treasures. I think of the priest hole that leads directly into the house. These men think nothing of venturing into an underground tunnel. Will one of them use it to access the manor and steal Felix away?

It feels like an eternity, but at last I hear Felix's cheerful chatter. The small group emerges from the building at last. Felix is jumping about like a spring rabbit. Robert is lagging behind with Mr Bray, both of them solemn and pensive. Mr Pengower is talking to his brother. His gait is buoyant. He is chipper. Whatever they did, Mr Pengower considers it well done.

Felix scampers up to me, his face aglow with pleasure. 'We went into the tunnels!' he informs me, his voice pitched high with excitement. 'We were like moles under the ground. I want to be a miner when I grow up!'

I force a smile. 'I'm sure you'll make a good miner,' I tell him, putting my hand on his head and ruffling his hair. My heart aches because I know he will never have the chance to make a good anything.

'Master Felix is fearless,' Mr Pengower tells me proudly. 'You should have seen him, Miss Swift, scurrying up and down the tunnels like a mole. Yes, a mole, I tell you! You should have been there. Like his father, he is.'

'How about you, Master Robert,' I ask, turning to the boy. 'Do you want to be a miner when you grow up, too?' His face is pale, and I see that he is shaking. He's clearly terrified.

'No.' He scowls. 'But not because I was afraid. I don't need to be down there. I'll be in charge of it all.'

I look at Mr Pengower, self-satisfied and arrogant, and think how foolish he is. By taking the children down the mine, he will have rubbed salt into the wound of the poor father whose child was killed in the catastrophe. I wonder how Cordelia could have married him. I wonder too whether, deep down, she wishes she hadn't.

I'm relieved when the carriage leaves the mine behind and carries us into the sunny countryside once again. I relish the sight of lush green fields, of yellow buttercups and pink campion, of white cow parsley and daisies. I relish the sight of life, after the sterile landscape of the mine.

Cavill's gentle gaze settles on mine and holds it for a long moment. I daren't smile for fear of giving myself away. But Mr Pengower is not interested in me. He's listening to Felix, who is entertaining us with his breathless descriptions of the mine and endless questions that please his father. 'What is the blue stuff on the walls, Papa?' he asks.

Mr Pengower is thrilled by his son's interest. 'That's copper, my boy, leaching out of the rock. How clever you are to notice it. A true Pengower, full of interest and curiosity.'

'I want to go down again,' says Felix, basking in the praise he's getting from the father who perhaps has never really noticed him before. 'Please, Papa, can I go down again?'

'Of course you can, Felix.'

'I want to be a mole and dig about. Can I dig a tunnel, Papa?'

Taken by the idea, he adds, 'I am going to dig a tunnel in the garden. A proper tunnel, like a proper mole.'

Mr Pengower laughs. 'Do you hear, Cavill? Felix wants to be a mole. I dare say he will make a very fine mole. The finest mole in St Sidwell.' Felix beams at his father and his eyes shine with happiness.

'You see, Miss Swift,' the child says with a grin. 'I am the finest mole in St Sidwell!'

Mr Bray, who is sitting beside me, is preoccupied. He rests his elbow on the side of the carriage and thoughtfully rubs his chin thoughtfully. He's still cross that Mr Pengower insisted on taking the boys down the mine. I can feel his fury, even though he's doing a good job of containing it. I glance at Robert, who's sitting up on the box with Mr Grantly. He's quiet too. He's not saying a word. I wonder what's going through his head. But Robert is no concern of mine. Felix is, and I must watch him closely.

As we turn into the gates of St Sidwell Manor, I notice for the first time, on one of the pillars, the smudged remains of the graffiti Miss Prideaux told me about. Someone has tried to wash it off, but the red paint can still be seen on the stone. *An eye for an eye* . . . the thought of it turns my blood to ice. Mr Pengower doesn't look at it, but Mr Bray does. He looks at it and then he looks at me. His eyes seem to darken with concern, and I feel his fear roll over me like a prickly wave.

When we arrive home, I leave the children with Gwen and go in search of Cordelia. I find her sitting alone on a bench in the garden, a basket of sunflowers at her feet. She's wearing a wide-brimmed sunhat and looks for a moment as if she's dozing. But then she sees me and beckons me over with a wave of her elegant hand.

'You are back,' she says and forces a wan smile.

I sit beside her. 'I'm sorry, I didn't have time to warn you.'

'I knew he would take them,' she says dully, and knits her fingers in her lap. 'I knew I wouldn't be able to stop him. At least it is done now, and they are home and safe.'

'I think Mr Pengower will always do just as he pleases.'

'He is so stubborn. I begged him not to take them. They are too young. What are they to gain from such an expedition?'

'Maybe it was beneficial for them to see how the mine works?'

Cordelia sighs. 'At a different time, I would have agreed with you. But things have changed. The miners are resentful and angry. Did you see what was written on the gate?'

'I did.'

'Someone wants to do us harm.'

'I'm sure no one would do that,' I tell her, but the truth is I'm not sure at all. 'If they want to hurt their master, I'm sure they would not do it by hurting his child. What person would do that? It's unthinkable.'

She wrings her hands. 'Because he hurt one of theirs.' Her eyes fill with tears.

'Oh, my dear Mrs Pengower,' I exclaim. 'He did not do it on purpose. It was an accident.'

She looks at me fiercely. 'It was negligence,' she replies, spitting out the word like venom. 'Carelessness. It could easily have been avoided. Mr Pengower is a stubborn man. When he gets an idea into his head there is no shifting it. He will not be challenged. He is very set in his ways. I know it is not my place to argue with him, but sometimes gentleness is a more effective way of getting the best out of people than severity. Mr Pengower does not understand that, to his cost.' She laughs through her unhappiness and drops her gaze to her fingers that are now pulling at her white lace handkerchief. 'Do you know the story of the sun and the wind, Miss Swift?'

'Aesop's fable,' I reply. 'I know it well. But tell me again.'

'They were arguing, the sun and the wind, you see. The wind was boasting of his strength whereas the sun was explaining that there is great power in gentleness. They spied a man on the path below. He had on a heavy coat. The wind said he would prove his strength by blowing the coat off. He blew and he blew, and the leaves flew off the trees, but the man held his coat ever more tightly about him. He would not let it go. Eventually, the wind went quiet, and the sun shone warmly upon the man, who grew so hot that he took off his coat himself.' She chuckled sadly. 'I wish my husband would take heed of those words. I read that story to the boys every now and then and hope that the lesson might be learnt. There is, indeed, great power in gentleness. I have found, in my own small way, that kindness brings out the best in people.'

'And you are right,' I agree. 'Mr Pengower will learn, in time. But it might take something . . .' I hesitate, not wanting to alarm her. 'Something painful to wake him up.'

'I do not wish that on him,' she says.

'Of course not. You are a positive influence on him. If each of us has a purpose in our lives, perhaps yours is to encourage him to find his gentler side.'

She laughs softly. 'That would be quite an achievement, Miss Swift. I am not sure I will fulfil it.' She turns to me and there's a knowing look in her eyes. 'But let us talk of happier things. Mr Cavill is very fond of you.' She smiles. 'I think you are rather fond of him, too.'

'He is kind and sensitive,' I reply carefully, my cheeks flushing. 'I do not think I have met a more admirable man. But he is above my station; it is unthinkable.'

'Don't be so sure! Let me tell you a secret, Miss Swift,' she whispers conspiratorially. 'I was a governess once, just like you. I was tutoring two young girls at a house in Somerset when Mr Pengower came to stay for a shooting weekend. The man I worked for happened to be his godfather. A girl like me would not have dreamt of marrying a man like Mr Pengower, but I was fortunate, he chose me, and I was flattered.' She sighs. 'I did not love him, but it pleased my mother. Like you, my father had died and my mother depended on me. I believed that in time I would grow fond of him.' She turns to me and smiles bitterly. 'One does not always fulfil one's intentions. He is a difficult man. I try to feel fond, but I'm afraid I fall short. God forgive me, but there is little in him that inspires fondness.'

I feel an ache in my heart. I envisage her stuck in Felix's bedroom as an earthbound spirit and pity her. 'I'm sorry your life is so difficult,' I say. 'We all want to love and be loved in return.'

She takes my hand and squeezes it. 'How sweet you are, Miss

Swift, to care like you do. You're becoming a dear friend to me.' Her eyes shine with tears. 'I have made my bed and I must lie in it. But I can confide in you. I have, in dark moments, entertained the idea of leaving my bed and no longer lying in it. Of taking control of my destiny and living the way I choose.' She sighs and drops her shoulders in defeat. 'But it is impossible, of course. I have too much to lose. However, I know I am loved.' I imagine she means by her children, because she cannot mean by her husband. 'Perhaps that is enough. Just to know it. One cannot have everything, can one? Sometimes one has to accept one's lot and be grateful for the small glimpses of light that shine through the shadows.'

She lets go of my hand and wipes her eyes. The conversation is over. She picks up her basket of flowers. 'Come, let us go inside,' she says, standing up. 'I'm sure the boys will want to tell me about their adventure. I will have to pretend that I am happy to listen.'

That night, I decide to read to Robert. He's had a difficult day being outshone by his little brother and I want to make him feel better. I choose a book of Aesop's Fables. I start the story about the north wind and the sun, but he puts his hand on the page and grumbles that he has heard that one already. He prefers stories with foxes in them. Reluctantly, I read *The Fox and the Grapes*. He's satisfied with that and asks me to read more. At length, I close the book and say goodnight. It is time for me to dress for dinner. As I'm walking towards my room, I meet Cordelia on her way to say goodnight to her boys. She takes the opportunity to ask me to join the family this evening. 'I have spoken with Mr Bray,' she tells me in a low voice. 'He was unaware of Mr Pengower's plan to take the boys down the mine and is very unhappy about it. He is coming to dinner tonight and I fear there is going to be an argument. Mr Bray says that the men have taken it badly. They don't feel reassured at all, they feel resentful. They think Mr Pengower takes them for fools.'

And they are right. 'Mr Cavill tried to talk to him at the mine,' I reply. 'But he wouldn't listen. I know that Mr Bray was unhappy about it too.'

She sighs. 'My husband doesn't listen to anyone, but I shall try again. It makes me shudder to think of another accident happening when it can so easily be avoided.'

I go to my room, bathe and change. When I come down I find Cavill on the lawn. He's standing alone on the terrace with a tumbler of whisky in his hand, looking out over the gardens. Mr Pengower and Cordelia have not appeared, and Mr Bray and Mrs James have not yet arrived.

It's another hot evening. The air is thick with midges and the sweet scents of the garden. The sun is the colour of a blood orange sinking slowly towards the treetops, setting their tips aflame. It's beautiful but melancholy, as the end of the day often is. I feel a heaviness in my heart. I have but one day left with Cavill before he leaves. Then I will never see him again.

'Cavill,' I say. He turns and his delight at seeing me lights up his face and lifts my deflated spirit.

He comes towards me. 'Hermione,' he replies softly. 'I was just thinking about you.'

'Oh?'

'I found myself wishing that I could turn the clock forward and instead of leaving on Friday, I could be returning instead.'

'I wish for that too,' I whisper. A lump lodges itself in my throat because I know he will never return.

'I will write to you, whilst I am away,' he says fervently, and his eyes burn. 'I will tell you about my adventures and you will write back and keep me in touch with life here at St Sidwell.'

'Oh, Cavill, I . . .'

At that moment Cordelia steps out onto the terrace in a pretty duck-egg-blue dress. She is smiling at us, a knowing smile, and looking upon us with affection. 'Isn't it a beautiful evening?' she says, joining us.

'It is all the more beautiful with you two lovely ladies in it,' says Cavill with a grin, and Cordelia beams.

'Doesn't he always say the right thing?' She laughs.

'He thinks flattery will get him everywhere,' I add, trying not to flirt in front of Cordelia.

She gives me a quizzical look and Cavill chuckles. I realise that that might be an expression they haven't heard before.

Mr Pengower appears with Mr Bray and Mrs James. I sense that the two men have already had words because neither is looking particularly happy. I feel Cordelia stiffen at my side.

I catch Cavill's eye. He takes a breath and blinks. It's going to be one of those nights where we all pretend everything is fine, while the subject of Felix and Robert being taken to the mine sits in the middle of the dining table like a festering carcass that no one wants to acknowledge is there.

And so it is. On the surface, the conversation is light; Cordelia is charming, Cavill witty, Mrs James a delight as she laughs at everything Cavill says. But beneath the cheerful surface, the atmosphere is tense. Mr Bray is reticent. Mr Pengower grudgingly agreeable – his foreman has offended him with his criticism, and he does not want to forgive him. I notice he has two large glasses of whisky, neat, and asks for a third. Perhaps it is the whisky, but, towards the end of dinner Mr Pengower decides to assert his authority and explain why he decided to take the boys down the tunnels. 'What you do not realise,' he begins, looking at Mr Bray and Cavill in turn, 'is that the men look to me for leadership. If I give in to their demands I will only make a cross for myself that I will have to carry for years to come. They want more pay.' He waves his glass in front of him and slurs his words. 'If I give in, what is to stop them asking for more in, say, six months' time? And then more in, say, eight months' time? And so on. I have to be strong as my father was before me. He ruled them with a rod of iron. That is the only way. They are a rowdy lot and capable of rising up and making a great nuisance of themselves. Today, my dear Mrs Pengower,' he turns to his wife with a snarl on his lip. 'I took the boys down the mine to show the men that I deem the tunnels safe. If they are safe enough for my sons, they are safe enough for them. It was a show of strength, not weakness.' He smiles triumphantly. 'Did you see Felix? What courage that boy has. What vim! Scampering along those tunnels like a rabbit. Like a rabbit he was, I tell you.' He chuckles.

Mrs James laughs with him. 'Was he really, my dear? Like a rabbit?'

'Indeed, he was, Mother. Like an intrepid little rabbit. Never been so proud of him.'

Cavill arches an eyebrow. 'Better late than never,' he says.

Cordelia doesn't smile. She plays with the stem of her wine glass. 'It is a shame that it took a potentially dangerous excursion for you to see his value.'

Mr Pengower's face darkens. 'My dear, I am growing weary of your nagging. You are beginning to sound like a fishwife.' He drains his glass and slams it on the table.

'Ivan.' Cavill bites back on Cordelia's behalf. 'We are all concerned about the potential danger in those tunnels.'

'Then you need to find something else to complain about, because I am weary too of repeating myself. It is *my* estate. *My* mine. *My* men and *my* jurisdiction to do what the hell I like. Mr Bray, Cavill, Mrs Pengower? Is that understood?' There is fire in his eyes, blazing out of his dark and furious face. We sit in stunned silence. I want to tell them that on Saturday night, someone will take Felix. That they will steal him out of his bed and spirit him away through the priest hole into the night and he will never be seen again. That would shut Mr Pengower up. If I told him there's a very strong chance that the perpetrator is a disgruntled miner, would he see sense and do as Mr Bray, who is obviously both sensible and compassionate, suggests?

I bite my tongue. This is one of those moments where I can only sit back and observe. I am now pretty convinced that Felix is taken by a miner – and it appears to be his father's fault.

Mrs James turns to Cordelia. In a sweet and placid voice, she says, 'Will you play the piano again, my dear?'

'Of course,' Cordelia replies, getting up from her chair. I realise that everyone is relieved that they will be permitted to sit in silence and listen to music until it's time to go to bed.

Night has only just fallen when we retire to our rooms. Twilight has given way to darkness and the moon shines upon the gardens with a melancholy light. The air is heavy and moist, hanging over the grass and shrubs like a damp blanket. I feel there's going to be a storm. This weather will have to break at some point and there will be rain, and lots of it. The men don't remain in the drawing room smoking, but retire also. Mr Bray escorts Mrs James home without shaking Mr Pengower's hand. It appears that the two men are at odds and will be for some time. I wonder how this will pan out. Will Mr Bray be proved right when one of the miners steals Felix from his bed? I push the thought away.

Tomorrow is Thursday. I can slide through time, that is magic, but I cannot, even with all the will in the world, slow it down.

It's not long before Cavill's familiar knock is heard upon the door. I wish I had the strength to turn him away. But I can't. I open it and he slips in as he did the night before. We don't speak. He presses his lips to mine and wraps his arms around me, and I close my eyes and commit myself with all my heart to the eternal present.

Chapter Sixteen

Gwen is sullen and unforthcoming at breakfast. The colour has drained from her face and her eyes betray her worry. I go to the window and look out. The stable yard is quiet. I wonder whether John has been climbing the drainpipe again and keeping her up all night with his demands.

I glance at the clock on the mantelpiece. The hands move inexorably forward. The local newspaper on the table reminds me of the date: 27th June, 1895. In two days' time I shall know who steals away the child. I shall witness it, God help me, because I will lie in wait in his bedroom and watch, and then I will follow and see where he's taken. I'm terrified of what I'll witness, but I'll have to endure it. It is my job. It's what I'm here to do. I'll want to prevent it, but I'll have to be strong. I remember the words of the old gypsy woman at the encampment: *It is a dangerous game to play with time.* Indeed, it is.

I feel Gwen's heavy eyes watching me and turn around. She smiles absentmindedly and sighs. I tell Robert to go and practise the piano, and give Felix paper and colouring pencils, which ensures his total absorption, and sit down at the table beside her. I look at her steadily. 'You are not well, Gwen,' I tell her quietly. 'Is there something you would like to tell me?'

She drops her gaze onto her hands. I notice that she's been chewing her nails. They're ragged and raw.

I lower my voice further. 'You can trust me, you know. I am neither a servant nor a member of this family.'

She lifts her eyes off her hands and faces me squarely. Her lips tremble and a tear slides down her grey cheek. 'I think I'm carrying a child, miss,' she says in a voice so tiny I can barely hear it.

I wasn't expecting that. I take a beat, lost for words. If it was 2013 that would not be dire, but it is 1895 and Gwen is unmarried. The implications are horrendous. 'Does the father know?' I ask, my heart flooding with pity.

The word 'father' releases more tears. She shakes her head.

'Are you going to tell him?'

She shrugs. I sense her dilemma at once. John Snathe has no intention of marrying her. He never has and he never will. Gwen has given herself to him in the hope that he will marry her, and he has allowed her to believe it just so that he can satisfy his lust. It's all so obvious and sad. Gwen is a fool, but that's no crime. I could bloody kill John Snathe!

'Perhaps you should tell him,' I suggest.

'I don't know.' Gwen's eyes darken with fear.

'Has he told you he loves you?'

'Oh, yes.'

'Has he mentioned marriage?'

Her shoulders slump, uncertain suddenly. 'He ought to, but . . .' Her voice trails off. She averts her eyes. 'If he does not, what will become of me?' She begins to cry.

Her distress alerts Felix. He stops drawing, holding his pencil above the page and staring at her with big round eyes. Then he starts crying too. Seeing her upset like this shakes his little world. Gwen notices at once and hastily wipes her cheeks. 'Oh, look at the two of us. What are we? A pair of sillies! Come and give Gwen a cuddle then. That'll make us both feel better.' Felix slips off his chair and runs round to be gathered into her fervent embrace. 'I love you so much, Master Felix. You know that, don't you?'

He puts his hands on her cheeks and presses his face to hers. 'No more tears, Gwen,' he says.

She smiles happily, forgetting her dilemma in the warm light of the child's affection.

Gwen looks at me over the boy's head. 'I'll tell him,' she says firmly. 'I think it'll be all right.'

I hope for her sake that she's right.

*

Later that morning we are to have our photograph taken. The entire household, including me. Symons has organised for chairs to be arranged in a row upon the gravel in front of the house. Those are for the family. We will stand in a row behind them. A photographer has come down from London especially. He's called Mr Pringle and is apparently quite celebrated. Everyone is very excited.

I go to my room to tidy my hair and make sure that I look my best. I gaze into the glass and run my fingers over my face. How strange it is that I have a completely different appearance to Pixie Tate. I am Hermione Swift and comfortable in her skin. I feel the same inside. I always feel the same inside, in my core. The deepest part of me, the quiet, still awareness that observes, is eternal. But my outer appearance changes with every slide I make. It never ceases to amaze me how I become someone else and yet, at the same time, remain unchanged inside. I take in my hazel eyes, the dark lashes that frame them, the slim, straight nose and full pink lips, the creamy skin and delicate sprinkling of freckles. I would quite like to take this face with me back to my own time. But that's not the way it works. When I slide back, I'll leave everything behind. Except for love. My love for Cavill. That I will take with me. It's a part of me now.

I turn away from the looking glass with a sigh. I'm enjoying this dream and do not wish it to end. But end it must. Time is ticking and will not wait. It will draw me closer and closer to the tragedy, and then I will be gone.

It's another hot day. The sun sits restlessly behind cloud that's as damp as a sponge. There's no breeze to blow it away. The heatwave has lasted over a week. It started a few days before I arrived and is perhaps going to see me out. The air is heady with the floral scents of the garden. It's luxurious and lifts everyone's mood, for how can one not feel blessed in such a paradise? Even Mr Pengower is cheerful. I notice, however, that he ignores Mr Bray, and Mr Bray, in turn, ignores him.

Cavill draws my attention away. His obvious affection softens

241

his features, and he takes me in with eager eyes. 'Beautiful Hermione,' he breathes.

I laugh and glance about to make sure we are not being overheard. 'I think I am only beautiful in your eyes,' I reply quietly.

'Mine are the only eyes that matter,' he whispers.

I look at him lovingly and, as I do so, I feel him slipping away. Tomorrow he will be gone and I will be alone, to do my duty. A duty I don't want to do. 'Yours are the only eyes that will ever matter,' I respond, and he cannot imagine how deep is the ache in my heart, or why.

'Your face will be immortalised in this photograph, Hermione,' he says. 'I will have it sent to me in South America, even though I will not need it, for I will carry your image in here.' He presses a hand to his chest.

Mr Pengower orders everyone to go to their places. To my surprise, Cordelia asks me to sit on one of the chairs with the family and I take my chair beside her. The two boys sit cross-legged in front of their parents. Behind us the entire household assembles with those who work outside it. Mr Grantly, John Snathe and the stable boys join those who work in the gardens. It's a surprisingly large group. Mr Pringle stands before us like a conductor about to lead an orchestra. He has a bushy black beard and a big, bulbous nose on which sit round glasses. He fusses about his camera which he has set up on a tripod a short distance from us, and makes sure we are all where he wants us to be, silent and still. He tells us that we must not move until he lets us know that we can. 'Are we all ready?' he asks.

'As ready as we'll ever be,' replies Mr Pengower merrily.

'Now, remember. No smiling, no fidgeting, you are as statues. Is that clear?'

'As clear as it will ever be,' Mr Pengower replies. 'Now let us get on with it, Mr Pringle.'

I glance at the boys and hope that Felix is able to sit still for as long as it takes.

Mr Pringle disappears beneath the black cloth. 'Still as statues,' he repeats. 'Go.'

*

'At least we're not dead,' says Rose when it is done. She's standing directly behind me.

I turn to her and laugh. 'What do you mean?'

She grins down at me, brown eyes lively with mischief. 'The last time I had my photograph taken was when my father died. We sat him in a chair, in his Sunday best, and gathered round. I hope they don't take my photograph when I'm dead. I don't think I'm going to look my prettiest that way.'

'Oh, Rose. What a thing to say!' I exclaim. But it's true. Victorians have a certain fascination with death. Where I come from, we'd rather have photographs of the living.

Everyone returns to their work. Felix takes Gwen's hand and they go inside. I notice John watching her as she disappears into the house. I wonder whether he has any idea that she's carrying his child. I return to my duties, accompanying Robert upstairs to resume his lessons. I look forward to the afternoon when we'll ride out with Cavill. I'm acutely aware that it'll be the last opportunity we have.

Mr Pringle stays for lunch. I'm not required, but when I come downstairs to search for a book on Greek mythology in the library, I hear him holding forth in the drawing room. Mrs James Pengower is also present, and I hear Cavill's laughter erupting at something Mr Pringle has said. If I didn't have to leave, this is the life I would expect to have. A life of endless lunches and dinners, of dressing up and socialising, of riding across beautiful countryside and picnicking on the beach. A life like that of Cordelia. If I didn't have the perspective I have, I'd probably accept it without question, without analysis, and be satisfied. But if I stayed, if I left my world for this one with the knowledge I have, would I be happy as Mrs Cavill Pengower? Would I eventually forget where I come from and sink into this reality until it covered my head like water? Until this was all there was? All there ever was. Until Pixie Tate was a distant memory, like a wisp of a past life relived only in dreams? Would loving Cavill be enough? I don't know.

I'm in the library when there's a sudden commotion in the hall. A cold wind seems to blow in and sweep through it, reaching me at the bookshelf. I hear raised voices. There's a sense of urgency in them, and fear. I rush to the door to see what is going on. The lunch party is spilling out of the drawing room as curious as I am.

It's Mr Bray. I hear him say that he needs to speak to Mr Pengower urgently. I sense there's trouble at the mine. The two men exchange words. I can't hear what they're saying. But Mr Pengower's face reddens. He summons his brother. The two of them leave with Mr Bray. There seems not a moment to lose. The front door slams behind them, leaving us in the wake of the ruckus, reeling from the shock of it.

Cordelia turns to Mr Pringle and tries to hide her fear behind a smile. I'm familiar with that smile now, the way it conveys serenity while beneath, her whole being is in turmoil. 'I think we should eat,' she says bravely. 'My husband and his brother will not be joining us, I'm afraid.' She feigns laughter. 'They are like the Three Musketeers, riding off to fight for their sovereign.' No one laughs with her. They are too shaken. There's trouble at the mine and no amount of fake good cheer can disguise it.

I retreat upstairs, hoping that Cavill isn't in danger. I find it difficult to concentrate on the lesson. Robert doesn't know that his father and uncle have ridden off in haste. I keep looking out of the window at the stables, hoping to see them return. But the sun moves across the sky, and still they do not appear.

Robert and I ride out at our usual time. When we return home for tea, I recognise Cavill's horse immediately as I walk mine beneath the clock tower. The grooms are busy in the stable yard watering down all three who are steaming hot and covered in sweat. The men must have ridden them hard. I don't linger but take Robert inside. I'm keen to know what has happened. I send Robert upstairs to change out of his riding clothes and loiter on the landing to find out what happened.

The family is gathered in the drawing room once again. From what I can hear of their conversation the man engine that Mr Pengower is so proud of broke and sent thirty men plunging into the chasm. It's a miracle that no one was killed, but some of the men were badly hurt. As a consequence, the miners rioted. This is not the first time a piece of machinery has failed and caused injury. The miners set fire to some of the wooden structures and threw stones. It took all three men and the police who joined them, to quell the revolt.

'You are so brave, Ivan,' I hear Mrs James gush in her sweet, girlish tones and Mr Pengower continues to boast about how very brave he was, as if Cavill and Mr Bray, or, indeed, the police, had little part to play in the drama. By the animated tone of his voice the crisis has clearly excited him.

I listen keenly for Cavill, willing Mr Pengower to stop talking for a moment to give his brother the opportunity to speak. I need to know that he's there and that he's all right. Mr Bray insists that measures must be taken at once to ensure the safety of the mine and the adequacy of the equipment. 'These things can no longer be ignored,' he says firmly. Mr Pengower announces, in a tone that implies magnanimity, that he will take steps to guarantee that the mechanism is repaired and that more time and manpower are dedicated to fortifying the tunnels. 'We'll have no more accidents on my watch,' he announces. It's breathtaking how he accepts no responsibility for the substandard conditions of his mine or the welfare of his workers.

At last, I hear Cavill's voice and I'm filled with relief. 'You must go further than that, Ivan. You must give the men more pay,' he says. 'And there must be a review of their housing. Their living conditions are squalid. And those children are too young to be down a mine – they must be educated. It is within your power to raise them up and give them opportunities. At the very least you must talk to them to show that you care, or they will come and burn down this house, or worse. You owe it to your family to make peace.'

'I will go as far as I deem fit,' Mr Pengower growls, his exuberance now deflated. 'I will not be told by you, Cavill, or indeed anyone else, how to run my business. I am not a charity nor am I a bottomless pit of gold.'

I notice Symons then. He's in the hall, listening too. We catch eyes. I expect to see disdain, but something surprising passes between us: an understanding. In that moment we are united in condemnation even though neither of us has uttered a single word. I shake my head sadly and walk slowly on up the stairs. I'm sure now that Felix's disappearance must be linked to the events at the mine. Evil's dark tentacle has already climbed these steps. It's making its way to the nursery, and there's nothing I can do to stop it. Even if Mr Pengower declared today that he was going to make amends, it would be too late.

That evening I'm included at dinner. It's only the four of us for Mr Bray has escorted Mrs James home in her carriage and gone home himself. We don't discuss the trouble at the mine. It's another festering carcass in the middle of the table that everyone pretends is not there. Cordelia's eyes are red. I can tell that she's been crying. And there's an obvious tension between husband and wife that they take trouble to conceal. I sense there's been an argument and that Cordelia has lost. My heart floods with pity for her, for what she is to become. There's nothing anyone can do to avert it. I watch her and for the first time, see the light around her grow dim. Her jawline is stiff, her lips pursed into a thin line, her eyes dull and her skin pale. Everything about her face betrays defeat. In the golden glow of the gas lamps she looks beautiful but wretched, as if she senses intuitively the tragedy that is to come, even though she does not know what form it will take.

Cavill barely speaks to his brother, and I sense a gulf widening between them. They simply cannot see eye to eye. In order to change the subject, and investigate further, I ask Mr Pengower to tell me about the priest hole here in the dining room, which Robert showed me on my first day. He launches into a soliloquy about the persecution of Catholics and the clever Pengower family who built hideaways all over the estate to enable priests to flee from the soldiers who came often to arrest them. 'There's one in the chapel,' he tells me. 'A hole concealed beneath the altar, as well as a secret stair in my dressing room, barely wide enough for a child, which takes you down to the kitchen.' He doesn't mention the one behind the bookcase in the library, and Cordelia doesn't volunteer its existence. I can't believe he doesn't know about it. Cavill eats his dinner in silence. I catch his eye and he blinks back at me despondently. Today's events have really shaken him up and it seems as if he can't forgive his brother.

The sky darkens outside the window, the pale blue of dusk deepening to a beguiling indigo, and finally to black. Stars twinkle and the waxing moon shines through a halo of mist and illuminates the gardens so that one could walk in them without needing a light to guide the way. I would like to walk with Cavill, but the grandfather clock in the hall chimes eleven and Cordelia stands up. 'I will retire now,' she announces. 'Tomorrow Mr Trimlock is coming to paint me.' She sighs and lifts her chin. 'I am not in the least enthusiastic about it.'

'Tomorrow is another day,' I say, quoting Margaret Mitchell's classic that hasn't been written yet.

'Indeed, it is,' she says, smiling forlornly.

Mr Pengower insists that Cavill accompany him while he smokes a cigar and drinks another glass of whisky. He kisses his wife goodnight; I notice she gives him her cheek and grimaces as he presses his prickly moustache against it. Then the two of us leave the room.

'I am beside myself, Miss Swift,' Cordelia says as we lift our skirts and set off up the stairs. 'I do not know what to do. What I can do? But he will not be told. He will never be told. That is his greatest folly. He is too proud to admit that he is in the wrong. Mr Bray has told him a thousand times and even Cavill is at the end of his tether.'

'One can only learn wisdom through experience,' I reply. 'Perhaps today will give him the wisdom he needs to make the mine work for both himself *and* the miners.'

'I am afraid he is too stubborn to learn anything.' She turns to me and her eyes are wild with fear. 'Oh, Miss Swift, I have a dreadful feeling roiling in the pit of my belly.' She puts a hand there. 'Something terrible is going to happen, I just know it.'

'Your priority is the children,' I remind her.

She nods keenly. 'At least they were not in the tunnel when it happened.' Her hand shoots to her breast. 'I thank God for that. I

247

thank God for the children. If it wasn't for them . . .' She stops on the landing and takes my hand. 'I envy you, Miss Swift. You have your whole life ahead of you. There are choices you are yet to make. I have made mine and I must live with them.' She turns away a moment and inhales through her nostrils. Then she looks at me fiercely and squeezes my hand between hers. 'You have the chance to find true love. If I had known then what I know now, I would not have made the choices I did. I would have held out for someone who was compassionate and kind. I would have followed my heart not my head. I would have been wise. But we are not wise when we are young. We know nothing of the world. We do what we're told, and we don't expect too much. We are taught, as women, not to expect too much. But I tell you, expect the world, Miss Swift, for you can have it. Don't compromise. Don't think you don't deserve it. You deserve to love with all your heart and to be loved in return. Don't do what I did and marry a man who . . .' Her breath catches in her throat. 'Does not know how to love.'

I don't know what to say. What *can* I say? I wish I could be a better friend to her.

We part ways, she to her bedroom and me to mine. I stand by the window on the landing, watching the wind rustling the branches in a melancholic dance, and ponder on her words.

I think I'm falling in love with Cavill, but I cannot have him. Tomorrow he will leave, and I will never see him again. When I slip back into my own time, he will have left this world long ago. I can do nothing about that, but I can help Cordelia Pengower. Poor, sad Cordelia Pengower. I can and will help her find love and happiness in the light.

I hear the familiar knock on my door and see the turning of the brass knob. He enters. 'Cavill!' I exclaim and run to him. 'I thought you might not come.'

'My brother . . .' he begins, but I do not let him finish. I press my lips to his in a fierce kiss. I want this moment to last for ever. If time can be manipulated, why is it, I ask myself in frustration, that I cannot *halt* it?

Present

Chapter Seventeen

Tabitha hurried back through the trees in the direction of the gardens and house. Daphne ran behind her, surprisingly swift and light-footed for such a big dog. As they left the wood the mist cleared and the sun shone in watery beams through the crisp air. She reached the vegetable garden and slowed down to a walk. Who was that boy Felix, she wondered, and why was he warning her about the wood? What did he mean? And where did he go?

Making her way through the gate at the other end of the walled garden, she spotted Zach on the other side of the lake. He was skimming stones over the water. She decided she wouldn't confide in him about Felix. He'd probably accuse her of making it up anyway, especially the bit about him not wearing shoes. Who walked barefooted in winter?

'What are you doing?' she asked when she reached him.

He sent another stone bouncing across the surface of the lake. 'Nothing. Bored. I think Dad should buy a boat.'

'Where would you sail to?' Tabitha asked. 'There's nowhere to go.'

He shrugged. 'I wouldn't have to go anywhere. It would be fun just sitting there, in the middle, don't you think?'

'Maybe.'

He searched for another stone. Daphne stuffed her nose in the reeds, sending a moorhen shooting out of the other side and escaping through the water.

'Do you think Pixie is getting somewhere with the spirit?' Tabitha asked, looking longingly towards the house. She'd tell Pixie about the boy. *She* wouldn't disbelieve her.

'I just want whatever it is that's making that noise to go away so that we can have friends to stay,' said Zach. 'You know, if she doesn't get rid of it, we'll have to move back to London.'

Tabitha was horrified. 'You think so?'

'We're not going to stay here if we can't have people over. We're in the middle of nowhere.'

'Is that what Daddy said?'

'It doesn't need to be said. I know what they're thinking. No one wants to live in a spooky house.'

'You don't like it here, do you?' said Tabitha resentfully.

Zach found a stone and turned it over in his hand. 'I like it. It's a cool house, a real flex. I just don't like the fact that it's creepy.'

'You said you weren't afraid. You said you don't believe in ghosts.'

'I'm not afraid. I didn't say I don't believe in ghosts, I just don't believe in the sort of ghosts you believe in. You know, dead people who can't find their way to Heaven. That's just rubbish. When you're dead, you're dead, and there's no coming back. But I *do* believe in poltergeists.' He grinned. 'They're really scary.'

'So, you agree the house is haunted?'

'Well, something's not right.' He sent the stone jumping over the water. 'Probably a poltergeist. How will your "ghost hunters" get rid of a poltergeist, I wonder?' He laughed.

'Pixie can get rid of anything.'

Zach grinned cynically. 'What do you think they're doing in there? Probably sitting on their phones or watching a film and talking shit.'

Tabitha was horrified. 'That's not true.'

'Of course it is. They're hiding up there pretending to get rid of the so-called ghosts, waiting for enough time to go by so they can come downstairs and say they've done it. They'll take their money and leave, having done nothing.'

'You're such a cynic.'

'And you're so gullible. So is Mum, and Antoinette. Well, she's a fruitcake.' He chuckled, pleased with the description. 'Antoinette has always been a fruitcake.'

'You're an ignorant idiot.'

Goaded by the look of disdain on his sister's face, Zach set off up the lawn.

'What are you doing?'

'I'm going to prove I'm right.'

'You're not going in there, are you?' Tabitha began to panic. Surely, he was joking.

'Yes, I'm going in there. I'm going to expose them as frauds. You and Mum won't thank me, but Dad will.'

'Zach! Come back!' Tabitha followed him at a run. 'You're not really going to disturb them, are you?' She hoped he just wanted to scare her.

'Come and watch if you don't believe me. Ghost hunters, my arse!'

Past

Chapter Eighteen

I awake with a sick feeling in my belly. It's five in the morning and the grey light of an overcast dawn is seeping through the gap in the curtains. Today the sun isn't shining – today even the eternally optimistic sun is hiding her face.

I gaze up at the ceiling. My heart is a leaden brick in my chest. Cavill has not yet departed for the Argentine but I already feel bereft. My whole body anticipates the impending emptiness and aches with longing. I cry as despair overcomes me. I'm not strong enough for this. I don't think my heart will survive it.

I drag myself out of bed and dress. It's a long process. Layer upon layer of cotton and lace until finally I'm presentable. I pinch my cheeks, but they're as sallow as Gwen's. We make quite a pair the two of us. I breakfast alone in my room and then wake up Robert. He's too young to need those extra hours in the morning and springs about like a young dog, excited to be starting his day. He's even enthusiastic about practising the piano.

I accompany him downstairs. The house is quiet. The family is still asleep. Cavill is still asleep. How I would love to visit him now, but I don't know where his bedroom is. How I would love to slip beneath the sheets and into his arms. But I'm with Robert and so I continue on to the drawing room. Robert settles himself on the stool and lifts the lid. He opens his score and places it on the music desk. He positions his fingers over the keys and takes a breath as he's been taught to do. Then he begins to play.

I go to the window and gaze out over the lawn. The run of good weather is finally breaking. Damp clouds have moved inland from the sea and are thickening over St Sidwell. The gardens look dull in this lacklustre light. I fold my arms and sigh. My chest is tight with foreboding, the tears ready to break free again and expose me. I'm meant to be detached. I'm meant not to fully engage. I'm supposed to be on my mettle, but all I can think about is Cavill. And losing him.

But lose him I will. We are from two different times and there's nothing I can do to reconcile them. Today he will leave for South America and he will never come back. He will die on the voyage. I cannot bear it. I wish I didn't know it. I wish I were the real Hermione, ignorant of the future. But I'm Pixie Tate and the dreadful awareness of what is to come has overshadowed every moment of joy with Cavill. If only I could exist within the present and bask in the light of his love.

Robert plays falteringly, but I'm not really listening. I'm wallowing in my pain.

I put my thumb in my mouth and chew the nail. A pair of crows land on the grass just outside the window and hop about in search of worms. It's going to rain and then there'll be a banquet for the birds to feast upon. I wonder whether Cavill has ever drawn a crow. I wish we could spend another day sitting on the bank of the estuary sketching birds. I wish with all my heart that I could have another day.

Gwen and I meet in the nursery as usual. Her face is white, even her lips have been leached of colour. She smiles at me wanly, and I sense that she's grateful to be able to confide in me, not to have to carry the burden of her condition alone.

While the children eat, I sit beside her and put my hand on hers. In spite of the warm room, her skin feels cold. 'Have you told him yet?' I ask.

She shakes her head. 'It's not so simple, miss.'

'What do you mean?'

Her gaze drifts to the window and she bites her lip. 'I should have told you before. He's married.'

John Snathe is married? I hadn't even considered that. My heart goes out to this poor, hopeless woman who faces nothing but ruin. 'How long have you known?' I ask softly.

She shrugs in defeat. 'I have always known. That's why I can't tell him, you see. He already has a wife.'

'Where is she?' I ask. I assumed John lodged above the stables.

'She lives with her mother who is sick. But when she dies, his wife will come back.'

I take her hand. 'I'm so sorry.'

'No one is more sorry than I.' Her shoulders shake. She turns to me, her eyes large and pleading. 'What am I to do, Miss Swift?'

I cannot answer that.

After breakfast, instead of going to the schoolroom, I take Robert down to the library under the pretence of looking for something interesting to read. I hope Cavill will find me here and say goodbye. I linger about the shelves, my eyes running over the spines, but not reading the words embossed upon them. Robert pulls out a book. It's about inventions. He takes it to the leather sofa and starts looking through it.

I hear voices in the hall. Cordelia is talking to Symons about Mr Trimlock, who is coming to paint her this afternoon. She wants him to set up in the blue drawing room. Her voice fades as she leaves the hall. Perhaps she has gone to her study to attend to her correspondence. She likes to do that in the mornings. The grandfather clock announces the hour and I put a hand to my chest. The time of his departure is approaching.

Panicked, I tell Robert to take his book upstairs, assuring him that I will join him in a few minutes. As Robert leaves, Cavill finds me. 'There you are,' he says, relieved. He's not the same carefree man I first met on the stairs, but a man consumed with apprehension. The events at the mine and his disagreements with his brother have robbed him of his insouciance. He strides straight over and takes my hands in his. 'I must go,' he tells me, his brow furrowing and his eyes dimming, and that beautiful mouth of his turning down at the corners. 'I admit that I am happy to leave St Sidwell and my brother, but I wish to God that I did not have to leave you.'

His eyes caress my face as if he wants to commit to memory every contour. 'I love you, my darling Hermione,' he murmurs.

My throat tightens. I want to stop him going, I know I mustn't. But I can't help myself. I care too much. 'Cavill . . .' I look into his eyes and tears mist my vision.

'Hermione, this is simply farewell.'

If only he knew that it is the end.

'Cavill . . .'

'What is it?'

I see Symons over Cavill's shoulder. He stands in the doorway and coughs. Cavill lets go of my hands and turns. 'Your carriage awaits,' says the butler solemnly.

'Thank you, Symons.' He turns and leaves the room.

I hear Mr and Mrs Pengower in the hall. They wish him luck but panic sends the blood rushing into my temples and I hear nothing more but the drumming in my ears. He is leaving and I will never see him again. I put a hand on the back of an armchair to steady me. I cannot let him go. I cannot.

As my heart floods with despair, he reappears suddenly. He strides across the floor towards me. 'I want you to have this, Hermione.' He holds out a small, leatherbound sketchbook. He runs his fingers over the cover, as if caressing an old friend. He puts it in my hands. 'It is full of sketches of birds I have drawn down on the estuary and the beach. I want you to have it, so that you keep me close to your heart.' My eyes blur with tears. 'Open it.' I turn to the first page. Beside a beautifully drawn little egret are the words: *To my beloved Hermione.* I catch my breath. It's so special, I don't know what to say. He lifts my chin and kisses me gently on the lips. 'Wait for me,' he adds quietly. I nod because I cannot speak. I press the book against my chest. Beneath it I feel my heart breaking.

He walks away, and this time he doesn't come back. I glance out of the window and see that it's started to rain. His carriage is indeed waiting in the forecourt. Grantly, in a cloak and hat, sits hunched on the box seat, waiting to drive him to the station. The horse looks bedraggled and miserable. I go to the glass and gaze out. Cavill climbs in. Then he turns and his eyes find me. They look inordinately sad.

I cannot bear it. Despair takes me over. I will not remain here and do nothing. I cannot allow the man I love to leave and die. I cannot. I forget the Butterfly Effect. I cannot worry about the consequences when the man I love is about to face his death. When it's within my power to change what's written.

I place the book on the table and hurry from the room and across the hall to the front door. The carriage is already making its way towards the avenue of plane trees.

I lift my skirts and rush past them, into the rain. I don't care that I'm getting wet. I just care about Cavill. 'Stop!' I shout. Mr Grantly cannot hear me above the clopping sound of hooves. 'Stop!' I shout again. 'Stop!'

At last, I'm heard.

Grantly draws the horse to a halt and turns to face me in alarm. I run to the window of the carriage. 'Cavill!' I cry, the tears misting my vision so that the carriage is just a black smudge in the rain. I put my hands on the window frame, out of breath and panting.

Cavill looks at me in fright.

'Cavill, please don't go . . .' I cannot get the words out.

I feel a sharp pain in my chest. I cry out and press my fist to my breast. It's as if my lungs are on fire, as if my throat is burning too – as if I'm being consumed by flames. I lift my gaze to see him opening the carriage door. I see his eyes, his beautiful blue eyes, so full of concern . . .

Then everything goes black.

Present

Chapter Nineteen

Pixie felt an intense pain in her chest, as if it were on fire. As if something was weighing down on it and squashing the life out of her. Fighting for breath, she opened her eyes. She was lying prostrate on the floor. Staring down at her were three horrified faces: Ulysses, Zach and Tabitha.

'Pixie, Pixie, *você me ouve?*' Ulysses was shaking her by the shoulders as she twitched and writhed. 'Pixie, *escuta-me*! Pixie! *Pelo amor de deus, fala alguma coisa!*' Ulysses always broke into Portuguese when he was frightened.

Pixie took a great gulp of air. She realised suddenly where she was, and the shock hit her like a blow to the stomach. 'No!'

Her scream startled the two children and they recoiled as if they'd been bitten by a snake.

'No, no, no, no, no, no! This cannot be!' Grabbing Ulysses by the arms, she pulled herself to her feet and stood gaping in bewilderment at the three terrified faces, astonished to see them there. 'What just happened?' She stared at them in horror. 'Tell me! What the hell just happened?'

'You were having a fit!' Ulysses replied. 'Are you okay?'

The pain in her chest was beginning to subside. Pixie rushed to the window. She looked out at the winter's day. There was no mistaking it – she had slid back.

Banging her forehead against the glass she closed her eyes and cried out.

Ulysses turned to the children. 'You'd better leave us,' he said. Then more urgently, 'Go!'

The children bolted into the corridor. Tabitha turned on Zach. 'You idiot!' she cried. 'What were you thinking? How could you?'

Zach felt terrible. 'I didn't know. I'm sorry.'

'You might have killed her. You're so stupid!'

Zach's cheeks burned scarlet. He felt like a fool. What had he been thinking? 'I know. I'm sorry. I shouldn't have . . .'

They made their way down the stairs in silence.

'What happened?' Pixie asked Ulysses.

'Zach burst in,' he explained with a shrug.

'He just burst in? Why?'

'I don't know. I was watching my movie. I didn't expect anyone to disturb us. Then he burst in and said something about this being a big joke. The next thing I know, you're convulsing on the floor. You really worried me, Pix. I thought you were going to die.'

'Shit!' Pixie turned back to the window. How different the garden looked in winter. She glanced down at her jeans and trainers. They felt odd after the long skirt and boots she'd been wearing. 'Oh, Ulysses. I was so close to finding out who takes Felix.'

Ulysses didn't know what to do. He'd never seen her like this before.

'It's ruined!' she exclaimed. Then she burst into tears, banging her forehead against the glass again. 'It's ruined. All ruined.' She felt as if she'd hit a brick wall.

A moment later he was behind her. He put his arms around her in a hug, but it was of little comfort. 'It's okay, Pix,' he murmured softly. 'It's okay.'

'No, it isn't. How am I going to slide back to where I left off? If I link into the locket again, I might slide back to another time. A month before, who knows? I can't control it. I put out the desire and leave the details to divine power. Now it's ruined. You can't play around with time.'

'Stupid boy,' Ulysses exclaimed crossly.

'He's a boy. How could he know?' She turned around and let her friend pull her against his chest. If only he were Cavill.

'I should have been on guard!' he said. 'I'm sorry I fucked up.'

Pixie began to sob. 'Someone is going to take Felix away . . . and I won't be there to see who it is.'

'It's in the past, Pix.'

'Not for me, it isn't,' she snapped, shaking him off.

'Then you have to find a way to slide back.'

'It's not so simple.' She swore again, loudly. 'How long was I out?'

'Three hours.'

'Three hours!' She laughed bitterly. 'I was there for ten days.' She thought of Cavill and a sick feeling crept into her breast. 'Cavill!' Her stomach cramped with guilt. Had she stopped him from leaving? She couldn't recall what she'd said to him. Had she affected time?

'Who is Cavill?'

Pixie didn't anwer him, and rushed towards the door.

'Where are you going?' Ulysses asked, chasing after her.

'Come.'

She did not want to bump into the family, at least not yet. There was something she had to do first.

Pixie now knew the house well. Surprisingly little had changed since it had belonged to Ivan and Cordelia Pengower. Certainly, the structure was the same; it was only the decoration and some of the furniture that had been altered – like an elegant old dame who has simply slipped into a new outfit. The smell was the same too, of woodsmoke and antiquity, and it brought Cavill back to her in a sudden assault of memory and she suffered once again a searing sense of loss. Suppressing the desire to cry, she led Ulysses down the corridor and the old servants' staircase, and out through the back door into the January afternoon.

The cold took Pixie by surprise. She had never seen the gardens in winter. Gone were the summer flowers and foliage and immaculately cut grass, and in their place naked, shivering branches and overgrown and tangled borders. The ground was soggy where the frost had melted, and her trainers squelched as she strode purposefully through the vegetable garden and on into the wood. It compounded her sadness to see such neglect. Under Cordelia Pengower's loving eye, this place had been a utopia.

'Where are we going?' Ulysses asked, struggling to keep up with her. 'I'm not wearing the right shoes. You could have told me we were going to be in the mud.'

'We're going to the family chapel,' she answered curtly.

'Isn't there a path, or a track? Do we have to wade through wet grass? I'm wearing suede.'

'There *is* a track, but we're going the shortcut.'

'What's the hurry?'

Pixie stopped and glared at him. 'Look, you don't have to come.'

Ulysses' face fell. 'But I want to come,' he protested in bewilderment.

'Then stop complaining. You're behaving like a child.'

'And you're being horrible. You're not being *you*!'

She sighed in frustration. 'Look, I'm sorry, Ulysses. I'm just devastated. I was so close to finding out what happens. I was living it. Every minute of it. That child is real to me. He's not in the past. He's in the present, and he's going to vanish. He's probably going to die.'

'But you can't stop it, Pixie.' Ulysses reminded her gently.

'I know. But I can find out what happened. I can see who takes him and with that knowledge I can settle Cordelia's soul. I know her, I have to help her. I need to find out what happens to Felix and bring her peace.' Pixie turned to Ulysses, her eyes welling with tears. 'I care for these people, Ulysses. And I fucked up. I'm hating myself right now.'

'Being mean to me won't make you like yourself, you know.'

'I'm not being mean to you.'

'Maybe not intentionally.'

'This isn't about you.'

'You're making it about me.' He drew his lips into a thin line. 'Just be nice.'

'I haven't got the energy to be nice. I just want to curl up and die.'

He rolled his eyes. 'So, what are you going to do at the chapel? Pray or dig your own grave?'

She had to laugh at that. Pixie had never been religious, so praying wasn't an option. 'I'm going to look at the graves, not dig one.'

'*Bem.*' He was still none the wiser, but he ran after her all the same. He glanced down at his brown suede shoes, now darkened with moisture, and marched on regardless.

At last, they emerged out of the trees. In the middle of the pasture the chapel was bathed in silence and cold sunshine. It looked almost exactly as it had done in 1895. Perhaps there were more gravestones, she couldn't tell. If Ulysses hadn't been beside her, and she hadn't been wearing jeans, she might have thought she had slipped back in time. If only she had.

Leaving Ulysses picking his way carefully over the soggy ground, Pixie ran towards the graveyard. A pressure built in her chest, rising into her throat. Her vision misted and she blinked away tears. Frantically, she moved through the gravestones, memorials and tombs that were littered over the grass, searching for one name. She did not notice Ulysses or hear him speak. She was alone with her purpose, and nothing could distract her.

She saw the memorial to Cordelia Pengower, and a larger, more ostentatious one for Ivan. She found Mrs James Pengower's headstone and her husband's obelisk. She passed other Pengowers whom she had never met, and then she found the one she was looking for.

Her legs gave way beneath her. The pressure in her chest was released in a sob and she threw her arms around the headstone. Beneath her the words *Cavill Henry James Pengower* were carved into the stone, along with the sentence *Go forth into the light* and the date: *1857–1943.*

She stared at the numbers in amazement. *1943.*

According to the book Bruce had found, Cavill had died in 1895. But now the gravestone indicated that he had lived into his eighties.

'Oh my God. I've changed the future,' she murmured in astonishment. However, an assault of guilt and terror quickly followed. She wasn't meant to change events. She was meant to observe and change nothing. But she had prevented Cavill from dying on the way to Argentina. She had saved his life. The implications of that were tremendous and terrifying. A sick feeling churned in her belly. What were the consequences of her meddling?

Ulysses stood a short distance away, tactfully leaving her to her sorrow. He could not imagine what was going through Pixie's mind.

Kneeling before the gravestone, Pixie trailed her fingers over Cavill's name. It was unimaginable to think of him dead. Unbearable to envisage those beautiful eyes closed for ever. Right now, it didn't matter that his soul lived on, because it felt like mere minutes ago that she had been in his arms. He'd been real and solid, warm-bodied and breathing. He'd been living and loving, but now he was gone.

Now he was gone.

Slowly, Ulysses approached. He looked at the gravestone and read the words. 'Who was Cavill?' he asked again.

Pixie felt drained and deflated and very tired suddenly. 'I loved him,' she replied.

'You fell in love?' Ulysses asked, amazed.

'I love him with all my heart, Ulysses. I have never loved like this before, and I suspect I never will again.' She sounded different, not at all like the Pixie he knew.

Ulysses screwed up his nose. How could this have happened in three hours? 'What about Pablo?' he asked.

For a moment Pixie didn't recognise that name. Then it registered. How insubstantial it sounded compared to Cavill. 'Pablo is nothing to me,' she replied, and indeed the name sounded hollow and weightless, like a husk.

'Who was he?' Ulysses crouched beside her, wary of getting his trousers dirty. They were designer and very expensive.

'He's Cordelia Pengower's brother-in-law. He's leaving now for South America, and I can't bear to see him go.'

Ulysses put a hand on her shoulder. '*Meu amor*, he died over seventy years ago. You're talking in the present tense. He's not real.'

'He is real to me,' she bit back.

At length she stood up and sighed in defeat. The hard winter sun was low in the sky, turning the ribbon of the sea to a dazzling blue. In her mind's eye she saw herself riding through the long grasses with Robert and Cavill. It had only been a few days ago. She could feel the wind in her hair and smell the sweet scents of wild flowers and brine. The vision was almost tangible, as if she could reach out and touch it. But it was gone, all gone.

She turned to her friend. 'What do I do now?' She looked small and pitiful and lost.

Ulysses shrugged. 'You have to find a way to go back.'

'Going back is not a challenge,' she told him. 'Going back to the moment where I left off, is. Timesliding is not an exact science, or perhaps I'm just not very good at it. It isn't like waving a magic wand.'

'You have to try,' said Ulysses with a shrug.

'For Cordelia,' she added, motivated suddenly by thought of that poor, wretched soul. 'I have to try, for her.'

They walked through the wood. The gardens of St Sidwell might have changed but the woods had not. Only the season was different, stripping the trees of their leaves and sending the birds away to warmer climes. It was as if the place had died with Cavill. While they made their way back to the house, Pixie told him about her adventure. He listened in wonder as she described the family and the events leading up to Felix's disappearance. 'I'm convinced it's a miner,' she told him. 'There were other possibilities, but knowing what I know now, I think it's someone who wants to hurt Ivan Pengower. If I manage to get back, I'll find out simply by being there. But there's more going on that I feel is significant. You see, when I slid, I put out the desire to find out what happened in the past to prevent Cordelia moving on in the present. It's one thing holding an object in order to link me with the person I need to know about, but it's another to travel on the energy of that desire. It's the desire that determined the date of my arrival. Do you see?'

Ulysses frowned. 'Not really,' he confessed.

'By the law of attraction, my desire took me to a point in time where I could find out what I needed to know. Well, if all I needed to do was lie in wait in Felix's bedroom on the night of the 29th June 1895 and watch who came in to abduct him, then surely I would have slid back to the morning of the twenty-eighth. But I didn't. I slid back to eleven days *before* the abduction. That's not accidental. That's deliberate. The law of attraction is the most powerful law in the universe. Nothing happens by chance.'

'So you think there's another reason why she won't move on?' Ulysses asked.

'I do. And I was given eleven days to find out what that is.'

'Then you have to go back and live the last day.'

'I do. I just have to find a way to do it. I've never been in this situation before. I can link into the locket again, but I can't guarantee that I'll slide back to the same moment in time. I might slide back to a different time and then have to relive the whole thing again. I can't do that, Ulysses.'

'Is there anyone you can call? Another timeslider?'

Pixie looked at him askance. 'Oh, do you know one?' she asked sarcastically.

He shrugged. 'Clutching at straws, Grumpy! How about calling the college?'

'And how are they going to help? I think even the College of Psychic Studies would find my claims of sliding through time a little too out there! I don't even think my mentor Avril can help me. Her knowledge of timesliding was limited to what an Indian guru told her, and what she'd read in a book she lent me. Basically, theory. She had never done it herself. But, following what she'd learnt, she taught me how to link into an object and put out the desire of what I wanted to achieve, and she taught me about the law of attraction and how it works. But I can't be specific about the exact time and place I want to arrive in. I've tried that and it doesn't work.'

'You're giving me a headache,' Ulysses complained. 'I was never good at physics at school.'

'It's really hard to understand, especially because no one else seems to do it. When I was a child, it happened by default. I'd desire safety and slide back to a time before my house had been built. Of course, back then, I didn't realise I was sliding through time. I'd find myself in a meadow and feel safe. I thought it was Heaven. But as I grew up and began sliding, quite randomly, to different eras, I realised that I was sliding through time. I began playing with it. It was entertaining. I'd put out the desire to go back to a certain year and I'd find myself there, observing. That was when my grandmother found me in a trance and shook me out of it. I ended up having a fit and being taken to hospital.'

'Lucky we didn't have to take you to hospital this time,' said Ulysses with relief.

'Very lucky,' Pixie agreed. 'But that was when I realised it wasn't something I could play with. I also learnt that sliding back as *me*, with my astral body, meant I could only stay a short time. I didn't have the energy to remain for long.'

'So, if you don't slide as *you*. Who do you slide as?' It had never occurred to Ulysses that, when Pixie went back in time, she was anyone other than herself.

'When I met Avril at the college, as well as learning to link into an object to take me back in time, I learnt something else.' She glanced at Ulysses, doubting suddenly whether she should tell him. She decided she should. She needed to share it with someone, and he was the only someone she had whom she could trust. 'I learnt to slide into another person's body. That's what I do, you see. I slide into someone else's body.'

Ulysses stared at her in puzzlement. If he didn't know her so well, he wouldn't believe her. 'You've never told me that before,' he said.

'I know. I'm embarrassed because it's weird. Usually, I slide back as me and observe, and you keep me safe. But recently, I've been experimenting with possessing another person's body. There, so now you know.' She shrugged. 'You're the only person, besides Avril, who knows.'

Ulysses laughed. He thought it sounded absurd. 'Are you serious, Pix? You really do that? You possess someone else's body? Isn't that a bit gross?'

Pixie was put out. 'Look, it's the only way it works. Sometimes I can't do it being me, all right? I have to be someone else.'

'Can you slide into a man's body?'

'No, by the law of attraction, I slide into a body that's close in energy to mine. It's a relatively new skill, to be honest. I'm still learning how it works. I think this slide has taught me that the universe, or God, or whatever you want to call it, helps me to slide into the best body for my desire, which is why I didn't slide into Cordelia. I needed to observe her, not *be* her.'

He nodded, taking it in. 'So, when you say you fell in love. The man you fell in love with, Cavill, actually fell in love with—'

'Hermione Swift,' Pixie cut in. 'I've been living in the past as Hermione Swift, the governess. Cavill fell in love with her.'

'Which means, if he were to meet *you*, Pixie, he wouldn't know you?'

'That will never happen,' said Pixie sadly. 'But you're right. He wouldn't know me.'

Yet, if Cavill looked into her eyes, looked *deeply* into her eyes, might he . . .? Pixie so wanted to believe he would.

'What are you going to tell Olivia?' Ulysses asked.

'That I'm not going to give up. I just need time to work it out.'

'There has to be a way.'

'Trust me, I'll move heaven and earth to get back and finish the job. I owe it to Cordelia. She's not just a spirit who's trapped on the earth plane, but a friend too.'

And she'd move heaven and earth to have one final moment with Cavill.

Zach and Tabitha went out into the garden. Neither spoke; Zach was feeling guilty; Tabitha was still furious. The light was already fading even though it was not yet three. Purple shadows were lengthening over the wet grass and the air was growing heavy with moisture. There would be another frost tonight. They wandered miserably down the stone path. Even though it wasn't Tabitha's fault, she felt bad. She should have stopped Zach from barging in. The sight of Pixie falling onto the floor and convulsing was one she would never forget.

Zach thrust his hands into his pockets and kicked a stone out of his path. 'I'm going to be in shit now,' he said eventually, looking to her for support. Not that he deserved it, Tabitha thought. He knew he'd done wrong.

'You're going to have to say sorry,' she said.

'I know. Should we go back?'

'No. I think we should steer clear for a while.'

'It's getting dark.'

'I don't care.'

'Just saying.'

Tabitha sighed. 'If we're going to stay out, we might as well explore.'

'What's there to explore?' he asked dully. The last thing he felt like doing was exploring.

'Loads.'

He didn't look keen, but Tabitha wanted to go back to the cottage. 'Come with me. I'll show you something interesting.' She decided not to tell him about the boy, unless he showed up. But it was getting dark; he was likely at home with his family.

Tabitha led Zach through the wood. The smell of pine and wet soil saturated the air, which felt colder in the trees. It was darker too. There was no birdsong, only the cawing of rooks and the screeching of an owl. 'Where are we going?' Zach asked.

'To a secret place,' Tabitha answered, delighted to have something to show him that he hadn't already seen. 'Have you brought your phone?'

'Yes, why? Do you want to make a call?'

'We might need the torch.'

'You're not going to send me down a hole, are you?'

She laughed, no longer cross. 'No, but I doubt there's electricity.'

'Sounds great,' he said unenthusiastically.

At last, they reached the clearing. The cottage stood still and silent like a tomb, sinking slowly into nature's embrace. 'Wow!' Zach exclaimed, cheering up. 'This is awesome.'

'Pretty cool, right?' Tabitha strode towards it. 'Let's go and have a look inside.'

'When did you find this?'

'This morning. But I didn't go inside. I was going to, but I got distracted by Daphne.'

'It's a ruin. I love ruins.'

'So do I. No one's lived here for years. I suppose Daddy's inherited it as well?' Tabitha asked.

'He's inherited the whole place,' Zach replied. 'We should rebuild it.'

'Like we need more space!' Tabitha pushed the door. It opened without resistance, only a gasp as if surprised by the intrusion. The thick mesh of spider webs that tore around the frame revealed that no one had been through it in a very long time. She wondered where the boy had come from. If he hadn't been inside, where had he been?

The first thing that struck Tabitha on entering the house was the dust. It covered all surfaces in a thick grey blanket. There was little furniture in the main room. Just a wooden table and a few chairs, a dresser and a fireplace. The cottage had clearly been vacated years ago. Windowpanes were broken or hanging off their hinges. Damp stained the walls in patches of brown. Mice had eaten through the curtain, or perhaps the fabric had been devoured by moths. It was bitterly cold. When she exhaled, her breath misted.

'I wonder who lived here,' Tabitha mused, gazing around her in awe. 'I'd like to know, wouldn't you?'

'Yeah,' Zach agreed, lifting a rusted red-and-yellow tin off the table and wiping away the dust with his fingers. 'I'd like to know why Mrs Delaware left it to rot.' He blew the remaining dust away to reveal the words *Gold Leaf Honey Dew* on the lid.

'Maybe she didn't have the money to repair it,' Tabitha suggested.

'I suppose she let her own house go to ruin.' Zach opened the tin. To his surprise he didn't find tobacco, but a folded piece of yellowed paper.

'What's that?' Tabitha asked, drawing close.

Zach lifted the paper out and unfolded it.

'Give me your phone,' she said. 'And I'll shine the torch onto it.'

He put the tin down and opened what turned out to be a short letter. While Tabitha shone the torch, Zach read it out loud. It wasn't easy to read for the writing was very tight and slanted.

September 1895

Beloved. My suffering is total. I am in torment. I cannot live without you in my life. I simply cannot. I carry our child in my belly and that keeps me from giving up. This child is my hope and the only thing that gives me a reason to live. It is a part of you and a part of me and was conceived in love. Indeed, there is no child on earth that was conceived in more love than this blessed soul. Adultery is a sin we are told, and yet how can love such as ours be a sin? God is love. These laws we must abide by are simply human constructs. Loving you is not a sin but a God-given gift.

I love you, my dear one, and I pray that we may find a way to be together. I hope this letter finds its way to you. I hope you read it and that it gives you hope, too. Hope now is all I have, and I cling to it with all my strength.

Your loving friend

'Wow!' Tabitha exclaimed. 'I wonder who wrote it?'

'Someone who was pregnant and shouldn't have been.'

Tabitha laughed. 'Scandal! Let's take it back and show Mum. I bet she doesn't even know about this cottage.'

'Of course, she doesn't. She's barely been outside,' said Zach. 'It's too cold for her.'

Tabitha grabbed the tin. 'Nice. A real relic.'

'There are plenty of those back at the house,' said Zach. 'I've seen them. Let's see if we can find anything else interesting in here.'

The two children wandered from room to room then climbed what remained of the staircase. The upstairs was in worse condition than the downstairs for the roof had fallen in leaving it open for the rain, and the ivy and bindweed to steal in with their boundless appetites.

'Come on,' said Zach, making his way back down the stairs. 'Let's go and show Mum the letter.'

'And apologise to Pixie,' Tabitha added.

Zach groaned. 'I suppose I should,' he said.

'You can redeem yourself with the letter.'

'Yeah. I hope it's important.'

Pixie and Ulysses found Antoinette and Olivia in the drawing room. The two women sat up expectantly when they saw them. 'How did it go?' Antoinette asked. 'Did you get rid of her?'

Pixie shook her head. 'I'm afraid not.'

'Oh.' Antoinette was disappointed.

'What happened?' Olivia asked.

'I was disturbed,' said Pixie awkwardly, not wanting to get the children into trouble.

'Who disturbed you?' Olivia asked. Then her expression hardened. 'Not Bruce?'

'No, the children,' Ulysses interrupted. 'Zach to be precise. He just burst in, and Pixie was woken out of her trance.'

'Dear girl—' Antoinette exclaimed.

'It's okay,' Pixie cut in hastily. She didn't want them to know how dangerous it was to interrupt her when she was in that state.

Olivia was cross. 'That's not on. Where are they?'

Pixie shrugged. 'I don't know.'

'I told them to leave,' said Ulysses. 'Pixie wasn't right, and we needed space.'

'Good God!' Antoinette gasped. 'Are you all right, my dear?'

'I'm fine. But I need to find a way to get back.'

Olivia looked anxious. 'Can you do that?'

'I don't know,' said Pixie. 'I was so close.'

'To finding out what happened?' Olivia asked.

'Yes.'

'Tell us,' said Antoinette, lighting another cigarette. 'What have you found out so far?'

Chapter Twenty

'It's gripping,' said Antoinette when Pixie had finished. 'It could be anyone, really, couldn't it? The obvious culprit is one of the miners. Olivia and I went to the local library and found out that the boy killed in the mining accident was called Billy Tonkin. According to the librarian, who just happens to be a very keen local historian, it was the boy's father who sought revenge on Ivan Pengower and hid the child's body in the mine. No one bothered to look there, or to question the men, apparently.'

'He might be right,' said Pixie.

'I suspect he was murdered,' Antoinette added, before taking a long drag. Something in Pixie's heart snagged. The very idea of that innocent child being killed was unbearable. To Antoinette, Olivia and Ulysses, Felix was simply a name, but to Pixie he was a sweet child, a sweet living-and-breathing child who, when she'd last seen him only hours before, had been very much alive.

'Could it be someone in the house, do you think?' Olivia asked.

'It could be,' Pixie replied, but she wasn't convinced. 'I did find out that there's a secret passage leading from a hidden door in the library to a shed by the stables. A priest hole. This house is full of them. So, if all the doors and windows were locked the night he was taken, he could only have been spirited away through that passageway. But I don't believe that anyone in the house has – had – a motive to hurt Felix.'

Olivia's mouth opened in amazement. 'There's a secret passageway in the library?' she gasped.

'No way!' exclaimed Ulysses. 'The plot thickens!'

'Really,' said Pixie. 'There's one in the dining room too. Come, I'll show you.'

The four of them gathered in the library. Pixie pulled the lever and the door clicked open, revealing the staircase behind it. Olivia stared at it, dumbfounded. She had been in this room many times and not noticed it. 'This is incredible,' she said.

'Astonishing,' Antoinette added. She looked at Pixie with admiration. 'You really do slide back in time, don't you? I wasn't sure, to be honest. I don't think either of us were. But now I know. How else would you have found this?'

'I agree,' said Olivia, feeling a wonderful sense of justification. This would prove to Bruce that timesliding wasn't a fantasy.

Pixie nodded thoughtfully. 'Whoever takes Felix very likely comes and goes from the house through this tunnel.' She folded her arms as her skin prickled. It was horrendous to think of Felix being carried down this hole and never coming back.

Just then Zach and Tabitha appeared in the doorway. Both children looked sheepish.

'Well?' said Olivia, putting her hands on her hips. 'What have you got to say for yourselves? I hope you're sorry.'

'We are,' said Zach quickly. 'I mean, I am. I'm sorry, Pixie.'

'It's okay,' said Pixie. 'You couldn't have known.'

'I thought—' he began.

'It doesn't matter what you thought,' Tabitha cut in sharply. 'Look what we've found.' She held out the tin.

'What's that?' Antoinette asked.

'A tin,' said Ulysses.

'It's what's *inside* the tin that's interesting,' said Tabitha with a grin. She opened it and lifted out the letter. She handed it to Pixie.

The room fell silent as Pixie read it out loud. When she finished, she folded it up and gave it back to Tabitha. 'It's from Gwen, the nursemaid,' she said. 'It's sad to read. Women like Gwen didn't fare well in those days. I don't imagine her story is written up in any history book. We'll never know what became of her or her child.'

'We will if you manage to slide back,' said Ulysses.

Pixie sighed. 'I will think of a way,' she said. 'I'm not leaving without settling Cordelia's soul.'

Olivia called the children over to the bookcase. 'Look what Pixie's found,' she said. Zach and Tabitha stared into the priest hole in wonder.

'Wow!' said Zach. 'This is really cool!'

'Can I go down it?' asked Tabitha.

'Go and find your father and see what he says,' Olivia suggested.

'You said there was another one in the dining room?' Antoinette reminded Pixie.

'There is. I'll show you. And apparently there's one in an upstairs bedroom that has a secret staircase going down to the kitchen,' she added, remembering Mr Pengower mentioning it.

'How exciting!' Olivia gushed, clapping her hands. 'Let's go and see if we can find it.'

While the children went in search of Bruce, and Olivia, Antoinette and Ulysses went upstairs to look for the secret staircase, Pixie returned to Felix's bedroom in the hope of persuading Cordelia to move on. Maybe Pixie could suggest that one of the miners had taken him. Cordelia might accept that and agree to leave. After all, if Felix was in spirit, Cordelia only had to move into the light to be reunited with him. What did it matter what happened to him in the past, if he was here in the present?

Pixie wasn't confident that her idea would work and was concerned that Cordelia would sense that she hadn't really found out the truth, but she decided to give it a go anyway. She sat on the chair and closed her eyes. She quietened her breathing, focused on the gentle rise and fall of her chest, and slowly sank into trance. Then she reached out to Cordelia.

She waited, but she sensed only the empty room and the stillness. *Cordelia* she said in her mind, but Cordelia didn't appear. *Cordelia, I have found out what happened to your son.* Nothing. Perhaps Cordelia intuited that she was lying. Frustrated, Pixie remained on the chair for another half an hour. She could feel the heavy, desolate energy and the damp cold that the spirit carried with her, but, however much she called out, Cordelia herself did not appear.

Finally, she had no choice but to give up. Cordelia didn't show herself because she didn't want to. It was obvious that she was determined to stay where she was. She didn't want to be helped. But why?

There was nothing for it. Pixie had to think of a way to get back to her in the past. She had to finish the job she had set out to do. What happened on that fateful night of the 29th of June? Unless Pixie found the answer to that question, Cordelia would remain for ever *here*.

When Pixie came downstairs, Antoinette, Olivia and Ulysses were back in the library with the children and Bruce. Elsa and Tom were there too, discussing the priest hole. Tom was making his way up the stairs with a torch. 'I'd say it's safe,' he announced, brushing the dust off his shoulder.

'Ah, Pixie,' said Bruce. 'I don't know how you discovered this, but it's a genuine, Elizabethan priest hole. Extraordinary!'

Elsa scratched her head. 'In all the years I've worked here, I've never seen this one. I don't even think Mrs Delaware knew it was here. She never once mentioned it.'

'We knew about the one in the dining room,' Tom added, climbing out. 'And the one upstairs, but this one has blown my socks off.' He grinned. 'It takes quite a lot to blow my socks off!'

Antoinette laughed. 'Good to know you have an escape route, should you need one,' she said to Bruce.

Tom handed the torch to Zach. 'You want to go down?' he asked.

Olivia was quick to intervene. 'I don't think the children should go in there,' she said. 'Don't you agree, Bruce? It might be dangerous.' Zach pulled a face.

'Yes, you wouldn't want to get stuck. We might never find you!' Bruce chuckled.

'Oh, Daddy!' Tabitha exclaimed.

'Don't "Oh, Daddy" me! Ground rules. No going down holes, do you understand?'

Both Zach and Tabitha nodded.

'I'm not sure I believe in all this mumbo-jumbo,' Bruce said to

Pixie. 'But you clearly have a gift of sorts. If you find secret treasure hidden beneath the floorboards, let me know. We'll go halves.'

That night, Pixie couldn't sleep. Her heart pined for Cavill, while her mind ached with the effort of trying to think of a way to get back to him, and to Cordelia. The next twenty-four hours were crucial, and she had missed them. She *had* to slide back. But this was uncharted territory, and she didn't want to get it wrong. How could she guarantee that her desire would take her back to the moment she'd left? It just didn't seem possible. She could hold the locket and put out the desire, she could even picture the very scene, but how could she be sure that that would work? It was too much of a gamble.

Antoinette noticed Pixie's pallor in the morning when she walked into the dining room at breakfast, but she was too polite to say anything. She buttered her piece of toast and told Daphne to go and lie down. 'Not everyone wants you drooling over their breakfast,' she added, giving the dog a gentle push. But Daphne had her eye on the toast and wasn't going anywhere.

Bruce, who had already been out milking the cows with Tom, was reading the newspapers on his iPad while Olivia was busy scrolling through her emails on her phone. She didn't want to let on how worried she was, how much it mattered to her that Pixie got rid of the spirit. Both said good morning and then returned to their business. Elsa came in with a fresh pot of tea and toast, and offered to make Pixie and Ulysses a full English breakfast. They both declined. Ulysses never understood how the British could eat so much food in the morning. He typically drank just a strong cup of coffee and mushed avocado on toast.

Tabitha, who had already eaten, went and sat beside Pixie. She put the letter on the table beside her. 'I think you should keep this,' she said.

'Thank you, Tabitha,' Pixie replied. 'You're clever to have found it. You'll make a good detective one day.'

'I want to be like you,' said Tabitha quietly.

Pixie laughed. 'If you knew what I was really like, you wouldn't say that.'

'Did you go down the priest hole?' she whispered.

'I did.'

'Was it dangerous?'

'Not at all. But that was over a hundred years ago.'

'Will you come and look at it with me after breakfast?' Tabitha glanced at her parents, but they were too busy engrossed in their devices to hear her.

'Let's go now,' Pixie replied. 'I'm not hungry.'

Pixie left the room with her young friend. Bruce didn't take his eyes off his iPad, but Olivia watched them leave, a frown furrowing her brow. She silently prayed that Pixie would send the spirit on its way, and make the house feel nice. If she couldn't do it, Tabitha wouldn't be the only one to be disappointed. She took a sip of tea and shivered. She really couldn't last much longer in a house this cold.

Antoinette noticed that Daphne was drooling again and accused Zach of teaching her bad habits. Ulysses had received a text from Jean-Michel and was too busy writing back to notice Pixie heading off without him.

In the library, Tabitha found the secret lever in the bookcase and pulled it. 'Can we go down the stairs, just to the bottom.'

'Well, your parents don't want you going down it. It might be dangerous.'

'Tom said it was fine,' Tabitha argued.

'I'm sure he's right. When I went down it, it was very well made.'

'Then let's have a little look.' Tabitha grinned mischievously. 'Just a little look,' she added.

'All right. But let's be quick.' Pixie didn't want to be found breaking Bruce and Olivia's house rule.

By the light of her mobile phone, Pixie led the way down the steps. It was cold and damp underground and smelt, not unpleasantly, of earth and mould. It had smelt like that in 1895, she recalled. 'Wow, it's amazing!' Tabitha exclaimed. She put a hand to the wall. It was wet.

Pixie thought of Cordelia stealing out in the night, and of Felix who was very likely spirited away down this tunnel, and her stomach twisted with anguish.

'Can you feel anything spooky?' Tabitha asked hopefully. She was glad she wasn't down here on her own.

Pixie narrowed her eyes. 'A place like this is never going to have good energy. It's underground for a start, and it's abandoned. For a place to feel good, it has to be loved. There's no love down here.'

'Is that what it takes to make a place feel good?'

'Yes, everything always comes back to love.' As Pixie said those words she was struck suddenly by a flash of inspiration. She heard the words of the old gypsy woman echoing through time: *Love will always bring you back.* Pixie gasped as the truth of that phrase illuminated her mind with a dazzling light. How come she hadn't thought of that before? It was so simple, like Alexander the Great and the Gordian Knot. 'Oh my God!' she exclaimed excitedly. 'I know what to do.'

Tabitha frowned. 'About what?' she asked.

'I know how to sort this out,' said Pixie, hope flaring in her chest. 'Come on, let's go back to the house. I know what needs to be done.'

By the law of attraction, love would take her back to Cavill.

Ulysses made himself comfortable on the old iron bed in Felix's bedroom while Pixie settled into the chair. He had a strong cup of coffee to keep him focused, and another Ingrid Bergman movie on his iPad to entertain him. This time he chose *Gaslight*. Before he pressed play, he watched Pixie close her eyes and settle herself. 'Good luck, Pix,' he said. 'I hope your love is strong enough to take you back.'

'So do I,' she replied, but something told her that it would be. It just felt right.

With the door locked and the children safely at the other end of the house, Pixie pressed the locket between her hands and closed her eyes. She concentrated on her heart and thought of Cavill. As his face materialised in her mind, she felt her chest flood with love. The more she envisaged him at the moment they'd been separated, the more intense the feeling grew. Like a sun it was, burning behind her ribcage, expanding, bigger and bigger, brighter and brighter until she felt herself surrounded by a white light. A light so powerful it seemed to dissolve her body until she herself was made of light too.

With a sigh of relief, she was lifted out of her body. As she floated a moment above it, she made up a mantra in her mind that she hoped would carry her back to Cavill: *Love is eternal. Love is beyond time and space. Love connects us to those we believe we have lost. Love ensures that we never lose anyone, not really, not ever.*

Then the walls of the room began to fade.

As easily as a swirl of smoke curling through gauze, Pixie slid through the veil.

Past

Chapter Twenty-One

I open my eyes. Cavill is staring down at me in alarm. I'm lying on the ground, on the wet ground, and rain is falling gently on my face. But I don't care. I'm here, in his arms, and I never want to be anywhere else.

'Hermione!' His eyes are very blue. He has no idea how relieved I am to see them. How relieved I am to see *him*. To be back, exactly where I left off, as if I had never gone. I can scarcely believe it. But the law of attraction, the most powerful force in the universe, has drawn me back to *this* moment. 'Can you hear me?'

Mr Grantly's worried face appears beside Cavill's, and I'm brought to my senses with a jolt. I allow Cavill to lift me onto my feet. I put a hand on my heart. Love did, indeed, bring me back. Back to Cavill.

'I'm all right,' I reassure him, feeling a strange swell of happiness.

'You fainted,' he says, perplexed. He's white. I must have given him a great shock.

'I am well,' I reply, slipping once again into the Victorian mode of speaking.

He looks at me searchingly. 'I have to leave, Hermione. You must understand that. But I will come back.' I recall his memorial stone that declares the date of his death to be years from now and know that he doesn't die in South America. He lives a long life. It isn't cut short, after all. I feel a sting of guilt for having changed the future, but there is no time to consider what the implications of my meddling might be. No time to think about how my meddling might affect Hermione. It is done. I have to accept it and concentrate on what I am here to do.

I put my fingers against Cavill's cheek. 'I just needed to tell you that I love you,' I say quietly.

His expression relaxes. He puts his hand on mine and presses it into his face. I have never said those words to him before, but I say them now and I mean them with all my heart. 'And I love you, my dear Hermione,' he replies. 'I hope you will wait for me,' he adds, releasing me and sweeping my wet hair off my forehead. 'But stay not a moment longer in the rain. You will catch a chill.'

I nod, overwhelmed with sorrow, but also with gratitude for these stolen extra moments with Cavill. I lay my eyes on his face and commit it to memory – his gentle gaze, the lines that fan at his temples when he smiles, his sensual mouth and straight, patrician nose. Most of all I commit to memory the love reflected in it.

I watch him climb into the carriage. Mr Grantly shakes the reins, and the horse walks on. I remain there until the carriage has disappeared out of the driveway into the lane. Then I turn and make my way back to the house. I have a mission. That is my focus now. And I must not fail.

I remember where I am in the past. It's still Friday. Tomorrow night Felix will vanish. Tomorrow night I'll discover what happened. But there is much to do before I leave.

I retrieve the sketchbook Cavill gave me and then go up to my room and change out of my wet skirt and blouse. I appraise myself in the looking glass and bemoan my bedraggled appearance. I tidy myself up as best I can – I could really do with a hairdryer. Then I go and check on Robert. He's in the schoolroom studying the book on inventions that he found in the library. I tell him to search for his favourite invention and write a short piece on why he likes it so much. Then I go and look for Gwen. When I enter the nursery, she's not there. Instead, Rose is sitting on the rug, playing with Felix, who's in his den. 'Where is Gwen?' I ask.

'She's sick, miss,' Rose replies. 'I've been told to look after Felix until she's better.'

'Has someone called the doctor?' I ask.

'She says she doesn't want a doctor.' Rose shrugs. 'She hasn't got a fever. She just looks tired.'

'Yes, she's been complaining about being tired. A rest will do her good. I might go and see her.' I leave them to their play and head upstairs to Gwen's bedroom.

Motivated by the hope of being able to help Gwen as well as Cordelia, I knock softly and open the door. Gwen is in bed, lying on her back. She's been crying. 'May I come in?' I ask.

She nods. Her white face peeps at me from beneath the cover. It's heartbreaking. I perch on the edge of the bed. 'How are you feeling?' I ask, but it is a stupid question. Her anguish is obvious.

'I think the pain in my head is worse than the sickness,' she says, glassy eyes overflowing.

'You have to tell him.'

'What can he do? He's married.'

'You can't be left to deal with this on your own.'

'Yes, you're right. It's not fair, is it, to be left to deal with it on my own? It takes two to have a baby, after all.'

'You need to tell him, Gwen. Write him a note.'

'I can't write, miss.'

The world stops turning. I stare at her in astonishment. How is it possible that a woman of her age can't write? But this is 1895; illiteracy was common. 'You can't write?' I repeat.

'I can't write.'

'But . . .' I stop myself. If she can't write, then who writes the letter? For a moment I'm baffled. Then I come up with a plausible theory. Maybe she asks someone to write it for her?

Gwen doesn't notice my confusion. She can't imagine what's going through my mind. The letter from *Your loving friend* hasn't even been written yet. It's dated September 1895, over two months from now, around the time, I imagine, that the pregnancy starts to show. 'If they discover that John . . .' she begins, then her round eyes widen as she realises that she's just revealed the identity of the father. She doesn't know that I already know it.

'John Snathe?' I ask. 'I did suspect it was him.'

She nods and sighs helplessly. 'Well, you suspected correctly. The father is John Snathe.' She smiles feebly. 'You're sharp, you are, miss.' She takes another full breath, as if trying to relieve a weight bearing down on her chest. 'John will be in terrible trouble if they find out that he's the father. And they will ask me, won't they? And I'll have to tell them.'

'John has to take responsibility, Gwen. This isn't your fault alone. This is the fault of the both of you. Like you said, it takes two to make a baby.'

She nods, but I can tell she still believes the fault is hers entirely.

There's nothing more to say. I pat her arm. 'You rest now and don't worry about Master Felix. Rose is looking after him and he's very content.'

'He might come looking for me.'

'We'll make sure he doesn't.'

'Tell him I'll be back soon. Tell him Gwen needs to sleep and then she'll feel better.'

'I will.'

I leave the room and linger a moment in the corridor. The letter has to be from Gwen. If it's not her hand, I wonder then who she will ask to write it.

I remind myself that I have already interfered by unintentionally preventing Cavill from dying on the way to South America. I can't allow myself, however great my desire, to interfere again. I'm here to observe. I mustn't forget that. Events must play out without me trying to influence or alter them. I'm a timeslider. I don't belong in this dimension. I'm merely a visitor. This time, I won't sink into the dream, but remain awake, alert and ready to witness whatever may unfold. Without Cavill, this world has lost its sheen. The sun has retreated and the once vibrant colours in the garden have grown dull. Heavy clouds hang over the land like sodden linen in the wash. They're grey and dense and unmoving. There's little wind, only a blustery breeze blows in from the sea, bringing with it the sulphurous smell of the estuary. I think of the birds there, the spoonbills and yellow-legged gulls, the plovers and greenshanks, and Cavill's face appears before my eyes with his tender gaze, and my heart aches with longing. I put him to one side. I can't allow him to distract me now. I go to the schoolroom and resume lessons with Robert. He has eagerly written out a page on why he's so enamoured of photography. I read it with amusement. If he were to see the films that are available in my time, he'd be truly flabbergasted.

I'm uneasy. I will time to move faster so that I can get the job done and return to my own time. Instead of remaining in the schoolroom I suggest to Robert that we go into the garden. I feel like a caged tiger inside. I need the air. I need a diversion. As we walk downstairs there's a loud knock at the front door and Symons strides out from the direction of the kitchen to answer it. I'm curious, and wait to see who it is, for the usual stream of vendors and labourers call at the tradesmen's entrance at the back of the house.

Symons opens the door. A woman stands on the step with a child. A boy about the same age as Robert. They're not wearing travel coats so they can't have come far. I imagine they're from the town. The woman asks to see Mrs Pengower. Symons is about to turn them away when she says, clearly and in a firm but tremulous voice, 'Tell her it is Mrs Tonkin. Billy Tonkin's mother. She will know who I am. Tell her I want to see her.' I know from having slid back and talked to Olivia and Antoinette that Billy Tonkin is the boy who was killed in the mine. I know from having talked to Cordelia that his mother put a curse on Mr Pengower. My heart starts to race. It's beginning. That dark tentacle is unstoppable now.

Symons asks Mrs Tonkin to remain outside while he goes to see if Mrs Pengower is at home. He turns and walks into the hall. When he spots me, he shakes his head. We both sense trouble. I put a hand on Robert's shoulder. 'Go into the drawing room, Master Robert, and play something nice on the piano. I want to have a quick word with Mr Symons.'

Robert does as he's told. Symons sucks the air through his teeth. 'I know what that woman is after,' he says in a portentous voice.

'That's the mother of the child who was killed in the mine, isn't it?' I ask, although I know the answer.

Symons nods gravely. 'She's after work for her other son.'

I imagine that Cordelia will give the woman whatever she demands, out of both fear and charity. She might hope that, by helping the family, she will break the curse. But if she employs the boy, she'll infuriate her husband. When Mr Pengower hears of it, he'll be outraged. They'll have a terrible row. Cordelia will want to appease the Tonkins. Her husband will want nothing to do with them.

'I would defer to Mr Pengower,' says Symons dolefully. 'But he is out. Mrs Pengower is having her portrait painted in the blue drawing room.'

I haven't yet been into the blue drawing room. 'What are you going to do?' I ask.

'I will go and tell her. But Mr Pengower will not want to hire the Tonkin boy. I can tell you that.'

'But Mrs Tonkin has lost a child,' I remind him. 'Perhaps it would be wise and compassionate to take pity.'

'Does Mr Pengower appear to you to be a man to take pity?' says Symons and I'm astonished to hear him speak ill of his employer. 'Frank Tonkin is an angry, vindictive man, Miss Swift. He believes his son died because of Mr Pengower's negligence. I would not suggest allowing him to infiltrate this house by way of his son. It would be prudent to keep him at arm's length.'

'Would it not be prudent to make a friend of Frank Tonkin, and not an enemy?' I suggest.

'He is already an enemy, Miss Swift. And once an enemy, always an enemy. That man is as likely to transform as base metal to gold.'

Symons leaves me in the hall. I wait for him to come back. I listen to Robert's playing, but my mind is focused on the events unfurling before my eyes. Tomorrow night, Felix vanishes. Frank Tonkin's son will very likely be denied employment in the house. Maybe that will be the straw that breaks the camel's back and lead the man to do something terrible out of anger and frustration. Perhaps Frank Tonkin seeks a terrible revenge. I want to persuade Cordelia to give the boy something – a job in the kitchen or the garden. Anything, to keep Mr Tonkin sweet. But I must not change the sequence of events that are now developing fast. I feel in my gut that this moment is significant.

Eventually Symons reappears. 'Mrs Pengower must speak to her husband first, as this is not a decision she can make. Mrs Tonkin will be disappointed.'

'And Mr Tonkin will be even angrier,' I add with a shudder.

Symons walks past me to relay the message. I remain in the hall and listen.

'You tell your mistress that she owes me!' Mrs Tonkin exclaims, and I feel her pain. She's lost a child. There's no greater suffering than that. My heart goes out to her. But I sense foreboding in her husband's wrath, for surely Mr Pengower will never give their son a job. I fear that grief will make Mr Tonkin do something he'll later regret.

I take Robert into the garden. It's no longer raining but the air is damp. 'Let's see if we can name some of your uncle's favourite birds,' I suggest as we walk across the lawn. Robert is delighted with the idea and spots a couple of thrushes on the grass.

The day drags. I can think of little else but Felix. At lunch I look at him across the table as he forks his fish into his mouth, and my heart hurts. I can't bear for this child to suffer, and I hope that whatever happens to him is swift. It might be a gift to be able to slide through time, but it's a curse to know of something as dreadful as this, to have to watch it take place, and to be compelled, out of a sense of responsibility, to stand back and allow it to happen. Because I *could* prevent it from happening very easily. I could. Have I not already changed events? But I know I mustn't. Who's to know that if I prevented it, it wouldn't simply delay it for another night? Maybe you even meet your destiny on the road you take to avoid it.

After lunch, we go for a walk. Rose accompanies me with Felix. The four of us set off down the track where Robert, Cavill and I used to ride out together. But Cavill isn't here and I have therefore lost the will to remain. I take Felix's hand and he skips along merrily. This cheerful, innocent child who has never known anything but security and joy. I decide to make today special for him.

We enter the wood and I suggest that we see how many creatures we can find. I know how much Felix and Robert both love insects and animals. Rose is enthusiastic too and sets about searching the leaves for caterpillars and butterflies. We immerse ourselves in our task and the minutes pass rapidly. I don't think about what's to come, but only of what's happening right now. There's pleasure to be had in nature whatever the weather, however sick the heart – pleasure to be had in the ferns unfurling gently, in the red campion and cow parsley, in the wild jasmine and elderflowers. Those simple things never fail to lift one's spirits. It's impossible to be unhappy in the midst of such abundance. As long as one remains in the present, one can find joy.

Felix delights in the fat bees that toddle into the trumpets of the foxgloves and lifts them up with his unsteady hands to watch them feast upon the nectar within. He chases butterflies and laughs at the skittish darting of dragonflies. I show him a quail and we listen as a woodpecker makes rat-a-tat noises against a tree with its beak. There are wonders to be found in the woods and we encounter many and are delighted by them. The cloud breaks and the sun beams through in luminous shafts of gold. We watch the midges dancing in the warmth of those sunny shafts, and the butterflies soaking up the energy with their wings outspread as they rest upon the hogweed. A blackbird sings from the top of a sycamore tree, and I hold Cavill's image close while the beautiful tune floods my heart with a bittersweet yearning for what I've lost and will never get back.

When we return to the house for tea the boys are weary but happy. They've enjoyed their afternoon. So too have Rose and I. We discover that Gwen is still in bed. I wonder how much of her sickness is in her body and how much is in her heart. Rose suggests that, if she's still unwell tomorrow, we should call a doctor. I know Gwen will protest. She won't want anyone to know about her condition. If the doctor comes and detects that she's pregnant, he'll surely tell Cordelia and then I don't know what will happen.

That evening I read to Felix. He requests I read from a book of fairy tales. His favourite is *Rumpelstiltskin*. He sits up in bed in his pyjamas. 'Why isn't Gwen going to read to me?' he asks.

'Gwen is not well, Master Felix,' I tell him. 'But I'm sure she will be better tomorrow.'

Satisfied, he listens to the story. He likes the happy ending. Don't we all like happy endings? 'Rumpelstiltskin is a bad imp,' he says.

'He is a very bad imp,' I agree. 'But the Queen is much too clever for him, isn't she?'

'What happens to the imp?'

'I should think he disappears into the forest and is never seen again.'

'Where does he go?'

'I don't know,' I reply.

'Does he come back?'

'I don't think so.' A lump lodges itself in my throat and I'm assaulted by a wave of sorrow.

That night, Cordelia requests that I join them for dinner. It's just the two of them and me. Cavill has left and she's nervous about being alone with her husband. 'I fear we are going to have a fight about the Tonkin boy,' she explains anxiously. 'I need you to be there to support me. He will behave better if you are present.'

'Of course I will join you,' I reply.

'He has been under a great deal of strain recently. After those menacing words in paint on the gate and then the accident in the mine and the riot. But instead of reaching out to people and making peace, he digs in his heels. He will not yield, even though his resistance only makes him unhappy. He's too stubborn and proud, and will not admit that he is in the wrong.'

'After the riot, did he agree to improve the conditions in the mine?'

She laughs bitterly. 'Some of them, yes. The machine will be mended. Limbs will be mended too. But spirits will grow harder and more resentful.'

'If he won't listen to you or Mr Bray, or even acknowledge the evidence of his own eyes, who will he listen to?' I ask.

She gives a pitiful shrug. 'There is no one, Miss Swift.' She sighs in defeat. 'But I must try to be heard. I must not give up. Even though it would be easier to step aside and let him continue in his folly.'

At dinner, Mr Pengower declares that the Tonkin boy will not work at the manor. 'I sent word to them that there will be no employment for him here,' he says in a tone that indicates the subject is not open for discussion. 'I will not permit that family to gain a foothold in our home,' he adds. 'I am glad you deferred to me, my dear.' He pats her hand approvingly. 'Very sensible of you. Very sensible, indeed.'

Cordelia stiffens. She's not happy. 'I wish you had taken pity, Mr Pengower,' she replies, taking her hand away. 'They lost a child . . .'

'It was an accident,' says Mr Pengower through gritted teeth. He feigns a chuckle to mask his irritation and takes a swig of wine.

'Accident or not, it is your mine, Mr Pengower,' Cordelia insists bravely. 'They blame us for it. They always will. Mrs Tonkin says we owe it to her.'

'We owe her nothing. Employing her son will not redress the balance. It will not bring their dead boy back. I am sorry for it. Very sorry, indeed. But I will not change my mind. Frank Tonkin is a menace, and I will not bring his child into the fold.'

'He will be angry when he hears,' says Cordelia apprehensively.

'Let him be angry. He has been angry for years. He was angry even before his child was killed. He was likely born angry.' Mr Pengower chortles and forks a potato into his mouth.

'But he might do something . . .' she begins.

'Like what? Burn our house down? I think not.' He laughs. 'Really, that is absurd, my dear. Sometimes, you are quite hysterical.'

Cordelia is affronted. 'Now you are being absurd, Mr Pengower.'

'Do not raise your voice at me,' he growls and glares at her.

But tonight she will not be cowed. 'They are decent people,' she continues, lowering her voice a little. 'They lost a child. They are only asking for employment for the brother. We can put him to use somewhere. You do not have to pay him very much. But it would be a way of making peace with them. Of being kind. Can you not, Mr Pengower, find kindness in your heart, somewhere?'

'Kindness,' he scoffs. 'More like weakness.'

Cordelia bites her lip and her eyes shine. She plays with her food a moment. Then she takes a breath and looks at him steadily. 'Do you know that after their Billy was killed, Mrs Tonkin cursed you.'

Mr Pengower sighs wearily. 'I imagine they all cursed me that night.'

'Her words were, and I think I have them right: "I curse Ivan Pengower and his blood line, that they and their house may be dogged by unhappiness. That tragedy will follow them like a shadow and not release them, so they know what it is to suffer loss."'

'Is that meant to intimidate me?' he asks.

'It has frightened *me*,' Cordelia returns.

Mr Pengower narrows his eyes. 'And how did you come by it? Who was the fool who told you?'

'I do not wish to say.'

'Tittle tattle. You should not listen to it.'

'Please, I beg you, Ivan. Give the boy something, anything. You might not believe in the curse, but I do. I do not wish ill on our house, on your bloodline – on our children.'

Mr Pengower's face darkens. 'Enough, madam. We will speak no more about this. Not a word, do you understand?' He takes a slurp of claret. It has stained his teeth red. 'I am sick of hearing about it. Sick, do you hear me?'

There is a long silence. Only the scratching of Mr Pengower's knife on the china plate disturbs it. Finally, Cordelia turns to me. 'I hear that Gwen is still unwell,' she says, changing the subject. She looks pale and there's a shadow of defeat about the eyes, as if she's lost the will to fight.

'Yes, she is. I'm afraid she spent the day in her bed.'

'D'you know what's wrong with her?' Mr Pengower asks. I don't imagine he has much sympathy for sick servants.

'I do not,' I reply. 'I imagine she will be better tomorrow. She does not have a fever.'

'That's good,' says Cordelia.

Mr Pengower nods. 'We do not want her spreading disease, now, do we? If she has something that is catching, she must remain in her bedroom.' He turns to me specifically, wielding a potato on the end of his fork. 'Do not let the children near her, do you hear?'

'Absolutely not, Mr Pengower,' I reply. 'I am keeping them apart.'

'Good, good, Miss Swift.' He smiles and looks me over appreciatively as if seeing me for the first time. 'I am beginning to feel that I can rely on you. Yes, indeed, you are a good sort, Miss Swift.' I wonder if he is saying that in order to hurt his wife. Perhaps he wants to put a wedge between us. Maybe he senses we have grown close and doesn't like it.

'Thank you.' I lower my eyes.

Cordelia smiles wistfully. 'It was sad saying goodbye to Mr Cavill this morning. But he will return soon. We must all write to him. Perhaps you can write, too, Miss Swift, and tell him about the birds on the estuary. He will miss them, I'm sure.'

Mr Pengower is no longer listening. He's pouring another glass of claret and summoning the footman to bring him more potatoes. Cordelia gives me a knowing look. 'I think the birds and you are what he will miss most about St Sidwell Manor,' she adds.

It is past midnight when I slip behind the curtain in the library. I imagine that tonight, after the tension at the dining table, Cordelia will need her solitary time on the bench. I presume she needs it now more than ever. But I wait until the grandfather clock in the hall chimes two and realise then that she is not going to come. I imagine her crying into her pillow, alone in her bedroom, believing the worst has happened, when the worst is yet to come, and feel ever more intensely the desire to help her find peace.

Chapter Twenty-Two

I awake with a belly full of ants. At least, that's what it feels like, a nest of ants wriggling about in all directions. I lie in bed not wanting to get up. It's five a.m., and the dawn leaks through the openings in the curtains to tell me that it'll be a fine day. The light is white and radiant and full of its usual enthusiasm. Yet it fails to uplift me. I'm terrified. Tonight Felix vanishes, never to be found, and I'll witness it. I wish to God that I didn't have to.

I turn my thoughts to Cordelia's spirit, earthbound with grief, and know that I must endure whatever takes place, for *her*, so that she might move on into the next world and find peace, with her son.

Reluctantly, I climb down from the big bed and dress. This is the last time I'll wash myself in this bowl. The last time I'll put on these clothes. The last time I'll look upon this face reflected in the mirror, because tomorrow *I* will have vanished too. They won't miss me, for Hermione will still be here. I wonder what they'll make of her, though, and how different she'll be to *me*. I hope that I haven't made her life too difficult, leaving her with Cavill, who is in love with her.

Even though Saturday is my day off, I know that I must help out because Gwen is off sick. So, I wake up Robert. He dresses and diligently goes downstairs to practise the piano. To him it's just another day. I take the sketchbook Cavill gave me and return it to the library. There's no point leaving it in my room, and I can't take it with me. I can't take anything with me except the memories, and the love. Before I hide it in the bookshelf, slipping it behind a set of encyclopaedias, I take up a pen from the desk and write in small letters in the corner of the first page, beneath his sweet inscription: *PT.* I look at it for a moment and then slide it back among the other books. Perhaps the real Hermione will find it and cherish it as I would like to do, and I feel a stab of jealousy for the woman who will carry Cavill's heart in her hands and not even know the treasure that she holds.

While Robert plays, I take a walk around the garden. It's resplendent in the morning sunshine. Everything gleams from yesterday's rain. The dew on the grass shines like diamonds and the flowers glow, their colours vivid in the dazzling light. I can't help but think of the terrible thing that's about to strike at the heart of this family. For all its beauty St Sidwell Manor will be plunged into foulness. Those tentacles of darkness have now reached the child's bedroom and are creeping slowly across the walls, poised to steal the innocence and the light.

When I go up to the nursery for breakfast, I find Rose with Felix. Gwen is still in bed. Rose informs me that Cordelia has sent for the doctor. My first thought is to try to put her off, but then I remind myself that I'm just an observer. That I must *not* try to influence events. If this is the way the story unfolds, I must stand back and allow it to take its natural course.

Felix is desperate to see Gwen. Rose tells me that Mr Pengower has forbidden anyone to go into her bedroom in case she's infectious, but I can see that Felix's tears are softening her resolve. I make no comment. It's not my job to tell her what to do. 'She's not infectious,' she says, taking the child by the hand. 'She's just run down, poor lamb. Come on, Felix, you can talk to her through the crack in the door. There's no harm in that, is there?' The two of them leave and I hear her voice as they make their way down the corridor. 'You promise you won't whine about it anymore, Master Felix? And you won't tell your papa? He'll have my guts for garters, he will.'

The artist arrives at the front door to paint Cordelia. The postman and usual vendors flock to the tradesmen's entrance. The servants are busy in the house and the gardeners toil away in the gardens. There's nothing out of the ordinary. Nothing to raise suspicion or to suggest that anything untoward is about to happen. Mr Pengower sets off in his carriage. Robert and I ride out after lunch. When we return, the artist has left and the doctor's gig is on the gravel.

As I'm climbing the stairs with Robert, I meet Cordelia and the doctor on their way down. They're both looking grave, talking together in voices so low that I can't hear what they're saying. I nod respectfully as they pass. Then I send Robert to the nursery and quicken my step up to Gwen's bedroom. To my surprise, I find her all smiles. 'Gwen, what happened?' I ask.

She's sitting up against the pillows. 'I'm not pregnant,' she informs me happily.

'You're not?' I exclaim, thinking of the letter. If Gwen doesn't write it, who does? If Gwen isn't pregnant, then who is? I only have a few hours now to find out. But my detective work is unravelling. Is the letter even relevant to my mission? Something in my gut tells me that it is. I have never been wrong when I've followed my instinct.

Gwen shakes her head. 'I'm overtired and need to rest. That's all,' she says.

I sit on the bed and take her hands in mine. 'This is good news, Gwen.' It *is* good news, but I feel deflated. I simply can't work it out.

Gwen nods. 'I will get back to work tomorrow. I imagine Master Felix is missing me.'

'He is, Gwen,' I say.

But tomorrow I won't be here. Neither will Felix.

'You rest now, and God bless you.' I don't imagine I'll see her again.

It's early evening when Mr and Mrs Tonkin appear at the front door. They've left the boy behind. Mr Tonkin has dark brown hair flecked with grey and a thick beard to match. His eyes are deep-set and surprisingly light, like marbles. Beneath them are purple shadows. But there are crows feet fanning out at his temples and lines around his mouth that suggest laughter. Maybe he laughed a lot before Billy was killed. Perhaps he wasn't born cross as Mr Pengower suggested. He's dressed in his Sunday best, with a waistcoat and jacket and a cap on his head. I notice that his black lace-up boots are scuffed and wearing away at the toe. Mrs Tonkin is in a drab brown dress and a mob cap. They both look impoverished and old, and I question whether they're as dangerous as Symons suggests they are. Perhaps they're just desperate. After all, why have they come back if they are not desperate?

Mr Pengower is home and prepared to deal with them. Symons shows them into the library. He lifts his nose as if there's a foul smell beneath it and tells them to wait. I hover on the stair, eager to hear what they say. Mr Pengower makes them wait a good fifteen minutes. I shuffle on the landing, as impatient as they are. Finally, I hear the tapping sound of Mr Pengower's shoes on the wooden floorboards. I shrink back against the wall. He enters the library but doesn't close the door behind him. I imagine he's done that on purpose, for everything Mr Pengower does is carefully thought out and measured. Perhaps he feels that by closing the door he's giving their visit an importance it doesn't deserve. Whatever his motive, I hear almost everything he says.

'I have already told you that there is no work for your boy here,' he begins.

'He's a good lad,' says Mr Tonkin in his thick Cornish drawl. 'He'll work hard and not let you down. I only ask you to give him a chance. Just one.'

'I have no intention of employing him, Mr Tonkin. I do not require another servant.'

'Times are hard, sir . . .'

Mr Pengower cuts him off brusquely. He only ever wants to hear his own voice. 'And you think they are not hard for everybody? Am I to hire everyone's sons, Mr Tonkin? Is that what you suggest I do?'

'Our boy died in your mine,' says Mrs Tonkin, and I admire her courage. Perhaps despair has made her brave. 'You owe us.'

Mr Pengower snaps back, angrily. 'I owe you nothing, madam.

It was an unfortunate accident. I am sorry you lost your son. I wish to God that it had not happened, but God saw fit that it did. *He* took your son, Mrs Tonkin, not I. If you have words to say, then say them to God.'

There's an awkward pause. I don't imagine the Tonkins expected Mr Pengower would dismiss them so cruelly. 'We need the wages to pay for food. We are hungry, sir,' Mr Tonkin says. His voice isn't angry at all. It's soft and pleading.

'Everyone is hungry,' Mr Pengower replies. 'Am I to feed the entire population of St Sidwell?'

'You don't know what it's like to lose a child,' says Mrs Tonkin, her voice low. 'Our Billy was a good lad, he was. A good boy. A hard-working boy. He toiled away in that mine and what did he get in return for his labour? A five-foot coffin and a hole in the ground. He didn't deserve to die.' Her voice cracks. She rallies before Mr Pengower can interrupt her. 'Our William is strong and willing. He can work in the garden. He'll do anything for a few bob. It'll mean the difference between going hungry and having a morsel to eat. Have pity, sir.'

Mr Pengower has gone quiet. I wonder what he's thinking. 'I cannot imagine anything worse than losing a child,' he says at last, and his tone has changed. Perhaps he's thinking about his own children and, for the first time, putting himself in their shoes.

I feel someone beside me. I turn to see Cordelia. She's come down the stairs without me noticing. I'm horrified that she's caught me eavesdropping. I'm about to move away when she puts a hand on my arm to detain me and places a finger across her lips. She then turns her eyes in the direction of the library. Neither of us can see what's going on within, but we can both hear the silence as Mr Pengower reflects. I hope that he's going to give in.

But he doesn't.

'That is all,' he says at last. 'I will not be manipulated. If I employ your son, I will have to employ everyone else's son. I simply cannot do that.'

'May God see fit to give you what you deserve,' says Mrs Tonkin. 'You have no heart, Mr Pengower.'

Cordelia and I watch the couple leave through the hall. They seem smaller than they did when they arrived, as if defeat has shrunken them. Symons is waiting at the door to let them out. A moment later Mr Pengower steps into the hall. He raises his eyes to the landing. He looks steadily at his wife and his face is as hard as granite. His cold eyes glint. He is the master of the house and he wants her to remember that. He returns to the library and closes the door behind him. A moment later the smell of cigar smoke wafts out from beneath it.

Cordelia summons me to the blue drawing room with a brisk toss of her head. I follow her through the house. Her whole body is stiff as if she's drawing on every muscle to contain her fury.

The blue drawing room is sumptuous with tall windows framed by long, pale blue curtains. The walls are covered in blue damask paper and paintings of ancestors in gold frames that hang on chains. The ceilings are high and adorned with white mouldings. This room must have been added on later, for it's not Elizabethan in style. A screen is set up at one end, depicting a landscape. A chair stands in front of it. This is where Cordelia has been sitting for her portrait. I go to the easel, which displays the beginning of a painting. There's not much to see, only the bare outline of a figure and something of the background. I suspect it will never be finished.

She strides into the middle of the room, puts her hands on her hips and swings round. 'I hate him,' she seethes and bursts into tears. 'I hate him.' She begins to pace the floor.

I want to put my arms around her, but I don't know whether that would be appropriate.

'I'm so sorry,' is all I can say. 'I truly thought he would give the boy work.'

'He is a cruel and selfish man,' she hisses, stopping suddenly and then resuming her pacing. 'But I will give them what I can. Tomorrow I will go into town and pay a visit to Mrs Tonkin. Yes, I will take matters into my own hands.'

I know that she'll have other things on her mind tomorrow. 'I think Mrs Tonkin will be grateful for anything you can give her,' I say, but, really, I have no idea how Mrs Tonkin will feel.

Cordelia stops and sighs loudly. Tendrils of hair have come away from the pins and are hanging loose about her cheeks and neck. 'Life is so unfair, Miss Swift. Why is it that for some it is hardship and poverty and for others it is comfort and joy? I simply cannot understand it.' She swipes aside her skirts and sits down on a pretty blue chaise longue. Then she waves her tapering fingers at the sofa, and I go and sit opposite her.

'I wish I knew,' I reply, smoothing down my skirt. 'We each have our own path to tread,' I add. 'And every path is different. Life appears unfair to us, but I do believe every one of us has a purpose. Maybe, on a soul level, we have chosen this life for the opportunities in it to learn and grow. Perhaps we have more lives than one.'

She's listening to me with intent, thirsty for enlightenment. I don't feel qualified to instruct her, for what do I know of the meaning of life? I have no doubt that there is no death, for I've seen the continuation of life with my own eyes and my own being, but to talk to her about reincarnation seems somehow a step too far. I don't think she'll accept it. She might even think I'm mad. But life is short; how are we to learn all that we need to learn in just one lifetime? A prince in one, a pauper in the next, like actors in a play. Endless productions, many actors, a wealth of different parts to perform. It's all theatre.

She wrings her hands. 'There is so much misery in St Sidwell. So much poverty and hopelessness. And here we are, bathing in our abundance and good fortune. I cannot rest knowing that just outside our property there are those that have scarcely enough to eat.' Her beautiful eyes flash with disgust. 'And my husband, who has it within his power to alleviate their suffering, does nothing.'

'Life is a long time,' I say, not wanting to be drawn into criticising her husband for that is not my place. More specifically, it's not Hermione's place, and I'm acutely aware that tomorrow I will be gone and Hermione will be left to carry on from where I departed. I don't want to leave her in a difficult position. 'Perhaps Mr Pengower will change his mind one day. It happens sometimes, doesn't it? That people see the error of their ways and make amends.'

Cordelia nods. 'You are right. I must hope for that.' She turns her face to the window and looks sad, suddenly. 'But I am also thinking of myself. Of my own good fortune.' I watch her put a hand on her stomach and leave it there, resting on the curve of her belly. I feel a prickling sensation crawling over my skin. I stare at her hand in amazement. Is it possible that the woman who is pregnant, is *her*? 'I feel guilty,' she adds in a quiet voice, unaware that I'm adding two and two and getting four. 'Guilty for having so much, and guilty for wanting more.'

'Don't feel guilty, Mrs Pengower,' I say, trying to keep my voice even as my mind weighs up the possibilities. Now I consider it, the letter was intelligently written, the language that of an educated person. She speaks of hoping that they can find a way to be together and asks how it is possible that a love such as theirs is a sin. These sentiments are very much Cordelia's. She claims that her suffering is total and that the child she is carrying is the only thing that gives her a reason to live. Bearing in mind that she writes it *after* Felix has vanished, her sentiments are understandable. Yes, the letter has to be written by her. I'm now sure of it. But to whom is she writing? 'Enjoy your good fortune while you have it,' I continue. 'For life is peppered with ups and downs, and you cannot avoid the downs any more than you can avoid the ups. You will face your own set of challenges. Then you will have to find the strength in you to weather them. But know that when you rise and face those challenges, you are growing and expanding, as you are meant to do.'

Perhaps when she has lost Felix, she'll be able to look Mrs Tonkin in the eye and feel true empathy and compassion. I silently ask God to give them both strength. This is her karmic path, and she can't avoid it. I would give anything to help her avoid it, but I can't. It's destiny, and she must live it. It's what she came here to do.

'You are wise, Miss Swift,' she says, and smiles softly with gratitude. 'Young though you may be, you seem to have the wisdom of an old person. Yes, you are an old woman in the body of a young one.'

I glance at the clock on the mantelpiece. It's six o'clock. I need to go upstairs and start my vigil in Felix's bedroom. I stand up. 'I will bid you goodnight, Mrs Pengower,' I say.

'Wait,' she commands. She goes to a walnut table set against the wall and picks up what looks like a tobacco box. Not unlike the one the children found in the cottage. 'I want you to have this,' she says and gives it to me.

I smile, bewildered. 'But I do not smoke,' I tell her.

She smiles knowingly. 'Open it.'

I do as she asks and lift the lid. Inside, is a locket and a note. 'I want you to have this locket. You have been a true friend to me, Miss Swift. Someone I can confide in. Someone I can trust.' I open the locket to find the miniature portrait of her. The very same one I used to slide to this time. So, this is how the locket brought me to Hermione instead of to Cordelia, because Cordelia gave it to her as a gift. If the locket belonged to Hermione, that means that the two women must have grown close. It begs the question, then, how much of what I, Pixie, am doing through Hermione, is what Hermione herself did? I believe I have taken her over completely and am living a life independent of her wishes and desires, but perhaps I am living some of those wishes and desires. How much of Hermione is me? How much of me is Hermione?

'It's beautiful,' I say, because it is. I unfold the note. I'm struck immediately by the handwriting. It's exactly the same as the handwriting on the letter I'd attributed to Gwen.

To thank you for your friendship, dear Hermione. Your loving friend.

So I am right. The letter is from Cordelia. Cordelia is pregnant, and not by her husband. Cordelia notices the astonishment on my face and smiles affectionately, believing my reaction to be on account of her kindness. 'I mean every word, Hermione,' she says. It's the first time she's called me by my first name. 'You came when I needed you most.'

I hide my confusion and thank her. She bids me goodnight. They have guests for dinner, and I'm not invited. She doesn't know it, but this is not simply goodnight, but goodbye, until we meet again in the future.

*

As I climb the stairs, I stare down at the tobacco tin and silently process the shocking information I've just learnt: Cordelia Pengower is the writer of the letter that Tabitha found. That letter was dated *after* Felix's disappearance. So, who is the letter to? Who is the father of her child? Who could it be? Have I missed something? While I was sketching birds and riding out with Cavill, did I allow clues to pass me by? And why is it significant? For surely it is, otherwise it would not have been found. Nothing happens by coincidence. Nothing.

I read a fairy tale to Felix even though my throat is tight with anguish. I tuck him up in bed, fussing about the covers, wanting him to feel cherished and safe even though nothing is going to keep him safe tonight. I sweep his blond hair off his forehead and press my lips against the soft, warm skin. He smells of soap. His mother has already kissed him goodnight. I am the last person to see him before he is taken away. My heart breaks at the thought of what is to come. He asks why Gwen isn't here to kiss him goodnight. I tell him that she'll be well tomorrow, even though I know that he won't be here to see her. I feel sick in my heart and my soul, and yet I can do nothing. I have to be strong, to witness what unfolds, and not try to stop it. It's then that I notice he's wearing the bracelet the traveller woman gave him. It's tied loosely around his wrist. He must have put it back on by himself. Why would he do that, I wonder, when his father got so cross about him wearing it? Not that it matters now. He won't be seeing his father again.

But his mother must have seen it when she came to say goodnight. Did she deliberately leave it on in a small act of defiance towards her husband? I wish that it did have the power to keep him safe.

Felix asks for Gwen one last time. I remind him that he'll see her tomorrow. Tomorrow she'll be well. He snuggles up with his toy rabbit and closes his eyes. How innocent he looks with his eyes closed, sinking into dreams. I stifle a sob and leave the room. I go to mine and change into my nightdress and dressing gown. I give Felix time to fall asleep and then return, quietly opening the door to his bedroom and slipping inside. I tiptoe across the carpet and climb into the wardrobe to hide. I'm shrouded in darkness in there, alert to every sound and sense. I wait. Like a spider, I wait. I know that it won't be long before a fly drops into my sight. I wait for the fly. I feel nauseous with anticipation. Who will come? Will it be a traveller, jealous of the Pengowers' wealth and good fortune? Will it be a miner, angry and vindictive? Will it be Frank Tonkin? Or someone in the house who wishes Mr Pengower ill? Or will it be someone I haven't yet anticipated, who wishes to destroy the Pengowers' happiness? I don't know. I sit in wait like a predator expecting the arrival of its prey and then I will follow them and see where they take him. As far as I can go, I will follow.

I'm not sleepy. I'm not faint-hearted, but I *am* afraid. I'm *very* afraid.

I'm afraid that I might try to intervene and thus alter what should not be altered.

Chapter Twenty-Three

Through the crack in the wardrobe door I see the shadows of moonlight slowly creep across the floor. I hear the distant screech of an owl in the woods and the light scampering of mice beneath the floorboards, but other than those nocturnal sounds, the house is silent. The sheer force of my resolve prevents me from falling asleep. I have one chance and one chance only to find out what happens to Felix Pengower, and I will not fail. I expect an intruder to come into the room and I focus on the door. I wait for it to open. It's a surprise, therefore, when Felix himself wakes up and climbs out of bed. I expect he wants to use the chamber pot. I'm astonished when he makes his way to the door. The moon is full. Indeed, tonight it is a fat, luminous moon. It fills the bedroom with a translucent light, as if we are underwater. As if we are underwater but able to see every object, clear and sharp and bright.

Felix makes for the door. He looks small and vulnerable in his sailor-suit pyjamas. My heart lurches with dread, but I know I mustn't do anything to stop him.

I get up and follow him out of the door. He turns towards the servants' staircase. I imagine he's going to Gwen's bedroom. He has wandered there before, many times. In spite of his mother putting a stop to it, he's determined to see his nurse. She's been sick and he's been denied her. Tonight, he wants to steal into her bed and be enveloped in her warm, maternal embrace. I feel an anguish almost too much to bear, but I know what I have to do, and I walk on.

By the light of the moon, he treads confidently. Silently, I walk behind him. He doesn't sense me here. I'm as quiet as a mouse. He climbs the narrow wooden stairs, one at a time, holding the banister and pausing after each step. My heart goes out to him, this little person climbing to seek comfort, ignorant of the fact that he won't find it.

He pads along the corridor to Gwen's bedroom, scampering quietly over the shafts of silver that beam in through the small windows and slice through the darkness. He knows the way and trots with confidence. The last time I saw her she was feeling better, sitting up in bed, happy to have discovered that she wasn't pregnant. She wasn't sick at all, simply sick in the heart because she can't have the man she loves because he's already taken.

I wonder how this child can come to harm in Gwen's bedroom. Gwen loves him. She would give her life for him. How is it that tonight, as he makes his way to her room, he vanishes, never to be seen again? Surely, he's safe in her loving arms?

At last, he reaches her door and hovers there in a puddle of moonshine, uncertain suddenly. The door is ajar. Inside, there are hushed voices. I stand behind him, in the bathroom doorway that is cast in shadow. He doesn't sense me here. It's as if I don't exist.

I listen to the voices through the gap in the door.

You know I can't marry you, Gwen.

But you don't love her.

Love! You know nothing of love.

I know I love you, John.

Listen, let's not talk of marriage. Let's just enjoy each other. Why do you have to ruin it? You always have to ruin it.

I'm not ruining it. I just deserve more.

I'm risking my job coming up here to see you. Isn't that enough?

Well, I'm risking mine too. If we're found out, we'll both be dismissed.

Felix pushes the door.

Master Felix. What are you doing up here? Go downstairs at once.

I can tell by Gwen's tone of voice that it gives her pain to send the child away.

What's the boy doing here? What's he heard? He'll sneak, he will. How much have you heard? What have you heard? Tell me, you little blighter! What have you heard?

Lay off him, John. He's only little. Go back to your room now, Master Felix. Be a good boy.

Felix begins to cry. My heart freezes. Is John Snathe going to kill him? Surely, he wouldn't hurt a child?

Lay off him, I tell you. Stop!

I'm not having him sneaking on me. You sneak on me and I'll cut out your tongue, do you hear me? I'll cut out your tongue so you'll never speak again.

I hold my breath. But to my relief the child runs out of the room with a sob. He hurries down the corridor and I lift my nightdress and gown and pursue him. Moonlight, pouring in through the small attic windows, lights his way back. He stumbles down the stairs, quietly crying. I fear he might fall. His white hand holds the banister, but he's trembling and unsteady. I expect him to fall, and through my mind passes a possible scenario – that he falls and breaks his neck and Gwen and John have to hide his body. But I'm wrong. He makes his way down safely. When he gets to the bottom, he hesitates. He doesn't turn right towards his bedroom, but left towards his mother's. I follow him at a safe distance. He is, indeed, headed to his mother's bedroom even though she has forbidden him to go there. I imagine that was a rule she made when she started her affair. She didn't want anyone to discover her absence. I imagine it's been years since Ivan Pengower visited her bedroom. But Felix is making his way to her bedroom none the less. He's frightened and he wants his mother.

He stops suddenly in his tracks. At the far end of the corridor is the faint glow of a gas lamp turned down low. His mother's unmistakable figure is briefly silhouetted against it. She turns the corner and the glow recedes, her shadow sliding down the wall after her. Felix takes a breath, gathers himself, and then scampers in pursuit. He's no longer crying. Making sure that I'm a safe distance behind him, I walk silently on.

The house is quiet, not even the mice can be heard scratching beneath the floorboards. All is still. I follow at a distance. Felix descends the grand staircase, trailing the lamplight. He doesn't cry out for his mama. Perhaps he's afraid that he'll be in trouble.

Felix reaches the library. Large silver squares shimmer on the floor where the moonlight shines through the big, mullioned windows. The room is as bright as day, but the watery blue light is eerie and confusing. It has a dreamlike quality. But this is not a dream. For Felix and his mother, this scenario is all too real.

Felix hovers in the doorway as his mother pulls the lever to open the secret door and then disappears inside. I imagine this must fascinate him, a hidden door in the bookcase. The boy walks slowly towards it. Curious. Fearless now, and I remember how delighted he was by the tunnels at the mine. How thrilled he was that his brother was frightened while he wasn't. This door, concealed in the bookcase, must be magical for him. By the way he's striding towards it, light on his feet, a bounce in his step, I sense that inquisitiveness has overridden his fear. He wants to be a mole and he's not afraid of the dark.

Cordelia has left the door ajar. This is a fatal mistake. This, I imagine, seals the child's fate. If only that door was closed. How different things would be. I feel the frustration burning in my chest.

Felix slips through the gap and makes his way down the steps. I plunge into the darkness after him. The tunnel is lit by the gas lamp that Cordelia has left at the other end, presumably to light her return. It burns like a star and Felix is drawn towards it. Outside, she doesn't need it, for the moon is full.

When I get to the stairs at the end my attention is diverted by Felix's bracelet. It has come off his wrist and is lying across my path on the paving stones. It resembles a thin little snake. My instinct is to pick it up, but I pull back. I mustn't change anything. I must leave everything exactly as it is. But my throat tightens with anguish, as if an invisible hand is squeezing it. I want to take Felix by the hand and lead him back to bed, to safety, but I cannot. I must not. I have to see this nightmare through, and keep my attention focused on the reason I am here.

I follow Felix up the steps and into the shed. He's hurrying out in pursuit of his mother, around the back of the shed and into the copse behind it. I haven't been this way before, but I soon recognise the landscape. We're making for the wood.

There's something mystical about the moon tonight. It's big and round, shining brightly in a deep indigo sky studded with stars. The trees are silhouetted against it, strange and otherworldly, swaying gently in the balmy breeze. Soft light is fragmented by the branches into hundreds of milky beams, which act as spotlights, shining onto the ground, illuminating our path, showing Felix the way. Drawing him towards his destiny, and me to my purpose. I sense it is almost done.

Shortly we come upon a cottage, snuggled in a clearing. It's a romantic-looking building with pointy gables and latticed windows. The spine of the roof sags, as if it's old and weary and taking a rest. As Cordelia approaches it, the door opens and Pascoe Bray stands in the frame, ready to greet her.

Pascoe Bray is her lover. I never guessed. But I suddenly recall the many times he was present, and Cordelia Pengower's happiness. It hits me now, the realisation that she was always happy when he was around.

Felix stops short.

I stop behind him, hidden behind an ash.

We both watch as Pascoe pulls Cordelia into his arms and kisses her. Entwined, they retreat inside, and the door closes on their adultery.

The child seems too shocked to cry. He stands there, staring in bewilderment, not knowing what to do. My heart breaks for him, this little person, alone in the night with no one to turn to.

How appalling it must be to be betrayed not only by his nurse, but by his mother too.

Felix goes to the window and peeps in through the glass. It's human nature to be drawn to things we know we shouldn't see, and to watch in horror and be repelled. Felix remains there, standing on his tiptoes, his nose pressed against the glass, for a moment only. Something he sees sends him into a panic because he springs away as if the windowsill he's holding onto suddenly scalds his fingers. He turns on his heels and runs.

He doesn't return the way he came. He runs in another direction entirely, stumbling over fallen branches and fighting his way through the bracken, which is thick and tall. He runs blindly, clearly lost. I struggle to keep up with him, my long night-dress getting caught in the undergrowth and snagging on the brambles.

Shortly, he slows down to a walk. His panic abates and he begins to look around him and trail his hands over the vegetation. He stops here and there, detained by a sound in the bushes perhaps, and crouches down to search for things in the grass. An owl hoots, but he doesn't seem to mind. Perhaps he's living his fantasy of being a fox or a mole or a rabbit. Maybe he's consoling himself with that and sinking into the comfort of play.

I cannot imagine what harm can come to him here, in this wood, unless he stumbles across vagrants. I remember the two I saw at the chapel and shiver. One of them was carrying a knife. Is that what happens? He comes across vagrants and they seize the opportunity and take him? It seems implausible, somehow.

Felix is now pretending to be an animal. He's on all fours and he's found a giant laurel. He crawls beneath it. I hide behind a tree trunk and watch him disappear.

I wonder what he's doing in there. I hear rustling, a murmur and then a thud. The thud turns my blood to ice. It was like something dropped from a height. What on earth is inside that bush?

I remain for a long while behind the tree, petrified with anxiety. What was that sound? Did I imagine it? Was it something else, far away? A branch falling or something? Or was it Felix? If I crawl under that bush, will Felix, pretending to be a fox, see me? Will I interfere and alter the chain of events? Or is there a hole and he's fallen down it? If he's fallen down a hole, can I walk away and leave him there? Can I leave him to die?

Is he dead already?

My breathing grows shallow. My heart races. My body bristles with fear. My legs weaken and shake. I'm too frightened to do any-thing. I remain paralysed to the spot, unable to leave it.

I hear nothing.

My heart lurches. It's seized by a cold and icy hand. It's happen-ing. It's happening now.

SHADOWS IN THE MOONLIGHT

Felix has been swallowed into the bush. I have to go in after him and find out what's there.

I force myself to take a step and then another. I crouch down and part the branches of laurel. Inside, on the earth, is a grey flagstone. It's mottled with lichen and moss, like a gravestone. Beyond it are narrow steps. I know at once that it is a priest hole. *Another* priest hole. This place is indeed riddled with them. I doubt very much that anyone knows it's here. It might have saved the lives of priests in Elizabethan times, but it's taken Felix's.

I kneel and crawl on in. There are steps and they appear to lead down into a dark hole. I cannot bear to look down it. Even if I could, it would be too dark to see anything. I suspect there was once a ladder, but that must have rotted centuries ago. It's a deep hole and Felix has fallen down it.

I crawl out. My mind is spinning. I want to throw up. My head tells me I have to leave, but my heart is begging me to stay. To call for help. To rescue him. I could never have predicted this.

No one has taken him.

No one has murdered him.

He's fallen down a priest hole, by himself, in a horrible accident, and there's no one around to save him.

No one, but me.

Oh, if only his father hadn't taken him down the mine. If he hadn't encouraged him to be a mole. If he hadn't celebrated his bravery in those tunnels. If his mother hadn't forbidden him to go to her room. If she hadn't left the secret door ajar. If the child hadn't had a fascination for making dens and exploring tunnels. If only . . .

I remain standing there, as still as if I were made out of marble. I move nothing. Only my pulse throbs in my temples and my heart thuds in my chest.

I can alert Cordelia and Pascoe and they can rescue him.

I can.

But I won't.

I know I won't, because if I do, I will change the future – again. I have already changed it once with Cavill and who knows what *that* will do to the lives of others? One small flutter of the wings of a butterfly can cause a hurricane on the other side of the world. What hurricane have I caused by saving Cavill? What hurricane might I cause by saving Felix?

There is nothing I can do. Nothing.

With a sob, I turn and walk away.

It's the hardest thing I have ever had to do.

I return through the wood, my whole being heavy with sorrow. My legs feel like lead, my heart like a pebble. I ache all over. I can't bear to think of that child, stuck in the hole. I hope he died instantly. I hope he didn't suffer. *Please God, don't allow him to suffer.*

No wonder they never find him. That hole was built to be hidden. Hidden it is, and so is Felix.

I make my way back through the tunnel, leaving the gas lamp and the bracelet exactly where they are. Cordelia will find that bracelet and know that her son followed her. She will know that *she* is to blame for his disappearance, and she will never forgive herself. That's why she's stuck, refusing to move on. Because she knows what she did. Because she believes she is to blame.

My job is done.

I return to my room, undress and take to my bed.

I leave Hermione safely there, beneath the quilt. She won't remember anything of the last eleven days. Her amnesia will be put down to shock, I expect. And life will go on.

As I close my eyes and prepare to slide back, to leave this time for ever, I think about the real Hermione. Was she dear to Cavill as she was dear to Cordelia? Was it written in the Great Book of Life that she and Cavill loved each other? After all, didn't he say that he fell in love with me – with Hermione – the moment he laid eyes on me in the hall? Before he'd even got to know me? Perhaps he and Hermione were destined to be together. Maybe they fell in love. They might even have intended to marry. Did I simply step into her shoes and live her life? Was the life that I borrowed for eleven days not so very far from the one that was really lived? Or did Cavill and

I, Pixie, connect on a deeper level, on the level of the soul? Did we have something timeless, something unique?

I will never know.

I listen to my breathing and drift deep into trance. I feel myself slipping away. The vibration murmurs in my ears. My limbs grow heavy. It is time. My job is done.

Present

Chapter Twenty-Four

Ulysses was enjoying his film when he sensed movement. Reluctantly, he lifted his eyes off the screen. Shame, it was his favourite moment when Ingrid Bergman . . . never mind. He sighed and glanced at his watch. Pixie had only been in trance for fifteen minutes. He wondered how long she had spent in the past this time.

He swung his feet off the bed, sat up and closed the lid of his laptop. He watched quietly as she opened her eyes and remained still as she slowly adjusted to the change. He was ready to help her transition. After the last episode, he was prepared for anything. He hoped that she had managed to complete the mission this time, and not mess it up by trying to be clever.

Pixie looked around the room, *Felix's* room, where only a short while ago that sweet child had been sleeping soundly and safely in his bed. Now he was gone. There was the wardrobe where she had hidden, the bed where Felix had slept, the window through which moonlight had shone so keenly. She thought of his body, his small, fragile body, broken at the bottom of the priest hole, and began to tremble violently. Her eyes filled with tears and her chest grew tight as the nightmare she had experienced reverberated through her body like the final tremors of an orchestra that had ceased to play. Overcome, suddenly, by the need to vomit, she ran to the bathroom and threw up in the loo.

Alarmed, Ulysses waited outside the bathroom door, his ear pressed against it. On hearing her throwing up, he recoiled. He wondered what on earth she had witnessed to be so dramatically affected by it. It wasn't looking good.

Pixie splashed her face with cold water, trying to wash away the darkness she had brought with her into the present. Trying to bring herself back into the now, into the light. She stared at her face in the mirror and told herself that what she had lived through had been a nightmare and that now she had awoken. The horror she had observed had happened over one hundred years ago.

But that horror was still happening for Cordelia Pengower. For her, the nightmare went on every minute of every day. She was trapped in her guilt, like a glitching television screen that was stuck on a scene and wouldn't move on. It was time to release her from her suffering. But how? Pixie wasn't sure. She closed her eyes and took a deep breath. She would step aside, figuratively speaking, and allow her guides in spirit to show her the way. She couldn't do it on her own.

Ulysses knocked softly. 'You okay in there, Pix?' he asked.

She dried her face on a towel and opened the door. He winced. She looked like a ghost herself, even her lips were grey. 'God, what happened?'

'Felix Pengower fell down a priest hole in the wood,' she told him flatly. 'I had to walk away. It was awful, Ulysses. I just walked away and left him there.'

Ulysses put his arms around her and drew her against him. 'What you have to go through in your line of work, Pix. It's too much.'

'The worst is that I couldn't do anything about it,' she said. 'It went against every instinct. I wanted to stop it happening. More than anything in the world, I wanted to stop it happening. But I couldn't. I had to walk away. It was terrible.'

'But it's essential, Pix. If you could play about with the past and impact the future, we'd all be in a mess. We couldn't have you running amok like that, trying to make things better, but probably making things worse.' He kissed her temple. 'But your job isn't over yet.'

She took a deep breath. 'I know. There's still work to be done. The most important work.' She walked past him, into the corridor. 'Let's go to the wood.'

*

Pixie and Ulysses found Olivia, Antoinette and Tabitha in the dining room. Antoinette was enjoying another cup of coffee while Tabitha was on the floor, stroking the dog. When the two of them walked in, Tabitha jumped to her feet. 'Did you do it? Did you release the spirit?' she asked.

Pixie nodded. It was a relief to be able to give them some good news. 'I know now what needs to be done.'

'Sit down, my dear,' said Antoinette, patting the chair beside her. 'Tell us all about it.'

Pixie and Ulysses sat down. Ulysses helped himself to coffee. Pixie was too fidgety to drink anything, least of all coffee.

'Cordelia Pengower was having an affair with the foreman at the mine called Pascoe Bray,' she began. 'The night Felix disappeared—'

'Felix?' Tabitha interrupted excitedly. Her eyes widened with astonishment. 'Did you say Felix?'

Pixie frowned. 'Yes, Felix was Cordelia's six-year-old son who went missing.'

'I know a little boy called Felix. I met him in the wood.'

They all stared at her in confusion. 'You met a little boy in the wood?' Olivia asked. 'When?'

'You didn't tell us?' said Antoinette.

'I didn't think it was important,' Tabitha replied.

'Tell us now,' said Pixie. It hadn't occurred to her that Felix might be earthbound too.

'He was wearing a white-and-blue sailor suit and his feet were bare. I did think it strange that he wasn't wearing shoes. He said he didn't feel the cold.'

'What was he doing?' Olivia asked.

'Playing. He was at the cottage.'

'What cottage?' said Olivia.

'Pascoe Bray's cottage,' said Pixie slowly, the pieces falling into place.

'On this estate?' said Olivia. 'I didn't know we had a cottage.'

Tabitha stood up. 'It's a ruin,' she told them. 'I went exploring and found it. The little boy was there. He wanted to play

325

hide-and-seek, but, when I went to find him, he'd disappeared. I thought he'd gone home. Then he appeared again and told me that it wasn't safe to play there. In the wood. He told me to go. He disappeared again, into the mist.' She looked at Pixie, eyes shining. 'Is he a ghost? A spirit, I mean.'

'He's an earthbound spirit,' said Pixie sadly. 'I didn't expect that. I thought he would have gone straight to the light. You see, the night he disappeared, he followed his mother out through the priest hole in the library to Pascoe Bray's cottage. Cordelia was pregnant with Pascoe's child. It was she who wrote the letter, not the nursemaid, Gwen. When Felix saw his mother and Pascoe together, he ran off and fell down a priest hole hidden in the bushes. He was never found, which isn't a surprise because the priest hole was built never to be found. I suspect Cordelia realised her son had followed her because a bracelet he was wearing fell off in the tunnel and she would most definitely have found it on her way back. Plus, the door in the library, which she usually closed, was left ajar. Poor Felix's spirit has been stuck in the wood ever since. He probably hasn't a clue that he's dead.'

'Can you show him the way home?' Tabitha asked.

Pixie nodded. 'I can.'

Just then, Bruce walked in with Zach. 'What's going on?' he asked. 'You all look very serious.'

'Apparently, there are *two* earthbound spirits,' said Antoinette gleefully.

'Goodie,' said Bruce, rubbing his hands together. 'The more the merrier.' He looked at the bewildered faces. 'We thought we'd go and help Tom on the farm. Does anyone else want to come? Tab?'

'I'm staying here,' she replied firmly.

'Very well,' said Bruce. 'We'll leave you to your earthbound spirits, then.'

Zach rolled his eyes and followed his father into the hall.

There was a moment's silence as they watched the air settle.

'What do we do now?' Olivia asked.

'I release the souls of Cordelia Pengower and Felix into the light,' said Pixie.

Antoinette pushed herself up from her chair with a groan. 'Can we come too?'

'I think it best if we leave her to do it alone,' said Ulysses apologetically.

'All right,' Antoinette agreed, although she'd love to have seen how it was done. 'We'll take Daphne for a walk.'

'Is it okay if Tabitha comes with me?' Pixie asked Olivia. Tabitha gave her mother a pleading look.

Olivia nodded. 'As long as it's not dangerous,' she said.

'It's not dangerous,' Pixie reassured her. She smiled down at Tabitha. 'I think you have the makings of a gifted psychic,' she said, and Tabitha beamed.

'I hope you manage to release them,' said Antoinette. 'I'd like to see happiness restored to this place.'

'So would I,' Olivia agreed, and watched Pixie and Tabitha leave the room.

How different the winter garden looked to the summer garden Pixie had just slid from. It was hard to get her head around the sudden change. Instead of the intense heat, a cold sun hung low in the sky, shining weakly through the branches and throwing damp shadows over the long grasses. Heaps of weeds had taken over the once immaculate borders, and shrubs and trees had seeded themselves in the middle of the lawn. Yet in spite of the neglect, there was beauty in the wildness. Nature had been left to her own designs, free to grow where she chose, and there was something delightfully extravagant about that. Even in the dead of winter, the gardens pulsated with aliveness.

They walked through the woods, retracing the steps Pixie had taken over a hundred years before, but only this morning. The trees had looked different in the moonlight. Pixie would have had to follow her intuition had it not been for Tabitha who knew the way.

As they neared the hidden priest hole, Pixie felt the energy change. The air grew colder and the light dimmed. It was as if a cloud had passed in front of the sun, even though the sky was clear. Tabitha felt the heavy energy too and stayed close to Pixie.

She was excited that she'd been included in the adventure and was determined to be useful.

Tabitha led Pixie to the place where she'd seen Felix. They didn't have to search for the hole, for Felix himself was there to show them. He stood in front of a tangled thicket of blackberry bushes in his sailor pyjamas, blinking at them impassively, as if unsurprised to see them there. His feet were bare, but, just like Tabitha had said, he didn't seem to feel the cold. Pixie's heart flooded with pity, but also relief, for the last time she had seen him he'd disappeared into the ground, and she had walked away. Now he was standing before her, as if it had never happened.

She peered into the thorny brambles. The priest hole was in the centre of it somewhere. They'd have to get a digger to find it, because it was too prickly with thorns to clear by hand. It was heartbreaking to think of Felix's bones lying undiscovered for over a century in that damp and lonely place. She'd suggest they fill it in and give it a headstone. Perhaps ask the vicar to come and say a few words. It would be nice to give Felix Pengower a proper burial.

But, right now, he needed to go home, with his mother.

Tabitha took Pixie's hand. Her heart was beating so loudly she feared Felix would hear it. Felix appeared not to, however. He was looking at Pixie, his expression one of curiosity. Tabitha wondered if it was because of her pink hair.

'Felix,' said Pixie. 'I've come to show you the way home.'

Felix frowned. 'I *am* home.'

'This was once your home. Do you remembering falling down a hole?' she asked.

Felix looked into the bush then back at Pixie. 'I was making a den,' he said happily. 'Daddy says I make a good mole.'

'I think you make a very good mole. But now you need to come with me. Your mother is waiting for you.'

He frowned, uncertain suddenly. 'She was over there.' He pointed in the direction of the cottage and his face grew serious.

'She's not there any more, Felix. She's waiting for you in the house, and I'm going to bring her to you now.'

He looked nervous. 'Will she be cross with me?' he asked.

'She won't be cross, Felix. There's nothing to be cross about. Your mother loves you with all her heart. She's been waiting for you for a very long time.'

Pixie closed her eyes and thought of Cordelia Pengower. She did not need to go to the house or take Felix with her, for Cordelia and Felix, as spirits, existed beyond time and space. All she had to do was reach out to her with her mind and ask her to come.

Pixie took three deep breaths and imagined Cordelia as she had seen her in Felix's bedroom, enveloped by grief and self-loathing. Tied to the earth by the weight of her guilt and regret. With all the energy she could muster, Pixie called to her with her inner voice, willing her to connect. *Cordelia. Cordelia. Cordelia.* Pixie envisaged a light emanating from her heart and expanding out towards Cordelia. She imagined it filling Felix's bedroom until everything in it was bathed in a golden radiance. Bathed in love. *Cordelia. Cordelia. Cordelia.* Pixie thought of Cavill and her light grew. She thought of Felix and it grew brighter still. She called to her again. *Cordelia. Cordelia. Cordelia.*

At last she heard a voice, so distant, it sounded like a faint echo. *I am here.*

Pixie held on to the vision. *Cordelia. I've found your son. I've found Felix. You must come to him now. He's waiting for you. Here in the wood. He fell down a priest hole. He followed you to the cottage and fell down a hidden hole in the ground. But he's here, and he's well. You must let the past go now, Cordelia. It's time to move on. Time to forgive yourself. Time to go home, together. Come.*

Pixie heard the echo of Cordelia's voice once again. *I am not worthy. I have done terrible things. You have no idea. I am not worthy of forgiveness.*

I know what happened that night, and it wasn't your fault. There is only one person who must find it in their heart to forgive, and that's you. You must forgive you. The only thing holding you to the earth plane is guilt. Let it go. It has no place where you're going. You cannot take it with you. You must let it go. Just let it go. Focus on the love, Cordelia. Let love carry you to your son. To Felix. Love will take you to him. He's waiting for you. So come.

SHADOWS IN THE MOONLIGHT

There was a pause, and then a quiet sob. Pixie sensed Cordelia was finally going to open up. That she was ready to unburden
herself.

I have done terrible things, she repeated in a voice so quiet Pixie
could barely hear her. *I must pay for my transgressions with suffering.*

There is only forgiveness, Cordelia.

I killed Felix. Me, who loved him the most.

You didn't kill him. It was an accident. You couldn't have known.

*You know nothing about it. Nothing. You do not know what I did
and what I am paying for.*

*I know that you sneaked out of the house through the secret door in the
library.*

You know about that?

*I do. I know that Felix followed you because you left the door ajar. He
wasn't afraid of the dark, in fact, he loved playing in tunnels. He was
pretending to be a mole, scampering along it.*

You know that too? What else do you know?

I know that he followed you to the cottage in the woods.

*Yes. He must have followed me to the cottage and seen everything. But
I didn't know. I didn't hear him. I didn't see him. I should have sensed
my son out there in the night. In the darkness. Lost. I cannot live with
the pain of knowing that it was my fault. I want to stop the pain, but
I cannot.*

You must let it go . . .

*I searched the wood the following day when we discovered he was
missing. But I couldn't reveal why I believed him to be there. I should
have owned up, but I did not. I couldn't admit to knowing or I would
betray myself and . . . I loved a man who wasn't my husband. Do you
know that?*

Pascoe Bray. And you were pregnant with his child. I know that too.

You seem to know it all. But you do not know everything.

Then tell me. I'm not here to judge you but to help you find peace.

*My husband knew that the baby growing inside me was not his. He
sent me to a nunnery, claiming I had gone mad with grief after losing
Felix. I languished alone for five months and then gave birth there in
secret. Ivan gave my child to Pascoe on the condition that he left St Sidwell*

and never returned. I mourned my baby with all my heart because he might as well have been dead. I lost two children, you see. Two . . .

Pixie was astonished that the baby had survived. She had assumed, because it wasn't included on the family tree in the book Bruce had found, that it had died. *It's all in the past, Cordelia. You must let it go.*

Cordelia laughed bitterly. *How could you possibly understand? It is not so easy to let these things go. You know nothing of my greatest sin.*

What is that? Pixie couldn't imagine what else there could be.

There was a long pause, and then Cordelia finally reached the core of her anguish.

I hanged myself.

Pixie was astounded. The light in which she held Cordelia inflated with compassion. *You hanged yourself? Oh, Cordelia . . .*

I could not live after I had lost everything, you see. After I had lost Felix, the man I loved, and our child, a boy. A little boy. I could not live after my baby had been taken away from me. Only poor Robert remained but he clung to his father. I was alone. I had no one. This house became a prison and I a prisoner in it. There was only one way to escape. To be free from the pain.

But it didn't free you. It anchored you to the earth.

Do you still not see? Cordelia's voice quivered with frustration. *I did not deserve to be freed. I do not deserve to be freed now. I must pay the price for defying God and taking my own life. I must remain here. I am not worthy to go to God's house. You think you know me, but you do not know me at all.*

Pixie realised then that Cordelia was stuck in the house refusing to move on, not only because she believed herself guilty of causing Felix's death, but also because she deemed herself unfit on account of taking her own life. For a God-fearing woman like her, suicide was one of the greatest sins, and she'd committed it. She did not believe herself worthy of God's love, or His forgiveness. What she didn't realise, however, was that she was worthy of both.

You must let it all go, Cordelia. Pascoe and your child are waiting for you. Felix is waiting for you. Come to Felix now and the light will find you. It's a fallacy that suicide is against God's will. God is love. The only person condemning you, is you. Forgive yourself and go in love into the light. You will see that there is nothing but love there. Trust me, Cordelia. You have nothing to fear but fear itself.

Tabitha stood very still. She didn't want to frighten Felix away. She held Pixie's hand and glanced up to see that her eyes were closed, but her eyeballs were moving very fast behind the lids. Tabitha wondered what she was doing. But then she knew, for another figure slowly materialised in front of them. Tentative at first, then with more confidence, a woman in a long black dress and veil appeared. The energy around her was so dark that Tabitha could scarcely make her out. She looked like a funnel of black smoke. Tabitha could see, however, the glimmer of tears behind the veil, like tiny stars twinkling through it.

Pixie opened her eyes and watched as Cordelia became aware of her son. With a cry, she put out her arms and Felix ran into them. She pulled him against her, burying her face in his hair. *I'm sorry,* she whispered, holding him tightly. *I'm so sorry.* The child wrapped his arms around her and seemed to melt into her.

The love that radiated from them burned away the darkness. Like sun dissolving fog, it emanated from them, and around them, filling the wood and everything in it. Cordelia shed her darkness like ashes falling away and revealing a beautiful golden phoenix beneath. The golden brilliance of Cordelia's soul.

Cordelia turned to Pixie. *Who are you?* she asked. *I know you.*

A friend, Pixie replied. Then she opened her hand and revealed the locket.

As the light grew brighter, so bright that Tabitha and Pixie had to close their eyes and shield them with their arms, Pixie heard Cordelia's voice for the last time, so faint that it might have been a slip of wind through the branches.

Hermione Swift.

Tabitha waited until the light had gone then she tentatively put down her arm and opened her eyes. She was still holding on to Pixie's hand, squeezing it so tightly it had gone white. The wood looked different. The heavy energy had lifted and sunbeams streamed through the trees, softly luminous. The darkness had gone.

'You did it,' she whispered to Pixie. 'And I saw it happen.'

Pixie smiled down at Tabitha. 'I'm so glad you did,' she replied. 'It's a true gift to witness spirits moving into the light.'

'Are they in Heaven now?'

'They're in spirit. What happens after that, I don't pretend to know. They're on the next stage of their journey, and my job is done.'

'Does that mean you'll leave now?'

Pixie laughed. 'I'll leave after you've shown me the garden.'

Tabitha looked downhearted. 'Will you come back?'

'If you want me to.'

'I do,' Tabitha replied. 'I want you to very much.'

Chapter Twenty-Five

When Olivia and Antoinette entered the house after their walk with Daphne, they were immediately struck by the warmth, and by the soft, luminous quality of the light. The brittle, unhappy energy had evaporated, and in its place was a feeling of harmony and joy. 'She's gone,' said Antoinette with satisfaction. 'By God, she's gone. Good old Pixie. I knew she'd do it.'

Olivia's relief was immeasurable. She had doubted there even was an earthbound spirit, but the difference in the feeling of the house was so great now that she couldn't deny it. Her heart lifted. They wouldn't have to leave. They could stay and make their lives here in this truly special place. With a renewed sense of optimism, Olivia knew she could restore the house and gardens to their former beauty, and she couldn't wait to get started.

As the two women settled in the drawing room, where a vivacious fire gave out both heat and a real sense of hospitality, Elsa wandered in with a tatty cardboard box. 'Can you feel the difference?' she declared, putting the box down on the coffee table and running her eyes over the room in wonder, as if seeing it for the first time. 'The house feels happy!' she declared. She had never known St Sidwell Manor to feel like this. It no longer felt so big and hostile, but homely, as if a veil had been lifted and the sunlight allowed in. 'The past has been laid to rest,' she stated solemnly, and her vision misted; Mrs Delaware would be so pleased.

Ulysses, who had been waiting in the library for Pixie to come back, heard the voices in the drawing room and went to see what was going on. He was crossing the hall when Tabitha and Pixie came in through the front door.

'Any luck?' he asked Pixie hopefully.

'Cordelia's gone,' she told him, taking off her coat and boots. 'She and Felix. They've gone home together.'

Ulysses smiled. 'Great!' he exclaimed, relieved. 'Now *we* can go home too.'

Pixie rolled her eyes. Ulysses had been away for only one night; Pixie had been away for two weeks! He had no idea what she'd been through. However, although she was emotionally drained and exhausted, she was deeply satisfied. She had acomplished what she had set out to do, to help a lost soul find her way into the light. It was a privilege to witness an earthbound spirit's release; in this case she had witnessed two. 'Let's go and tell your mother,' she said to Tabitha.

They found Olivia and Antoinette in the drawing room with Elsa. When they saw Pixie, their faces lit up. Antoinette clapped. 'Well done, Pixie, my dear. You did it.'

Pixie was thrilled that they felt the change in the house. Sometimes people didn't. 'The souls are settled,' she confirmed and sank into the sofa with a sigh.

'Well done, you,' Antoinette gushed. 'No more crying in the night. Wonderful. I knew you'd succeed. There's no one like you, Pixie.'

'It was a challenge,' Pixie replied. 'But sometimes challenges are the most gratifying.'

'You look like you need a stiff drink,' Antoinette added, raising her eyebrows and glancing at the drinks cabinet.

'It's too early for that.' Pixie laughed. 'I'm fine, really. Success is reward enough.'

Olivia smiled sheepishly at Pixie. 'Thank you,' she said with emphasis, and the unspoken addendum to that was *I'm sorry I ever doubted you.*

'It's a pleasure. I'm just pleased that everyone is happy, both the living and the dead.'

Antoinette turned to Elsa, who was hovering by the coffee table. 'What's in that box?' she asked.

'A photo album,' Elsa replied, brushing dust off the top with a tissue. 'Mrs Delaware kept it safe in the library on the very top of one of the bookcases. I knew I'd find it eventually.'

They gathered round and Antoinette lifted out a red leather-bound album, which was closed with a brass clasp. Embossed into the cover was a bouquet of roses and the name *Cordelia Pengower*. Antoinette unclasped it and opened the first page. There, in black and white, was a photograph of Cordelia herself. For Pixie it was like looking into the face of an old friend, but to the others it was a case of putting a face to a name they had heard so much about. She was sitting on a velvet chair, looking over the back of it with her arms crossed. She wore a dark-coloured dress buttoned up to the neck with long slim sleeves that reached her wrists. At her throat was a pearl brooch. Her fair hair was curled and pinned upon her head. Her beauty was remarkable. She had a steady, gentle gaze that stared gravely out of the photograph. Her skin was flawless and about her was an air of serenity and calm. 'She was very beautiful,' said Antoinette.

'But her eyes are sad,' Olivia added.

Tabitha thought of the statue at the fountain. She hadn't seen Cordelia's face when she had appeared as a spirit, because of the veil that covered it. But now she knew that she was right. The statue *was* of Cordelia Pengower, gazing sorrowfully up to Heaven. Searching for Felix, perhaps. She couldn't wait to show it to Pixie.

Antoinette turned the page. The next photograph was of Ivan Pengower. 'What a horror!' Antoinette gasped.

'Ivan Pengower looks mean,' said Tabitha.

'He was mean,' said Pixie. 'He was pompous and selfish man.'

'But what wonderful photographs!' Antoinette studied them closely. 'It's fascinating to put faces to the story, isn't it?'

Ivan's photograph revealed a severe-looking man with a big, sweeping moustache and heavy black eyebrows. His eyes were small and black in a hard, humourless face, his neck short and thick. Antoinette turned the page to find an oval photograph of two young boys. Blond-haired Felix was seated in a chair. Robert, who was darker like his father, was standing beside it. The two of them stared out with round eyes and wary expressions, as if they had been told not to move and were trying very hard to be obedient.

'This one is Felix,' said Pixie, tapping her finger on the picture.

'He looks adorable,' Olivia mused. 'How sad that his life came to such a tragic end.'

'But he's happy now,' Tabitha added cheerfully. She'd seen him herself, fading into the light. It should have been extraordinary, but there had been something strangely familiar about it, as if on some level, she had witnessed that sort of thing happening before.

At last, they reached the photograph that Pixie had been waiting for. The group photograph, taken outside the house with family and servants, the day before Cavill had left and two days before Felix had vanished. She examined it in detail. She recognised herself at once, as Hermione Swift, seated beside Cordelia, in front of Rose. Had that really happened, she wondered? Was that truly her? Were the eyes that stared out of that beautiful face, Pixie's? It seemed so farfetched now that she was sitting in the drawing room in the present day.

Eager to see more, she reached out and turned the page. As it fell, revealing a large black-and-white photograph of two people on their wedding day, something in Pixie's heart snagged. She took a sharp breath. *Cavill and Hermione, October 1896.*

1896!

Pixie stared at it in amazement.

'Who's that?' Tabitha asked. 'She's pretty, isn't she?'

But Pixie wasn't looking at Hermione.

For a moment she couldn't speak. The sight was extraordinary. 1896 was the year after Felix had died. A year after Cavill *should* have died. She coughed to release the tightening in her throat.

'That's Hermione Swift, the children's governess, and Cordelia's brother-in-law, Cavill,' she answered vaguely, feeling strangely lightheaded.

He didn't go to South America, after all.

He came home. *To her.*

*

337

Pixie needed space to think. She mumbled something about being back in a moment and left the room in haste. She made her way straight to the library. With her heart thumping in her chest, she went to the bookcase. It didn't take long. She knew where to find it. Just as she had hoped, the sketchbook that Cavill had given her was precisely where she had left it back in 1895, hidden behind the encyclopaedias. No one had moved it. In all the years that had followed, no one had moved it.

With a trembling hand she took it out and opened it. There were Cavill's words: *To my beloved Hermione.* She ran her fingers over the ink, feeling his energy reaching her across the years, bringing him back to her in a wave of memory and sorrow. Then her eyes dropped to the corner of the page. Exactly as she had written them were her initials, *PT.* She blinked at them in wonder. She had been there. She had really been there.

She pressed the book to her breast and took a deep breath. For a moment she felt dizzy. *Cavill.* She closed her eyes, her heart aching with longing, and pictured him. He had come back, and he had married Hermione. She put a hand to her forehead. It was a mind boggle. Had Pixie changed the future for them? Had she stopped him going? Had the Butterfly Effect of her actions changed their destinies and enabled them to marry and have a future?

She couldn't help but feel envious of Hermione Swift living the life she couldn't live.

Pixie opened her eyes to see Tabitha standing shyly at the door. 'Daddy and Zach are in the drawing room and Antoinette is trying to tell them what happened,' she said. 'I think you'd better come. She's getting it all wrong.'

Reluctantly, Pixie put the book down on the table and followed Tabitha into the hall. She decided that now was a good time to tell Bruce where he came from. 'Your father might not believe in spirits, Tabitha, but he's interested in history,' she said. 'Let's go and enlighten him on his own.'

Tabitha looked up at her and frowned. 'You've found out how he's related to Mrs Delaware, haven't you?'

Pixie laughed. 'You're very intuitive, you know, Tabitha,' she said as they crossed the hall.

Tabitha beamed. 'Do you think so?'

'Absolutely.'

'How do I get good at it?'

'By acknowledging that it's there. By being alert. By focusing on the present moment and not cluttering it with thoughts. Spend time in nature and look and listen and feel. Don't think.' She put a hand on the child's shoulder. 'And if you're interested, read books and learn from them. Follow your instinct and you'll be guided to which books are best.'

'Is that it?'

Pixie shrugged. 'That's it.'

'Will I be like you?' Tabitha asked hopefully.

'You never know,' Pixie replied, but *she* knew – there was no one like her.

Pixie perched on the club fender with a cup of coffee. Elsa and the family sat around on the sofas and chairs, watching her expectantly. Even Bruce had a genuinely attentive look on his face. 'I've discovered something that might interest you,' she began.

'More revelations,' exclaimed Antoinette happily, rubbing her hands together. 'Let's hear them.'

'All right,' said Pixie. 'As I already told you, Cordelia Pengower was having an affair with the foreman at the mine, called Pascoe Bray. He was a kind and compassionate man who cared very deeply about the way the miners were treated. He fought with Ivan Pengower often, because they had very different views about how the mine should be run. In fact, there was an accident up there in eighteen ninety-four and a young man was killed. Pascoe Bray was a hero that day, saving lives, but he couldn't save that boy. The boy's mother blamed Ivan for her son's death and Cordelia believed she put a curse on the family.'

'I don't believe in curses,' said Bruce.

'Good, Bruce,' Pixie replied, holding him with her cool blue gaze. 'Then they have no power. Curses only have power if they are believed, like superstitions and predictions. If you believe the number thirteen to be unlucky, it will be. Your thoughts manifest, so take care what you focus your attention on. The thing is, Cordelia believed the curse. It went something like this: "I curse Ivan Pengower and his bloodline, that they and their house may be dogged by unhappiness. That tragedy will follow them like a shadow and not release them, so they know what it is to suffer loss." I think I've got that right. Well, Ivan and his bloodline certainly suffered loss. Felix fell down a priest hole and died. Cordelia was pregnant with Pascoe's child. Ivan knew it wasn't his and didn't allow her to keep it. He gave the baby to Pascoe to bring up. And, as a consequence, Cordelia hanged herself.'

'Good Lord!' Antoinette exclaimed. 'She hanged herself? How terrible!'

Olivia gasped. 'That's horrible. Poor woman. I suppose she couldn't find a way out. She'd lost so much.'

'Gruesome,' said Zach. 'Do you think she hanged herself here? In this house?'

'She did,' Pixie answered. 'Which is why the energy was so negative. It filled the entire building.'

'Go on,' said Bruce. He wasn't interested in hearing about energy, and he certainly wasn't going to believe that Cordelia Pengower hanged herself simply because Pixie told him so. But he was curious to hear what she had to say about *him*. 'I think I know where this is leading,' he added.

Pixie smiled over the rim of her coffee cup. She took a sip and then resumed. 'I suspect Mrs Delaware knew about the curse. The whole family must have. It would have been something they discussed, certainly after Cordelia hanged herself. Mrs Delaware miscarried three children. I think she believed in the curse and therefore gave it power. So, in order to lift it, I suspect she tracked down the descendant of Cordelia and Pascoe's child.' Pixie turned to Bruce and grinned. 'You.'

'Me?' Bruce asked.

'I suspect, if you dig into your ancestry, you will find a Bray. Pascoe and Cordelia's child was a son.'

Olivia looked at her husband. 'That's interesting, isn't it?' she said. 'It shouldn't be too hard to find out. People find out about their ancestors all the time. We just need to do a little digging.'

Bruce arched his eyebrows. 'It makes sense,' he said. 'I'm not sure how you came to that conclusion, Pixie, as I don't buy into that timesliding stuff. But you might be onto something. We'll let you know.'

Elsa coughed and everyone turned to look at her. She'd been sitting quietly on a chair, taking it all in. Now she had something of her own to share. 'As we're talking about ancestors, I have something that might interest you, too,' she said. 'I'm descended from the gypsies Pixie talked about,' she declared. 'My grandmother was a little girl when Felix Pengower disappeared. Her father was one of the men who were taken in for questioning. Of course, there was no evidence that any of them had taken the child. My grandmother remembered Mrs Pengower. She came with gifts, things she no longer wanted. They were grateful to her for that. My family came back the following summer, and every summer after that, to help with the harvest and fruit picking. Years later, when Robert Pengower was master of St Sidwell Manor, my grandmother was given a position in the house. She said Mr Pengower was sad and full of regret. He was lonely, too, and spoke often of his mother. But there were a few things he did that made a great impression on my grandmother and her people. He made sure that the mine was safe. He spent a lot of money doing it. He improved the miners' living conditions and gave them more pay. People thought very highly of him in St Sidwell. Eventually, he closed the mine in nineteen twenty-nine, and gave my people the land, so they had somewhere to camp that was legal. They're a small community now, but every summer they return for harvest time, and some of them work in the local shops and on the beach, when it's full of tourists. We have Robert Pengower to thank for that.'

Pixie was moved. She thought once again of the Butterfly Effect and wondered whether, if Cordelia hadn't died, her son might never have made those changes and more people might have been killed in those unstable tunnels. It was heartening to think of the travellers having a safe place to camp. Robert had clearly changed his opinion of them. Cordelia had been a positive influence on him, after all, and, maybe, just maybe, Pixie had been too.

'That's a nice end to the story,' said Antoinette.

'It certainly is,' Bruce agreed, getting up from the sofa. 'So, is your job done?' he asked Pixie.

'It is,' she replied.

'We should be going,' said Ulysses.

'Not before I show Pixie the statue,' said Tabitha, jumping off her chair. 'Come on!'

Pixie smile apologetically at Bruce. 'I'm sorry, but I can't say no to your daughter. We'll be out of your hair very soon.'

'Please,' said Bruce. 'Take all the time you want.' He ran his eyes over the room, sighed with satisfaction and put his hands in his pockets. 'I don't know what you've done, but the house does feel very nice suddenly. Perhaps the heating has come on at last. If it continues like this, I'll have to turn it down.'

It was early afternoon and a grey mist was settling over the garden when Pixie, Olivia and Antoinette followed Tabitha down the path towards the statue. The temperature had dropped and it was bitterly cold. Tabitha hoped it might snow. Thick cloud had drifted in to make a flat white sky. Darkness was sure to come early. They made their way along the path. Antoinette and Olivia walked behind Tabitha and Pixie, going over the extraordinary events of the morning, and Elsa telling them that she was descended from the gypsies. 'You'll be able to find someone to replace her now,' said Antoinette.

'I know, but I don't want to,' Olivia replied. 'I'm very fond of her. Perhaps she'll stay on for a while longer if I find a couple to do the hard work for her.'

'That's a good idea. It would be a shame if she were to leave just when the house has been put right. She deserves to enjoy it after so many years tolerating it. She deserves a medal for having put up with all that negativity.'

'She must have loved Emily Delaware very much.'

'And it was a family tradition for the women in Elsa's family to work here. I don't suppose Elsa ever contemplated working anywhere else.'

'I will beg her not to retire,' Olivia added decisively.

Antoinette laughed. 'I don't think you'll have to. I don't imagine she wants to be anywhere else but here. It's her home too, and now it feels so nice.'

Tabitha heard the fountain a short while before she saw it, the merry trickling of water. Excitedly, she ran to see what had happened. To her surprise, the round basin at the base of the statue was full and water was raining down cheerfully in graceful arcs. 'There was no water here when I first saw it. It's magic!' she exclaimed.

'I think you're right,' said Pixie, amused that these sorts of miracles still surprised her.

'Who turned it on?' Olivia asked. 'I didn't even think it worked.'

'Bruce?' Antoinette suggested, but they all knew he hadn't. It had started on its own.

'It's magic,' Tabitha repeated. 'I feel it.' She was going to feel a lot of things now that Pixie had told her she was intuitive. 'Isn't it amazing?'

Tabitha gazed upon the stone figure of Cordelia Pengower, her hands reaching up to Heaven, her beautiful face gently tilted, her long hair softly waved. She didn't look sad any more. In fact, as Tabitha examined her more closely, she was sure she could see a barely perceptible curve upon her lips.

Pixie was sad to leave St Sidwell Manor. It was as if she was leaving Cavill there, and Hermione Swift, and all those characters she had grown to love. She had to remind herself that they were long departed and that nothing good would come of dwelling in the past. She was here to live and learn and grow, and that meant committing fully to the present moment.

Tabitha was sorry to see Pixie go. She hugged her fiercely. 'Can I text you?' she asked.

'You can text me whenever you like,' Pixie replied, embracing her back. 'I'd love to hear from you.'

'I'll tell you whenever I see a spirit, although I probably won't see any here now because they've all gone.'

Pixie laughed and looked down at her with affection. 'There are no *earthbound* spirits, you're right about that, Tabitha, but you're surrounded by spirits all the time. You don't realise how busy it is. Spirits come and visit because they love you; some are here because they're protecting you and guiding you, and some are here because they're fond of the place. You're never alone – you only think you are because you can't see them.'

Tabitha's eyes lit up. 'So, I might still see a spirit?'

'You'll very likely see them and that's nice. Only, you might not want to tell your friends about them. Most people aren't as keen to see them as you are.'

'I'll tell you,' Tabitha whispered. 'It'll be our secret.'

'I'd like that,' said Pixie.

Olivia thanked her and then stood on the step as Ulysses climbed into the driver's seat of his funny old Morris Minor and started the engine. The family waved them off with Elsa and Tom, and Pixie stuck her hand out of the window and waved back. Even though it was getting dark, the house did not look forbidding as it had when they'd first arrived. The lights glowed golden in the windows, like vivacious eyes beckoning visitors with a warm, benevolent gaze.

Pixie lifted the sketchbook of birds out of her bag and opened it.

'What's that?' Ulysses asked, glancing across at it.

'A book from the library,' she replied.

'You stole it?'

'I did.'

'You stole a book?'

'I did.'

'Pixie, are you out of your mind?' Ulysses was appalled.

'They won't notice! Who's interested in a sketchbook of birds? It's been there, untouched, for over a hundred years.'

'It's the principle. It's unprofessional. You're despicable.'

She laughed. 'I know, but you love me anyway.'

He laughed with her. 'Why are you interested in the book?'

'Because it's Cavill's sketchbook and he gave it to me.'

'That's just weird. You're in love with a dead man.'

'I am. That's the price I have to pay for being a timeslider.'

'You need to find someone like Cavill in *real* time.'

'I'll never find anyone like Cavill, ever,' she told him seriously.

'Rubbish. The reason you loved him was probably because you knew you could never have him. Impossible love is irresistible.'

'I just loved him, Ulysses,' she replied resolutely, stroking the book, for that was the only tangible thing that connected her to him.

'You'll fall in love again, Pix. I know you. It won't be long before you lose your heart to another Pablo, or Pedro, or Pancho.'

She looked at him askance and frowned. 'Does he have to be Spanish?'

'You seem to have a penchant for Latin men.'

'Cavill could not have been more English.' She sighed wistfully and closed the book. 'But you're right. He's in the past.'

'He's in the ground.'

'He's in spirit,' Pixie corrected.

'Then he might pay you a visit.'

Pixie turned her eyes to the window. It was now dark, and her reflection gazed disconcertedly back at her. 'He loved Hermione Swift, Ulysses, and I was never really her.'

'Does it matter? We live our dreams for ourselves, don't we?'

'Maybe it doesn't matter,' she conceded. 'I've lived an experience that was very real to me. I'll carry it in my heart for as long as I live. That's what's important – what I've learnt from it.'

'So, what *have* you learnt from it?'

She smiled bashfully, aware that she was going to sound silly, but knowing Ulysses would never judge her harshly. 'That I'm lovable,' she replied, folding her arms and turning her face to the window again. She thought of her dead, alcoholic father and her mother who'd killed him. Then she thought of Cavill and that hard place in the core of her heart softened.

'You see, Ulysses, I really needed to know that.'

Epilogue

Spring brought warmth and colour to the gardens of St Sidwell Manor. Delicate green leaves opened on the beech hedges and lime trees, and daffodils turned their vivid yellow trumpets to the sun. Weeping willows trailed their leafy tentacles in the water and ducks glided upon it as serene as sailing boats in a gentle wind. But something unexpected happened that took everyone by surprise. Heaps of forget-me-nots appeared suddenly in the wood where Felix Pengower had died. After Pixie left back in January, Bruce had called the police and, after going through the required formalities, the child's bones had been buried alongside his family in the chapel on the estate. Tom had cleared the brambles that covered the priest hole and filled it in with earth, and Olivia and Tabitha had bought a small memorial stone with Felix's name engraved on it to mark the place where he had died. It wasn't his grave any longer, but they both felt strongly that they wanted to honour it.

One morning in May, Olivia had gone for a walk there and been struck by the vision of flowers. There they were, radiant in the dawn light, as beautiful as they were miraculous. The place where Felix had died had been found at last and embellished with the full force of nature's extraordinary imagination. The tiny blue flowers were such a deep blue and growing so abundantly that Elsa hadn't known what to make of them. In all the years she had worked at St Sidwell Manor, she had never seen anything like it.

Word had got around and people from the town had asked to come and view them. They'd stood at Felix's memorial stone, scratching their heads and marvelling at the miraculous sight.

Even the vicar had come and confirmed that it was, without doubt, something spiritual. A local photographer had taken pictures, which were published in a national newspaper and for a while those photographs had trended on social media, much to Tabitha and Zach's excitement. They'd suddenly found themselves in the centre of a delightful furore. Their schoolfriends had been more enthusiastic than ever to come and stay.

Olivia had been busy with the team of local gardeners she had found on the internet, cutting back, weeding and planting, and the place began to re-experience something of the beauty of Cordelia Pengower's lively creativity. After years of neglect the flora had seemed to thrive on the attention, shooting up from the earth with all the energy and colour of those bygone days. *How intrepid is nature*, Olivia had thought, marvelling at its power of rebirth. *Nothing is ever really lost.*

Bruce's health improved. He took an active role in the farm, getting up before dawn to milk the cows and relishing his new life outside the office. He was home every day for lunch, which Olivia enjoyed, and was full of enthusiasm. Moving to Cornwall was the best thing he'd ever done, he told her, and he laughed in his good-natured way about the ghosts. He hadn't noticed much of a difference in the feel of the house besides the temperature. According to him, it had always felt good.

However, to his astonishment, Pixie was right about his ancestry. He discovered, after some research, that Cordelia and Pascoe's son was called Ruan Bray. Ruan Bray had had a daughter called Jenifri, who'd married a man called Jonas Talwyn. They, in turn, had had a son called Edgar. Edgar Talwyn was born in 1944 and had emigrated to Australia, where he married and had had a son: Bruce. That made Pascoe Bray Bruce's great-great grandfather. How about that? Bruce couldn't work out how Pixie had found that out. One thing was for certain, it wasn't from sliding back in time!

Elsa was happy to remain in the house with Tom. She had never really wanted to be anywhere else. It was her life's work and her home – and Tom wanted to keep an eye on his mother as well as doing odd jobs around the house when he wasn't busy on the farm.

Olivia had found a young couple to clean and cook, but only after inviting almost the entire town to a drinks party to show them how the energy in the place had changed, and how the ghost that had haunted it had moved away.

Victor Pollard had been the first to arrive and the last to leave and had subsequently inveigled his way back on numerous occasions to read Cordelia Pengower's letter, which Tabitha had innocently told him about, and to look around the historic building that was full of priest holes and other treasures. Having anticipated his visits to be a great bore, Olivia had discovered that not only did he and Bruce have much in common in terms of their interest in history, but Olivia was beginning to enjoy his company too. He was passionate and knowledgeable, and it was uplifting to have a cheerful person around the house.

Olivia hired a building company to put in a planning application to open up the attic to make a children's floor, and she settled happily into her studio overlooking the newly restored box garden. She'd agreed to a new project illustrating a children's story about litter and a riverbank and the animals' quest to clean it up. It felt good to be working again.

Tabitha kept in touch with Pixie. She texted her often and, when term ended in July, she dyed her hair pink for the school holidays. Olivia was horrified, but Bruce and Zach thought it funny. Tabitha sent Pixie a selfie, and Pixie replied that it was a prettier shade than her own and really suited her. Tabitha would have to dye it back for the new school term in September, but for now she enjoyed her new identity, and it made her feel close to Pixie, who she missed.

Tabitha's favourite place was the churchyard. She would wander among the graves and ponder on life and death and spirits. Pixie had encouraged her to learn as much as she could about the paranormal through books, and Tabitha had taken her advice and borrowed from the local library in town, and also ordered esoteric literature from Watkins Books in London, which Pixie had recommended. The spirits of Cordelia and Felix might have departed, but Tabitha's interest in the unseen world was only just beginning.

Sometimes, as she sat on the bench against the church wall, she saw movement out of the corner of her eye: a dance, a leap, a skip, a mischievous attempt to get her attention, perhaps. There would be many who would dismiss those sightings as tricks of light, but Tabitha knew very well what they were. She'd been aware of something there the first time she'd visited the church with Zach and her father back in December. Maybe, if she honed her ability, she might one day be adept enough to engage with the spirit who was so clearly trying to get her attention. She knew it wasn't an earthbound spirit, for Pixie would have picked up on it when she'd visited and released it. No, this was a cheerful spirit who simply wanted to play.

Tabitha hadn't forgotten what Pixie had advised her to do. She closed her eyes and emptied her mind by focusing on her senses. She became aware of the breeze on her face, the scent of the sea in her nostrils, the aliveness in her body and the gentle beating of her heart. She sank into the moment, into the vast, timeless space of her mind. Then she asked for the spirit to make itself known.

Pixie thought of Cavill often. She knew it was mad to pine after a man who'd lived a hundred years before. Who she'd never see again – at least, not in this life. Yet her heart would not give up its attachment. In the evenings when she was in bed and alone, she opened the book he'd given her, and remembered the birds they had watched together, on the bank of the estuary and in the wood. She could picture his face so clearly. The tenderness in his eyes, the mischief in his smile, the affection that fused them in an unbreakable bond. She thought often of Hermione – the real Hermione – and wondered what had become of her. Had she and Cavill had children? Had they remained at St Sidwell, or had they moved away? She could have done some research, but there was no point; she had to move on with her life. *This* life. And commit to it fully.

But one question niggled – one question that could never be answered. When Pixie had left, had Cavill noticed a difference in Hermione? She hoped, jealously, that he had. That he'd found something missing. A spark, a connection, something that was unique in Pixie that she'd taken with her when she'd slid back. Had he looked into the eyes of his beloved and found them wanting? She would never know.

Pixie kept herself busy. She'd had a lot of work, clearing earthbound spirits, laying crystals, and other psychic work. She hadn't had to slide since St Sidwell, and she was relieved. It took a lot of energy, and emotion. She wasn't sure she wanted to slide again for a while.

Then, in September, she returned home one afternoon to find a letter among the bills. She rarely received letters. People emailed or texted – and even they were rare for she had few friends. Actually, she had only one: Ulysses. This letter was handwritten. Intuitively, she knew who it was from, even though she didn't recognise the writing. She stared at it for a long, long time, deciding finally to wait until Ulysses was home before she opened it.

Ulysses returned at the end of the day having been in Manchester, interviewing an up-and-coming pop star for a music magazine. From the pleased look on his face, the interview had gone exceedingly well. Jean-Michel's time was up.

Pixie opened the letter. It was only a few lines.

Dear Penelope, it's time we talked. Please call me. Mum.

Penelope! No one called her that but her mother.

'I have a job for you,' said Ulysses, flopping onto the sofa and looking at his phone. 'A linguini. And before you object—'

'Where?' Pixie interrupted keenly. Right now, she'd slide anywhere just to avoid her mother.

Ulysses was surprised. 'Oh, okay. I thought you were going to fight it. You know, the usual, *I'm not ready for this . . .*'

'Where?' she repeated.

'New York?' He winced. 'I know you're going to say—'

'Great. I'm going. When?'

He raised his eyebrows in surprise. 'As soon as we can go.'

'Tomorrow. I want to go tomorrow,' she said, tearing up the letter.

Ulysses watched her drop the pieces of paper into the bin. 'What's that?'

'Nothing,' said Pixie tightly. 'At least, it's nothing now.'

'Right.' Ulysses noticed her sudden pallor, but he decided not to mention it. If Pixie wanted to share the contents of the letter, she would, in her own time.

'So, tell them yes!' Pixie insisted.

'I will.'

'I've never been to New York.'

'Well, you're going now. And, by the way, I think you're going to love this one.'

Acknowledgements

I'm excited to introduce the first book in a brand new series. Having adored writing the Deverill Chronicles I was keen to get into another saga, but this one is very different. Pixie Tate is an intriguing heroine and I've loved creating her and her unique world. It's been a challenge, but often the most ambitious projects push us to surpass our perceived limitations and reach greater heights of creativity.

I would like to thank some very bright lights who have illuminated my spiritual path over the course of my life and inspired me to search and learn and grow. I couldn't have begun to write this book without them. My father was my first mentor in that field, giving me books on the esoteric to read, which we then discussed at great length on those long drives to school. From then on my interest in the subject grew and I have been guided and taught by some wonderful people: Susan Dabbs, Avril Price, Robin Lown, Tony Stockwell and Lucie Rowe. I thank them all.

Producing a book is not a solitary endeavour. I'm fortunate to work with some really dynamic, brilliant people. I would like to thank my agent Sheila Crowley at Curtis Brown, for her mastery, her wisdom, her strength and her friendship – and for being simply a lovely, positive, uplifting person. I'd also like to thank her colleagues at Curtis Brown who work so hard on my behalf: Katie McGowan, Tanja Goossens and Aoife MacIntyre. Thank you, too, to Addison Duffy at United Talent Agency in Los Angeles, for representing me on the film and TV front.

I feel that Charlotte Mursell, my editor at Orion, has put her whole heart and soul into this book as much as I have. She could

353

not have worked harder or been more dedicated to the task. I thank her for her enthusiasm and expertise, but also for her creativity, her imagination and her tact, for we authors are very sensitive. I thank the Managing Director Anna Valentine for her belief in me and for her passion for this story. She has an unbeatable team at Orion, and I would like to take this opportunity to thank them too: Jen Wilson, Tara Hiatt, Snigdha Koirala, Lynsey Sutherland, Cait Davies, Leanne Oliver and Paul Stark. I also extend my gratitude to Suzanne Clarke who copy edited the book, her meticulous attention to detail has been invaluable.

I thank my readers wherever you are. If it wasn't for you, I wouldn't be able to do what I love and my books would never come into the light. I also thank all those in the book trade who produce, buy and sell my work. It's an industry that attracts the nicest people and I'm so lucky to be a part of it.

Most importantly, I thank my family from the bottom of my heart. They are my greatest joy. My husband Sebag, and my children Lily and Sasha. My parents Charlie and Patty Palmer-Tomkinson, my brother James, and his family: Sos, Honor, India, Wilf and Sam.

Credits

Santa Montefiore and Orion Fiction would like to thank everyone at Orion who worked on the publication of *Shadows in the Moonlight* in the UK.

Editorial
Charlotte Mursell
Snigdha Koirala

Copy editor
Suzanne Clarke

Proof reader
Linda Joyce

Audio
Paul Stark
Louise Richardson

Contracts
Dan Herron
Ellie Bowker
Oliver Chacón

Design
Charlotte Abrams-Simpson

Editorial Management
Charlie Panayiotou
Jane Hughes
Bartley Shaw

Finance
Jasdip Nandra
Nick Gibson
Sue Baker

Marketing
Cait Davies
Jennifer Hope

Publicity
Leanne Oliver
Sian Baldwin

Production
Ruth Sharvell

Sales
Catherine Worsley
Esther Waters
Victoria Laws
Toluwalope Ayo-Ajala
Rachael Hum
Georgina Cutler

Operations
Dan Stevens